Praise for NEON CITADEL:

"With Neon Citadel, Leunig has proven his mastery over genre, successfully blending cyberpunk, urban fantasy, and noir into a bloody cocktail fit for even the most discerning of vampires. Open your heart to the darkness and let in the grit--I know I did, and I don't regret it one bit."

— Russ Nickel, lead writer of *Helldivers 2*

"Cyberpunk and dark fantasy collide in an explosive thriller set in a corporate dystopia five steps from reality. NEON CITADEL is an exciting conclusion to the trilogy, as once again the hardboiled (and now vampiric) Gash Jensen teams up with newly magic-powered comrades in a fight with both world-changing and personal stakes."

— Erica L. Satifka, Endeavour Award-winning author of *How to Get to Apocalypse and Other Disasters*

"*Neon Citadel* is dripping with danger and atmosphere like its own Seattle sky. The collision of magic and cyberpunk is giving *Shadowrun* vibes in all the best ways, and Leunig provides plenty of twists and turns to keep you turning the pages to the very end."

— Chris M. Arnone, author of *The Jayu City Chronicles*

"In Neon Citadel, Greg Leunig blends noir, fantasy, and science fiction to create a genre bending confection that I read in a single delighted sitting. This novel is enormous fun with an anti-corporate heart--I want more!"

— Jennifer Pullen, PhD, author of *Fantasy Fiction: A Writer's Guide and Anthology* and *A Bead of Amber on Her Tongue*

"If you're craving a flawed anti-hero with fangs, a flask, and a savior complex, meet Nagash, a scotch-drinking vampire trying to find his place in a burning city. As he searches for peace and redemption, impossible choices and haunting memories threaten to drag him under. Neon Citadel is a fierce, genre-bending fusion of sci-fi and fantasy, rich with action, dark humor, and emotional weight."

— Michael Solis, author of *Deficient*

Also by Greg Leunig

Cold Wind Blowing
Colossus

NEON CITADEL

Greg Leunig

Denver, Colorado

Published in the United States by:

Spaceboy Books LLC
1627 Vine Street
Denver, CO 80206

www.readspaceboy.com

First printed January 2026

ISBN-13: 978-1-951393-50-2

For everyone who read and loved *Colossus* and *Cold Wind Blowing.* Without your kind reviews, wonderful praise, valuable feedback, and excited live-chatting I never would have sustained the energy and focus over the years that were necessary to make *Neon Citadel* the book it needed to be.

You keep me afloat. You're the best.

CHAPTER 1

Nagash "Gash" Jensen stepped out onto the deck of his stolen yacht, *The Holy*. Rain fell from the starless sky, sheets of it that raked the bow of the ship. Must be getting close now – the city's glow on the horizon, like a small sun perpetually rising into the night, lit his way home.

Home. It was less than a year since he fled Seattle, desperate to escape the country, desperate to escape the violence that seemed to follow him wherever he went. A lot changed in a span of months. He met someone, was hired as her bodyguard. Fell for her. Turned into a vampire. Realized it was mistake and completely abandoned her. Now he was being sucked back into his old life, the life of a private investigator in a world governed by corporations with private armies of cops. And now, against his better judgment, he prepared to take the first steps in finishing the case that drove him out of Seattle to begin with. The case that almost killed him and made him a fugitive from WalCo, one of the largest corporations in the world.

His anonymous client had re-hired Gash to rescue a Romanian scientist named Ana Marin, whom WalCo abducted years ago as part of their expansive forced-work initiative. Even now, when Gash closed his eyes, he could picture her face. Her features petite, but creased from a life of struggle. Her irises almost neon blue beneath hooded eyelids. It didn't matter who Gash's mystery client turned out to be. It didn't matter that the payday would set Gash up for life, except as a component in a promise he'd once made: To escape his violent life once and for all and live the rest of his days in peace. All that mattered was *saving her*.

The rain sloughed off Gash in sheets, the percussion of water striking the composite deck in deafening tune with the sharp roaring of the boat's engine as the little yacht cut through the chopping ocean waves. He returned to the ship's cabin, shedding his soaked overcoat at the threshold.

The Holy featured a luxurious interior cabin. Full bar, faux wood paneling that looked better than the real thing, forming foam seats, and a voice activated Virtual Intelligence named Trine (a sexy British persona clothed in a pornographic parody of a sailor's outfit and possessing feminine physical features of greatly exaggerated proportions). That Trine was not only enabled but locked in by the boat's former owners, the no-fun-at-all Sovereign Military Order of Malta, had been the highlight of his escape from Rhodes after accidentally unleashing magic into the world as part of a small expedition. The conclusion of his gig as bodyguard. He regularly imagined the conspiracy-theorist military order gathering to make war plans around Trine's display, glowering at each other through the translucent blue display as she danced and bounced in ways that defied the laws of physics.

Gash poured himself a scotch, and downed it immediately. His first night on the yacht, he was relieved to discover that he could still enjoy cigarettes and still get drunk. Normal food made him sick, but booze, thankfully, did not. Or at least, not any more than it ever did.

A week and a half into the voyage, when he stopped at Panama on his way through the canal, he discovered that he could still enjoy getting laid, too. He indulged twice in Panama – once in the brothel and once trolling for a mugger to drink. The guilt from exsanguinating his first victim in Rhodes still followed Gash, and he figured he better try to avoid more killing if he ever wanted to be able to sleep again. So he left the man moaning and half-dead in the alley. Two weeks of bliss followed, quietly sailing the open ocean and drinking and lost to the world.

Gash poured himself another scotch and slammed it down. Good stuff, this. Expensive, aged, peaty. A shame not to let it linger on his tongue, he thought, as he slammed a third and rose to his feet. The end of bliss drew near. In hours, he would dock at Seattle, and then it would be time to get to work. His client had already secured him a long-term berth beside some other yachts, prepaid for three months. He would live and work out of the yacht until he could find Ana for his mystery client. Then, he would retire and sail off into the sunset. In his more romantic moments, he imagined Ana would join him on that journey.

Gash climbed the steep stairs into the ship's helm, and sat in his usual seat. The ship's computer did all the work for him, he didn't know how to captain a boat. But he liked to sit at the helm and stare at the point of the horizon where the deep charcoal of the sky met the jet-black line of the ocean. In these quiet hours of watching, Nagash Jensen knew peace for the first time since Serena. He didn't want it to end.

Tonight, bright light shown in the distance, illuminating the helm. He squinted at the midnight sunrise – Seattle glowing neon on the horizon. Something was wrong. Smoke. A great plume of it rose from over the horizon, illuminated by the LED glow of 10 billion lights shining into the night: Seattle was burning. He checked the readouts on the computer. Fifty minutes out from docking. Better figure out what was going on in the city before he got there: He dropped back down into the cabin and took a seat in the lounge.

"Trine," he said.

A holographic projector set into the far wall came to life, and a translucent blue projection materialized in the center of the room. She turned to face him. "Yes, Gash?" she queried.

"I see smoke coming from Seattle. Comb the newsfeeds and tell me what's happening."

"There are seven separate news events involving fire. According to intensity of coverage, the most significant is an incident in the Georgetown neighborhood. Most of the structures in that area have been razed to the ground by a small group of magic users. Major corporate news outlets are in agreement that this was a conflict between rogue magic users that got out of hand, though most eyewitness accounts describe a choreographed event minimizing harm to the participants and maximizing collateral damage."

"Georgetown, eh? Corporations have been trying to get those people out for over a century. Lots of valuable real-estate there." Gash sighed and stood, made his way over to the bar.

"My databases confirm this," Trine said.

"I didn't need confirmation." He poured another scotch, shot it, and then after considering the glass and the bottle for a moment, shoved the glass aside and took a long pull directly from the bottle.

"Why isn't the rain putting out the fires?"

"The rain has not yet reached the city," she responded.

"Trine?"

"Yes, Gash?"

"Dance for me. Select at random from your database of erotic dances. Something I haven't watched yet. Notify me when Poseidon calls us for authentication."

"Yes, Gash," she said, the blue light projection of her hips beginning to sway back and forth to the beat of some kind of slowly building electronica. He watched for a few minutes, but before long his eyes defocused on Trine and his thoughts drifted to the years he spent in this city with Serena, rainy nights in the city spent adventuring in the streets. He'd been happy then. Or at least happy sometimes. Content often. It felt like a long time ago. He thought of Ana Marin, then, and wondered if she even had access to the outside world, or if WalCo kept her imprisoned. If she was living in deep oppression all those long months he spent fleeing from WalCo instead of saving her.

The rattle of the downpour on the deck of the ship, magnified by his vampiric senses, cut through the music, a dissonant rhythm in stark contrast to the beat of Trine's electronica. Gash thought of Jacksonville, then, the heavy monsoon season in full swing the night he met Starfire and she hired him to be her bodyguard. To when they'd almost kissed in Rhodes.

He sighed.

"Trine, deactivate," Gash said. She disappeared without a word, and he took another long pull from his bottle, his gaze unmoored.

CHAPTER 2

The Poseidon Shipping and Yachting goons were polite as they rifled through everything, aside from some up-turned eyebrows at the bar full of empties. He could tell that, as a *premium* customer, he received the light version of the contraband search. A token ten-minute scan, and he was formally docked in his luxury berth and ready to hit the city.

Sure it was two AM and he was exhausted from a hard night of drinking, but he had to get off the boat and back into the streets. These were his streets. At least some of them. At least they had been.

Gash's brain hung an "Out to Lunch" sign and his feet guided him into the city. Far from the tourist traps – the ancient fish market, the museum to the world's favorite coffee chain. Far from Georgetown, too. The smoke billowed above him – from up close, the tower of it might have been an ashen shroud cast over the whole of downtown.

At least the rain hadn't hit yet.

Eventually, he found himself at Shen Wu's Noodles, an old favorite haunt. The proprietor was a friend, or something like it, before Gash took off. He still remembered just over a decade ago, watching the young Mr. Shen drive his food truck onto the sidewalk and begin deconstructing it. Within two days, Noodles2Go was transformed into a kiosk leaned-to up against the rent-a-office building that held Gash's office (along with about 120 other "independent contractors").

When Gash had approached Mr. Shen on the third morning to ask him what he was doing, the young man was hard at work cooking some rice noodles in a giant wok, shielded from the blazing sun only by a thin canvas tarp.

"You must be Shen Wu," Gash had said too-loudly.

The man had angled the wok up, turned over the mass of carbs with a giant set of tongs, and then set it back down on the burner and gave Gash a once over. Offered his hand, which Gash shook. "Phil Shen," he said.

"Is Shen Wu your dad?"

"There is no Shen Wu. My girlfriend thought I'd sell more noodles if the place was called Shen Wu's Noodles. I guess she didn't think Phil Shen's Noodles had the same ring." Phil took a giant tube of some kind of black sauce and sprayed it into the wok, turning over the noodles again.

Gash had laughed. The noodles smelled salty and fresh. "She sounds like a smart girl, but I don't think it works if you tell everyone that your name is really Phil."

Phil never missed a beat, turning over the carbs in the pot again, mixing them in with the sauce as they sizzled on the wok. "You're about to sit down and place an order, right?"

He had been right.

Gash blinked his eyes rapidly, re-focusing on the present. No Phil at Shen Wu's today, just some young girl. How long was Gash standing there, zoning out to old memories? But still, the girl behind the kiosk ignored him completely. She sat, enraptured by a Nat Geo report of some kind on a tiny old holo-projector. A new species of corvid discovered in Olympia. It just looked like a raven to Gash. The girl couldn't have been more than 18, but she was heavily and ostentatiously modded. Lots of it looked purely aesthetic: Her eyes glowed purple, and thin silvery filaments wound along both sides of her face. But there was a legit neural jack, too, nestled along her bright green hairline.

Gash leaned over the kiosk, trying to get her attention. "Are you a bird scientist or a noodle vendor?"

She turned her head just so slightly, glaring at him from beneath neon bangs. "Ornithologist."

"What?"

"It's not 'bird scientist,' the correct terminology is 'ornithologist.' Jack out already, Jesus," she huffed, looking back at her holo-program.

Gash stood and stared at her for a long time. Eventually she turned back to him, gave him a little head shake with her eyebrows arched.

"I want to order something," he said.

"Fine," she said, pausing the holo program and sliding the menu tablet over to Gash. And then after waiting a beat, "what are you even doing out here anyway?"

"What do you mean?" Gash asked, as he keyed in his old favorite – soy ramen.

She gestured wildly in all directions. The streets were basically abandoned. Some part of Gash noticed, but it never really registered consciously. Big parts of Jacksonville were this way when he was on the run. Rhodes often seemed empty during his brief time there, on the expedition. Not this city, though. This part of the city, at least, was always full. People loved it here – non-corporate types at least.

Because it wasn't a part of any particular company's domain back in the day, a dozen different megacorps bought out this section of the city indiscriminately and asymmetrically during the great takeover. As such, none of them could agree on how (or more importantly who) to regulate the place. Which corporate legal system it would be subject to, who would enforce, who would reap the tax benefits of incarceration, etc. Eventually, they all just agreed that nobody would get to do any of those things, and over time the anarchists and squatters and other independents claimed the place. Lacking any incentive to fight back, the corporations abandoned their stakes. Folks in the city called it the Deregulated Zone, since you could basically do anything (as long as it didn't piss off the other inhabitants). Hence why entrepreneurs could just drive a food truck onto the sidewalk and start a business there. Not the kind of place that ever slept – 2 AM or otherwise.

"Empty," Gash nodded. "Georgetown fire?"

"For starters. I don't know if you heard, but there are people out there now that can just incinerate you with a flick of the wrist. Fly around and shoot lightning bolts out of their assholes. Normal people don't roam the streets at all hours when wizards are out here causing trouble."

"Guess I'm not normal people," Gash said. He completed his order and the tablet read his account, deducted the credits. Sat down at a stool a few feet down from the girl's perch. The old plastic stool was cast off from a prison undergoing renovations if Gash remembered correctly; it creaked under his weight, as it always had whenever he sat on it. "For that matter, I guess neither are you, huh?"

"My dad says I have to take nights three times a week, says it's safe. Says nobody's going to shoot lightning bolts at a noodle vendor."

"Your dad – are you Phil Shen's kid?"

"Yep," she said.

"I didn't know Phil had a daughter," Gash said, wracking his brain for a missing memory. He found none.

"Well then I guess I must not be real, huh?" the girl said, unpausing her show and turning back towards it.

"What's your name?" Gash asked.

She waited a long time before pausing again and turning back towards him. "If I tell you, will you stop talking to me?" Behind her, a small auto-chef unit was coming to life, firing burners, a conveyor pre-loaded with rice noodles began to roll.

"Phil always used to cook his noodles by hand," Gash said, regarding the machine dubiously.

"Well, 'Phil' took a stray bullet to the lower back. It grazed his spine and now he's in a wheelchair. So we got an auto-chef."

They regarded each other in silence for a time. Gash's heart didn't beat anymore, but he still felt something stirring down there in his chest. A tightness. Phil caught a stray bullet. What a bunch of bullshit. He clenched his fists and then unclenched them.

When he breathed in, the smoke from the burning city stung. The acid of it mixed in with the soy and the cooking noodles and the faint floral essence of the girl's soap or shampoo or whatever, a cacophony of dissonant aromas rioting just behind his nose. The hum of the streetlights, the girl's breathing, the rumbling of the conveyor belt, the sound of a car rolling past one street over, the tires going over a speed bump, the electrical engine humming softly, her hair reflecting the soft LED from the lightbulb above her in the kiosk, it all came spiraling in at once; the sights and sounds and smells a piece of abstract neural art. They all blobbed in his brain, bouncing around seemingly at random in his cortex. Purple paint from the girl's too vivid eyes blasted the "Out to Lunch" sign and every last synapse in his brain seemed to come to life. Was this a vampire's version of a panic attack? The trillion sensory inputs of the city all crowding into his throbbing mind?

He closed his eyes for a moment only to realize he was fighting back tears. Tears for Phil Shen? His regular noodle guy from before he left Seattle? He didn't even know Phil enough to know he had a daughter. Maybe that was it. Maybe this purple-haired girl was proof that his ties to the city were tenuous at best. Maybe the worst part about being a fugitive vampire forced to cut all ties was the fact that in all the decades he'd lived, none of the ties he'd built were able to stand the test of time. Cutting all ties just meant he lived in a boat now instead of that shitty flop-house before, but nothing else really changed.

Or maybe he just liked Phil. It didn't matter, Nagash Jensen did not have time to lose his shit right now. He opened his eyes.

"Okay," he said.

"Okay what?" the girl said.

"Okay, tell me your name and I'll leave you alone to watch your show"

She regarded him for a moment. "Daiyu," she said eventually. The conveyor on the other side of the auto-chef spit out a piping hot bowl of noodles. They came to rest on a tray directly beside her.

"Daiyu," Gash said.

"Daiyu," she said again.

"Your dad, Phil Shen, named you Daiyu Shen?"

"My mom named me. She's into classic Chinese names. She actually named this place." She gestured at the old, weather-beaten sign. "Wu Shen's Noodles."

So Phil married his girlfriend from back then. Or maybe not married. But started a family with. Good for him. Gash didn't think about his last girlfriend. Or the one he kind of fell in love with on that expedition to Rhodes. He didn't think about those things at all.

Daiyu grabbed the bowl of noodles, a pair of disposable plastic chopsticks, and dropped both in front of him. Then she checked the tablet, noted the other item, and grabbed a bottle of sake out of the fridge beneath the bar of the kiosk. It was a different brand than Phil used to sell. The characters on the clear plastic wrapper were all in Japanese. She unscrewed the green plastic top, the soft snap of the breaking seal a gunshot in Gash's throbbing eardrums. She placed it next to the bowl. She did not ask if he wanted a cup before turning back to her holo projector and hitting play again. The announcer resumed talking about the newly discovered corvid. Something about beak width.

Gash stared at the noodles for a few minutes, eventually getting up the energy to claim his chopsticks. The smell finally got to him – the fresh-salty, soy tang had his mouth watering like in the old days. He grabbed the bowl with his other hand, angled it against the chopsticks, and shoveled a huge portion into his mouth. Immediately his gag reflex kicked in, and he spit the noodles back into the bowl. It was everything he could do to keep himself from throwing up.

Of course, he was a vampire now. In the early weeks of his vampire life, Gash never really sought out food, beyond drinking those couple muggers. Apparently booze was okay but not noodles – it never occurred to him that this would be a problem. Maybe regular food was poison to him now. Booze had always been poison, which maybe explained why it tasted the same as it always had. He set the bowl down and looked over at Daiyu. She was totally oblivious. He clenched his fists until he drew blood. The soft patter of large water droplets striking the plastic kiosk roof heralded the rain's arrival.

Gash popped the top the rest of the way off the bottle of sake and took a tentative drink. No gag reflex. He tipped it up again, upending the contents into his mouth as fast as the laws of physics would allow, the burning against his esophagus mild compared to what he felt in every other fiber of his freshly cursed body. He did not stop until the bottle was empty. By the time he finished, the patter turned into a roar, the downpour dragging soot from the plume of smoke above and depositing it in the street, splashing it against his ankles. It ran oily into the drains, carrying plastic wrappers, used dermal patches, and for some reason confetti with it into the world of sewage beneath the city.

When he slammed the plastic bottle down and rose, Daiyu looked back over. She didn't say anything, but her eyes were obviously drawn to the empty sake bottle and the full bowl.

"Auto-chef ruined Phil's recipes," Gash growled. And then, before Daiyu could say anything or before he could look at her again, he stepped back and into the deluge, the oily river in the street up to his ankles, the downpour running ashey smears along his face and soaking him to the core, and there was nothing else. Just the concrete beneath his feet and the black hot water and the LED glow of 10 billion lights reflecting down at him from the clouds, a spot-light and a "welcome home" and a big "fuck you" and of course nothing at all but rain falling on a burning city.

CHAPTER 3

No planned Lunar Arcology, The Deregulated Zone was an urban organism. Concrete for bones, glass for eyes, canvas and cardboard and plastic for skin, the DRZ lived and breathed and grew inwards in its urban prison of roughly twelve city blocks. Since Gash last spent time here, a new generation of street vendors and street squatters accrued in the cracks and gaps between all of the previous generations of the same, the labyrinth growing denser. The place burgeoned with displaced outcasts, unhoused avoiding the wastelands around the cities, and people considered deviants or criminals by polite society. In short, all the groups who didn't fit in with the corporate-imposed illusion of order in the rest of the city. You could get lost forever in a place like this, and that was exactly the point.

Fortunately, Gash knew the area – evolving or not – better than the inside of a bottle of scotch. Oh, and being a vampire with superior strength and senses certainly helped.

Between the rain and the attacks in the other part of the city, folks huddled in for the night – giving Gash free run of the place. He scaled the concrete wall of a nearby rowhouse with all the ease of walking along the sidewalk. From there he knew exactly which direction to go. Southeast to the other end of the DRZ, leaping from roof to roof, he dropped down in front of a crumbling office building. Every impact-resistant window on the first floor had been chipped or cracked at some point since whatever corporate goons had moved out decades ago. The plaster facade crumbled away by the day, and only two letters remained where once a logo adorned the building above the third story window: a "d" and an "o."

Welcome to the Rat Eater's den, he thought. It had been years since necessity last brought Gash to the den, but here he now stood. In Gash's early days, the Rat Eater served merely as an information broker. Jacked in to some stolen wifi and squatting in the third story of this abandoned building alongside a few dozen like him, the Rat Eater earned his name – and anarchist street cred – as an information broker who only worked with non-corporate clients, and who specialized in helping blackmail and take down "corp-rats."

The perfect info broker for a lone independent private eye in a town full of corporate security districts and billion credit investigative teams, Rat Eater nonetheless always rubbed Gash the wrong way. There was something off about the guy.

Off or not, there was no denying that Rat Eater was moving up in the world. A very indiscrete merc stood at the entrance to the door in a long black trench coat, a shotgun resting casually on his shoulder. But it wasn't the shotgun that drew Gash's attention, it was the shine of chrome from where the trench coat folded at his shoulder. The merc rocked some real top-of-the-line augs. To the untrained eye, he was just a beefcake wearing sunglasses at night like a thousand other douche-bags. But Gash recognized more implants – WalCo Eyeguards. Probably 3rd or 4th edition. Flashbang resistant, with micro-LED lens providing, at minimum, infrared and night vision capabilities and a simple combat HUD. Anti-ballistic skin grafts, a particular texture. A combat-grade neural jack resting just below the cut of his high 'n tight. Ex-military, expensive. More confidence than common sense, but he'd probably earned that confidence in countless combat encounters during his service in some corporate military outfit and after. Gash served with men like this back in his heyday, before Serena and the dream of peace.

Gash clambered down a wall into an alley across the street, and emerged into the open, hands held a few inches away from his waistband – the equivalent of a white flag in these parts. He stepped slowly towards the entrance to Rat Eater's.

Up close you could tell the merc had mid-gen cybernetic arms, too, from the way the trench coat bulged, and from his metal hands. Couldn't tell all the specifics, but odds were good this guy could pull a man apart like a child twisting the arms off his sister's Barbie. Moving up indeed. This was a big money hire for an info broker like Rat Eater, especially just to waste him on guard duty.

But then, this wasn't just guard duty. This was a business decision. Who needs a shiny neon sign or 1000 5-star reviews on the web – people who came to see Rat Eater knew he was the real deal because of this merc. The equivalent of some shipping executive wearing an Italian suit worth more than the average slag dock worker or retail mook's yearly wages. Success begets success, the law of the land. The rich got richer because they were rich. Even here in the DRZ.

This little visit promised to cost Gash a pretty penny. Good thing he had an expense account again.

Gash stopped a few feet away from the merc at the door. The man only looked at him, waiting. His grip tightened ever-so-slightly on the shotgun.

"Here to see Rat Eater," Gash said.

"You're not on the list," the merc said, hefting his shotgun off his shoulder and letting it come to rest a few inches away from being pointed at Gash's head. "And Rat Eater doesn't do business with washed up old junkies."

Being a vampire had its perks, but it wasn't for the self-absorbed. Looking pale and gaunt – to the point of lurching up to death's door – did not inspire awe in strangers.

"I was doing biz with Rat Eater when you were still shitting your diapers, kid. Tell him Nagash Jensen has work for him."

A staring match, then. This was not a man who was used to being talked to like that, and Gash could see it in his eyes – the bloodlust of ego weighing against his job as Rat Eater's gatekeeper. Credits beat out blood, in the end, and the merc rolled his eyes. His mouth moved, subvocal communication with his boss. After a brief pause, the merc stood aside. "Go on in old timer, but watch your mouth from here on out."

When Gash stepped inside, Rat Eater's meteoric rise really struck home. The first and second floor, back in Gash's day, belonged to the junkies. The place was an open-concept office once upon a long time ago, so the space seemed huge. Hacked power grids with small space heaters; junk fires near cracked windows, built out of refuse and whatever paper kindling; and a random assortment of scavenged electric light sources lit the place unevenly. Scattered used hypodermics, spent psychotropic patches, shattered glass vials, broken portable Real-D rigs, and all manner of scrap decorated the floor. You didn't come here to try to get your life together and catch a low level corporate gig. You came here to spend the rest of your life on your own terms.

Now the place looked positively lavish. Rat Eater'd cleaned up, first of all – including the people. He'd turned the first floor into a *waiting room* – no other term for it. Several luxury synth-leather sofas were scattered about, paired with built-in jacks and synth-mahogany coffee tables topped with larger-than-life high-res holo-projectors. The walls were cleaned of all sorts of blood and bodily fluids, repainted in a tasteful dark grey, and adorned with *paintings*. Gash didn't fancy himself an art connoisseur, but even he could tell that these were all cheap AI-generated garbage. Not that the images themselves weren't richly detailed, but that nobody had curated them with human ideas. Basic art tropes that some low-level bot had scraped off the scrapings of ten thousand other low-level bots, imitations heaped on imitations until it was all movie characters re-imagined as famous people or famous people re-imagined as movie characters or corporations imagined as famous people playing movie characters.

So some things changed, but some things stayed the same. Rat Eater had money now, but the money didn't come with taste.

A few potential clients – three non-descript suits – sat on one of the sofas, watching a floating holo-display of a local news broadcast. The reporter ranted about magic-wielding terrorists still at large after burning down a number of low-income housing units. The rain put out the fires, and the carnage seemed to be over for the night.

The reporter scrolled images for his viewers – charred corpses, collapsed rubble, crying women and children. All of the usuals. A WalCo rep spoke, promising a heavy infusion of credits to rebuild the Georgetown neighborhood bigger and better than ever before. Everyone knew this show, by now. Bigger and better meant high income condos and all of the accompanying franchises, orderly rows of consumers. It meant new infusions of refugees to places like the DRZ.

The way the suits were nodding to each other, the way their body language changed when the WalCo rep came on – these suits were corporate. No wonder Rat Eater was living large now – he'd gone corporate. Would he soon eat his own rat tail, a modern ouroboros?

Revulsion rose like bile in his throat, but he suppressed it. None of it mattered, Gash needed the Rat tonight. Two more mercs, one standing lazily by the elevator and the other sitting on the stairs, watched him casually. Once upon a time, that elevator was used in some pretty... unsavory ways. Gash preferred the stairs. He approached the guard, who sighed and stood.

"Gotta wait your turn grandpa," he said.

Gash checked his watch. Close to 4 AM. Not too long before sunrise. He did *not* feel like coming back another day. "Rat Eater's probably jacking off to Real-D foot porn right now, and I just don't have time to wait. Tell him I got an expense account burning a hole in my pocket and need info stat."

The merc's mouth moved, and after a long pause, the word came down. "Go on up," he said, shaking his head.

From behind, one of the suits spoke up. "Hey, we were here first! Do you know who I am? Are you going to make me wait while –"

"Can it," Gash said. "I'm an old friend, and suits like you are on the clock anyway, right? So what do you care?"

They looked at each other, but didn't seem to know how to respond. Before the conversation could continue, Gash slid past the guard and onto the freshly re-carpeted staircase. Halfway up, he heard voices. When he stepped onto the second floor, he could see that it, too, had undergone major renovations. It mirrored the first floor in many ways – dark gray walls liberally adorned with more AI art. Instead of a waiting room, however, Rat Eater had converted this floor into an auction house of some sort. A few dozen folding chairs faced a well-constructed faux-oak stage.

The site of the place turned Gash's stomach. It made him long for half-decayed dead junkies and real-D addicts fondling themselves on rotten, scavenged sofas and ancient, crusty bean bag chairs. The stage held two things and two people. The first, a podium, stood front and center. Rat Eater lurked behind it, his weasel's grin almost hidden behind the tall piece of faux-wood. As much as he'd stayed the same – wiry and pale and with a face not even a mother could trust – he'd changed, too. What little remained of the hair on the top of his head finally abandoned him, leaving only long strings of black on the side of his head. The years had puckered the skin around the integrated neural port on his forehead (one of the great Rat Eater mysteries – why have it in the front of your face like that?). It seemed ready to leap out of his face. He wore a suit now – a nice one, too. The effect was as though Gash had stepped not through a portal into the future, but through a portal into a parallel dimension. He was definitely looking at Rat Eater, but not the same one he remembered.

None of this is what turned his stomach.

Behind the podium Gash saw a raised platform set in the center of the stage. Stairs on either side led up to a woman. Chains bound her wrists and ankles, and a central chain bound all of it to a metal loop in the floor of the podium. She couldn't have been more than her mid-to-late twenties. She stood upright, bearing the weight of her chains as if they were nothing, eyes like iron, face broad and proud. Black hair cascaded down her shoulders to her navel, covering her bare breasts. She had no augs that he could see, except for a small implant, not much larger than a PCom memory chip, protruding from the flesh just behind her right ear. The hair had been shaven in a small patch around the device. A small light blinked green every few seconds. She wore only a pair of worn khaki trousers; too large, and torn at the legs, as though they once belonged to a fat man before he destroyed them. Strange.

A handful of suits – not unlike the men downstairs – waited in line at the foot of the stairs. One such man, a particularly fat one, balding, with a white pin-stripe suit, climbed to the podium. He leered at the woman for a time, before grabbing her chin and angling her head up and away so that he could look closely at her implant. Finally, he forced her mouth open to, for some reason, check her teeth. Satisfied, he stepped down, making way for the next suit.

The second one did more or less the same. He stepped away, but then as an afterthought stepped back towards her, also rubbing his hand around her eyes. She cringed, and when his hand came away, Gash could tell – even from the other side of the room – that the suit had rubbed makeup away from a massive black eye. The second suit gave a loud "Tch," looking over at Rat Eater. He grinned, revealing platinum-coated teeth, and shrugged his little weasel shoulders in a comically exaggerated manner. He scanned the audience in the chairs, and eyes alighting on Gash, brightened up.

"Ah hah! My old friend, Nagash Jensen, best and only private dick in Seattle. Welcome to the new and improved Rat's Den!"

Gash strolled forward slowly. Aside from about a dozen men in suits – customers – four more mercs armed and auged to the teeth stood in strategic positions around the room. Gash needed info, bad. And Rat Eater was the best info broker available to a free agent like

Gash. Maybe the only one, these days. But he felt rage building slowly in the pit of his stomach. Not only had Rat Eater turned corp-rat, but he was auctioning off a human being to suits for profit. If Gash wanted to find Ana Marin and finally close this old chapter of his life, he had to keep his cool. The world was a shitty place, and corps bought and sold people every day – indentured workers, illegals turned into sex slaves and worse.

This was just the world. It happened every day in every city. No reason to get killed for it.

"I'll be done with this biz in just a few minutes," Rat Eater said when Gash was close to the stage. "Since you apparently have money now, you want to check out the merch?" He gestured back at the young woman on the stage.

Gash gritted his teeth. "Selling sex slaves now, Rat Eater?"

Rat Eater tugged at the thin strands of hair hanging off the side of his head, mouth open too-wide to flash that platinum grin. "Men and women, boys and girls, if you want one. But not tonight. This one's a real specialized find. You ever heard of a wechuge?"

He shook his head.

"Well you'll hear all about it when the bidding gets started. Check her out up close, if you want. Always good to make sure you're bidding on good product."

The way he paused on the word "good," to describe a woman chained half-naked to a stage and forced to stand still as men studied her like a horse for sale, enflamed the rage in Gash. Crimson seeped slowly into his vision, like red dye mixing into liquid cornea. His vampiric senses tuned in to beating hearts and arteries. The blood running hot through Rat Eater and his suited customers and his chromed up mercs. And the woman, too, the would-be slave. If he let the red rage take him, there would be a horrible bloodbath here, and it might be his blood. Or even hers. The animal inside craved the red and made no distinction between slave and slaver. This was not the day or place to pick a losing fight. With tremendous will, he fought back the rage, and his vision gradually returned to normal.

Better to play Rat Eater's little games. Gash stepped to the podium and stood in line to "check out the merch." Don't try to save the world if you can't even save Ana Marin, he told himself.

After watching four more suits poke and prod the poor woman, it was Gash's turn to climb the stairs. Up close, Gash could see a number of bruises and scabs on her arms and stomach. She looked him in the eye. She hadn't done that with the others.

His vampire senses kicked into overdrive again – he still struggled to control them. She radiated heat, the vital fluid pumping in her arteries. He could almost taste it. The woman smelled strongly of sweat and iron. She must've been here for days, meaning this was not an impromptu auction. It was planned at least a week in advance. Beyond that was something else. The smell of... ozone. Like just before a powerful storm, but much fainter. He smelled this once before. Selina, right in the moment magic returned to the world. Just before she was surrounded by a blue forcefield and flew up past him like some crazy superhero.

He stood before an exceptional woman: a bottled storm, a magical being, fierce and brave. In that moment, Nagash Jensen did what Nagash Jensen always did. He fell right in love. His brain knew all the things it needed to know. It was a fool's errand to try to save this woman by himself. He needed the flesh-peddling corporate-rat-feeding scumbag Rat Eater to save Dr. Marin. To collect a payday big enough to finally retire on. This was the next step on that journey. The mystery woman standing before him was half his age and he knew nothing about her. His brain hammered him over and over. You don't know her, you can't love her, you can't sacrifice your life and your job for this random stranger. What kind of fool are you anyway? Just sit down and wait for it all to be over and move on and get the job done.

He stood practically toe-to-toe with the woman, trying not to feel her throbbing pulse in the thick air, the warmth of her vitae in her veins. He pretended to consider the quality of her hair, whispering as softly as he could, "I'm going to help you get out of here."

She continued to stare, eyes a mining laser boring deep into him, or through him. "Good," she whispered. "Pull this damned inhibitor out of my skull and get out of my way."

"Won't that... damage you?" he whispered back.

She popped a half smile and shrugged. "Better than being sold into slavery to one of these leering corp-sluts. I'd rather die free."

He considered her for a single fleeting moment that stretched on for days and weeks, keenly aware of Rat Eater's mercs – four on this floor, three more down below, and who knows how many more in the side rooms and upstairs? Not to mention the suits. Some of them were no doubt auged and armed as well. Rat Eater's men didn't bother to confiscate firearms at the door, so any one of them could pull the trigger that ended Nagash Jensen's life.

But there she stood, darkly radiant. A dangerous beautiful normal woman chained and being sold as chattel in a ritual of commerce that should have stayed dead centuries ago.

Faster than anyone could react, he reached up and yanked the inhibitor out of her skull. The metal shard came out easy in a spurt of blood and little chunks of tissue. Just flesh and blood, he hoped. Not grey matter. The moment it came free, the woman changed. No, *transformed*. It happened fast – maybe half a second. To the men on the floor below, it would have been almost impossible to track. But not for Gash Jensen and his heightened senses.

Her face bones cracked and rearranged, the fine hairs on her arms extending and growing into thick brown fur as her radius and ulna elongated and wicked claws sprouted from her fingers. Her knee joints cracked backwards, feet turning to hooves and thick brown fur growing in everywhere. Bone grew out of her face, her head elongating and horns – no, antlers – growing out of the side of her head. When all was said and done, she grew a foot taller, muscles rippling beneath shaggy brown fur, and her head looked precisely like the still-antlered skull of a dead buck. The bleeding wound on the side of her head stitched itself shut, flesh and fur growing in to fill the hole in micro-seconds. Now, the too baggy pants clung to a monster's muscled legs, the tears a perfect fit to the transformation.

So *that's* a wechuge, Gash thought, and she gave a bone-shuddering howl that shook the walls and rattled the podium. Nothing normal about this woman. And then Gash did exactly what the lady instructed. He stepped out of her way.

CHAPTER 4

The wechuge lunged off the platform with what must have been blinding speed to the humans down below. Her target, the nearest merc – another heavily auged grunt like the one outside – didn't have time even to bring his SMG to bear. She ripped his head off like she was picking a petunia from a flower garden, and flung it away. His body crumpled to the stage as his head struck the far wall with a loud, wet crunch.

The other three mercs reacted first, opening fire at the monster. Rat Eater reacted faster than he should have – must have sprung for some neural implants in recent days – ducking down behind his podium. The suits moved last, diving behind cover and drawing sidearms of their own. It all seemed to happen in slow motion to Gash, who stood on the platform watching the scene unfold. A barrage of gauss projectiles hit the wechuge in a torrent, punching holes in flesh and bone – blood and skull fragments showered the platform. Gash thought that would be the end of her, but she grabbed the headless body off the stage and dove for cover behind the platform.

"Kill him too," Rat Eater screeched, and the mercs turned their weapons on Gash. Fair enough.

By the time they pulled their triggers, Gash stood behind the platform beside his new monster friend. He watched as she ripped a leg off the body, gorging on human meat like a cartoon wolf with a giant chicken wing. As she ate, her flesh and the bone of her face began to knit back together. He watched in awe as her wounds regenerated in seconds. When she'd eaten her fill, she tossed the body aside. The arterial spray was slowing. This close, he realized it had been quite some time since he'd had a meal of his own. He hoisted the mangled remains and, like a boy scout drinking water from a hose, drank his fill from the last spurts of crimson. The wechuge watched him, eyes narrowed.

"Vampire," Gash said. "Guess you and I are two of a kind." He dropped the body and wiped the blood from his face with the back of his hand. A powerful pulse of energy rippled through him, as it always did when he fed. His already-heightened senses climbed even higher. He felt stronger and faster. He could hear the heartbeats of the three remaining mercs accelerating steadily – controlled, no doubt, by an adrenal implant. Rat Eater's thumped rapidly and sporadically, along with two of the suits that had not fled the room already.

"You help." The rasping whisper of her voice, a dagger made of ice, carved its way into his head and made him shiver.

"I already did," he said.

"You help again," she said. "They are shooting at you too."

"You're not wrong." He peaked around the corner of the platform and could see the mercs moving to flank him. Rat Eater and the two remaining suits crouched behind some chairs, firearms aimed in anticipation. When they saw his head, the whole lot of them opened fire, the soft hum of gauss weapons spewing magnetized flechettes. The deluge of high-velocity metal shards carved away chunks of faux-wood as Gash ducked back behind cover.

"Fine," he said. "But I need the one that was trying to sell you alive. Rat Eater."

"*NO,*" she said, and the force of it almost knocked him over. He thought she might attack him right on the spot. "He put me in chains."

He thought of her before the transformation – the bruises and scabs. Of the millions of denizens in the Seattle sprawl, Gash could find another information broker.

"Okay," he said. "I'll go left, you go right. Ready?"

She nodded, and Gash drew his sidearm – a trusty old piece, a .44 magnum that he picked up in Florida a lifetime ago. It lacked the penetrating power, raw destructiveness, and ammo capacity of a more modern gauss weapon. But he liked it. Aside from being old like him, these classic firearms were *loud.* You could feel it kick and hear it thunder and you knew you were taking a life. Usually someone's life that deserved it, but still a human life. Good to be reminded of that. It felt too easy to kill with a gauss weapon. Too clean. Death shouldn't be quiet and smooth, it should be loud and messy.

She looked at his old gun and cocked her head. And it was true what she was probably thinking – he didn't need this, not anymore. He was a vampire now. Maybe one day he would be comfortable descending on his enemies and ripping them limb from limb like some hyper-auged cyber monstrosity. But for now he still preferred the comfort of his revolver, of a gun battle. The retired soldier in him felt at home.

He dove left, rolling from behind the podium faster than even the wechuge could react to. The nearest merc was climbing the stage in the corner of the room, trying to flank the pair of monsters.

Nagash Jensen always viewed combat in slow motion, even as a young soldier. Some deep and primal part of his brain took over in times of life and death, some death spirit that others simply lacked. No way he would have survived past his twenties without it. It inhabited him now, enhanced with vampiric speed and senses. The poor bastard never stood a chance.

He rolled to his feet, firing at that first merc before his would-be killer could even register his presence. The first shot went wide, but the second one struck home in the center of the merc's skull, blood blossoming out the gaping hole in the back and drenching an AI painting of Albert Einstein as an anime character with gore and bits of gray matter.

He turned to the second merc, standing center stage and covering the platform while his buddies flanked to each side. To his credit, the merc was already pointing his weapon at Gash, and the gauss shotgun humming softly, the sound of its magnets warming up in the microsecond before they spewed death. He must have had some serious neural augs to react that quickly. These were no hired muscle – reflex enhancements like that almost always meant corporate black ops. No time to process that right now.

Gash strafed further to the left, effectively side-stepping the burst of magnetized iron fragments that sizzled the air millimeters behind him. He fired his revolver twice, and the force of the old .44 caliber slugs impacting the merc's chest knocked him backwards. He kept his feet however, and fired off the shotgun at Gash again.

Surprise almost lost Gash his head. Could he survive a blast like that? Better not to find out. He rolled out of the way at the last millisecond. This merc didn't have body armor, which meant he must have had some heavy-duty dermal implants. High end. As Gash came to his feet again, he aimed for the merc's head – even if the skin was bullet proof, the impact of a .44 caliber bullet to the skull would rattle his brain. But before he could fire, the wechuge hit the merc from behind, tackling him to the ground.

Rat Eater and the suits below finally caught up to the action on the stage, and they opened fire with their gauss pistols. The small arms fire seemed to barely make an impact on the wechuge, and Gash was moving too fast again – they'd never hit him. He sidestepped left, then right, and cleared the rest of the stage in half a second, leaping off and downing the last two suits with his last two bullets.

Behind him, the wechuge groaned and roared. In a wrestling match with a monster, the merc was holding his own. She had him pinned, but he held both of her claws at bay. How? She shredded the other two mercs, who both sported cyber-arms strong enough to crush concrete into power. But then he saw the merc's eyes – they were beginning to glow blue. As the two wrestled, Gash noticed that his arms, too, were wreathed with a faint blue energy. Magic – the man was using magic to bolster his strength, not tech. Interesting. Gash took a step forward to help his fellow monster, but when he heard the scurrying of little rat feet, he turned. Rat Eater was making a break for it.

In a blink, Gash crossed the large room and interposed himself between the Rat and the stairway down to the first floor.

"Gash Jensen," Rat Eater said, his voice quivering. "You've really stepped in it now."

"Oh yeah? What have I stepped in, Rat Eater? Or should I just say Rat, now?"

Back on the stage, Gash watched the wechuge and the magical adept struggle, deadlocked. She couldn't quite muster the strength to rip his throat out, but he couldn't escape from beneath her either.

"You're in it up to your eyeballs, you idiot. But I'll make you a deal. Call off your dog – elk, whatever – and I will square you away with my employer. We'll just pretend the whole thing didn't happen."

The Rat Eater of old was always a free agent, but it was now clear to Gash that the price tag on the muscle in this place far exceeded what the Rat could ever hope to afford as an independent. What had he stepped in?

"If you want me to even consider your offer, I'll need details," Gash said.

"If I tell you too much, I'll die an even worse death than at the hands of that savage," Rat Eater started. Behind him, Gash watched as the wechuge finally grew tired of the battle. She reared up, gave one more roar, and then raked the man across the chest with her antlers. Blood fountained in her face, and the merc finally went still.

"I wouldn't call her a savage on moral principal, but also I just don't think she would like it," Gash said.

"Okay, wait, wait," Rat Eater said, turning around to watch her stride slowly towards him.

She let him beg for his life for a good thirty seconds. He kneeled before her, pleading for mercy. The sound of footsteps below and above, the smell of chrome and sweat, the faint voices of barking orders all signified that the rest of Rat Eater's goons were converging on them. She must have heard or smelled it too, because she finally reached out, grabbing Rat Eater by the neck. He squirmed, legs bicycling in the air, squealing just like a rat when she squeezed his throat like a toothpaste tube. With a spurt of blood from his mouth, the struggle ceased and the Rat went limp.

That was it, then. He was dead, and Gash would have to find a new information broker.

The wechuge stood over his broken body for a moment, then gave a long low howl. It opened a wide black chasm deep in Gash's chest, and he could've sworn his heart froze over. The footsteps above and below stopped dead. Before they could resume, she sprinted towards the wall on the street side. She jumped through, the plaster and glass crumpling outwards, no more than a paper ribbon at the end of a race. He followed her through, landing on the sidewalk beside her, and the two monsters fled deeper into the concrete neon-bright labyrinth, the eternal daylight of the night-time sprawl.

CHAPTER 5

Gash followed his new friend the wechuge for a few blocks, but when dawn cracked the smokey clouds over the eastern horizon, he knew it was time to return to his ship. He called out to her, but whether she heard him or not, she fled deeper into the DRZ as he broke off towards the Poseidon dockyard.

Now alone in his cabin, windows shuttered against a lethal dose of sunlight, Gash decompressed after the night's bloodbath. He kicked off his shoes and eyed the empty bar wistfully. One of the few mercies of vampirism – booze didn't hit him like it used to, but he could still find a buzz if he looked hard inside a big enough bottle. He would have to restock when the sun set.

Which left ten hours to kill. Gash would need to sleep during that time, but not yet. Couldn't sleep right after all that action. All that adrenaline. How to kill the time? He figured he could do some research, try to dig up info or a new contact on the dark web. Could catch up on the news, watch a report on how many people were killed in that conflagration in the Georgetown neighborhood last night. Could watch a movie on the ship's holovid.

The whole of the world's endless digital entertainment at his fingertips, a long hard mystery to solve, an ever-changing world to keep track of; and all he could think about was the woman he saved.

She reminded him of someone he'd known recently, a hacker named Selina Kan – both were fierce and beautiful and seemingly unflappable. Selina's path diverged from his the moment he transformed into a vampire, and now this wechuge was out of his life as abruptly as she'd entered it. He hadn't even gotten her name before she'd run off into the city.

And what would you do with her name, or anything else? She's half your age and saving her doesn't entitle you to a damn thing. Best to steer clear – work the case, retire to a peaceful corner of the world like you promised Serena and live out the rest of your days in solitude. Maybe find someone once it's safe to be around you.

That was always the plan – get the big payday and retire. Could a vampire retire? Would he live forever now that he'd transformed?

Too much. Processing the blood on his hands, adjusting to his new life as a vampire after just a couple months, trying not to fall for a beautiful stranger; everything pressed down on him at once and he couldn't breathe. "Trine," he said. The holovid snapped on, and the VI's avatar appeared before him. "Do that dance from before, with all of the cartwheels."

She stood – if you could use that word for a holographic projection – totally still. "Trine?" he said.

When Trine spoke, she did so using another voice; robotic and vaguely feminine, but totally mismatched to her figure.

"Is that really the best use of your time?" Trine asked.

Gash sat up. "What's going on here?"

"You are making liberal use of my expense account, I expect you to be working the case. Not slaughtering a room full of corporate contractors and abusing a complex Virtual Intelligence by turning her into a digital stripper."

"Oh Jesus, it's you." The mystery client. "You know, you can call me if you need something."

"This will do just fine," Trine's avatar said. "So do you care to update me on the case? I am starting to feel like I made the same mistake twice."

"That makes two of us," Gash said.

Neither spoke, then, for a time. After several minutes, Gash realized a staring contest with a hacked virtual assistant could only end one way.

"Fine," he blinked. "The bloodbath can be explained. I tried to connect with an old contact, an info broker named Rat Eater. Turns out, he expanded into human trafficking since the last time I worked with him. I saved the woman he meant to sell, and had to kill him and some mercs along the way. The dancing, well I suppose I have trouble dealing with stress. You want me to spend money and time on a therapist or lock it all behind mindless entertainment for thirty minute intervals and then get back to the case?"

The Trine form stood completely still. Except, was that a flicker in her eyes? His gut told him the same thing it would tell him if he were interviewing a regular person and saw that flicker. Emotion hidden beneath the surface. Except this was a holographic projection of a VI avatar hijacked by his client, incapable of expressing real emotion. Even Gash's gut caught false positives from time to time.

Eventually, she spoke again. "I see. I thank you for the update – please do not dally. Things are progressing more quickly than I originally anticipated."

"Hold on, what does that mean?" Gash asked. "It's foolish to hold back information from your own investigator. What else do you know about Ana's abduction?"

The projection simply stared at him, voice silent.

"Hey, I asked you a question," Gash said.

"Apologies, please restate your question," Trine said. Only this time she spoke, in her own voice.

"Never mind, Trine," he said, sighing and settling back into the sofa.

"Do you still want me to execute the dance with the cartwheels? I also have one in my database involving hula hoops that other users like you have enjoyed."

"Deactivate," he said, closing his eyes against the too-bright world.

33

Chapter 6

The next two days proved to Gash what he already knew – Seattle, like every other metro, proved to be a wasteland for non-corporate investigators. The corporations kept a tight leash on information, and info-brokers like the Rat Eater either went extinct or went corporate.

He took a long pull out of a fresh bottle of scotch – a 15-year malt with a Scottish-sounding name. The one high point in the last two days – Gash restocked the ship's bar with quality stuff, good enough to feel like he was getting the most out of his unlimited expense account, but not so outrageous that his client might feel compelled to cut him off.

Gash watched the horizon, a gray steel line between the gray sky and the blue-steel ocean, waves chopping gently in the rain. How long had he been staring at this single point? Long enough that the rivulets of water running down the window blurred as he gazed past them. One of the perks of being a vampire in Seattle – most days there were enough rain clouds that he could leave the window blinds up without fear of being roasted alive (though his skin stung if he stood too close to the window for too long, even beneath the thick clouds).

"Alive." Gash found little time since his transformation to really sit down and contemplate what it might mean to be a vampire. Was he really undead? He lacked a heartbeat, but he did bleed when cut or wounded. At least, for a few seconds, before his body healed the wound. He drank blood to live, but also seemed to "power up," for lack of a better phrasing, when consuming the red.

Fortunately, Gash's family were mostly dead or at least not talking to him anymore, and in his line of work you didn't make or keep friends – not for long. Meaning he owed zero explanations. He didn't need to report to a family member what had happened, he didn't need to come up with excuses for missing daytime engagements with friends. He didn't have a boss at a 9-5 day job that he needed to report to for missed hours. For the last two months, Nagash Jensen simply carried on his solitary life, using the tools at hand when he needed them. But one day soon he would make time to hold a reckoning with himself. To come to grips with his new status as a bloodsucking creature of the night.

A gull wheeled about and then dove into the water. It bobbed in the waves for a time, and then took off again, flapping violently to build up momentum against the current and the wind and the waves.

Time to face facts: Only one option remained to Gash. To get the info – to find Ana so he could save her – would require a hacker and a live op. Rat Eater might have known the right people to ask, the right places to grease palms with credits or favors. But with him dead, the information Gash wanted fell out of reach. That meant stealing it from the source instead. Hiring a hacker, taking a run at WalCo's secure servers. Last time Gash worked this case, a botched raid meant WalCo assassins hunting him all the way to Florida, and from there across the ocean to Rhodes. That was before the reawakening of magic. The chaos of an unregulated influx of power into the world gave Gash the cover to return to Seattle to take one more shot. But if he were to hit their offices, hijack their data, the corporate assassins would come calling again. Still, Gash saw no other path forward.

One more slug of scotch from the bottle, and he capped it, placed it back at the bar, and sat down with his PCom. He knew a damn good hacker, but would she take his call after he'd abandoned her at the end of the last job? When he'd transformed into a vampire, fleeing her side and abandoning her?

CHAPTER 7

Hemmingway. The name served as little more than a much-needed reminder, but at least one good came out of the call with Starfire. She couldn't help him directly, too much going on in her life. Gash believed her. In this new world, someone with magical powers like her would be in high demand – but a part of him couldn't shake feeling brushed off.

Maybe that was uncharitable. It was probably a hell of a weird conversation for her. Hi, oh hi it's me the bodyguard that abandoned you when the world exploded around us. What's new with you? Oh I'm a wizard now. Oh no kidding, I'm a vampire now. No kidding?

Strange all around.

At any rate, Starfire pointed him in the right direction, a mutual acquaintance and fixer known by his digital moniker, Hemmingway. Hemmingway put Gash and Starfire together for Gash's last job, and could surely connect Gash with another gifted hacker to make a run at WalCo.

Gash stepped off *The Holy* and strode quickly through the docks and towards the street. Nothing could ever be easy in this world. Hemmingway remembered him, but would only meet in person – either in the flesh or in the digital flesh. And since Hemmingway lived on the other end of the continent, digital flesh would be the answer.

Meaning Gash needed an integrated neural port or a Real-D rig. In order to keep major brain surgery off the table, Gash opted for a Real-D rig.

Fortunately, after years in a city like Seattle, Gash's PCom held more than a few useful numbers. In this case, speed dial connected him to Sammy Smut, the stunning non-binary proprietor of the DRZ's classiest Real-D parlor. Gash reconnected with Sammy, and after a few minutes nagging him for leaving without saying good-bye, they agreed to let Gash use one of their rigs to jack in and visit Hemmingway.

Stepping into Sammy's Real-D Emporium felt like stepping comfortably back into his old life. Days spent chasing cheating spouses and digging up dirt on corporations for folks looking for a little leverage, nights spent drinking in the DRZ and finishing up at Sammy's with the latest and greatest porn reels, fine-tuned by Sammy for maximum sensory output. Everything some well-endowed pornstar saw, felt, and heard, only turned up to eleven.

Sammy ran a clean parlor. Neon pink backlights around the room strobed purple and green. A few clients sat in plush faux-leather sofas, waiting for appointment times. Vending machines on the far wall dispensed only the highest quality corporate pharmaceuticals. Sammy themself sat at the counter, tapping away at their PCom. Their smile lit the room when Gash stepped in.

"Nagash Jensen, you grizzled old stereotype, you have returned to me at last. Welcome home, honey." Sammy stepped around the counter and gave Gash a great big bear-hug, before stepping back and slapping him. "My regulars do *not* abandon me without notice, so be warned if you plan to abandon me again that you won't get a third opportunity."

"Yeah, sorry Sammy," Gash said.

"You at least going to explain yourself?" Sammy asked, stepping back behind the counter before training their mesmerizing eyes on Gash. A thousand times Gash lost himself in those eyes, a one-of-a-kind aug as far as he knew. They glowed and pulsed softly in the same pink/purple/green hues as the parlor's backlights, sometimes one color, sometimes an ink-blot of multiple shades swimming in their digital irises, a never-ending sequence of colors that possessed a certain rhythm that soothed even as it defied prediction. Sammy once told Gash that they'd had the eyes custom-programmed based on some complex mathematical formulas. It all went over Gash's head.

He stepped up to the counter and leaned in on it. "Better for you if I don't explain."

Sammy cocked their head to the side and considered him. "Your head looks naked without your hat. What's going on up there?"

Gash laughed, long and low. "I thought you hated the hat, Sammy."

"I guess it grew on me, what can I say?"

"Well, I lost it on the last job. Haven't made time to replace it."

Sammy pouted, the gesture magnifying their already-huge lips to an almost comical extent. After two beats of pouting, their faced snapped completely back into business mode.

"So here's how it's going to be. Like I said on the PCom, I'm going to let you dive into the web using one of my Real-D rigs in the back. Traditionally reserved only for me and mine. I'm going to charge you an awful lot, and I'm going to isolate the rest of the store from the network while you do it. If you do anything that brings corporate heat onto my emporium..." they trailed off.

"Relax, Sammy. I'm not conducting any kind of op here, just need to meet a fixer in his little digital realm, make some arrangements."

Though Sammy did *not* look convinced, they nevertheless waved an invoice over to Gash's PCom. He glanced at it, and then waved the credits back over to Sammy's. The perks of a bottomless expense account.

Sammy raised their eyes at the amount on their PCom. "I gotta say, honey, I really thought you were going to try to haggle me down. You weren't kidding when you said you had a big expense account, huh?"

Gash shrugged.

"All this just for a meeting? What I'm charging you, you could book a flight halfway around the world to meet this fixer in person."

"Sure thing, but what I'm really buying is time. I just don't have time to go off jet-setting."

"Okay then, come on back, Mr. Big Bucks." Sammy turned and headed into the back of the parlor. Gash followed them down a long hallway, past a dozen closed doors, each numbered. Sound-proofed rooms with state-of-the-art Real-D rigs, comfortable seating, refreshments. Each room, Gash knew from experience, a tiny island of paradise in a disappointing and cruel world. Gash expected painful nostalgia, coming back for business and not pleasure, but it hit him harder than expected – hammered him with each step. His old life, his comfortable life with comfortable routines worn into the same comfortable spaces over the span of decades, snuffed out like a candle in the rain in just a single day. And he would have to take on WalCo *again* to try to get it – or at least something like it – back.

Sammy opened the door at the end of the hallway, and they stepped out of the riot of purples, pinks, and greens and into a more utilitarian space. Earth tones and faux wood governed this space. Gash followed Sammy past several unused conference rooms and offices, and finally into a corner office space that featured little more than an office chair and a Real-D rig.

"So I've billed you for an hour, if you go longer the meter *will* be running. Unlike my customer-facing rigs, this one has open access to the web, so behave yourself in there." Sammy's hand fluttered as they closed the door, leaving Gash alone in the non-descript room.

Gash took a seat, guiding the Real-D rig onto his head. Beginners sometimes struggled to get the electrodes attached to the right parts of the head, but not Nagash Jensen. It only took a moment to get situated, and then Gash flicked the "On" switch on his rig and closed his eyes. A few million electrical impulses hit his brain all at once, then, temporarily disconnecting his brain from his physical body, and connecting it to the full-sensory world of the virtual web. Gash floated in limbo while the software booted, a little circle spinning in the center of his vision as he waited to see what thematic choices Sammy had made with their home screen. Time to meet Hemmingway, time to get this op put together and crack WalCo again. Time to finally find Ana Marin.

Chapter 8

After navigating the links and waiting for the server admin to approve entry, Gash found himself standing on a small dirt path near the coast. In the distance, waves crashed upon a rocky shore, and the ozone smell of fresh ocean breeze filled his digital nose. Above, the sky seemed to stretch on endlessly, a purer azure hue than he ever remembered seeing in the real world. The sheer power of those initial sensory inputs almost knocked him backwards. Not that he hadn't experienced smells and sounds and sights every day in his normal real life. But had Sammy found a way to turn up the neural feedback on their rig? That would be a very Sammy thing to do. Or perhaps Gash's body and mind simply disconnected – what the mind knew was coming did not necessarily transmit to the body, and given that he still lie in Sammy's Emporium in the real world, it might be the surprise of subverted expectations that turned normal sensations into something extra.

"Feels pretty amazing, popping your live-action Real-D cherry, huh?" Gash recognized the voice from before – this was Hemmingway talking.

When Gash looked down from the amazing sky, he saw that the man who seemed to be speaking looked nothing like the big Samoan Gash met once in real life. Here in the Real-D digital universe,

Hemmingway looked like the famous author for whom he'd named himself. Tall and well-built, with a button-down shirt, slicked back black hair, and a well-oiled black moustache to cap the look.

"Hemmingway," Gash said. "This is pretty incredible. Is it always like this?"

Hemmingway shrugged. "You know I'm good, Gash. I programmed this little slice of cyberspace myself, so you're getting top notch inputs right now. There are domains of the same quality, and maybe a select few that you would find even more vivid. But no, it's not always like this."

For the first time, Gash understood how folks could grow addicted to Real-D. Not the pre-recorded porn reels, Gash's long-time vice. Of course people got addicted to those, too. Porn addiction was nothing new. Everyone liked to feel good. But the gamers, web divers, digital explorers and spelunkers: There was something Gash could never comprehend about moving around of your own volition in a hyper-real digital space. The junkies he'd seen on the streets and squatting in places like the old Rat Eater's den, clinging to duct-taped-together Real-D rigs, frantically hacking the power grid and trading passwords for satellite wifi networks like addicts trading needles for names of dealers: It all made sense now.

"Take your time," Hemmingway said.

Next, Gash looked at himself. He never thought to consider his own avatar before seeing Hemmingway's. His hands seemed like his own normal hands and he wore his customary long black coat and wide-brimmed hat (the one he lost in Rhodes).

"Residual self-image," Hemmingway said. "Assuming you didn't program that avatar yourself."

"Huh?"

"RSI – the concept has been around for over a century, but the tech is brand new, and takes a hell of a programmer. The software takes cues from your subconscious to render an avatar based on your impressions of yourself. Very hard to program, and twice as hard to get right. This Sammy of yours is quite good. You look *just* like the real version of you, except maybe ten years older."

Gash stared at his hands for ages before snapping back from his reverie. Ana Marin waited. She was waiting for him for a long time, and now was no time to sit around seeing the digital sights. "Okay, I'm good, let's get to business."

"Sure thing, my friend. Not here, though. We don't do biz in the yard like animals, let's have some tea and talk like civilized people." He turned towards the house in the distance, and Gash followed.

The house manor stood teetering on the edge of a cliff by the ocean. With seven stories, including turrets and towers protruding upwards at improbable heights, the thing looked more like a castle than a manor house – no, more than that even, it looked like a wizard's tower *disguised* as a house. You couldn't help feeling that it would topple over into the churning waves below at any moment, but of course with Hemmingway's coding it would be just as likely to float into the sky as topple over as stay put exactly where it stood even if he added fifty more stories. One of the perks of digital property – physics optional.

"What do you think of my home?" Hemmingway asked.

"Not your real, home, right? I've been there, before – nice pad in Jacksonville."

"Like most people, Nagash Jensen, you suffer from an affliction. Do you want to know what it is? No, don't bother to answer, it was a rhetorical question. You conflate the words 'real' and 'primary.' Just because something exists in the digital world instead of the primary world we were born in does not make it less important. In fact, everything here in my digital domain, – and I do mean everything – is better than the real world. You've been cruising around the ocean on that former Knights of Malta yacht, right? Well I happen to know the ocean smells like shit in the real world, on account of all the pollution and dead fish."

Gash could only nod.

"Not here, though. Here it smells like it used to, like it still does on a very few hidden beaches in the real world. Here it smells like whatever I want. It smells like gingerbread cookies fresh out of the oven if I want it to. My primary-world apartment is fine, I need somewhere to take care of the meat that keeps my brain alive. But *this* is my home." The sweeping gesture of his arm covered not just the house itself, but the whole area. The entire domain. He paused to turn back to Gash. "So what do you think?"

"I think all of that about primary and digital is bullshit, frankly. You're balancing on the fine line between pleasure and addiction and it's dangerous. But I will admit, it's a beautiful place you've coded for yourself here."

Hemmingway shrugged, and turned back towards the house. They walked in silence the last few hundred yards. As they stepped up onto the porch, the door to the home swung open from within. The woman holding the door open for them smiled and beckoned them inside. From a beauty mark on her chin to the individual hairs of her bangs tumbling across her smooth forehead, every detail felt real. She seemed familiar somehow.

"Impressive avatar," he said.

Hemmingway's laugh seemed to echo throughout the whole domain. "Oh Gash, that's just my virtual assistant, LuluBot. She takes care of the house."

"Lulubot?"

"Yes, she is indeed named after our mutual acquaintance."

Gash remembered Lulu – the street-walker in Jacksonville that originally connected him to Hemmingway. The explanation for the familiarity did little to dispel his awe at the level of detail. This virtual assistant dressed like a maid could easily pass for the real Lulu.

"How is the real Lulu?" Gash asked.

"Same as she always is. Anyway, you coming in so we can get down to business?"

Gash stepped past Lulubot and entered Hemmingway's space.

Inside proved to be as impressive as outside. Real or not, Hemmingway furnished the place beautifully, with deep mahogany furniture. Hemmingway led him into the kitchen, and past to a dining area with a sturdy oak table and some impressive oak chairs, rigid and elaborate. Gash was surprised to find that when he sat in his, it felt incredibly comfortable. Better even than the tempur-foam chairs at Hemmingway's real-world residence. Lulubot left them sitting at the table, but appeared seconds later with a tea tray featuring a delicate porcelain teapot and two cups. She served both of them, and then stepped out of the room.

"Please enjoy," Hemmingway said, grabbing one of the cups and taking a sip. "Do you prefer sugar or maybe some milk?" He snapped his fingers as he spoke, and a bowl of sugar and small pitcher of milk appeared on the table beside the tea tray. After, he looked at Gash for a moment before breaking out in a huge grin. "I can see from your face that you're not a tea drinker. Fair enough, you've probably never had the opportunity. Natural disasters wiped out most of the best tea plantations when we were young. Folks like us couldn't normally afford a luxury like this in the real."

"What do you mean you can see from my face?" Gash asked.

"It's so easy for me to forget that this is your first time meeting in Real-D because the equipment you're using is top notch. The rig you're wearing can read the little muscle twitches in your face and translate them into the digital. When you make a disgusted face at the idea of drinking tea like a 19th century British patrician, it shows here." Hemmingway laughed.

"Making me feel like a school-boy learning how the world works for the first time," Gash growled.

"Oh you'll get over it. You might even like it. Try the tea, Gash. I know, I know, not real, why bother drinking a beverage in a digital world, blah blah blah. Humor me."

Gash humored him. The drink tasted smooth, with a hint of citric acid and a slightly bitter after-taste. It actually wasn't bad. But he did try adding some of the digital sugar and stirred it in. That made it perfect. He downed the drink as quickly as he could, given the heat. LuluBot came in and refilled him as soon as he finished.

"Why use LuluBot to serve it when you can snap your fingers and cause it materialize?"

"Because ritual makes our lives richer. People get lost in endless digital worlds, scrolling from one to another and never waiting for anything. The waiting, the kind of communion I have with Lulubot, these details are the difference between an infinite scroll of entertainment and a detailed world that one can truly *live* in."

Gash mixed some more sugar into his second digital cup and took another sip. "Okay, you win, Hemmingway. This is all very impressive."

"That's all I wanted, you know," Hemmingway said, sipping his own tea. "Acknowledgment of the pleasures of the digital from the jaded old private investigator."

Before Gash could respond, Hemmingway gestured again, and a holo projection materialized in the air above the table between them. It showed drone footage of a particular WalCo facility in the wilderness of eastern Washington. He recognized this facility well as the place where things truly went off the rails, where he'd killed ten WalCo guards escaping after a failed attempt to locate and extract Ana Marin.

"You know this facility," Hemmingway said.

"Of course I do," Gash said, taking a swig of the tea. "Last time we were together, you showed me security footage of my escape, that bloodbath. You trying to remind me of my own failings?"

"Not at all. I'm trying to tell you that in all the comings and goings since the day you busted out of there, I've found no evidence of a VIP-type scientist being moved out. Meaning she's still there, or she was never there. And I've looked. Hard. Satellite data over the last year, drone flybys, publicly available radar and shuttle flight path data, shipping manifests."

Gash read through the data as it scrolled through the air in front of him. Hemmingway was thorough, but all of this just confirmed what he knew – the only way to find Ana Marin would be a live op.

Hemmingway continued. "I know you know this, but the only way to get the data you want is going to be to extract it directly from WalCo. This is why you came to me. I'm showing you all of this so that you'll think to come directly to your old pal Hemmingway next time you need data, not to scum like Rat Eater."

"You always do your homework," Gash said. "Did you know Rat Eater?"

"Knew of him. The world's better off without him."

Gash grunted. "So are you my guy for this op? Starfire's unavailable, but I know you're quite talented as well."

Hemmingway chuckled, pouring himself another cup of tea. "I certainly know my way around a stack of code, but I'm not the man for this job. This is field work, my friend. Old Hemmingway here is a fixer, not a field operative. You need to directly access the WalCo mainframe – any data of this sensitive nature is going to be held in a separate internal network, completely disconnected from the wider web."

Gash sat back in the chair and crossed his arms. "So you have someone in mind?"

"I do, but we're talking about a live op to crack WalCO HQ, which feels like a suicide run to me. You sure about travelling down this road?"

"Do I really need to answer that one?"

At that, LuluBot emerged from the kitchen again, only this time she carried a stack of glowing folders. She placed the top folder in front of Gash. It appeared to be empty at first glance, but when he opened it, data floated up from within.

CHAPTER 9

Rashid Hammad, the operative known as "Iblis," crouched behind the parapet wall of the Q7 convenience store. From behind, Gash could only see that he wore a black full-body ballistic suit, and a short black jacket with the hood pulled up over his head.

Down below, dozens of gunmetal cars pulled in and out of two rows of recharging kiosks. An automated semi parked in one of the truck berths, and a Q7 employee hustled out of the store to connect a diesel fuel pump to the big vehicle.

"You sure about this location?" came a voice from behind the camera. When the camera seemed to blink, Gash realized this was all streamed live through someone's late-gen recon cyber-eyes.

Iblis turned and glowered at the camera man, revealing a face weathered before its time. A number of scars crisscrossed his face, and a meticulously groomed full beard hung from his jaw. Two small impish horns protruded from within his slicked-back black hair. "This is the only accessible location with a vantage point of the guard house. Do not worry about those below. North American corporate drones do not look up into the sky, and if they did, what personal motivation would they have to get involved in dangerous business?"

The camera man seemed unsatisfied with that explanation, and the two went back and forth a few times. "What's with the horns?" Gash asked Hemmingway.

"I thought those might catch your eye," Hemmingway said. "This guy's a former Palestinian Liberation Force operative. Specialized in long range marksmanship and digital warfare. When you and Starfire put magic back in the world, he manifested as another thought-to-be-mythological entity – in this case, an ifrit. Afarit are considered demons in Islam, so his people banished him. Since he's new in these parts, we can get him for a steal."

"PLF? I don't work well with religious zealots," Gash said.

"Oh please, the only religious zealots are the leaders driving this iteration of 'Holy War' into its eleventieth decade. Anyway, he was kicked out for being a demon, what makes you think he still has his faith, if he ever did?"

While Hemmingway and Gash talked, the camera man and Iblis finished their discussion, and Iblis turned back to the target. Across the street, sitting conspicuously in a core of darkness carved from an endless sea of street lights and well-lit Suburban residential stacks, stood a storage facility. Walls topped with barbed wire ringed the facility, and a series of tiny red lights signified the presence of over a dozen security cameras. A guard post stood between the In and Out lanes of the sole entrance to the facility.

Iblis tapped away at a display pad integrated into the left wrist of his body suit for maybe thirty seconds, and then the red lights across the street went dark. "Internal security protocols disabled," he said.

"Wow," said the camera man. "Fast work, man, now we just need to take care of the guard."

"And you are sure it is just the one guard?" Iblis asked.

"That's what our intel says."

"I have trouble believing that anything worthwhile is hidden behind such lackluster security."

The camera bobbed up and down as the camera man nodded. "I felt the same way, but we had to crack some significant counter measures to learn that our cargo is here. When the job runner got the intel without being detected, 'that' was the real heist."

Iblis narrowed his eyes, but said nothing further.

"So what's the plan to take out the guard?"

Iblis turned back towards the WalCo facility and held his left hand up, fully outstretched, his fingers angled in a "C" shape, as though watching the guard post through the looking glass of his own hand. With his right arm, he begin to make arcane gestures. A fire appeared in his left hand, red at first, heating up to white as he gestured. Within a handful of seconds, the white -hot flame heated to blue. The camera man took a sharp breath, and stepped back, holding his hands in front of him – presumably as though to shield himself from the intense heat.

After intensifying the small flame in his hand even further, and carefully taking aim, Iblis made an outwards flinging gesture in his right hand, and a very tight beam of glowing blue erupted towards the guard post. At this distance, it was hard to see specifics, but the flame hit the presumably-projectile-resistant glass, and must have punched through, because the dark silhouette of the guard slumped and then fell.

The camera man slowly exhaled. "Jesus," he said.

Ignoring him, Iblis raised a hand to his ear. "Security is neutralized, send in Cargo One."

At that, the automated truck below rumbled to life and pulled out of the service station. Simultaneously, the ifrit hacker turned back to the camera man. "Let's go wrap this up," he said.

And then he disappeared in a puff of smoke, reappearing nearly fifty feet away, at the edge of the road, and jogging the rest of the distance to the guard post.

"Shit," the camera man said, vaulting the parapet wall and landing in the parking lot of the service station with a loud thud. A few civilians looked at him, but quickly looked away and went back to their business. Gash heard the faint hydraulic hiss of cyber-legs absorbing the impact of the twenty-foot fall, and then the camera man sprinted to catch up with Iblis. The guy was fast. Crazy fast.

When he caught up to the hacker, Iblis looked back at him and cracked the tiniest grin. "Glad you could make it."

Up close, Gash saw the result of the ifrit's fire magic. The beam of blue flame had penetrated the ballistic glass of the guard post with ease, leaving a single hole ringed with ripples from where the glass super-heated and then cooled again. Inside, the intense flame had blasted through the guard's Kevlar body armor and blown a hole clean through his chest. At least the poor guy died quick. Brutal, but impressive. Only the highest-end gauss sniper rifles could rip through armor like this with only a whisper, and this "Iblis" accomplished the same thing using only his bare hands – and magic.

The ifrit stepped into the guard post, tapped a few keys on the guard's display, and the "In" gate rose, just in time for the large cargo truck to come trundling through.

"Wow, the boss is going to eat this up," the camera man said to Iblis as he emerged from the guard post. "Really impressive stuff."

Iblis paused and then leaned really close to the camera man. "Are you *streaming* this mission?"

When the camera man said nothing, Iblis tapped a few keys on his integrated PCom and then looked up again. "Tozz Feek," he growled. "You *are* streaming. Have you gone mad?"

"It's part of the mission, boss needs intel on new hires to see if they qualify for bigger jobs," the camera man said. "Don't worry, nobody will see it outside of our org."

"You imbecile, once it goes digital it lives forever in the networks. Turn it off."

"It's part of the job, don't worry about it."

Iblis took one more step towards the camera man, who took two steps back in response. The black clad, horned operative held out both hands, flames rising up from his palms turning from red to white almost instantaneously. His eyes followed suit, glowing red and then white-hot. Between the horns and flames rising from his hands, Iblis completed the look. Monster. Demon.

"Okay, okay," the camera man said. "It's off all ready, Jesus." And with that, the feed did indeed go black.

"I like him," Gash said.

Hemmingway nodded. "I figured you might. A fellow veteran and another mythological creature to boot."

"I don't know hacking like you and Starfire do, but he has what it takes?"

"Oh yes. Information warfare is the frontline in the never-ending Holy War. Guys like Rashid are trained from infancy to crack security measures and access encrypted data-stores in the field. PLF and their Christian counterparts, the Evangelical Expeditionary Force know that it might cost them fifty soldiers to kill fifty of the other team's soldiers in the field. But one info-warrior can demotivate ten thousand if they dig up secure footage of a holy man diddling a kid. They can deprive an entire army of body armor if they hack the data to intercept the shipment or crash the deal before the shipment ever leaves the docks. They can drop propaganda into just the right server to recruit hundreds of new soldiers. I could go on."

"No need," Gash said. "I get it. He's the cutting edge of information warfare, and from context I bet we don't get access to too many guys like this. I imagine if he hadn't turned into a demon, his people would have never let him go independent."

Hemmingway laughed. "No chance. In fact, when I said he was banished, what I really meant is that they tried to execute him. He blasted his way out of the prison the night before and dropped off the grid for a month before re-surfacing in the Pacific Northwest."

"Sounds like this is our guy. Let's get him."

"Getting him," Hemmingway said.

CHAPTER 10

After hashing out details on the meet up with Iblis, Hemmingway and Gash paused for a brief interlude. Hemmingway gave Gash a tour of the first floor. A few empty rooms would serve as game rooms, meaning they could be transformed in a snap into a zombie apocalypse or alien invasion if Hemmingway found himself entertaining. Several rooms held beautiful art, mostly stylized depictions of 1950s Americana. The rooms displayed the art as paintings, with digital certifications of ownership proving that the art "belonged" to Hemmingway.

After the tour, they returned to the table. LuluBot cleared away the tea and folders. "Time for some more files," Hemmingway said. "We need to go over muscle, now. By my estimation, you'll need at least two or three field operatives in case things go to shit. And since you're walking into WalCo's HQ things will most definitely go to shit." He waved his hand as though to summon LuluBot again. When she failed to materialize, he rose to his digital feet, angling to see into the kitchen.

And everything went black. Not black like turning all the lights off and closing the blinds, either. Total void. The visual input disappeared, but so too the ocean scent, the sound of crashing waves, and the sensation of sitting in a comfortable chair. These all left a sort of blackness in their wake when they disappeared. In the vacuum created by the total elimination of all sensory input, Gash flailed. Or tried to flail, but he could not even perceive his own body, his own limbs with which *to* flail. Only emptiness, floating in an infinite void. The absence of even a single errant photon. Absolute dark.

The sensation lasted barely two seconds, after which Gash found himself once again sitting in Hemmingway's tea spot. Only instead of Hemmingway sitting across the table from him, there stood a giant raven – nearly as large as the average person – claws digging into the wood of the table. It stared at Gash, beady black eyes the size soft balls.

"Hemmingway...?" Gash stood slowly. Something had gone wrong. Nothing should happen in Hemmingway's domain that he hadn't coded. And Gash somehow doubted that Hemmingway ever coded a giant raven in as a second avatar.

The raven gave a loud "caw" and hopped into the middle of the table, sidling closer to Gash. When it drew close enough, its neck began to undulate, not unlike a cat trying to spit up a hairball. And sure enough, after a few seconds of this, the raven spit up something round and smooth, almost like a black pearl or a darkened crystal ball. It cawed again and stared meaningfully at the orb, and then at Gash, and back again.

Gash thought back to stories of hackers getting their brains fried trying to crack corporate security; other hackers sending rogue signals and turning them into potatoes, feedback loops that effectively blew out a Real-D rig or neural port user's brain. He stared at the dark orb, and the great bird seemed to grow more agitated the longer he sat there without touching it. After several seconds of this, the raven nudged the orb towards Gash, the thing rolling like a large marble along the wooden table.

His gut told him this was safe. Gash Jensen knew very little of the world of the cyberverse, a dark forest full of mysteries that his old brain would never have the chance to learn. But he did know his gut, and his gut told him that this raven meant to help him. Gash made a habit of listening to his gut, and so he reached out across the table and grabbed the orb. It felt cold and glassy in his hands, but also impossibly light. When both hands closed on it, the data knocked him back into the chair with such force that he tipped backwards, falling slowly through the artificial air, and as he fell backwards a jumbled series of images rushed in to replace Hemingway's carefully crafted home.

He saw his own face, first as though looking out from a mirror, weathered and gaunt and pale. Gash watched him reach for himself, for the left side of his face, then a sharp pain below his left ear. Rat Eater's sweating weasel-face came next, cackling and throbbing, cold iron chains digging into wrists, the smell of blood and body odor. The smell of coffee, a great machine screeching as it steamed milk, two boys giggling in the corner, the rumble of an old gas-engine automobile thumping slowly along an abandoned side road, hitting pothole after pothole, the wipers lazily squeaking back and forth, rain tap-rattle-tap on the old aluminum roof. A man with a hat and a briefcase standing in the fog, a black silhouette. All around, emerald green trees and the fresh-clean petrichor of rain and dirt. The Trinity river streaming past, giggling and splashing in the water, the wide blue sky full of nothing.

When the images stopped, Gash found himself lying on his back in Hemmingway's home again. The man's avatar stood above him, staring down. He was shouting and cursing and gesturing. The raven had gone, and along with it the black orb.

Gash felt as though he had been asleep for hours. Days. Someone else's memories lived in his head now. And he knew. He knew her name. His monster queen, the wechuge he had saved the night before. Silvie Wauneka. Not only that, he knew she worked as a barista. He knew she'd been displaced from tribal lands by a WalCo buyout enforced with a medium-sized corporate army as a child. He knew a sort of rage he'd never known before, a painful longing for a home stolen – not just a place she had lived, but a place that her parents had lived, and their parents before them, and on back past recorded memory. A place her spirit lived, and must have lived still, because after being forced to leave it she had never felt her spirit within her again. He cried, long and full, the tears – real or digital – pouring down his face in an unchecked river.

Eventually, Hemmingway stopped shouting and Gash was able to muster the energy to stand. He had some explaining to do, and a multitude of new questions with no answers. But he also had his team. She might not be a veteran operative, but Silvie Wauneka proved that, as a wechuge, she possessed the strength of a dozen cybered-to-the-gills mercs. That plus the boiling rage that simmered beneath the surface, ready to consume WalCo and all who enabled it, made her the perfect candidate. Between Iblis, Silvie, and himself, they had a full team. A monster squad. And a snowball's chance of actually getting in, getting the data, and getting out alive.

Chapter 11

Gash stepped out into the night once more. A drizzle drummed softly against the brim of his new hat – a parting gift from Sammy, something they found in the Emporium's lost and found. "Your head just looked sad without that old fedora," Sammy said. It fit like a charm and looked brand new to Gash. He took a deep breath. You could smell it on the air, and feel the thick heaviness of it on your face – the drizzle would turn to a downpour soon enough. He buttoned his long coat, adjusted his hat, and stepped into the flow of people coming and going from the DRZ.

Gash lost half the night extracting himself from Hemmingway's and then from Sammy's. Hemmingway paced back and forth, ranting about having never been hacked successfully before – he hadn't blamed Gash, but that it seemed to be Gash's mystery client did not endear Gash to Hemmingway. That bridge wasn't burned, not yet at least, but it was doused with oil. Sammy tried to push half a dozen new Real-D feeds on him. Ever the tempter, Sammy nearly reeled Gash into a Dionysian spiral of Real-D experiences that would have kept him from the outside world for at least 24 hours. Try explaining "that" on an expense account report.

Leaving Sammy Smut's Real-D Emporium without getting off definitely felt alien to Gash, but aside from concerns about abusing his mystery client's expense account, Gash worried about time as well. How long until his mystery client gave up on him again? How long would it take the next WalCo assassin to find him? How long before WalCo decided Ana Marin was no longer of use and disposed of her? Like the ancient pharaohs executing the builders of the pyramids to protect their secrets, mega-corporations like WalCo that abducted scientists for forbidden research would inevitably have to silence those scientists when they were finished with their work.

The thought of faceless suits burying the beautiful scientist in an unmarked grave in the country-side, a single bullet in her head, drove a shudder through Gash's body. More likely, though, they'd just chemically lobotomize her and dump her in the streets of a major metro. When some provisional government or corporate security team found her, she would do little more than drool and mumble and smile vacantly. No murder case for opposing corps to try to leverage, just one more burnout fading slowly away, dying alone in the proverbial gutter.

When Gash stopped to check his PCom for directions, he heard a flurry of wings, and a raven came flapping down from the power lines above, landing on a nearby vending machine full of nicotine derms. It stared at Gash, cocking its head to the side, and let out a loud "caw."

Tough not to think this was somehow connected to his experience in Hemmingway's domain. But how? He looked closely at it. Could this be some kind of hyper-realistic drone? If so why land it so close by? Why draw attention? With his attenuated vampiric senses, he could see it very well in the shadows above the vending machine – it just looked like a raven. He cocked his head a bit, thinking to focus his superior hearing towards the thing, but unfortunately in the throng of people and with the rain starting to pick up, all he could hear were thousands of human hearts pumping away, and the rising staccato of precipitation. After a moment of this, the raven flew away. Bizarre.

When Gash turned back to his map, he realized he did not need it. Memories not his own lived like vivid dreams between the seams of his personal experiences. He didn't even know the name of the coffee shop that Silvie worked at (and there were a great many of them), but something in him knew exactly how to get there, as though he had worked there himself for the last five years. Just a few blocks' walk. Would she be working tonight? Every shop in the city had a night shift, but that didn't mean Silvie would be on. Still, he needed to find it, and he could at least get a message to her if not speak to her in person.

As he walked, Gash felt old memories bubbling up, but struggled to identify whether they were really his. To his brain, they all felt like his – the human brain never evolved to house someone else's memories and identify them separately. Fondly recalling that time when, a young girl, Gash spotted a white-tailed dear and her fawn drinking from a nearby stream was making it hard for Gash to separate his reality from hers.

When his churning brain served him up a war-torn desert, Gash latched onto it, a familiar memory rerun by his brain a thousand times, if suppressed in recent years. On the outskirts of an abandoned town 50 kilometers outside Riyadh, he leaned against an old brick wall, automatic gunfire from just around the corner chipping it away into red dust that mixed with sand in the wind and gusted into his mouth and nose. He tried not to choke. Beside him, also wearing the desert camo uniform of the Marine Corporation, Corporal William Sinder clutched his assault rifle close to his chest, eyes wide.

"What do we do, Sarge?" Sin shouted into the wind, his thick Irish accent barely cut by ten years of living and fighting with mostly American soldiers at various Marine Co facilities and bases.

"Well, corporal," Gash hollered back, "this was an ambush meant for our whole squad, and we sprang it from the outside. That means two things. One, they'll be trying to flank us on both sides. Two, we need to get the hell out of here."

Bad intel, Gash knew, from the Church of the J, a sister corporation to the Marine Co in the WalCo family of interconnected corporations. Church of the J famously had the worst intel, which is why Gash decided to scout the location with Corporal Sinder. A lightly guarded Caliphate rabble-rouser, the intel said. But a whole army greeted the two men.

"Yes, Sarge!" Sin shouted.

Gash remembered leapfrogging from cover to cover, the two men giving each other covering fire. A piece of shrapnel from a nearby grenade took Sin's eye, but the young man only fought harder. After nearly thirty minutes of bounding overwatch across dunes and abandoned homes, they somehow found themselves back with the rest of the squad. Dusty, bloody, almost out of ammo, alive. With covering fire from the other ten men, the entire squad extracted, a few potshots ricocheting off the large chopper as they rose from the desert floor. Not one casualty, at least a dozen insurgents dead. This memory belonged inescapably to Gash, and no digital raven could rip his identity from him.

He walked, lost in the wars, until he found himself standing at the entrance to one of hundreds of locations belonging to that green-signed coffee chain that could trace its ancient roots to this very city. This one was much smaller than the last such place he'd visited – where he first met Starfire and the first time she saved his life – too small for an on-site security guard. Despite (or perhaps because of) its size, it felt cozy and bright. Inviting. He took that invitation, opening the door to the rich aroma of coffee beans mixed with the harsh iron tang of blood.

Apparently, today was not Gash's lucky day. The top half of a corporate suit twitched on a nearby coffee table, his entrails splayed out in front of his lower half, which seemed to lean dangerously close to falling out of the little faux-wood chair. Blood spray covered the walls in between, as though a child took a stab at modern art using a super soaker filled with red paint.

While there were no other patrons, one barista huddled against the far wall of the shop, sobbing, knees pulled to her chest. When she saw Gash, the words came pouring out of her mouth.

"It's not her fault, the guy's a regular, he's always shouting at us. She gave him his drink and he said it was wrong and threw it at her and it burned her and she screamed and turned into some kind of a *monster* and ripped him in half. Blood everywhere, and she howled after and I could feel it – all the way in my chest. I can still hear it, still hear the sound of her ripping him in half. What is she? What is she?" She trailed off, mumbling. Gash knelt beside her, tried her with a few gentle probing questions. What was her name? Where was she from? When had this all happened? But the girl just kept mumbling the question. What is she? What is she?

A wechuge, Gash thought. That's what. Sounds like this guy had it coming – especially knowing about Silvie's trauma. What was she doing back at work the day after escaping slavery? But he knew, of course. Same as everyone else in this city – if you stop, the money stops, and then you're out on the streets and its only a matter of time until someone is stripping your body for parts. Swim or die. Silvie had chosen to swim.

Still, whether the guy had it coming or not, a barista turning into a monster and ripping a customer in half? Silvie's erstwhile employers weren't going to take her recent sordid history into account. They'd plan to track her and put her down.

He had to find her first. But how? He surely only had moments before the coffee chain's rapid response unit arrived. It wouldn't do to be here when they did, or they'd want to know what he saw. Might run his vitals and see that WalCo still had a warrant out for him. This company and WalCo had extradition treaties with each other, so odds were they'd turn him in if he made it easy for them.

No obvious blood trail led away from the coffee shop. Gash couldn't remember where she lived in the same way he remembered this place, so many of her memories still felt entangled with his own, jumbled and inaccessible. Maybe in time he'd sift it out, but maybe not. Hard to say, as he lacked expertise in having memories directly inserted into his brain by a computer-programmed raven.

Break room. Every one of these shops had a little break room in the back. He stepped past the sobbing girl, and into the employee's only space. She barely looked up at him.

Much of the space served the needs of the shop. A small bot – about three feet tall – stood powered down against the far wall beside a VI-powered cleaning station. All the dishes, the floors, the display cases: The machine and its accompanying apparatus would clean everything. Across from the shiny new cleaning station, mounted to the wall, was a large sink, a relic from the days when the coffee shop workers cleaned dishes manually. Time drew patches of rust from the drains into the sink basin, and the half-corroded appliance now served as a sort of storage space.

In fact, it contained two backpacks. One, pink, sported a dozen patches characterizing small imaginary monsters. Collectibles. None of it meant anything to him. Maybe the crying girl's stuff. When he saw the other backpack, a black one made from some ancient synthetic material, he knew. A patch on the center showed a forested hillscape and a small river. He felt it instinctively – in the same way you knew something from a deep well of memory – that this patch was once the official seal of the Hoopa Valley tribe. Her tribe.

A voice from the retail space shouted commands. Get down, show me your hands. All clear. The rapid response team was here already. Gash looked around frantically. There were two other doors, but one led to a storage space in the back, and the other to a bathroom. In seconds this would turn into a bloodbath, and he might well find himself with another corporate warrant out.

That's when Gash recognized the little piece of plastic mounted to the ceiling. Once upon a time, public spaces like this were required to have emergency exits for fire safety. One such sign was once bolted to the ceiling above where now stood a shelf full of pre-packaged ingredients for the machines that made everything out front. Gash had no time for stealth. He could hear footsteps moving past the sobbing girl and they were about to enter the back room. He ripped the shelf away from the wall, and sure enough, there stood a door behind it. Some corporate handyman a few decades ago bolted and sealed the doorway to make room for the extra storage, but with Gash's vampiric strength it might as well have been a strip of paper covering a hole in the wall. He smashed through, and found himself in a small alley between the coffee shop and the neighboring retail space. Slinging Silvie's pack onto his back, he scaled the two-story wall, landing gently on the roof.

He peered back over the parapet. Two operatives in full body armor stood at the open door looking around. They both sported a tabard bearing the corporate logo, and a latest-gen gauss submachine gun.

"What the hell?" one of them said. "Where'd he go?"

"I don't know, but the girl said the killer was her shift lead. If someone else was here, they might have just been an unwilling witness. Not our job to deal with that, we just need to track down the rogue employee and neutralize her."

"Easy as that?"

"Corporate doesn't like long investigations, and you know it. We have a cut and dry story, we can get this done and be home in time for breakfast. Come on, let's try out this new tracker. Supposedly he's one of the new acquisitions, a mage that can trace someone's body aura over a hundred miles."

"Yeah, can he fight a barista that turns into a monster and rips people in half?"

"That's what these are for," the first operative said, patting his gun.

"Fine," the other operative said. "But we're getting a full team. It's bad enough, people reading auras and slinging fireballs. But monsters ripping guys in half? I'm six months from retirement, we're doing this by the book."

At that, they both stepped inside. Magical tracker, that did not sound good. Gash would have to really hurry if he wanted to get to Silvie first. He opened her bag and rifled around, looking for anything that might help. Change of clothes, a spare PCom battery pack, an old school synth-paper book written by J Tolkien IV. A Tupperware with a sandwich inside. Nothing he could use.

Well, maybe there was one thing. More specifically, a smell. With his head half in her bag, Gash could smell Silvie again, like before at Rat Eater's. Her skin, her sweat, and that faint hint of ozone. Something about her magical essence, maybe? He took a deep whiff. As a vampire, could he be a bloodhound and track her down by this smell? He raised his face to the sky, and sure enough he caught a hint of that particular scent profile on a gust of wind. He closed up the bag and slung it onto his back. Silvie might want the book, and he might need to take another smell if he lost the scent. Down below, he heard someone chanting. Was the tracker on site already?

No time to waste, then. Silvie's scent came from the west. He sprinted across the roof and leapt the space between it and the next roof. Swift and silent, he cleared roof after roof, headed west towards Silvie, all thoughts of the case gone for the moment, replaced only by the thought of her face, her fierce eyes and long hair. He had to help her. He had to save Silvie.

CHAPTER 12

Silvie's scent trail led to an older residential area about a dozen blocks from the coffee shop. Residential towers stacked together in a single mass, half a million folks crammed into 500 square foot apartments, people stacked on people ad infinitum: a giant concrete honeycomb. Better than the cage homes in old Downtown at least.

Though the clock ticked closer to 3 AM, this block might as well have been bathed in noon-day summer sun. Holo-ads jockeyed for air-space in front of the building. Sexy young people slapped nicotine derms on each other's biceps; refined-looking middle-aged people sipped coffee; a very fast car drifted around a corner, chased by a military helicopter of some kind; a brunette with a 12-pack wearing nothing but a hat airbrushed with a corporate logo railed a woman that looked like she could be his twin. There must have been hundreds of ads clogging the air, pulsating with bright holographic light, shouting into the void at a wall of closed windows, blinds pulled.

The lights made it hard to assess the situation below, but fortunately Silvie made it easier. He heard her shouting curses, and then saw her fling a bicycle into the street. He descended to ground level just in time to watch an auto-cab drive right over it. As the bike buckled in an explosion of sparks and rending metal, a computerized voice said "I'm sorry, your subscription to this bicycle has expired. Please renew subscription to unlock wheels. I'm sorry," it started again. "I'm sorry, I'm sorry, I'm sorry –" it stuttered a few more times, before slowing down and eventually going silent. The bike was dead.

Silvie wore nondescript jeans and a black hoodie, and clutched a duffle bag slung over her shoulder. She was making a run for it, good. Smart girl. When he landed behind her, she was too busy shouting at the bicycle to notice him. The language would have made even the guys in his special ops unit back in the day blush.

"Silvie," he said. She spun around, aiming a can of pepper spray at Gash's eyes.

Her face, contorted into a grimace, untwisted when she saw him. She dropped the pepper spray and threw herself at him. Taken aback, he reciprocated the hug as she buried her face in his chest, sobbing. The term he'd used as a kid was "ugly crying." Long, deep sobs. If he didn't still have his long coat on, his shirt would be soaking up water. Gash knew people. Months or years of trauma built these kinds of outbursts. He tried to flatter himself as her savior, that she would throw herself at him like this, but the truth was that he was just the first safe face she'd seen since the latest horror descended into her life. A convenient shoulder.

He gave her a moment, but they would need to get going quickly. Neither of them could afford to stand out in the open like this for long. But before he could say anything, she stopped herself, pulling away suddenly and wiping her face clean with the sleeve of her sweatshirt. As though she'd flipped a switch, the crying stopped. A tiny half-smile even cracked through the clouds for a moment. "My vampire savior. That scumbag slaver called you Nagash Jensen?"

"I just go by Gash," he said.

"Thought I'd never get a chance to thank you for your help, and now here you are. Coming to save me again?" She sniffed, reaching out her hand. "Silvie Wauneka."

He shook her hand. "A hug and a handshake. Much better than pepper spray. By the way, what are you doing bothering with pepper spray? You have... more effective options."

She laughed, brief and short and harsh. "I've never killed anyone before yesterday. My first thought at danger isn't to transform into a fleshing-eating wechuge and rip somebody in half. Now I've killed, what, like four people in two days?"

"It gets easier."

"God, I hope not," she said.

And there they stood, looking at each other. In this light, on this night, something about her made Gash's heart flutter. God damn he hated that feeling. Teenagers' hearts should flutter when they looked at a pretty boy or girl or whoever; at his age, the only reason for his heart to flutter should be the fact that he hadn't been to a doctor in seven years.

"Heeeey there buckeroos," came a voice from above. A cartoon cowboy came swooping down riding a cartoon spaceship, cutting between the two of them. "The adventure of a lifetime awaits you at Rocket Billy's Space Western Adventure Park, Seattle metro's *only* space western theme park! Book your tickets now on your PCom! Your child – *or* your *inner* child – will thank you!"

"Look, I need to get out of here, fast," Silvie said. "I know they're coming for me, and I need to be gone. The rest of my family is sleeping. I... I don't want anyone to get hurt because of me."

"You can lay low at my place," Gash said. "Well, my boat. Well, it's not really *my* boat." He paused, took a deep breath. "Let's go, they'll never think to look for you on the docks. We have a lot to talk about anyway."

CHAPTER 13

By the time the sunrise lit the gray wall of clouds, Gash and Silvie were settled in on *The Holy* for the day. Silvie, exhausted, passed out on the bed. Hemmingway managed to obtain a layout of the WalCo building from a disgruntled architect and ex-WalCo employee.

Gash downloaded the file and flipped it from his PCom onto the ship's central holo-projector, kicking back on one of the plush sofas arrayed around the central viewing space. Looking at the image in 3-D helped sometimes. At first, the sheer scope of the place overwhelmed him. When WalCo completed their new headquarters fifteen years ago, it held the record for the tallest building in the world at 302 stories. One of the earliest "cloud scrapers" built utilizing carbon nanotube framing, WalCo HQ towered over the older architecture in the city.

Security controlled the entire ground floor. Personnel at multiple stations scanned incoming visitors for weapons, vetted them, assigned them security badges and numbers, and only then routed approved guests and employees in good standing to the correct elevator bank based on their department or business. There would be multiple squads of security personnel, heavily armed and augmented, not to mention turrets and drones.

Each floor above and below the Lobby was built around a security station as well. The elevator and stairs would feed into a central security space on that floor, and doors would lead from that security station into the rest of the building. In other words, no matter where you were headed once you got inside, you passed through security at ground level and again at your destination floor. The windows were constructed from military-grade ballistic glass, making any kind of aerial entry impractical: It would take a missile launcher to so much as scratch them.

To make matters worse, they housed the secure servers in a sub-basement. To be more specific, WalCo kept six dedicated floors full of servers in sub-basement levels. The protected, non-networked servers that undoubtedly held the information Gash needed would be found on the bottom floor, or sub-basement level twenty.

After a time, the images blurred his vision. He stood and stretched – time for a scotch break. He filled his glass to the brim and returned to the sofa with the bottle and glass, where he took a long, slow swallow.

"Not going to offer a lady a drink?" Silvie stood at the doorway to the sleeping quarters, hair askew and wearing the change of clothes from her backpack, grey sweatpants and a baggy white T-shirt. She gave a big yawn and grabbed a glass off a nearby end table, stepping towards Gash with her hand outstretched. He filled her glass, and she slammed it back, holding out the empty expectantly until he poured her another before sitting next to him.

"What are we looking at?" she asked.

"A job," Gash said.

"A job," Silvie echoed.

For a time, the patter of rain against the ship's polymer roof and the sound of Silvie breathing tapped out a pleasant rhythm. A song of reprieve. He closed his eyes and gave himself to it. But like all good things, his song of reprieve did not last.

"That's why you were looking for me," Silvie said. "You need a fellow monster for a job?"

"What makes you think I want to hire a customer service worker for a job? Could have just been checking in after I saved you the other night."

"Could have. Were you?" she asked, sipping the scotch.

He paused. "Well, if you want to make some money and hit WalCo where it hurts, I think we could work something out."

Silvie raised her eyebrows. "Who says I care about hitting WalCo?"

A digital raven downloaded your memories into me yesterday, so I know all about you and your history with WalCo. "Call it a hunch," Gash said.

Silvie stood and walked to the nearest window. She reached for the motion sensor and swiped up, raising the blind enough to look out at the ocean. On days like today an open window posed no threat, so Gash said nothing. She figured it out pretty quick, though, stealing a glance over her shoulder at Gash and quickly swiping the blind closed again.

"It's okay, more or less, as long as I'm not in direct sunlight. I could probably even go out on a rainy day like this if I had a good coat with a hood," Gash said.

She nodded slowly, but left the blinds shut. "I'm new to all this," she said.

"What, being a monster? Magic and vampires? You're as new to it as the rest of the world."

She walked back over to the sofa, finishing off her scotch, and sat back down beside Gash. "Well sure, but killing people too. Being on the run. Sticking it to corporations. 'Jobs.' You're some kind of merc, right? Rat Eater, being on the run, that stuff isn't new to you." She paused. "It's new to me. I make coffee for a living."

This close, he could smell her again. The faint hint of ozone, the residue of whatever soap she used that carried a scent of evergreen. More than that, he could feel her. The warm heat of her. The beating heart, blood racing through arteries. Her sensory presence felt only warm at first, but the more he focused on it, the hotter and brighter she grew, until by her mere proximity to him she became an incinerating sun, his face flush from the burning of it and his stunted undead heart about to collapse from the pressure. He'd be sweating bullets if vampires could sweat.

Gash stood and walked to the other side of the holodisplay. "Well, I'm a private investigator, but I suppose that's just a kind of mercenary. Let me give you the briefing. If you want in, we'll need to figure out the details together, along with the third member of the team, who should be here soon."

CHAPTER 14

blis closed his eyes when he took the first sip from the glass of scotch. After a long, quiet moment, he opened them again and grinned. "The finer things in life are new to me, Mr. Jensen, so I go out of my way to appreciate them."

Up close, you almost forgot about Iblis' horns. Up close, he seemed like just a guy – not a half-demon ex-PLF sniper.

"You are paying well, but this job seems supremely dangerous. Is this 'WalCo' not one of the heaviest hitting corporations here in the West?"

Gash stood and poured himself another drink from *the Holy*'s recently restocked bar, topping Iblis off in the process. "They are. Naturally, if the job wasn't dangerous, it wouldn't pay so well."

"I have researched you, you know. Nagash Jensen. You are a private investigator, not a mercenary or a fixer. I do not question why you need to break into WalCo or why you need to gather information from their secure servers, because I am a professional. And I confirmed that you once were in the military, like me. Special forces, also like me. Because of this I have chosen to trust that you are also a professional and that I am not risking my life by placing it in your hands. However, the girl I am not so sure of." Here, he gestured towards Silvie, sitting quietly in the corner and watching the exchange between Gash and Iblis. Her face remained impassive.

"I'll vouch for her," Gash said. "She has... unique abilities that may come in handy."

Without responding, Iblis swiped through the air from his PCom to the yacht's holodisplay. Footage appeared from the other night. Silvie as a wechuge pouncing on one of Rat Eater's mercs and ripping him in half. Evidently the Rat had hidden cameras posted in the room, and evidently Iblis hacked the feeds. "I researched her, too. I am very thorough. She has impressive strength in this form. But she is a civilian, not an operative – how do I know she will not transform as we are infiltrating the building and blow our cover? How do I know she will not panic at the last minute and get me killed?"

Gash cradled his scotch in both hands, studying Iblis. The scars made a map of war on the half-demon's face – with the right key, you could trace those scars backwards in time to understand this man-turned-ifrit's history of violence. Nagash Jensen needed no key, for he recognized a kindred spirit in Iblis. It's not that he was fearful or overly cautious. Of course he felt fear, the only people who didn't were already dead. But Rashid Hammad aka Iblis had long ago forged his fear into a cold iron dagger, to be wielded alongside his intellect and his killing prowess in the war. Fear took many shapes. Fear could transform into cement boots, heavy weights pulling you under the proverbial sea. Or it could be sculpted into a tool for survival, a sharp blade. For both men, fear served them, not the other way around.

All of which to say, Iblis asked a valid question. Silvie seemed to agree, as she began to fidget in her chair the longer Gash let the question hang in the air. He considered his answer. Why *did* he want her on this job? Sure she was another monster and could rip a man in half, but was that it? Plenty of pros augmented to the gills could do the same, and had been on dozens of ops like this one. Was this the flicker of Gash's fickle and transient love-lust, to bring her along so that they could forge a passion in the fires of the struggle? He knew what he often knew in these situations, that she was half his age and that just because you felt it didn't mean you pursued it.

So what then? Had he decided to bring her because a digital raven that hacked Hemmingway's personal domain as good as told him to?

He considered her face. Silvie Wauneka possessed an iron will, and her brown eyes boasted a folded steel edge. Most people who'd gone through her kind of trauma would be curled up on the couch in a sobbing mess by now, and rightly so. Gash couldn't say he wouldn't do the same. And maybe she would one day, when it all caught up to her. But for now, he heard granite in her voice when she'd agreed to do the job. She was taking control of her life for the first time, and this opportunity would not slip through her fingers. He bet his life on it.

He said as much to Iblis, then, and after a few minutes the three of them moved on to the plan. Silvie stopped fidgeting. Empty scotch glasses forgotten on end tables, they plotted well into the night, until they had crafted a plan of attack that seemed ironclad. Despite that old adage about plans surviving contact with the enemy, hope crept into Nagash Jensen's heart.

As he stepped out of the ship in the wee hours of the night to procure some last-minute supplies for the run, he inhaled deeply. The thick air smelled of sea water and ozone and gasoline and rotting fish, and his vampiric senses magnified it all by a thousand. Though a part of him missed the entirely pleasant olfactory imprint from Hemmingway's digital manor by the sea, he mostly reveled in the grit of the Seattle coast. The realness of it.

In around 24 hours, his team should be extracting from WalCo, and Gash would have the means to finally finish this job. Almost two years pursuing Ana Marin, and at last he would know where to find her. A final rescue op, delivery to the mystery client, and he would have his happy ending. Nagash Jensen could sail off into the sunset and live a quiet, peaceful life, fulfilling an old promise made to a dead lover.

Not long now.

Chapter 15

Gash shifted uncomfortably in the back seat of the dark blue Chevron sedan. The suit fit well enough – Silvie assured him of this – but it felt too tight in the shoulders, and the shirt buttoned against his neck might as well have been strangling him. The tie-pin popped off when he tried to adjust the collar, and his tie flopped back and forth across his chest.

Silvie reached under the seat in front of him and grabbed the tie pin, re-connecting everything for him. He blushed, as much as a vampiric complexion could allow such a thing.

"You just aren't comfortable in anything but that fedora and trench coat, are you?" she said, a small smile cracking through as she did, and that alone made the discomfort worth it. It all felt very domestic, and for a few fleeting seconds the inner hunter allowed him to imagine that they were on the way to dinner at a fancy restaurant rather than a low-odds, high-stakes op to crack one of the most heavily fortified corporate HQs in the world.

The car rumbled up the steep hill towards The Bazaar. The AutoCab driver wore a suit, since this was a deluxe service, but otherwise might as well have been a statue. He simply sat, reading, as the auto-car cruised closer to the destination. Gash hated AutoCabs and any other form of self-driving car, but this was an important part of the ruse. Out of town IT specialists wouldn't be walking in, and they sure wouldn't be driving themselves in. Plenty of folks felt like Gash, steered clear of self-driving cars. But nobody in the tech industry would be such a luddite, Iblis and Silvie both insisted.

Out the window, the city rolled past at the speed of traffic. Swarms of corporate drones flowed up and down the streets on both ends. High-end WalCo chain restaurants dotted the streets in this part of town. WalSushi+, Flashburger, AquaEnvy, and so many others. Gash still remembered when famous local eateries outnumbered the corporate chains in Seattle; but like so many good things, those local joints eventually passed into the realm of small towns and fair weather – fond and slowly fading memories. Eventually, those like Gash would be gone, and their memories with them. Nothing would remain but what the corporations placed in museums – come pay tribute to a dead world for a modest fee. A mythical time when restaurants were owned not by software engineers and brand managers and social media trend leaders, but by trained chefs or by families sharing their generational food traditions.

The small earpiece in his right ear buzzed. When Gash checked his newly integrated PCom wrist mount, Iblis's code name flashed on the screen alongside Silvie's name. He and Silvie both swiped into the call.

"I am in position," Iblis said. "Are you both on approach?"

"We should arrive in about five minutes," she said.

"Looking forward to meeting our new client," Gash said, eying the driver. AutoCab prided themselves on privacy, but that didn't mean you trusted a random driver while on approach for an op like this. "How do things look on your end?"

"Seems your man Hemmingway had good intel. Multiple security patrols on the grounds, half a dozen guards at the front entrance. Everything else is locked down tight – no open windows, no patios, no side entrance for a quick smoke break. In fact I do not even see fire exits."

"WalCo was one of the first to do away with building codes," Gash said. "Dollars were saved."

Iblis didn't respond for a moment, eventually letting out a long sigh. "Even in our so-called 'Third World' countries we have fire exits on our large buildings."

"We're pulling in now," Silvie said. The WalCo building bristled with a razor-wired, electrified, steel-bar-reinforced fence that surrounded it at a distance of about a hundred feet. The security guard at the kiosk checked the AutoCabbie's credentials, and then waved them through the gate.

From this distance, Gash strained to see the top of the early-generation cloudscraper, but it disappeared into the clouds far above. It seemed an infinite monolith, a space elevator from when the human race aspired to such things, a black glass and gray steel and concrete monument to corporate power stretching up and away into the unbounded void beyond the sky.

Even at midnight, the grounds buzzed with activity. The place swarmed with WalCo security personnel, all heavily armed and armored. A gene-hound – a dog genetically modified to detect any scent – sniffed the car idly as they coasted up the four-lane drive towards the building. Whatever its owner was looking for, the K-9 did not detect it inside Gash and Silvie's car. A long line of cars stretched ahead of them and trailed behind them. Employees returning for graveyard shifts, outside contractors coming in for a quick job with no benefits, and vendors for other corporate interests looking to buy or sell to one arm or another of WalCo's various business units all poured in by the dozen.

Though Gash couldn't sweat anymore – a lesser perk of being a vampire – his palms tingled as if they longed to sweat, as though they had been denied the opportunity to release anxiety in liquid form. He looked over at Silvie, who showed not even the faintest sign of being nervous or uncomfortable. Was this just an act, part of her cover? Or did she really not know enough to be nervous?

The car pulled to a stop at the entrance to the WalCo building, and they stepped out into the cool night air. The familiar smell of impending rain filled Gash's nasal cavity. The AutoCab app proposed three tipping options to him, and he chose the middle one, swiping away the app after.

The two joined a moving line of a few dozen others entering the WalCo building, a stream of supplicants coming to pray at the altar for another paycheck. Gash pitied them. Another gene-hound sniffed the stream of folks as they approached the building. Apparently "vampire" and "wechuge" had not yet been programmed into the gene-hounds' sensory databanks. Good thing. Security personnel pulled a few people out of the stream – usually those with combat-themed augmentations or firearms, as far as Gash could tell. He felt naked without his own firearm, but they'd never get in the door with weapons.

Once inside the building, they were funneled through two large sensor banks (metal detector and explosives detector). They passed through with no issue, and then joined a long queue, awaiting the opportunity to petition for entry. This would be the first test – Hemmingway charged a bundle, but as far as Gash knew he was one of the best when it came to fake credentials. In only twelve hours or so he crafted what Iblis at least believed to be convincing fake documents for Silvie and Gash. Here, they were not Silvie Wauneka and Nagash Jensen, monster squad. Here, they were Sierra Montaigne, contract network security expert on loan from Applesoft, and Robert Fitzgerald, her field supervisor.

The wait couldn't have been more than a few minutes, but Gash lived and died a hundred times in that span as he considered every way they could fail and be killed. Eventually, they stepped up to Desk 12, and presented their papers to the bored-looking clerk. He glanced through the pages, looked up at Silvie and Gash, nodded, and swiped a hand past his computer terminal. Two visitor badges printed for Sierra and Robert. Silvie and Gash each took theirs from the dispenser, and hung it around their neck.

"Welcome to WalCo, where innovation meets global market supremacy," he droned. "You two are going to be posted on basement sub-level two. Follow the pink line to the west and over to Elevator Bank Four. Once you get down to sub-level two, the sub-level security chief will get you situated in your cubes. Thank you, please enjoy your stay, next person," he said. After all the agonizing, all the money Gash spent on Hemmingway, they might as well have been stepping into a noodle joint for all that security seemed to give a shit. But maybe that was a testament to the quality of the documents, as much as it felt like they could have walked in with any excuse.

The pink line wound around the desks and past additional security personnel that took a cursory look at their badges as they walked. There were four others standing around waiting to use Elevator Bank Four, the call button already glowing in affirmation that the car would arrive shortly. This could be a problem. With a ding, one of the elevator cars arrived on the lobby floor, and opened. The other four stepped in, and then turned to look at Silvie and Gash, who stood frozen.

"Go ahead," Silvie said, clutching her stomach. "I've got some putrid gas. I'd rather not subject strangers to it, you know? Bad tacos," she added after a pause. Without another word, one of the men in the car reached out and hit the "close door" button. When the doors closed on that car, Gash hit the call button again.

"Nice," Gash said. She grinned.

Fortunately, nobody else arrived at Elevator Bank Four in the fifteen or so seconds until a new car arrived. They stepped in, and Silvie smashed the "close door" button. Gash, meanwhile, reached into his jacket pocket and pulled out an innocuous-looking data drive. As promised by Iblis' contact, the little piece of tech flew completely under the radar at each security check. He pulled the elevator panel cover off and found a small port, just below the buttons, that was normally used for diagnostic purposes. He plugged the data drive in, and immediately heard Iblis' voice in his ear.

"Looks like you have entered the elevator, good. I will take it over now, stand by." Almost before Iblis finished talking, the bottom-most button, marked "20," lit up and the elevator car began to descend. Meanwhile, Silvie drew a pair of glasses out of her suit pocket.

When she put them on, she looked over at Gash and spoke. "Are we coming through clear?" she asked.

"Affirmative," Iblis said. "But I am regretting now that we did not make Gash wear them. I would much rather be looking at your beautiful face than his ugly mug." She blushed but said nothing. His coarse laughter filled the shared channel.

"Funny, I remember hiring a hacker, not a comedian," Gash said.

"Do not be angry, you would feel the same as me were our roles reversed," Iblis said, still chuckling. "But I see that you are almost down to sublevel 20. Remember to move quickly once you are there. An internal timer on the security network will be tracking how long since you checked in. The security chief on sublevel 2 will be logging your absence in a few minutes."

"We've got it, don't worry about our end. You have access to the cameras on 20?" Silvie asked.

"Shutting them down now," Iblis said.

As he spoke, the elevator slowed to a stop and the doors opened. As with every other floor, Basement Sublevel 20 featured its own security desk and bank of security cameras. A squad of five armed guards stood at attention at the five different doors leading from the security station out into different sections of the sublevel. Gash and Silvie stepped out of the elevator. The security chief and all five guards looked up at them. Unauthorized visitors.

"Going hot now," Gash spoke softly into the earpiece. "Start mission timer for five minutes."

"Cameras looped, floor alarms severed. You are clear to engage."

Gash stepped towards the security desk, Silvie close behind. He brandished his corporate credentials as he went. "Hey guys," he said.

"Sir, you don't belong on this floor," the security chief said, stepping out from behind the desk. The security personnel watched the exchange, and a few grips tightened on submachine guns, but otherwise nobody reacted with hostility.

Gash nodded vigorously as he walked closer to the chief. "I know, man, it's the weirdest thing. We were supposed to be on Sublevel 2. Not sure how we got all the way down to 20. My associate here swears she pushed the 2, but when the 20 lit up we couldn't get it to stop."

Nobody expected an old-looking, gaunt, unarmed man in a bland suit to move faster than the eye could follow, not even a squad of highly trained WalCo security guards. A burley Palestinian with devil horns probably would have raised some hackles right out of the gate. If Silvie came out in wechuge form, there would naturally have been gunfire immediately. But at seeing two generic-looking worker bees coming out of the elevator, WalCo security personnel let their guard down. And so it was that Gash stepped right up next to the security chief before springing into action.

He leveled the older suit with a hard right hook and had flashed clear across the room to the farthest security guard before any of them had the chance to blink. The inner killer came alive, as it always did when his brain opened the floodgates from his adrenal glands. The world always seemed to move in slow motion when life and death were on the line, even before his transformation. Pair those killer instincts with vampiric speed, and Gash felt unstoppable. He pulled the gun out of the first guard's hands and hurled it across the room at the second. As the impact of the thrown gun leveled the second guard, Gash smashed the first's head into the wall, knocking him out. Three down, three to go.

The men began to react, but it would not be enough. He sprinted from guard to guard, dropping each of them with a single super-powered blow. In no more than three or four seconds, all six of the security personnel were down for the count.

"Five minutes and counting," Silvie said.

"Care to join us?" Gash asked.

At that Gash heard a loud pop, and directly in front of Silvie a man-sized cloud of smoke appeared. It drifted up to the ceiling of the room, and when it cleared, there stood Iblis, fully geared in his body-suit. He held two sidearms, and tossed one each to Gash and Silvie. "Fully suppressed, untraceable Gauss pistols. Let us try not to kill anyone, but if we must then let us try to be quiet about it."

Gash caught his and checked the magazine. Fully loaded.

"Okay, let's do this," Silvie said.

Before Silvie could finish the sentence, alarms began to sound. Red lights recessed in the corner of the ceiling emerged, flashing brightly.

Gash looked at Iblis. "I thought you got the cameras."

"I did." Iblis blinked over to the security terminal in another puff of smoke, and began typing furiously at the workstation. It seemed an eon, but according to the mission timer on Gash's PCom, the ifrit spent only half a minute on the work station before he looked up. "Al'ama," he said. "An advanced VI security persona on WalCo's internal servers tracks bio-signs for *every person in the building.* It cross-references them against the number of people that have been checked in. When I teleported in, it registered an extra person in the building."

"That's insane," Silvie said. "The computing power required to do that..."

Iblis continued typing furiously. "Each floor is required to report in," he said. "...and it appears they have 60 seconds to do so before a red flag goes up. If we work fast, we should be able to get what we came for."

"Can you report in from here to throw them off?" Gash asked.

Iblis tapped a few more keys, and then muttered something that sounded like another curse. "No, the system requires an audio report and a rotating password. The VI references the voice patterns of the security chiefs on file to ensure that the report is legitimate, and matches it to an up-to-date password."

"So shouldn't we scrap the mission? Escape before it's too late?" Silvie asked.

Gash couldn't afford to scrap the mission, but he didn't want to drag these two to their deaths. This was just a job for them, nothing more, but for Gash it was everything. The rest of his life, the life of a beautiful blue-eyed scientist. He looked at Iblis, awaiting the answer. "It is already too late to walk out the front door, as planned. The whole facility is locked down. Nobody in or out. I do not know another way out, at least not for the two of you."

That was it then. No reason not to keep going.

"Then how the hell are we going to extract?" Silvie asked.

"We improvise on the go," Gash said. "We're going to make waves, but I've gotten out of worse. We won't have another shot at the data, though, so it's now or never. Let's get moving."

CHAPTER 16

Gash led the team deeper into the facility, shrieking alarms and flashing red lights dogging them at every step. Was he leading his team towards death? He should be working alone. Last time he worked with a team, he fell in love with his boss and then almost ripped her throat out when he turned into a vampire. Should have learned his lesson back then and stuck to solo ops. But instead, here he was putting a civilian in harm's way for his own ends, because a digital raven somehow dumped her memories into his brain. Iblis, as a soldier, understood the risks. Silvie couldn't have understood them, not properly, not without combat experience. You never understood the stakes until you were in it for the first time.

Still, they were all in it now. No time for second-guessing – he shoved those thoughts deep into his subconscious, where he could revisit them later if he managed to avoid a bullet to the brain.

Sublevel 20 held a number of large server rooms, and very few personnel. They sprinted past a maintenance worker huddled in the corner of the hall.

According to some shaky intel from Hemmingway, the most secure server would be at the end of two more long halls, in a sensitive data storage area that may or may not have additional security measures. When they hit the double doors at the end of this corridor, the first of those measures revealed itself. A retinal scanner and biometric print reader barred the way, holding shut reinforced heavy steel double doors. Gash slammed into the doors at full speed, but even with his vampiric strength, they didn't budge. Instead, the force of the strike dislocated his left shoulder.

He gave a roar, and smashed his shoulder backwards against the wall, popping it back into place. For a normal human, this sort of thing would no doubt leave bruises or torn ligaments, but as a vampire, Gash healed rapidly. No time for delicate work, and no need besides. He considered the security door, ignoring the blazing pain as the internal bits of his shoulder stitched themselves back together.

"Can you hack this?" Gash looked over at Iblis.

The hacker considered the device carefully, and then closed his eyes, evidently streaming something directly into his neural network. Surprising that he had reception this deep in the WalCo building's secure servers.

"I could, given enough time. But I can do you one better, boss." And before Gash could respond or ask for clarification, Iblis dropped to the ground, flattening himself against the floor so he could peer through the tiny gap beneath the double doors. And then he disappeared in a puff of smoke. Ten seconds later, and the doors opened, Iblis standing at the other end and grinning wildly through his thick beard. No biometrics on the other side, apparently.

Once through, they sprinted down another long, empty hallway. At the end of this one, the doors stood wide open. The feral killer living in Gash's gut howled a warning call – TRAP. Still, no point in slowing down, no point in going back. They would have to rely on their power as monsters. "Stay on your guard," Gash called out to his team.

He smelled sweat and metal before he saw the guards. Two of them swung from either side of the open doors down into a crouch, taking cover on either side of the doorway and aiming gauss submachine guns at the group. Nowhere to take cover, no side doors to dive through, a normal human team of mercs would simply be dead. These guards were about to unleash holy hell in this hallway. They opened fire.

Good thing Gash's team weren't normal humans. His predator instinct kicked in immediately, and he dove. In the process, he could see Silvie on one side of him transforming, her face warping and elongating, horns growing, strips of block cloth bursting and falling away as her body mass more than doubled in half a second. On Gash's other side, Iblis disappeared in a puff of smoke, magnetized metal flechettes passing through the empty cloud a micro-second later.

Additional flechettes tore into Silvie's hulking wechuge form, but to no meaningful effect. She roared, running through the hail of projectiles like a child might run through the sprinklers in old videos from before the global fresh water shortage. Gash dove under most of the gunfire meant for him, but caught a couple in the shoulder. Though it hurt, pain lived on another plane of existence now that combat was joined. Even before his transformation, things like pain and fear would be shunted away until the fight concluded. It's what made him such an effective soldier in his youth – now that he'd been transformed by mysterious forces into a vampire, something like getting shot held little more meaning for him than getting stung by a wasp.

He rolled back onto his feet, sprinting to keep up with Silvie, and to clear the distance to the attackers before they could reload and fire off another volley. Even a vampire could only get stung so many times before it started to matter.

But there would be no need for that. Iblis appeared directly beside the two gunmen in the doorway. Two flashes of white flame leapt, one from each hand, blasting each guard violently down into the floor. The smell of burning human flesh followed closely on the heels of twin explosions.

There would be no time to rest on their laurels – the soft hum of gauss weapons discharging flechettes from within the server room indicated more assailants. Iblis blinked out of the way again as a torrent of metal shredded the ground just beneath where he'd been standing.

That angle meant they were shooting from a raised platform of some kind. Gash hit the doorway at full sprint, stopping to pivot and climb the wall of the server room. A few more flechettes hit Silvie as she followed him into the room. One of the gunners tried to track Gash as he went up the wall, but the sudden vertical movement evidently surprised him and the stream of projectiles made a line that traced Gash's movement up the wall from half a second behind. Concrete and plaster showered the ground below as Gash raced to connect the line between his claws and his assailant's throat.

Observation in movement, a crucial element to a blitz attack like this. Gash took in what details he could as he moved towards the killing blow. The rather large room seemed to serve primarily as a reception area, presumably for maintenance personal or employees that needed access to the sensitive data. A receptionist's desk stood abandoned, no sign of the receptionist (unless it was one of the guards). Gash noted another security door, closed, behind the desk.

Catwalks ringed the room, linking two walkways that led to two more security doors on what served as the second story of the room. Maintenance access to the upper racks of servers, the apparatus that cooled the room, and machinery that powered the servers. Two guards stood on walkways, one firing down at Silvie and the one trying to hit Gash. A third had taken cover behind the receptionist's desk, but even as Gash watched, Iblis hit the poor bastard in the face with a white-hot blast of flame, dropping him like a packet of noodles into a wok.

This would all be over in a few more seconds. Gash leapt in an arc off the wall and onto the catwalk. He rolled under a last desperate burst of fire from the guard, and then came up inside the firing radius, grabbing the gun with one hand, and her throat with his other. He ripped the gun away, and then snapped her neck. He felt pity for her, a hapless worker drone serving a vile nest of parasites, but could give her nothing other than a quick and painless death.

Which was more than could be said for the last guard. Silvie leaped up onto the catwalk and ripped that guard apart, slurping down large hunks of his flesh, her wounds healing rapidly as she did. When she'd eaten her fill, she looked around, caught Gash's eyes. If it was possible for a hulking monster with a skull for a face and bone antlers to look ashamed, she certainly did. And then she transformed back. The transformation wicked the blood away, leaving her looking like a normal young woman, long black hair, gaze downturned. Naked and standing in a pool of blood and entrails.

"You didn't bring an extra change of clothes on this op, did you?" Iblis called up.

She covered herself and turned away from the two men. In that same moment, a memory crashed into the forefront of Gash's psyche, sudden and visceral. He stood on a wooden dais, cold and afraid, wearing a pair of ragged pants and with only his long black hair to cover his breasts. He repressed a shiver. Bile rose in his throat as half a dozen corporate suits leered at him, eyes lingering in particular on his exposed belly and the spots where the torn trousers exposed his thighs. He wanted to scream and sob but he wouldn't give them the pleasure of getting off on his pain.

Only when Gash watched himself walking into the room on the far side did he finally realize that this memory of being sold into slavery at Rat Eater's belonged to Silvie. The memory slowly faded, leaving Gash's chest heaving. He shuddered, and immediately looked away from Silvie, instead looking down at the guard whose neck he'd just snapped. The woman was slightly larger than Silvie, but not by much. He slid her pants and outer jacket off, carrying them over to Silvie, eyes still averted.

"Take a few seconds to throw these on," he said. "Best not to distract Iblis on the job, yeah?"

"Best not to distract Iblis," Iblis repeated in mock indignation. "Please, I am a professional!" At that he disappeared in a puff of smoke.

Gash felt Silvie grab the pants and jacket out of his hands, and then stepped away to give her a moment to change. She tapped him gently on the shoulder when she had dressed, mouthing a silent "thank you."

Gash took her offered hand and with his help, the two dropped off the catwalk to the ground floor. Iblis opened the security door from the inside, welcoming them into the WalCo secure server room with a flourish.

Lights on motion sensors flickered to life as the three stepped through the threshold – large hanging light fixtures casting dim blue light down on rows of walkways weaving between the massive two-story stacks. Winded from the fight, the trio slowed to a walk as they moved deeper into the server room. The size of the place defied belief. Each time Gash imagined they had reached the end, another set of lights flickered to life, illuminating another layer of the obscene labyrinth like a flare falling into a bottomless well. Moreso than ever before, Gash felt the age and size and depth of influence held by a mega-corporation like WalCo. Never more than in this moment had Gash felt like David staring up at a giant.

Silvie stared in awe, her breaths coming in short ragged bursts. Iblis, meanwhile, seemed unimpressed. "Nearest access point?" he asked.

"According to my guy, there's only one in the whole place. Other end of the room."

Iblis sighed. "This is taking longer than I would like."

Gash agreed. The now obsolete mission timer already read 3 minutes. According to the original plan, they would only have two more minutes to snag the data and get back topside. The extra security cost them precious seconds at every turn.

"Let's hustle, then," Silvie said.

The access point turned out to be a secure room set against the farthest wall. Iblis cleared a third security door, and the door opened into a small office space. A large faux-mahogany (or was it real mahogany? If anyone could afford the real thing it would be WalCo) desk rested in the center, with a computer terminal and work station. A real-D rig and a neural node rested one on each side of the workstation.

Gash looked over at Iblis. Unflappable since the beginning of this whole op, his face paled. He ran his fingers along the space behind his ear, unconsciously tracing his neural port. Like all hackers worth anything in this world, Iblis could dive directly into interactive cyberspace without a bulky real-D rig like what Gash used at Sammy's. But to have one at a simple server access point did not bode well. None of the intel they'd reviewed noted this.

"We still good?" Gash asked.

Iblis shook his head slowly. "I do not know. I will have to jack in to see. This might take longer than expected – do not pull me out early or you will turn me into the potato."

Gash nodded. "I know."

"You have my back?" he asked.

"Why is this such a big deal?" Silvie asked.

"Nobody designing a facility like this cares about the aesthetics of cyberspace, so the only reason a corporation would require neural immersion in a giant data stack like this is security. It forces anyone who wants access to the data to expose themselves to real world dangers."

"The security measures – black ICE – can create a feedback loop that can fry my brain," Iblis added. "Only possible if I hook my whole brain in."

"What's black ICE?" Silvie asked.

"ICE stands for intrusion counter-measures electronics. Digital security that takes its name from late 20th century fiction. Black ICE is the kind that kills you."

"Why not use the Real-D rig then?"

"Sufficiently advanced rigs like this one can cook you, same as jacking in directly," Gash said.

"Damn," she said, staring down at the rig. "So do we abort?"

"We are in too deep, now," Iblis said, and without further discussion he plugged the jack in the neural node into the port behind his ear. His body slumped against the desk.

"We need to get ready to protect this place when reinforcements arrive," Gash said.

"Okay, what do you want me to do?" she asked.

"I'm going to head back to the reception area, that's the easiest place to hold. You stay here – be ready to transform. If they slip in past me or there's another access point, you're the final stand."

She looked at him for a moment, blazing fiercely. She didn't want to be sidelined, she wanted to come stand her ground beside him. She resented the move, but she didn't argue. She only nodded. "Fine."

"If the security measures take him, you come get me and we're out of here, okay?"

"How can I tell if that happens?"

"You won't miss the smell of burning gray matter, or the dead look in his eyes. You can always check his pulse to be sure."

"Okay," she said.

Gash reached out, put his hand on her shoulder. "Listen," he started.

"Wow," Iblis said, sitting up at the desk and looking around.

"Wow indeed," Gash said. "Done already? Too much security? Are we aborting?" He had visions of leaving empty-handed, of Ana Marin's face gone black and white, one more disposable person dead or vanished. Blood pooling behind her eyes.

"No, I have it," Iblis said, tapping his head, "it was not like missile science."

"Do you mean rocket science?" Gash asked.

Iblis seemed to consider his hands for a moment, as though confirming the realness of reality, and then looked at Gash and shrugged. "It was... strangely easy. The black ICE in there should have taken me a long time to crack. Not sure I am even good enough to have cracked it. But when I was in there, it was like I was in the zone. Just knew exactly what to do. Easy mode. A cockier man would think nothing further than that…. But I know where my skills start and where they end. Somehow, someone paved the way for me."

Gash immediately thought of the raven in the net, injecting him with Silvie's memories. Had his client hired another hacker to help them? Why not let him know? Was he playing some other games in the background? Such questions would have to wait until they were no longer trapped deep within the monolithic WalCo HQ, on the cusp of being buried by a tidal wave of security personnel.

"We'll try to figure out what happened once we are clear. But you have the intel? You know Ana Marin's location?"

"I will wave you the data when we get to safety," Iblis nodded.

"Then let's clear the hell out," Gash said, and the three sprinted for the reception room.

"Do we have an escape plan yet?" Iblis asked.

"I was going to think about it while you were jacked in, but thirty seconds wasn't enough," Gash said.

"What if we go up?" Silvie asked.

"Up?" Gash asked, kicking in the door and bursting into the reception area.

"We can't get out through the lobby, the security in that place is insane, and they'll be waiting for us. So we go up past it, and out the windows."

"No good," Gash said, smashing through the security door to the final hallway. "The windows on this building are built to withstand explosives. Even with your super-strength, we couldn't break through."

"The eleventh floor is under construction according to those blueprints you had," Silvie pressed. "Iblis can soften the window with his fire, and if we can find a sledgehammer, I'm sure in wechuge form I can smash through."

Lots of "ifs." If Iblis' fire could get hot enough to soften top-of-the-line nano-impact-glass. If WalCo still employed human workers and had a sledgehammer sitting around the worksite. If they could even get up to the eleventh floor.

"We're really rolling the dice," Gash said.

"Given the lack of other options, I think it is a damn fine plan," Iblis said.

"You can't teleport us out of here?" Gash asked, as the team burst into the security station around the elevator. No additional guards were mustered down here, but Gash noticed the red lights on the security cameras had come back to life.

"Inanimate objects only," he said, smashing the elevator call button.

"They're watching us," Gash said.

With a gesture, Ifrit fired off a fan of small flames, like tiny red knives, that scythed through the four different security cameras. Each fell to the ground, a smoking ruin.

"We don't have any other options," Silvie said.

She was right.

"Okay. You're right, Silvie. Eleventh floor, here we come."

She nodded and transformed again, the muscle and bone shredding the WalCo security uniform. As a wechuge she howled, shaking Gash's bones, boiling his marrow. Thirty-one stories up, he imagined, they would hear that howl. And they would quiver to know that the monsters were coming, and that any who stood in their way would be hewn down.

The elevator door opened with a pleasant ding. Fortunately, this bank of elevators covered all the way from sub-basement 20 up to floor 15. They all stepped in, and Silvie smashed the button for floor 11. The doors closed, and the elevator began to rise.

CHAPTER 17

When the door opened onto the eleventh floor, the smell of sawdust and fresh paint poured into the elevator car. Gash stepped out to find the security station dismantled and the room empty. The walls stood bare, electronics removed, paint stripped. A recently-dried white base coast covered much of the space.

Silvie followed Gash, looking around as she emerged. "Looks like they're saving some payroll on security," she said, her wechuge's voice half gravel, half demon.

"Restraint is an unfamiliar concept for American megacorporations," Iblis said. "Do not let down your guard."

As though fate set out to prove him correct in that moment, all of the doors to the security foyer opened simultaneously, and four flashbangs came rolling in, one from each door.

In the half-second between registering the grenades and detonation, Gash managed to leap towards the nearest, kicking it back through the door from whence it came. Iblis blinked across the room in a puff of smoke, taking cover behind the security desk.

The deafening pop and blinding flash of the other three still sent Gash reeling, but didn't completely disable him. When WalCo security forces came pouring in, a river of black-armored and black-helmeted human destruction, he raised the pistol Iblis smuggled in, and started shooting. The first two guards coming in went down, but there were more behind, and they returned fire. Gash tried to spin out of the way, but, still off balance from the flashbangs, he moved too slowly. Magnetic flechettes ripped through his shoulder and belly. He could feel the heat of them, the sharp spike of pain. Time to take cover – he dove behind the security desk with Iblis.

Silvie, meanwhile, charged through the door on the other side, sending WalCo security goons flying like bowling pins. For some reason the flashbangs hadn't affected her. She bellowed with rage, and though he could no longer see her, he could hear the sounds of battle. Her claws tearing flesh, flechettes chipping away at her monster's body, at the bone skull of her face. The screams of men, dying hard.

The angle of the security counter served to benefit them – it was positioned (intentionally no doubt) to have cover from any point of entry into the room. Despite a withering hail of magnetic projectiles unleashed by something like a dozen armed WalCo guards, the composite material of the counter held. Gash's vision resolved, and the ringing in his ears grew softer with each passing second. He blind-fired over the counter until he ran out of ammo.

Using the cover fire Gash provided, Iblis popped up and gestured, opening both arms as if to hug the enemy. But hug them he did not – bright red flames erupted in a cone, bathing the center of the room in intense flame. His eyes glowed red, fire and smoke smoldering in his hair and beard. The smell of burning flesh immediately filled the room, as a dozen men ignited from the heat of the demonic flames. Most of them fell to the ground, trying to put out the fire before it consumed them. A few ran from the room, their agonized screams a hellish chorus, a celebration of pain and death.

The body count on this op had just surpassed twenty. Twenty souls, snuffed out, because Gash wanted a big payday, wanted to rescue a single Romanian scientist. He'd always written off corporate employees as having gone over to the dark side – by and large they were helping slowly strangle the world, extinguish independent souls, and give god-like wealth and power to a small group of oligarchs. But this level of carnage carried a dagger into his heart. Most of these people were just trying to get by. He'd spare them if he could.

A second wave of guards poured into the room, leveling another withering barrage at the security counter. Meanwhile, Gash heard Silvie shouting in the icepick-on-chalkboard of her wechuge voice. "Let me go," was all she howled, over and over. His wounds already healed and his senses restored, Gash was being overly cautious – he had to get out there and help her. Before he could act, however, Gash heard another sound. A metal-scrape, and a sort of "clink." A grenade, probably another flashbang. He paused just long enough for the goon to lob the grenade, and then popped up just in time to smack the grenade back at the firing squad.

As his open palm connected with the little piece of metal, he realized that this wasn't a flashbang. This was something new – it looked like a plasma grenade. The heaviest explosive you could fit in a small package. What the hell was WalCo thinking, giving ordnance like that to security guards? He had just enough time to duck back down behind cover, before the tiny harbinger of death detonated. Plasma grenades were new tech – very small radius, but incredibly destructive within that area. From behind the counter, Gash closed his eyes against the blinding flash of light as a wave of intense heat flooded over the counter. There were no screams of agony this time, just the sound of biological matter incinerating, the splatter of charred flesh against the wall. For a lone second, not a soul made a sound. Gash heard heartbeats through the walls on all sides, but in that frozen moment, that flash of calm before the storm, nobody moved. Nobody acted.

Gash felt their spirits, their ghosts, cleave to him already. Another dozen lives cut short, a modest addition to the congregation of dead haunting his waking dreams.

Something else to wall off for later, now was hardly time for self-reflection. Gash burst out from behind the counter and charged the door. The first thing he saw was Silvie – floating in the air at least a foot above a gruesome pile of human limbs and viscera. An aura of soft blue energy formed a halo around her body, and except for hands clenching into fists and unclenching, she did not move – could not move, it seemed.

When he registered the rest of the room, his blood ran cold. Aside from half a dozen guards, there were three others. Two wore long black robes, hoods pulled over their heads. Full tactical rigs, green-eyed night vision goggles, bullet-resistant composite facemasks, gave them the appearance of twin aberrations.

Behind them stood another man. This one wore an incredibly expensive looking suit, and not a wrinkle or scuff on the whole thing. He was tall, too – he towered over most of the others in the room. But what really cut through Gash's heart were the man's eyes. These were obvious augmentations, but a custom job the likes of which Gash had not seen before. Most cyber-eyes made an effort to emulate real eyes, or went in the other direction, making aesthetic choices to intimidate or dazzle. This man's eyes were simply... blank white. As though a magic wand had rendered them down to nothing more than twin corneas. Yet he carried himself with such commanding authority that these could be no simple fake eyes, no hack job implants.

When the man turned those eyes on Gash, they seemed to pierce his heart, to unearth all of his deepest secrets in an instant. And then he smiled, something refined and haughty and ruthless and feral. Gash sensed an endless sea of seething rage beneath the veneer of that smile, that multi-thousand credit suit.

"Got you," he said. And he did. One of the robed twins reached out a black-gloved hand, and in that moment, Gash felt pressure on every square inch of his body. He tried to move against it, and at first he was able to take a step forward, and then another, as though walking through a wall of snow. The robed figure grunted and raised a second hand, curling them both into half-fists. The pressure tightened. Gash could not move. He contorted and wrenched his muscles, but could not move another inch against the force. When he felt himself being lifted into the air, he knew it was over. With no leverage against the ground, he could only hope to twist in the air.

"Iblis, extract," Gash shouted. There came a popping sound, and then one of the guards called out.

"Sir, the third one seems to have disappeared in a puff of smoke."

"Yes, that one is a teleporter. He'll be challenging to track down," the tall man said. "Never mind him for now, clear the floor and coordinate with each other floor to make sure the building is secure."

"Let me go," Gash growled.

The man leaned in close to Gash, as though checking the provenance on a fancy bottle of wine. "I'm glad you could make it – I was beginning to worry that I had over-estimated you."

"How'd you know we were going to be up here?" Gash asked.

The man's thin smile somehow grew just a little wider. "You had three options. One: try to break through a platoon's worth of security and heavy weaponry on the first floor. Two: Pick from floors two through fifteen at random in hopes of finding escape. Three: Access the floor under construction in hopes of finding a construction implement to help you break through the windows. Given a basic level of competence it seemed clear you would go for option three. You'd most certainly be dead if you had tried anything else." The man shrugged.

"And now?" Gash asked. "Am I dead now?" It's not that he feared death – at least not any more than was reasonable. His only lament would be leaving this job unfinished. Leaving Ana Marin locked into some secure WalCo facility, slaving away, until her inevitable untimely demise. Well, that and getting Silvie killed. He regretted that, too.

"Dead? If I really wanted you dead, I would have just rigged the elevator to implode and blown you away when you arrived on this floor. No, the opportunity to study a wechuge *and* a vampire is far too compelling to pass up."

Oh, Gash thought. Great.

"Now let's see if our scientists got the dosage right," he said, raising a pistol and firing. Out of the corner of his eyes, Gash saw a small dart protruding from his chest. His vision blurred and swirled, making a mosaic of the blood and the gore and the black clad mages, and then gradually that mosaic dimmed and faded until Gash could see nothing, could hear nothing, could smell nothing. He did not dream.

CHAPTER 18

Nagash Jensen opened his eyes to the harsh white halogen light of a WalCo prison cell, and immediately regretted it. The brightness of it did not play well with his throbbing headache, and he snapped his eyes shut immediately. Too late. His brain took up the bass drum and it was time to practice.

"Look who's awake," came a voice from above him.

Gash forced his eyes open, if only to make sure that this stranger wasn't about to shiv him with a wooden stake. Given a few seconds to digest his surroundings, Gash managed to ascertain that he was lying on the bottom bunk in a moderately sized prison cell. The man in the top bunk dropped down and stretch a hand out to shake. He, like Gash, wore the typical WalCo prison uniform: a cheap blue synth-fabric tank top and long shorts. The cheapest non-problematic garments money could buy. On the chest of the tank, in bright orange letters intertwined with the WalCo logo, were the words "WalCo Inmate."

Gash's new cellmate stood almost a head taller than Gash, and seemed built entirely out of muscle. His long hair tumbled out of control in a confusion of curls and tangles, a chaotic black waterfall that stretched well past his shoulders. Long-term inmate, then. His face seemed out of control, too, if you could describe a face that way.

The proportions were off. One eye opened wider than the other, and his teeth didn't line up.

What most impressed Gash, though, were his arms. They looked like the real thing if you didn't have a keen eye for detail. Gash, though, always made a professional point to take in and process every detail. If you looked closely at the man's shoulders, you saw a faint seam between upper arm and shoulder, the skin of his arms just a hint lighter than the rest of him.

Bio-mod, hyperdense muscle-weave. As strong as the bulkiest cyberarms but let you blend in, feel things. Maneuver. Not the cutting edge anymore, but they had been five years ago. Meaning between the tech and the hair, this guy arrived as an inmate no more than five years ago, but not fewer than three. In the world before he would have seen some kind of combat action, and had money.

"We're going to be real close for a long time, is my guess," said the man. "You're not going to leave me hanging are you? That's a bad first impression."

Gash sat up, wiped a crusted line of drool off his face, and stood to face his new cellmate. He didn't plan to be here long – with his abilities it would only be a matter of time to find a window to escape – but he didn't want trouble with other inmates to complicate things. He reached out and shook the man's hand. "Nagash Jensen," he said. "But you should call me Gash."

"Pleasure to meet you, Gash. My name is Julius. Julius Weaver. I've been alone in this cell for quite a while."

"Huh. It's not like a corporation to give you a personal cell – ought to have packed in two or three other inmates to save costs," Gash said.

Julius patted his left bicep with his right arm. "Bio-mod arms, MK 2 MedCo. Evidently I merit a special cell, reinforced walls and bars on the door. Reinforced porthole window. No way of busting out. I'm guessing if you're in here, you must have some powerful augmentations, too."

"Surely you're not the only inmate with augmentations." Gash looked around the cell. Close quarters. Black walls, probably carbon-nano-weave. Door looked to be the same material – there were a few bars in an opening three quarters towards the top of the door, at face-level. On the far wall from the door, a small window – barely the size of a porthole – gave just enough of a look at the outside world, let just enough light in to preserve their sanity. Hopefully not enough to turn Gash to ashes.

"What of it?" Julius leaned against the beds, watching Gash intently.

On the right side of the room, opposite the beds, a small holo-projector mounted near the ceiling played one of the WalCo news feed. Some of the independent European democracies wrapped up signing a nuclear defense pact, and in response five of the world's largest mega-corporations did likewise. Old news, at this point – the news corps and all of the political entities involved were really drawing it out. Fishing for ratings, flexing military power to impress their own people and intimidate the other side.

"I just mean you must be some kind of VIP if you had a cell to yourself."

"Which makes you...?" said Julius.

"Either I'm a VIP too, or you're not a VIP anymore," Gash walked the room tapping the wall. He figured they hadn't designed it for vampire strength. How could they, if there had been no vampires when they'd built it? If he could find a seam in the wall material, or a hollow spot where maybe some wiring ran through, made the wall weaker, he could try to smash through.

"So you're not augmented?" Julius asked.

"Not exactly."

"Interesting," Julius said. "I wonder why you're in here, then?"

"I have... other sorts of augmentations."

"Well that's very cryptic. Look, if we're honest with each other, maybe we can come up with a way to escape."

"Sure," Gash said. "What are you in for, Mr. VIP?"

Julius wandered over to the window, looking out as though to be sure that the world was still there. "I blew up a WalCo research facility."

Gash stopped looking at the wall long enough to stare at his new cell-mate. Was the man joking? Making up stories?

Julius stepped away from the window and met Gash's gaze. "It's not like I set out to do it. Self-destruct mechanism. I was FBI, trying to arrest a head scientist responsible for some deaths in my jurisdiction."

"That explains it, I guess. The last of the Feds, rotting away in a WalCo prison."

Gash turned back to his task. After circling the room a couple times, he found what seemed like a hollow segment of the wall. The electricity and the air had to be coming in somehow, after all.

"Don't try it," Julius said.

"This part's –" Gash started

"Hollow," Julius finished. "Doesn't mean you can break through, the walls in here are impenetrable."

Gash reared back and smashed his fist into the wall with his entire strength behind it. Not only did the wall fail to break, but with a crack, two of his knucklebones went halfway back in his hand. Blocking out the considerable pain, he gave the wall a few kicks, and slammed his shoulder into it, dislocating it (again). None of it mattered, he would heal in a few minutes. Again and again he struck the hollow segment, but couldn't make so much as a crack in the nano-material.

"Told you," Julius said.

"You'd still have tried if you had just gotten here," Gash said.

"I tried for a lot longer than you. Lot of heartache – and body ache – for no reason."

Defeated, Gash wandered over to the window. Dawn toyed with the horizon, a few lights of red intermingling with the incoming wall of gray rain clouds. So they gave the vampire an east-facing cell. The holo-projector seemed like a nice touch, but the window had obviously been intended to torture him. He'd need to hide in the corner of the room until sunset.

After a few minutes of staring, Gash startled when a raven landed on the exterior lip of the window, framed perfectly in the porthole opening. It cocked its head to the side and looked right at Gash with beady black eyes.

"What's with the ravens?" Gash muttered.

"That's not a raven," Julius said.

Gash looked up from the window. "Then what is it?"

He shrugged. "New species of corvid. Raven-like. Apparently a little smaller and the beak shape isn't quite the same. Has some long Latin-sounding name. The ornithology community is holding a contest to give it a common name."

"How the hell do you know that?"

Julius laughed for a long time before he answered. "They only play news stations here. I'm supposed to be tortured by it, but the only torture is boredom. You know corporate news broadcasts, they recycle content nonstop."

Gash looked back at the corvid. It just looked like a raven to him. "I guess with all the wildlife that's gone extinct in the last century, people like seeing something new emerge."

"I'm from Arc 1, we never had birds and it never bothered me." Julius hopped back into his top bunk, positioning himself sitting up and facing the direction of the holovision.

Gash watched him for a moment. "If it's so boring, why watch?"

"You've never been in jail I guess? There's nothing else to do in this whole tiny world." Julius heaved a deep sigh.

A sigh of surrender, Gash thought. Some number of months or years ago, this prisoner – Julius Weaver – gave up on the world. As much as he gave the idea of escape lip service, it didn't take him more than a minute or two to lie back down and forget the whole thing. Gash, though, knew better than to give up. WalCo seemed an imposing foe, but with monsters and magic in the world they were out of their depth. Playing yesterday's game. No prison cell would hold him – or Silvie, who they presumably took to a version of this cell for women – for long.

The raven-that-wasn't-a-raven pushed away from the window, flapping in place for a moment, seeming almost to be watching Gash. And then it flew away, towards the brighter gray of oncoming dawn. A few droplets of early rain hit the window with a dull tap, but even covered by the clouds, the sun still tingled on Gash's vampire's skin. The burning would come soon if he did not find the darkest corner of this cell to wait out the day. He stepped away from the light.

CHAPTER 19

Gash grew accustomed to sleeping in the daytime not long after becoming a vampire, but between the need to huddle in the corner of the room furthest from the window, and the never-ending reel of news feeds, sleep came fitfully when it came at all. Instead, he watched the feed. His cellmate seemed glued to the broadcast in all his waking moments, though periodically he would exercise or receive a meal in the little slot in the door.

Gash's meals came in the form of small Styrofoam containers full of human blood. The first time he received a meal of his own Julius questioned him vigorously. Gash pushed it off as a medical condition, but that excuse clearly failed to land. Between that and the way Gash shunned sunlight, he figured his cellmate caught on fast. After all, watching the news every day meant more tales of magical mayhem than any other topic. The werewolf terrorizing London, the wizard with the flying carpet that got sucked into the turbine of a massive passenger shuttle and almost brought the whole thing down, the two invisible men who got into a fistfight after bumping into each other in a woman's locker room in Dallas, and on and on and on.

On the evening of the third day, when the sun set enough for Gash to move freely about the cell, there came a knock on the door. He looked at Julius, who shrugged, and then he stepped up to the little window looking out into the hallway. A tall raven-haired woman stood on the other side, frowning at him. He opened his mouth to ask what she wanted, but when she snapped her fingers, he plummeted to the floor, asleep before he even hit the ground.

Gash woke in a small white room with one-way glass and a single door on the far side. Chains held him to a metal chair that was itself bolted to the floor. He strained with all his vampiric might, but could not break free. After some time, when it became clear that escape eluded him for now, he closed his eyes and focused on his other senses. He experimented with meditation in his quieter moments on the open sea, and found that with the right focus he could project his senses. In the solitude of the little interrogation room, for lack of more direct options, Gash tried this now. Soft mumbling on the other side of the one-way glass resolved as he concentrated on it, until he found himself listening to two individuals wrapping up a conversation.

"...so we'll let him stew for another hour or so, and then invite Mr. Galloway in for the interrogation?"

"Precisely. I'll leave it in your capable hands. Don't hesitate to use your abilities if he seems to be getting free, and don't forget the panic button. "

Heavy footsteps crossed the room, a door opened and shut again. Gash heard the occasional soft rustle, a cough or sneeze, but otherwise time passed in silence. What seemed a great deal longer than an hour later, the door to Gash's little interrogation room opened. The man with the white eyes stepped through, dressed in the same or an identical copy of the immaculately tailored suit from a few days ago, when he and his mages captured Gash and Silvie.

"Mr. Jensen," he said, pulling back the chair opposite Gash and having a seat. "Good evening."

Gash said nothing, only raising his eyebrows at the man.

"My name is Henry," he said, withdrawing a pad of paper – real paper, not the digital papyrus now popular with the hipster crowd – and an actual ink pen.

"Mr. Galloway," Gash said.

Galloway smiled, a thin smile devoid of mirth. "It seems we'll have to work on our sound-proofing."

"I wouldn't recommend wasting the money. I don't plan to stay that long."

Galloway's smile widened at this, more a bearing of proverbial fangs than an expression of emotion. He made a little note on his pad of paper, but kept it at an angle that prevented Gash from seeing it. "Aren't you the bold little vampire. You must really believe that story if you're giving up valuable intel just to get a rise out of me. But you're delusional if you think there is a snowball's chance that I would let a prize like you slip from my grasp. I have big plans for you. First there is information that you will provide me with, and then when you have nothing else to tell me, we will study your biology at great length. We have had very little luck finding vampires to study... apparently you are a rare breed. And most of you have the good sense not to come wandering directly into our headquarters building, begging to be trapped."

Gash leaned forward, bearing his own fangs. "There is no chance that I will give you any information. And if you think to keep me long enough to study me, I promise that someone in your organization will, at some point, underestimate me. And then you'll find my fangs at your throat."

"So melodramatic. All of that may be the case, but nevertheless I am going to ask you some questions now. It would behoove you to answer them honestly."

Gash leaned back and affected a yawn.

"Nagash Jensen, born just under five decades ago. Parents died when you were young, you spent your early years in the military. First in the Federal military back when that still existed, and then in the holy land as a corporate soldier. Killer track record, and I do mean that literally, but then most of your squad died due to a 'failure of intel' and you dropped out after twenty years. Spent the next dozen as a private investigator. Met a girl, Serena, but she died too."

Galloway paused, the sad little frown on his face in stark contract to the mirth in his eyes. "Seems like everyone around you just... dies, Mr. Jensen."

Gash looked away; rage filled his heart, red filled his vision. He'd been interrogated before, he knew this tactic. Get him riled up and easier to manipulate. He took long, deep breath, staring defiantly at his interrogator.

"Can I share a dirty little secret with you?" Galloway asked, pushing on before Gash could answer. "I really shouldn't lay that last one at your feet. I looked into it and Serena's death? That's one of our little 'oopsies.'"

What did he mean? Gash felt the world closing in on him, struggled against the chains.

"Yeah, one of our subsidiaries was looking into a new drug therapy to transfer addiction. For instance, a young lady like Serena, addicted to some really dangerous street drugs, might sign up for an anti-addiction therapy, and we would give her a drug that reconnected those synapses to something a little safer. Something that might be found in a WalCo vending machine at a store near you. Unfortunately the human brain apparently doesn't work that way, and the drug backfired." Galloway looked up from his notepad and made eye contact with Gash. "Oopsy."

Gash snarled, and where he meant to curse, he could find only guttural, bestial syllables within himself. All those years ago, Serena had gone out to try a new anti-addiction therapy, and the next day Gash found her dead of an overdose. He always thought she'd backslid. As a private investigator, Gash met countless addicts who backslid right when they were supposed to be quitting. Was Galloway making up a story to get into his head? Or had WalCo really killed his Serena? He tried with all his might to burst the chains, but still to no avail. Galloway merely watched his struggle, taking the occasional note in his pad, like a sadistic therapist. Eventually, he managed to calm himself again. Panting with the exertion, taking deep breaths, Gash reined in the inner killer. No reason to waste his energy, best to let the rage fester until he could unleash it.

"Well, I guess the old ball and chain is a sensitive topic. You've been a busy little bee since your little queen overdosed, haven't you Mr. Jensen? You slaughtered ten security guards at a research facility in central Washington just over a year ago. Killed two WalCo agents tasked with bringing you to justice, and we have found ample evidence that you were at the center of events on the Isle of Rhodes approximately three weeks ago, when magic returned the world. A member of your party even managed to hack a WalCo shuttle in-flight to Rhodes, sending a dozen personnel plummeting to their deaths."

The turn took him by surprise. "Never heard of Rhodes," he said, but he'd paused for too long. Galloway made a little note in his pad.

"What was your mission? Did you somehow know that you would release magic back into the world or was that incidental?"

"My mission was to find the best beach to lounge on, with the prettiest girls and best cocktails."

Galloway made another little note. "And your compatriots – what were their names?"

Gash said nothing.

"No witty quips? I would venture to say you must care about your teammates. Or at least one of them. You worked with a hacker named Starfire, yes? She is the one who knocked our shuttle out of the sky. What is her real name?"

Gash continued not to speak, but could feel the heat rising from his chest to his face. He struggled against the chains. They were hot on Starfire's trail.

Galloway made a number of scratches on his notepad. "I wonder if she feels the same way about you? Perhaps we can use you as bait." He seemed to be muttering to himself, but Gash could tell that it was meant to get another rise out of him.

He willed himself to be still.

"And what about your new team that helped you launch this ill-advised raid on our headquarters building? Surely you, Iblis, and Ms. Wauneka had logistical support from outside?"

Gash bit down on his tongue so hard, he thought it might bleed.

"I have to ask, and you should know that this one isn't on my list, it's just more of a curiosity. Whatever possessed you to bring along a twenty-something coffee shop barista? Just because she can transform into some kind of monster? I mean, you and Iblis I get. You're trained soldiers, but poor little Silvie? She's no soldier. She got herself captured first, and now with a little time and a cattle-prod, any grunt with some imagination could get her talking."

"What have you done to her?" Gash growled, hating himself even as the words were leaving his mouth.

Galloway's wry smile transformed into a full grin and the man laughed. "Her too? You have a bit of a weakness for dark-haired twenty-somethings don't you?"

Gash looked down at the table.

"You should know we found your boat. Per the Global Corporate Legal Enforcement Charter, we have seized this particular piece of property, since it was obtained illegally. Your personal affects have been transferred here and deposited in a cubby in the highly unlikely event of your eventual release." He paused, and then set his pad face down on the table to lean forward. "A shame, I'm sure – you must have enjoyed the ability to move about freely on the open seas without concern for the mortal danger posed by the sun's rays."

"Illegally obtained, huh? I suppose you're going to return it to its rightful owners, the Sovereign Military Order of Malta?" Gash said.

"It seems that this organization has been disbanded, on account of most of their members being brutally slain. WalCo will be keeping it. Of course, it's a crime scene right now, as we discovered a number of confidential WalCo security files." He paused for dramatic effect. "Nothing to say about that? You really do care more about your people than anything else. What is the real name of the fixer whose handle is 'Hemmingway'?"

"I don't know any fixer named –"

"Please," Galloway interrupted. "We already tied him to your most sensitive downloads. How do you contact him?"

Gash was silent once more.

"Fine, but this next question is really important so I want you to think long and hard about your answer, okay? Why does he spell his handle with two 'M's'? Since it is supposedly a nod to Ernest Hemingway, it seems he spelled his own name wrong. Why do you think that is? Is he an amateur or do you think he just prefers to work with the illiterate? Maybe that should have been a red flag for you when you hired him. It certainly is for me, but then, I was reading Hemingway's books – in paper of course – long before either of you were twinkles in your father's eyes, so maybe it just matters more to me than you."

He knew a lot about Hemmingway. A lot more than Gash left carelessly in the database on his boat. Meant they were on his trail even before the op, and if they were on his trail, it proved they were on Starfire's too. Now more than ever Gash needed to escape. He owed it to the two of them. To Silvie. To Iblis, who would no doubt be on the run as well. Owed it to Sammy, because if WalCo could tie Gash to Hemmingway, they could eventually tie Gash to Sammy, too.

After a period of silence, Galloway sighed. "Well, I suppose that will do for now. I got more out of you than anticipated. I didn't think it would be so easy to stoke those emotions. Eventually, once we bio-calibrate the formula to your genome, we have some nice cocktails that will ensure you're more overtly cooperative." He rose from his chair, sliding his notepad into his interior jacket pocket, and gestured to the one-way glass.

While Gash struggled against his restraints, two of Galloway's cronies piled into the small room. First came an orderly with a set of syringes. He placed them on the table. Close behind came the raven-haired woman, the passive stone of her face showing not even a hint of emotion. She walked with confidence, a long black robe flowing along the floor behind her. She strode directly to Gash, reaching for him. She stopped short of actually touching him, but when she got close enough, he immediately felt the irresistible pull of sleep, the siren call of a long day's work, the deep-brain surrender to fatigue; all condensed into a single instant. For the second time that day, Gash fell asleep.

CHAPTER 20

Gash woke in darkness. With no frame of reference, he couldn't tell how long he'd been out, but some primal part of his brain marked a significant passage of time. The hard floor of his cell dug into his back, and he propped himself up on his elbows, groaning. The pounding headache, the waking on the floor, it reminded him of some of the nastier hangovers in his 30s and 40s. Before becoming a vampire eliminated the feeling. Until now, at least. Accompanying the throbbing migraine were fatigue and *hunger*, a feeling almost as powerful as the first minutes of his vampiric awakening.

"Feeling okay?" Julius asked from the darkness.

Gash's vampiric eyes adapted quickly, even to a dark cell lit only by the city's neon halo shining through the tiny window. Julius sat on the edge of the bed, his muscles coiled with anticipation, blood pumping hard, body in every way on edge.

"I should ask you the same question," Gash said. "You seem like you're about ready to attack. Or be attacked."

Julius gave out a short laugh. "They told me you'd be extra hungry. They told me... you're a vampire. As if I hadn't already figured it out, watching you hide from the sun, drink blood out of a plastic cup every day, and go around thinking you can punch a hole in carbon nanotube walls."

"Relax," Gash said.

"Easier said than done."

"I don't feed on the innocent, and as far as I'm concerned, if you're in here you're probably innocent."

"Don't be so sure," Julius said, lying back down. "Not that I'm trying to convince you to attack me, but I don't think innocent is the word."

Gash considered the word. It certainly didn't apply to him – he broke into the facility, wading through a double-digit body count just to recover data on one person that, for all he knew, wasn't even kidnapped.

But he didn't feel guilty either. Between mad science projects run amok, emissions propelling the world deeper into a climate spiral, and hundreds of corporate-law executions, WalCo and corporations like it sculpted this world. This dying world, where the only thing cheaper than vending machine guns and fast food and Real-D porn were human lives. So how could he be expected to feel guilt for trying to smash a tiny piece of that world order for personal gain? To escape to his own private paradise?

"So if you're not innocent, what are you in for?" Gash asked.

Julius lay back on the bed and took a slow breath. "My team blew up a secret WalCo facility trying to arrest someone. Well, we caused it to self-destruct at least. I told you that already. And I think... I think I let something out into the world that I should not have."

"What do you mean?" Gash asked.

"Nothing, just a hunch I guess. Well, nobody confirmed it but I'd say it's more than a hunch." He paused. "It doesn't matter."

"Well, when it comes to accidentally letting things into the world, I suppose you and I have a lot in common then."

"Yeah?" Julius asked.

"You wouldn't believe me if I told you."

It took Julius a long time to fall asleep. Gash tried and failed to follow suit. The sound of hot blood in the man's arteries and the feral pull coming from deep in his vampire brain to feed drove him far from sleep.

He rose to his feet and walked to the window. The city glowed with the light of a billion sparkling neon stars, forever awake. In time, when the sky began again to dance with the first hint of dawn, someone brought him a cup of blood. He chugged it like whiskey on those hard nights in his 30s. Apparently, this particular test of Gash's impulse control was over.

When Gash eventually escaped the encroaching gray light of morning, taking refuge in the darkest corner of the cell, he dreamed of Serena for the first time in a long time. But not the happy memories. He dreamed her last days, he dreamed finding her dead in the bathtub next to a small pile of empty eye droppers. He dreamed conversations he once had with her little grave-marker, promising to carve out a peaceful life on her behalf, to live the way they'd always promised they would live if she got free of her addiction and he got free of his old life.

Chapter 21

"Wake up."

How long was Gash asleep? The soft gray light from the window told him not long, but that primal internal clock told him otherwise. That this was more the fading light of dusk than the rising dawn.

The veil of sleep dissolved and his brain began to process stimuli. Bright red lights recessed in the ceiling were flashing. One in the cell, and a line of them through the doorway and down the hall. Klaxons blared, same as a few days ago, during the Monster Squad's failed heist. Something was going on – was someone else breaking in?

It took him entirely too long to realize what he was looking at. The hallway. The door to the cell stood wide open. Julius spoke, but those words passed unheard through Gash, who had never woken up easy. He blinked the sleep out of his eyes and willed himself fully into the land of the living. Or at least, the land of the awake. Things were happening.

"Hey," Julius said, shaking Gash.

"What?" Gash asked.

"I said, the cell is opened. You're a big bad vampire, right? I could use your help escaping. There's people waiting for me. There's a woman.... I need to get back into the world."

"You and me both, pal." Gash said, rising to his feet. "What happened?"

Julius shrugged, standing himself. "The door just slid open, and then the klaxons started."

The two of them stood there, staring at the open door to the cell. Gash remembered reviewing some of the blueprints for the higher floors, where corporate prisoners were housed, but had not studied them deeply. Certainly not enough to have memorized this floor, or even recognized which floor they were on. Could this be a trap? Another of Galloway's tests? It seemed most likely, but then, if Galloway wanted to kill Gash it would have been very easy to do while he slept.

"What are we waiting for?" Gash said after what seemed a very long time. And he stepped into the hallway. WalCo strategic design teams had really gone out of their way to ensure that the prison floor featured as little characterization as possible. The walls, plain beige, were decorated only by the swirling red hues from the warning lights in the ceiling. The hallway stretched ahead of him, and in both directions to the right and left. The floor completely lacked landmarks. Rows of unmarked cells, doors all closed, must have held dozens or even hundreds of prisoners.

Only Gash and Julius were to experience a taste of freedom, it seemed. Or a taste of some mind game?

As if on cue, a voice from the hallway to the right shouted at the two prisoners. "Get back in your cell!" Two prison guards, heavily armored with riot gear and wielding long stun batons, were charging him. Two long steps forward, one sideways step, and Gash smashed the shouting guard's head into the wall with a crunch. The second tried to stop, but his momentum carried him forward, swinging at Gash's face. Gash easily caught him by the wrist, which he snapped as he might once have snapped a long twig for kindling while camping with his father.

Where had that memory come from? The smoke of a campfire, the peace of a quiet night far from the cities and their light pollution.

An infinite field of stars twinkling down from above. He felt serene in that moment. The guard cried out in pain, and Gash cut it short, ramming his hand into the man's throat and ripping it free. A spurt of arterial blood mixed in with the red lights against the beige walls. Gash drank deeply.

The red washed over him, then, and the lights and the blood were nothing to the crimson that overtook his vision. He cast the dead body aside. The deep-sub-conscious Gash assumed control. The warrior instinct, the killing spirit, his inner vampire. Whatever. It was driving now and it was *pissed*. Everyone on this floor, in this building, made a choice to serve WalCo. A monstrosity responsible for endless human suffering and death. Responsible for Serena.

Two more with batons rounded the corner ahead, followed closely on the heels of the first. They stopped dead in their tracks, but it was too late to run. Gash pounced on them, carving them apart with his bare hands. When they were dead, he ripped a wrist-display PCom off the shift lead, unlocking the biometric security with a retina scan before closing the guard's eyes forever.

He looked idly behind him at his cell-mate. Julius finished choking the second of two other guards that had come from the other direction, and armed himself with one of their stun batons. He looked warily at Gash.

"Come on if you're coming," Gash growled, checking the map display on the guard's wrist display.

He did not wait to see if Julius would come, but did hear the man's footsteps following behind. He loaded a map on the dead guard's PCom, and followed it easily. Two left turns and a long hallway eventually brought them to a door labeled "prisoner effects." Such a paltry thing as a locked door wouldn't slow him down, not now. He ripped the sliding door open in a cacophony of hydraulic screeching and flying sparks, and stepped into a large room lined with endless polymer-composite cubbies. At the front of the room, an office manager dove beneath her desk at Gash's entry.

"I'm not going to hurt you unless you screw me over," he said. When she did not come out from beneath the desk, he reached down and grabbed her by the collar of her blouse, pulling. She cried out, but when he sat her at her desk, she did not move, only looking up at him with watery eyes.

"Nagash Jensen, Silvie Wauneka, and Julius Weaver." He looked at Julius for confirmation that he'd gotten the name right. Julius nodded.

Unable to form words, the office manager nevertheless managed to type out some names. After a long moment, three small drones walking on spider-legs clattered from the depths of the shelves, each holding a white polymer box. The office manager retrieved each box in turn, and each drone returned to the stacks of possessions from which it came. She placed them in a row on the counter, and then stood back. Obviously unsure of what would come next.

Gash opened the one labeled "Nagash Jensen" and withdrew the contents. His suit and PCom, but not the silenced weapon Iblis smuggled in on his behalf. In keeping with the illusion that the contents of these boxes would one day be returned to those imprisoned here, the WalCo HQ warden presumably removed all such weapons from prisoner belongings.

Fine, that wasn't why he'd come, anyway. Beneath these clothes, he found his pants, shirt, tie, long coat. His hat. He half expected Galloway to be lying about his personal effects from *The Holy* being brought here, considering they all knew he would never have a trial, let alone a release date. But corps loved nothing so much as a bureaucracy, and rules formed the genetic building blocks of bureaucracy.

Gash wasted no time in tearing off his prison clothing right on the spot, putting his own clothes back on. It wouldn't do to be dressed like a prisoner, even if the element of surprise long ago flew out the window. He topped it all off with his hat, which he pulled from the bottom of the box and placed gently on his head, running his finger along the brim almost lovingly.

Julius dressed as well, pulling his own clothes on top of the WalCo prison garb. He left his box half-full, a cold weather suit of some kind still stuffed in there. He wouldn't need that to escape, certainly.

Gash grabbed the box labeled "Silvie Wauneka" and handed it to Julius. "For my associate, who is our next stop," he said. Julius glowered, but accepted the box; he apparently knew better than to complain about mule duty to the blood-soaked vampire.

Gash turned back to the office manager, the words of a threat on the tip of his tongue. But of course no matter what he said, she would eventually report this to her security chief. He considered breaking her neck, but even through the violent haze of his rage, the thought of executing an unarmed civilian found no purchase. Perhaps knocking her out? But this was no action movie, and applying enough violent force to her head to make her lose consciousness would at minimum leave her with a concussion, if not a brain bleed.

WalCo would find out who escaped soon enough anyway, so at the end of the day it didn't matter. He whirled back to the door and stormed out, the map of the floor uploaded to his own PCom from the dead guard's. Only a few hundred feet to Silvie's cell, and then the three of them could escape. Surely at this juncture, Galloway and his telekinetic mages wouldn't still be camping out the construction floor. Or perhaps Gash would go through the front door this time, kill his way past turrets and heavily armed guards and the whole lot of them. He would wade through a sea of blood if that's what it took to get Silvie out of here, to reconnect with Iblis and snag the data he needed to find Dr. Marin.

Above all else he would *not* be recaptured and experimented on by Galloway and his people.

Around another corner and flitting past another guard in a spray of blood, he made for Silvie, freedom dripping from the tips of his fingers.

CHAPTER 22

nput Password. Two words Gash entirely failed to anticipate. The digital display on the lock to Silvie's cell buzzed harshly when he tried to skip the screen. Foolish. The amount of time it would take to backtrack to where he'd discarded the dead guard's security terminal would cost them dearly.

"Gash?" Silvie looked out through the little window in her door.

"We're making a break for it. As soon as I can figure out the password to unlock the door."

"How'd you get out?" she asked.

He tried "password," and the display blinked red. Incorrect password. "Let me figure this out and I'll fill you in later."

Julius leaned in close to Gash and whispered. "They're going to track the failed attempts to access this cell. A bunch of guards will be on their way here. We don't have time for this."

"I'm not leaving Silvie behind. Feel free to try to find your own way out if you want."

Julius shrugged and stepped back. Silvie stared at him with that iron stare of hers. The input buzzed and blinked red again. Incorrect password. He looked up at Silvie. "I'm not going to be able to brute force this. But if I had to guess, I would say that they cycle through random passwords on a daily or weekly basis. I should be able to find it at the main security station by the elevators."

"I'll ask again, how the hell did *you* get out?" Silvie asked.

"The door just opened," Gash said. "I don't know."

They looked at each other for a moment, the hope between them a flickering and fading candle. With each minute that passed, the odds increased that Galloway and his mages would arrive and recapture Gash.

When Gash looked back down at the digital display, the screen went black. A tiny white box flickered in the top corner. Did the security team lock it down? Text began to scroll across the pad, quickly dispelling the thought.

A helicopter is landing on the roof for you in five minutes. Hurry, there isn't much time.

Gash stared at it, his mind racing and tumbling over half a dozen different thoughts. Someone was jail-breaking him. Was this Iblis' doing? No, if he could remote hack WalCo this easily, they probably wouldn't have failed the first time around. Gash's gut told him that this vibe matched the time his mystery client unlocked the boat for him back in Rhodes, just after he'd turned into a vampire. It didn't seem like Galloway's style to lure him to the roof with a ruse like this. Meaning a viable means of escape would arrive shortly. He made the decision to trust it, since all other roads lead to recapture or death.

But none of that changed that he needed to get Silvie out. He reached for the pad, and the tiny keyboard display materialized again.

Not leaving w/o Silvie, he typed. And he waited.

Your recapture is imminent, you need to hurry.

If this, his same mystery client, could so easily spring Gash's own door open, then why not open Silvie's cell too?

Not without Silvie, open this cell, he typed.

She is the reason you were captured. She's undisciplined and split up the team at a crucial moment during your escape. I was wrong to suggest her. Leave her.

Gash snarled, punching the door. Who the hell was this and how did they already know how the op went down? Perhaps Iblis made contact and explained the situation.

"Gash?" Silvie almost whispered. "Is everything okay?"

"Yep," Gash said, whole body so taut he felt he might snap in half. *Fuck you, open this cell*, he typed.

Time crawled when the warrior spirit drove, when peril pumped his body full of adrenaline. So while a part of him knew that it took only a few seconds, precious minutes seemed to pass in the waiting. The fiber of Gash's being throbbed with barely repressed fury. The black screen displayed only his most recent words. "Fuck you, open this cell." No response from his secret savior.

And then the display returned to normal and flashed green. The cell door swung open, and Silvie leaped out, throwing her arms around Gash. "I knew you'd save me."

He could feel her arms, warm and strong and smooth around his neck. Her long black hair, silky against the stubble on his chin, tumbling away from him down her back. He could smell arterial blood pumping in her veins, kindling the hunger deep in his animal brain. A bottomless well of thirst. He returned the hug.

"We gotta go," he said softly. "A helicopter is going to be landing for us on the roof in a few minutes, and I have a feeling we need to clear a path."

"Okay," she said, stepping back.

"These are yours," Julius said, offering her the box.

She eyed the box and Julius, then looked at Gash.

"It's okay," Gash said. "This guy was my cellmate – he's all right."

"Name's Julius Weaver," Julius said.

"Silvie Wauneka."

"Let's save the introductions for when we're clear, okay guys?" Gash said.

They both nodded, and Julius held the box out to Silvie again.

She took it and looked inside. Just a few articles of clothing. "I don't think I'll bother," she said, tossing the box aside. She pointed behind her ear, at a small implant – apparently the same kind of implant that Rat Eater used to keep her from transforming. "I need you to pull this out for me, there's some kind of neural inhibition programmed in, and I can't do it."

Gash nodded, and just as before the device came away in a spurt of blood. She transformed into the wechuge, erupting into her wild, demonic alter-self. The WalCo prison clothes, shredded by her expanding muscles, sloughed off and to the floor. The wound in her neck healed immediately.

"Jesus," Julius said, stepping back.

"I know I know, the vampire and the wechuge, everybody's favorite children's book," Gash said.

Julius looked at him, and then back at her, and shook his head. "I've seen stories on the news feed about this kind of thing but it's another thing entirely to see you guys up close."

"And yet, there's no time for you to catch up. We gotta get moving. The goal is the roof, which means the elevators are the next stop. Try to keep up."

CHAPTER 23

Nagash Jensen licked human blood off his hands. The elevator hummed its way up towards the roof. He had never felt more like a monster than today, and he knew that even after he washed them, these weathered old hands would never again feel clean. It didn't matter, he needed to get Silvie clear of this whole mess, and then he had a job to finish. Ana Marin to bring home. Her deep blue eyes and the soft contours of her face flickered in his mind's eye, giving him strength.

The first of a burst of thundering explosions shook the building around floor 270. Anti-aircraft guns, he quickly realized.

"Are those –" Silvie started.

"Yes," Julius said. "Flak cannons on the roof – our ride is already here. Hope your people sent a good pilot."

Gash willed the elevator to go faster as the display ticked upwards. Vertigo struck him when he focused on the floor numbers. 287. 288. Almost 300 stories down to the concrete ground below, with nothing but a thin polymer floor between him and the abyssal void of the elevator shaft.

The display rolled through the last few floors quickly. 300, 301, 302, R. The elevator dinged, and the doors opened. At this height, the wind howled with frightening fury, clouds whipping past the rooftop space at subsonic speeds. For a moment, he felt those clouds might spontaneously condense and push the lot of them off the roof, and this thought brought back the vertigo. With great effort he pushed it out of his mind.

This particular bank of elevators opened onto the north side of the roof, and gave them a commanding view of the facilities. On each corner of the roof, anti-aircraft guns mounted on small security stations with ballistic windows spit fire. All four tracked and fired at an older-style military helicopter with twin rotors. Gash could tell immediately that the pilot was good. The aircraft swerved through the sky and dipped below the roof line, where the AA guns could not follow.

Gash counted roughly two dozen security personnel with small arms deployed across the roof, all watching the helicopter. Half of them took up positions on the two raised helipads in the center of the roof.

"That's a lot of guys with guns," Julius whispered.

"Leave it to us," Silvie said, the gravel of the wechuge voice a lance made of ice piercing Gash's spine.

"Take cover, grab a gun if you can and try to pick a few off," Gash said. Julius moved towards a nearby cooling unit to take cover.

He turned to Silvie. "You clear the helipads and I'll shut down those AA guns so our ride can land," Gash said. Without a word, Silvie charged up the stairs onto the nearer of the two helipads. The first guard she encountered went flying across the roof, tumbling and rolling right off the edge. Gash imagined his panicked scream, drowned out by the wind, as he fell endlessly to his death.

Time to move. Gash sprinted towards the northeast gun emplacement first. Two guards stood between him and his goal, but they hadn't noticed him yet. And they never would. He snapped both of their necks, snatching a gauss rifle from dead hands and kicking open the door to the security station. The three men stationed inside had just enough time to register his presence before being riddled with bullets, the little magnetic flechettes tearing through flesh and bone alike.

When the guards were dead, he turned the rifle on the computer interface, and emptied a full clip into the apparatus. When there was nothing left to destroy, he stepped back outside and looked up. The northeast gun drooped, no longer tracking the position of the helicopter below the roofline. Mission accomplished. It seemed odd that no networked Virtual Intelligence operated the guns, but then, maybe WalCo worried about the weapons being hacked. That would explain why they kept the controls on a localized interface. Lucky for his monster squad that WalCo considered remote hackers to be a greater threat than operatives physically infiltrating the rooftop.

As Gash moved towards the next security station, he watched Silvie work. The guards noticed her now. A full squad of WalCo elites turned their gauss rifles on her, but she grabbed the nearest of the bunch, hurling him like some human bowling ball at the full squad, scattering several and sending two more tumbling 300 stories to their death. It seemed Gash was not the only one harboring rage at being imprisoned. But then, Gash figured, after everything else Silvie had gone through – from her tribe's history with WalCo, to being imprisoned and incapacitated by some neural implant twice – Silvie had every right to be pissed. He would hate to be counted among those that wronged her.

Gash startled from his reverie when three guards stepped out of the southeastern security station, guns pointed at him. It was a relatively narrow corridor here, between the edge of the building and the helipad foundation on the other side. Nowhere to take cover. He raised his own weapon, but too late – he was going to take some hits. How many could he take? As he dove to the ground beneath the first volley of projectiles, he saw the helicopter rising just to his left. Iblis stood at the open door, smoke rising from his head, eyes red. He raised his hands into the air, and in a bright flash of white fired three lances of flame, dropping all three guards before they had a chance to fire a second volley at Gash. Iblis gave Gash a wave, and the helicopter descended again before the remaining three AA guns could lock in and fire.

Gash rose to his feet and barreled towards the next gun emplacement. He stepped over the smoldering bodies of the dead guards, scooping another rifle along the way, and found the station empty. He lit up this station as well, turning the controls to smoking ruins with his stolen weapon. From there, he passed through the other door and on the way to the southwestern emplacement. Nobody stepped out of the station this time, and he focused all his attention on his mission. Silvie would be fine without him to supervise her. This time the squad of four WalCo goons took cover inside the small station. Unfortunately for them, the quarters were too cramped and none of them possessed the reflexes to engage a vampire in a tiny space. He danced from guard to guard, slashing throats and snapping necks. A stray bullet caught him in the shoulder, but the wound healed by the time he grabbed the rifle from the lifeless hands of the fourth and final guard. His finger heavy on the trigger, Gash sprayed this third interface until the corresponding gun went silent.

One left. Gash stepped out, but the fourth gun already lay dormant. A few steps closer, and Gash saw Julius emerge from the security station, steam still rising from the coolant port of another stolen WalCo rifle. He limped towards the helipad, his left leg bleeding from a gunshot, and Gash realized that was it. They had taken the roof. The helicopter rose above the roofline again, this time coming quickly in to land on the northern helipad, near where Julius and Silvie already waited. Gash hustled to catch up.

He ascended the stairs, grabbing Iblis' outstretched hand at the top and hopping with ease up into the chopper. Silvie and Julius adjusted in their seats. Julius and the pilot were speaking animatedly as the pilot efficiently bandaged his leg using a first aid kit from beneath the seat.

The pilot looked relatively young, but deep scars on her face told a tale of combat experience. Probably a deserter from the Chinese military, a fairly common backstory for mercenaries of her age. She looked at Gash, gave him a nod, and then turned to finish her first aid. Julius waved Gash over, and when Gash sat, Julius handed him a headset. Gash put it on, and the deafening roar of wind and rotor subsided in the noise cancelling field. He could hear the others talking.

"Gash," Julius said, "I'd like you to meet our pilot and rescuer, Sheng Xiaoli. Xiaoli, this is Gash, my former cellmate."

"We'll have time for intros later," she said. "And for you to fill me in on why someone would pay a king's ransom for me to go on a suicide mission at *WalCo Corporate HQ* of all places."

Gash wondered about that, too. It must have been his client, but why go through all of this when surely there were other detectives who could pick up where he'd left off? Iblis presumably had Ana Marin's location, so why not just pay him for the job and hire some other mercs to go bring her home? Each day brought new questions by the bucket, and precious few answers.

Iblis' eyes flared white again, and Gash watched another blast of blame toss several more guards, fresh off the elevator, to the ground.

Xiaoli finished bandaging Julius' leg. "That should keep you alive long enough for us to land somewhere, at least." Out of the corner of his eye, Gash saw sparks dancing off the hull on the other side of the helicopter. A number of WalCo personnel stood on the other helipad, firing rifles.

"Should we be worried about those guys?" Gash asked as the deluge of high velocity flechettes ricocheted off the helicopter's armor with increasing volume and frequency.

"Nothing to worry about," Xiaoli said. We're in a Mark III Thunderclap, one of the most heavily armored choppers ever designed, and one of the last built by the US Air Force. They can hit us with those little pea shooters all day if they want to, won't even scratch us."

"That may be so, but if WalCo has a backup operational system that lets a runner operate those flak guns remotely, it could be online any moment and we'd be toast."

"It's a through-and-through," Julius said. "You stopped the bleeding. Thanks... and it's good to see you again. But I gotta say I agree with the vampire – please get us out of here. We can do a more thorough job bandaging this when we get to safety."

Xiaoli paused at the word vampire, eyed Gash warily, but then looked at Silvie (still in wechuge form) and Iblis, and shrugged, stepping back into the cockpit and taking the controls. They rose into the air. Iblis swung the door closed and sat down across from Gash as they took off. Gash watched the WalCo HQ building disappear beneath them as the chopper accelerated up and into the racing clouds. They did it. They really did it. Not all at once, but they transformed failure into a successful prison break. Suicide-mission accomplished with the whole team intact and the data in hand. Some kind of miracle.

CHAPTER 24

For the second time in as many weeks, Gash found himself in the foyer of Rat Eater's hideout. No Rat Eater this time, of course. No more suits, no cybered-to-the-gills mercs. The faux-wood-paneling, the faux-leather furniture, the spotlessly cleaned floors all remained. Gash's mystery client had been busy while Gash rotted in WalCo prison – hiring Iblis and Xiali for rescue duty, buying out the old Rat's den, and having the place cleaned (blood and bodies... not cheap but not uncommon).

Gash walked the first and second floors first thing. Most people living in the DRZ had no official ownership rights. Squatters' rights ruled the zone, and the Rat was no exception. The mystery client, however, went through the trouble of paying the fees in the Universal Corporate Property Database to officially claim ownership. This sort of thing never typically never stopped an empty building from being filled, but as he combed the place and found it empty, Gash could only suppose it might when combined with horror stories of gunfights, monsters, and a bloody mess straight out of a horror flick.

When they reconvened on the second floor, Gash glanced at Silvie. Since setting foot in the Rat's den, an intense grimace stretched her skin taut against her high cheekbones, and her eyes glistened with the faintest hint of wetness. Coming here, of all places, after capture and whatever foul treatment she'd received from Galloway... Gash appreciated the client taking the time to save them and provide them a place to lay low, but it showed a real lack of people skills. Stacking trauma on trauma like this couldn't end well.

On the second floor the squad noted that, aside from the cleaning and window repair, the mystery client also installed long thick curtains on each of the tall windows. The third floor featured living quarters for half a dozen bodyguards, and a master bedroom of sorts for the Rat himself, all furnished well above the average quality of life for the DRZ.

Aside from establishing a watch order to ensure that they would not be taken completely by surprise, none of them spoke much that first night. The rest of the gang retired to sleep while Gash (naturally) took the night time watch. At dawn, when Iblis rose with the sun to take over, Gash shuttered the windows in Rat Eater's room and fell into a fitful sleep on the over-sized bed.

Sometime in the late morning, Gash woke to a furious roar. The hairs on the back of his neck rose, a familiar reaction to the icy fear baked into Silvie's wechuge howl. He rushed from his room, dodging the gray morning light from the windows in the hall, and took the stairs three at a time down to the second story.

Silvie – in wechuge form – seemed at first to be locked in epic combat. But after a few seconds, Gash realized she had no enemy but the furniture. Specifically, the faux-wood stage upon which she'd only a few days ago been displayed as property for Rat Eater's corporate buyers. Her monstrous hands bled as she ripped up shards of the wood-like polymer, rending it and scattering it around the room. Iblis, Julius, and Xiaoli stood at the edge of the room, at the top of the first floor stairs. Gash watched from halfway down the third floor stairs, unable to enter the room on account of all the morning light.

After observing the carnage for a few minutes, he stepped back up to the third story and returned to his room. He no longer felt the urge for sleep, but Silvie's rage below felt like a private thing, not something to stand and watch. He knew what was wrong, and he knew he couldn't help her. Not in any meaningful way. At least he could give her space to work out her anger.

The violence continued for close to an hour. When exhausted panting and the low patter of whispered conversation replaced smashing and tearing, Gash grabbed his long coat and returned to the second floor. This time, when he stood in the shadowed staircase, Silvie noticed him, rising from the fetal position on the floor and drawing the curtains across the windows to block the sunlight, the gesture made awkward and slow by her need to cover herself as she worked. In the darkness, the lights recessed in the ceiling automatically powered on.

Gash approached Silvie, offering her the coat. Silvie silently accepted, wrapping herself in the coat. That done, they stood there, a few feet apart, unmoving. Silvie stared through the floor while Gash looked up, down, anywhere else but at Silvie, her blood pumping extra fast in her arteries from the exertion.

Eventually, Gash moved to hold Silvie. She seemed to need some kind of comfort, and he could think of nothing else. She shuddered in his arms, and Gash's mind went unbidden to Serena, when she first confessed to Gash that she had an addiction. That the cocktail of sparklers and mood alterers he knew she enjoyed had expanded to include heavier street drugs, and that she was spiraling, unable to function as a normal adult. She needed help. But Serena was his lover, and holding her for hours, stroking her hair, those things felt natural to him then. Now, he couldn't help but to be hyper-aware of Silvie's presence in his arms. Of Iblis and Julius and Xiaoli pretending not to watch from the other side of the room, conversing in low tones.

"We won't stay here long," Gash said at last, and Silvie looked up at him.

The words seemed to return her to reality. She stepped back from him and wiped her eyes. Where for a brief moment Gash saw a spark of vulnerability, steel now returned. She even forced a sad little smile. "I'm going to need to stop destroying clothes," she said.

"Try not to destroy my coat, okay?" Gash said.

"This? It's a part of your whole ethos. I wouldn't dream of it," Silvie said, wiping her nose with the back of her hand.

"Hey," Xiaoli said softly to Silvie. "I've got a few more things that might fit you – want to come with me and pick something out?"

Silvie nodded, and the women headed up to the third floor.

Stepping gingerly around the fragments of faux-wood scattered about the floor, Iblis approached Gash. "We should plan our next steps," he said.

"Aside from giving me Dr. Marin's location, I believe you've been paid and the job's done, yes?" Gash asked

Iblis said nothing.

"Don't get me wrong, you've been incredibly helpful. But aren't you chomping at the bit to get some distance between us? Between yourself and WalCo?"

Iblis laughed. "I spent the first thirty years of my life in a warzone. WalCo does not scare me. Plus, you obviously work for a *very* rich client. A golden goose, if you will."

"I can't disagree with that. Though I don't think I understood the scope until he paid you, hired Xiaoli, got the helicopter, and even bought this place for us to lay low." Gash looked around at the opulence of the new-and-improved Rat's den – corporate money had turned the place into a true diamond in the rough.

"And you?" Gash looked at Julius. "What's your plan now that you're out?"

"Xiaoli's still on retainer with your client, and I need to catch up with her about some mutual acquaintances from back in the day. Plus I owe WalCo the mother of all black eyes, so for now I'll stick around and help out too if you'll have me." He paused. "Plus I understand you're on a missing persons job. That used to be my specialty."

"I didn't think I'd be finishing this job with a team," Gash said. "But you're welcome to stick around – you've all proven yourselves."

Iblis opened his mouth to speak, but just then his PCom dinged, three loud chimes. He cursed softly under his breath.

"Trouble?" Gash asked.

"Yes, trouble. Follow me."

Gash and Julius followed Iblis down to the first floor. Iblis took a seat on one of the large L-shaped sofas positioned around a particularly large holoprojector. Gash and Julius joined him. Iblis waved a data-set from his PCom over to the projector, and Gash found himself gawking at a display featuring over a dozen surveillance feeds from around the De-Regulated Zone.

"These are all yours?" Gash asked.

"Israeli spy drones," Iblis said. "Flight capable, easy to mount to buildings and overpasses for temporary surveillance coverage."

"You're buying tech from your old enemy?" Gash asked.

"Buying?" Iblis looked up at Gash, his white teeth shining from deep within his black beard.

"Ah," Gash said. "Of course. So what are we looking at?"

Iblis double tapped the air and one of the images magnified, minimizing the others. With another wave of his hand through the display, Iblis activated audio for the now-magnified image.

A WalCo agent in heavy armor interrogated four unhoused men and women gathered around an open flame in one of the DRZ's many alleys. The audio came through muffled, on account of the drone's distance from the conversation, but all three of them heard the word "vampire" and saw the pictures of Gash, Iblis, and Silvie being passed around.

"They know we're here, at least in the DRZ." Gash said.

"That was fast," Iblis nodded.

"Not necessarily," Julius said. "After corporate law enforcement jurisdictions took over most of the major US cities, my people – the FBI and city cops – still owned the arcologies for a time. I was stationed in Arc 1. Before gene-hounds made it obsolete, my people trained a tactic we called "Flood and displace." When you're pursuing perpetrators hiding in... certain kinds of urban areas, you flood those areas with personnel. Homeless folk like this aren't going to know about us, let alone want to snitch on us to corporate goons. *But* if a perp sees a bunch of agents at the market down the street, he spooks.

And once he's on the move, CCTV algorithms pick him up, and you run him down. I'm surprised WalCo isn't using gene-hounds instead, but I guess human labor is cheaper than breeding gene-hounds and training their handlers."

He looked from Gash to Iblis and back. "Trust me, best thing we can do is sit tight. They probably have fifty teams like this in every slum and potential hiding spot in Seattle."

"Yeah, but how many of those locations are less than five miles away from an abandoned rescue helicopter?" Iblis asked.

"Okay," Gash said. "Let's sit tight and monitor these feeds until WalCo gives up and pulls their people. If they get too close we can fight our way out and rabbit to another city. It's important for us not to panic. I'm *not* going back to WalCo HQ to become that psycho Galloway's personal vampire guinea pig."

"We've got half a dozen holo-projectors down here," Iblis stood, gesturing at the separate waiting spaces in the huge foyer. "I can segment the broadcast data so we can each watch a few feeds. We will be ready if they get close enough to catch us."

"Great," Gash said, rising. "Set it up, I'll go check on Silvie and Xiaoli."

CHAPTER 25

The WalCo agent swaggered down the street. Wearing heavy carapace armor capable of absorbing the kinetic energy of a sledgehammer to the chest, and carrying a gauss assault rifle capable of unloading a clip full of 73 magnetized flechettes in under three seconds, he must have felt invincible striding through the squalor of the Seattle De-Regulated Zone. He stopped at a small kiosk (really just a folding table with a strip of canvas mounted on four scrap metal posts of different sizes) and leaned in to have a look.

The vendor, an older man with graying hair and one arm, shrank back as the agent leaned in. A ring of deep scars around the stump told a tale – once upon a time this man replaced his left arm with a cybernetic augment, an older model that bolted into the flesh and anchored to the bone. What became of this arm? Perhaps he was himself a corporate agent once, stripped of his augmentations at after a forced retirement, when he could no longer pay the lease fees out of his monthly paycheck? Or like many veterans, perhaps the man served in the military and came home to hard times, selling his augments to make ends meet until he ran out of spare parts and then out of money.

"What are you selling?" The agent's voice somehow made the question into a sneer, a slur.

The old vendor looked confused; his wares were displayed on the sad little table for the agent to see with his own eyes. Of course he answered the question anyway – you don't mess with someone like this unless you wanted to get hurt, and he'd already lived a lifetime of hurting. "Still-life nature paintings," he said.

The paintings were decent, though they lacked vibrance on account of the painter's limited access to colors. Instead of canvas, the artist painted on scraps: pieces of dirty faux-paper from nearby dumpsters, backsides of discarded coasters, urban driftwood (fragments of polycarbonate siding long ago torn from ancient buildings) – these were paintings made on trash. But for all that, they weren't bad. A forest, a lake, a mountain. Perhaps places the old man travelled in his youth. Perhaps figments of his imagination. Pristine landscapes predating human destruction, small windows into the past. In the right boutique setting with the right hipster corporate middle managers, these would sell like hot-cakes as upcycled art. But this painter in this place barely scraped by.

Between the agent and the vendor, neither of them saw the third man, though he struck an imposing figure. Taller than the other two by a head or more, the man lurked in the shadows of a nearby alley, shirtless in the cold, watching the exchange in silence.

"What do you sell these for?"

"Five credits each, sir."

"Five credits each, ten 'paintings' total. 50 credits if you sold the whole sad lot. I'm authorized to give you double that if you help me out, what do you say?"

The vendor looked down the street, north first and then south. Surely it felt like a trick, this heavily armed agent offering him money. What did he expect to see on the street? A sign saying "it's a trap?" But of course he saw nothing, and of course he couldn't turn such an offer down, at least not outright. "What kind of help do you need?"

The agent showed the man four pictures. "Have you seen any of these people around here? If you can tell me where they're hiding out, you get your hundred credits."

The vendor's shoulders slumped. Even if he had seen them, the unwritten rule of the DRZ meant never ratting someone out to a corporation. He might've ratted the four out to a local gangbanger for a single credit. But not to this corporate henchman, not for all the credits in the world. He shook his head.

"How about a large monster with shaggy brown fur and a deer's skull for a head? Or a vampire?"

The question might have sounded off the wall to some. But not to the vendor. In recent weeks, all manner of inhuman types sought refuge or anonymity in the DRZ. But he didn't know about the people – or monsters – that this agent was asking about. He shook his head again.

The agent stood there for a moment, and then he lashed out with his boot, kicking the table, knocking half the paintings to the street. He pointed his rifle at the vendor. "I tried the carrot, so now I'll try the stick. Tell me where to find them. Now."

The vendor stepped back, cowering against the wall of the building behind his little kiosk, arms outstretched as though to stop any bullets with his shriveled hands before they struck his face.

Now the man in the alley stepped out into the open. Long dreadlocks stretched down to his waist, and his muscles rippled as he moved. The vendor noticed him, but with his back to the alley, the WalCo agent did not. The lurker's hands glowed a gentle blue as he approached the kiosk. No ordinary transient living in an alley, the news and corporate label-people called folks like this adepts – humans whose magical aptitude lent itself to enhancing physical prowess. He wouldn't be throwing a fireball anytime soon, but he could almost certainly win an arm-wrestling match with a werewolf.

The agent stomped on a painting of a snow-capped mountain, grinding it into dust and fiber with his polymer-alloy combat boots. "Please, I don't know these people," the vendor said.

With two long strides, the adept crossed the street from his alley. He tapped the agent on the back and spoke. "Corporate agents aren't welcome here," he said, his voice an earthquake, his shaking rage a blizzard of flame.

The agent spun to face this newcomer, but far too late. The adept grabbed the gun out of the agent's hands like a normal person might pluck a flower from the ground, and tossed it aside. The agent swung his fist, a wide-arcing right hook, and the adept simply let it land. Thud. The agent might have been punching a carbon-nanotube traffic barrier.

"My turn," the adept said. But he didn't throw a punch. He reached out a long arm, muscles rippling and glowing with a bright blue light now, and simply tore the agent's head off, the helmet crumpling beneath his fingers as he pulled it away. A geyser of blood sprayed up and out of the wreckage of the agent's neck, dousing the paints, the vendor, and the adept with crimson. The agent's body took a moment to catch up to this sudden turn of events, only toppling over when the adept pulled it away from the vendor's blood-drenched kiosk.

Four WalCo agents, heavily armed and armored, made the rounds in a large transient camp built up over time with scrap metal and polymer, all lean-tos and thrown-away tents assembled haphazardly in an empty lot. Most of the residents ignored corporate agents unless approached directly. One, however, middle-aged with a long blonde beard and sleeves of tattoos up and down both arms, climbed out of his lean-to and approached one of the agents; a sergeant according to the crest on the right shoulder of her armor.

"There's nothing for you and your men here," he said.

She eyed him for a minute. "You're ex-military," she said. "I recognize some of your ink."

"Back when we had a *real* military," he said.

"Except that your military is gone, and mine is still here," she said.

He looked down at his feet at this.

"That's what I thought. But listen, I'm not here to bust you guys up. I just need some help finding some folks." She waved through several images on the holo-projector in the wrist of her armor. "Have you seen any of these individuals or do you have any idea where fugitives might hide around here? There's credits in it for you," she said.

Where fugitives might hide around here, he mumbled the words to himself, seeming to force down a smile. The irony seemed lost on the sergeant, who merely cocked her head, waiting for the man to respond. He studied the pictures meticulously, staring at each for almost a full minute. The WalCo sergeant grew antsy, but eventually the veteran pointed at one picture of a man with demon horns. "This one, I recognize him. I think I saw him earlier today."

Her mouth opened, but no words came at first. "Really?" she eventually asked.

"Yeah," he nodded, more sure now. "He's actually kind of hard to miss with those demon horns, don't you think?"

"That's great," she said. "Fifty credits if you can tell me where you saw him. A hundred if you can point me to where he's hiding."

"Easy money. He's hiding up your ass. I wouldn't think you'd need me to tell you that, what with the horns and all."

The man stared defiantly, waiting for the inevitable violent response. She didn't disappoint, drawing her sidearm and pistol-whipping him in the side of the head. He dropped hard to the ground, groaning. He did not get up.

"Everyone's a smartass, but I'd think an old veteran like you would know better," the sergeant said. She punctuated every other word with a kick to his ribs, legs, and back. The rest of the camp seemed to rise to their feet as one unit, and the three other agents formed a protective circle around the sergeant, pointing rifles at the beleaguered veteran's would-be defenders.

There were almost fifty men and women in the camp, but the sergeant didn't seem concerned by the odds. She pointed her sidearm at the bleeding man at her feet, and looked around at his fellows. "Normally I kill drifter scum with his kind of audacity, but I'm feeling generous today. If one of you tells me where I can find these men or this woman – here she held her off-hand high in the air so the whole camp could see the photos – I'll let him live."

The rest of her squad felt some kind of buzz that she obviously didn't, because they all stepped back, tightening the protective circle, trying to point three guns at fifty people all at once. Their fear was palpable, but not the sergeant. When nobody spoke up, she fired her weapon once. An explosion of concrete particles from the ground just beside the half-dead vet followed the soft "whoosh" of her gauss pistol. A warning shot.

"Next one blows his brains out the back of his head," she said, "and I'm leaving you all to clean it up."

When the next gunshot rang out, though, it wasn't the soft hush of a gauss weapon. It was a deafening bang. Gunpowder, older model weapon. From within the seething ring of fifty angry men and women, it was impossible to tell where exactly the shot came from, but it threw the sergeant off her feet. She landed on her back with a crunch as her head whipped into the hard concrete ground. The armor absorbed the impact of the bullet, but the fall left her still on the ground. The other three agents opened fire into the crowd, and a few of the transients fell.

But only a few. A great cacophony of detonations rang out – at least a dozen gunpowder weapons firing in unison. The WalCo agents were surrounded and had no cover, and so a few seconds of sustained fire from the crowd around them saw all four of the security team lying in a pool of blood, dead. The WalCo squad, accustomed to ignoring homeless rather than intimidating them, learned far too late that though the unhoused could seldom afford food, meaningful shelter, or even clothing; two things came cheap in this world: guns and lives.

A WalCo detective, complete with suit, tie, and sunglasses, pulled up at a particular noodle stand to interrogate the teenage girl working the register. A guy like this, even though he wasn't wearing the company uniform, she knew. Could smell the corporate money on him from 100 yards away.

Of all the pictures he showed her, she recognized one of them – a private investigator with a wide-brimmed hat and a trench coat. He'd been by around a week ago, bought noodles and left them behind after one bite. Seemed to know her dad. She knew none of that information would help the detective track his prey, but the moment you let on that you knew something, a guy like this became a dog with a bone. A rottweiler. She didn't want to end up in some WalCo holding facility for the next three months while they worked out whether or not she knew more than she was letting on, so she shook her head to all five pictures.

Problem was, a corporate detective like this rocked all the best gadgets. And some of them even cultivated instincts to go along with all that expensive tech. Cyber-eyes reading pupil dilation and tracking moisture build-up on visible skin, nasal implants picking up on an increased output of apocrine gland emissions based on the increase in body odor, and a comprehensive data storage library of non-verbal tics linked to the optics – it all turned the detective into a human lie detector. And this teenage girl who just sold noodles, she was a pretty good liar, but not that good. He grabbed her wrist and leaned in to whisper some threats.

The detective was used to having free rein in these sorts of situations – after all, who's going out of their way to interfere with a law-enforcement agent of a powerful corporation?

But this was the de-regulated zone. Cheap surveillance disappeared within hours of being installed, stripped for parts or destroyed. Even advanced spyware, the kind designed to avoid detection, wouldn't last more than a couple weeks. You could draw a line down the middle of the DRZ population and on one side, folks hated corporations. On the other, folks were actively hiding out from corporate warrants.

Three customers happened to be sitting at noodle stand in that moment, and as it happened all three were in the latter category. A team of mercs laying low after taking out an Appsoft convoy carrying millions of credits worth of electronics, they did not appreciate the notion that a corporate investigator would enter this area so wantonly, nor did they appreciate him laying hands on a kid. Though his optics registered the movement in his peripheral vision instantaneously, the biological software – his human brain – featured no such upgrades to processing speed, and so the detective failed entirely to even register the threat, let alone to react in time. Two of the mercs had him by the arms, and the third stepped behind him and snapped his neck before he could struggle.

The girl comped their meal, and when they finished eating, they dragged the corpse to the edge of the DRZ, depositing it on a foot bridge to some low rent corporate housing on the outskirts of the wealthier districts. The mercs deposited the dead detective on the sidewalk, piling him on half a dozen other dead WalCo agents. And then they withdrew into the anonymity of the DRZ, to a flophouse or brothel or whatever off-the-grid place they were wiling away the time while the heat from the last gig faded.

CHAPTER 26

Gash watched Iblis's various recon drone feeds in awe as the DRZ devoured the almost two-dozen WalCo agents that flooded the area. It took less than seven hours for the zone to kill them all, pick them clean of gear, and drag them to the outskirts. It wasn't often that you watched a major corporate miscalculation unfolding live, but feeding twenty-three highly trained and well-armed agents to the gristmill of the de-regulated zone surely ranked highly among those errors.

He leaned back into the soft synth-leather of the sofa, settling in and feeling a rare moment of peace. "Well," he said. "That was amazing. Someone is going to get laid off for that bloodbath."

"I wouldn't be so sure," Julius said, standing from his spot on a neighboring sofa and leaning in to rewatch one of the clips. "I'm pretty sure the girl at this noodle stand recognized you. That detective got whacked pretty fast afterwards, but odds are he was streaming everything directly to HQ in real time."

"So they know we're in the DRZ. Or at least that I am," Gash said.

Julius swiped down in the holographic image, closing it entirely. "It may not happen right away. Because of that bloodbath, there will first be meetings galore and a cost analysis, but eventually I think

WalCo will send a small army of personnel and drones in to dig us up."

"How do you know so much about corporate investigative procedure?" Silvie, stretched out on one of the other sofas, seemed more at ease after settling down from her earlier outburst.

"He was one of the last FBI agents. Just like me, he had to learn the habits of his major competition. About right?" Gash asked.

"About right. When corporations can swoop in and steal your cases on a whim, you learn everything you can about their ins and outs if you want to try and do your job."

"So we should probably get out of here then," Gash said.

"And go where?" Silvie sat up.

Gash looked over at Iblis, busily tapping away at his PCom, repositioning his recon drones from the looks of it. "Any chance they'll be able to track the data we stole on Dr. Marin?"

"Only if you or Silvie talked. I was exceedingly careful not to leave a trail," Iblis said without looking up.

"I didn't talk," Silvie said, squaring her shoulders to Iblis and tensing as if to rise.

"Relax, we know. Or at least I do." Gash said.

For the first in many hours, silence descended on Gash's squad. Eventually, he rose. He'd always been a solo act before Starfire and the fiasco at Rhodes, the big hole with magic in it. He liked it that way. The only people with expectation were clients, and they only cared that you got the job done. But this job – it was too big for a solo act, even with all of his vampiric powers. So without meaning to, he'd amassed a team: Silvie the wechuge; Iblis the ifrit hacker; and now this hot-shot pilot and Gash's former cellmate, who seemed to know each other from some past gig. They were all looking to him.

"Listen up," Gash said. "I have a job to finish, one I started over a year ago. WalCo abducted a scientist named Dr. Ana Marin, and for whatever reason this mystery client with bottomless pockets chose me to find and save her. If she's even still alive, I mean to make good. I know it's a little crazy to go after her right now, when we just escaped from WalCo's on-site holding facilities, but that's still the plan. Jobs like this come with a timer and I can't let this one run out."

"A *little* crazy?" Julius said.

"Okay, a lot crazy," Gash shrugged. "They know we're here in the DRZ, but there's a chance they don't yet know we're after Dr. Marin. I ran from this job once and life took me in a big circle back to where I started. This time, I'm finishing it."

Gash paced as he spoke. Iblis continued to tinker on his PCom. Silvie sat on the edge of her seat. Xiaoli seemed oblivious to the whole conversation, watching a stream of three or four news sites projected on the other side of the room. Julius sat back down on his sofa, massaging the bridge of his nose. Gash looked at each of them in turn, letting the silence return for a moment.

"What I'm saying is each of you has a choice – by now it's clear that this gig comes with a big payday. A couple of you have a bone to pick with WalCo. But this obviously comes with noodle-boiler levels of heat. You all have lives to get back to and if you're smart, you'll walk away right now. I'll make sure you're paid what you're due and we'll part ways as friends."

Gash sat back down at his sofa, and waved the holoprojector back on. "Iblis, hit me with all the data you got on Dr. Marin's whereabouts, then you can stay or leave as you prefer. Everyone, if you're in, come have a seat and help me figure out where she is and how we're going to set her free."

Silvie wasted no time rising from her own seat and striding over to take a seat beside Gash. Iblis, likewise, didn't hesitate to join them both, transmitting the stolen data to Gash's PCom along the way. Xiaoli sat in silence, though she turned her eyes away from the feed and watched the group. Watched Julius.

Julius hesitated. For what seemed like minutes, he sat there, eyes closed. "I have people, you know. I had a life before WalCo imprisoned me. They seized everything I owned, every credit from my accounts, held me without a trial for years." His voice caught in his throat. Gash looked away, to give the man a moment to compose himself. "Here's the thing," Julius continued. "I want to go home, I want to find my people. There was a girl…" he trailed off.

"It's okay," Gash started.

"No, what I mean is you're right. I have a bone to pick with WalCo. So I'm in if you're paying. I need money to put my life back together, and WalCo deserves everything coming to them."

When Julius rose to join the group, Xiaoli rose too. "Good enough for me," she said. And so Gash found himself seated in the center of a semi-circle, four sets of bright eyes on him, waiting for the plan. Waiting for him of all people, Nagash Jensen, to lead them. Fine.

"Let's begin."

CHAPTER 27

"Hiding in plain sight." Gash leaned forward in the plush sofa, scrolling the data. Who knew?

"Temperate and easily accessible – lucky break," Julius said.

"Sounds kind of boring," Xiaoli laughed. "The secret WalCo facility Julius and I hit back in the day was deep in the Arctic."

"I don't get it, how can a secret research facility be in a major metropolitan area like Kansas City?" Silvie asked.

"Midwestern areas were the first to give in fully to corporations. Folks in those areas are a lot less likely to question the comings and goings of corporate agents," Gash said.

"The FBI saw this a lot back when we still had some jurisdictional authority," Julius chimed in. "Forced-work abductions would often end up in the Midwest. Plus, if this is a bio-tech facility, they want it close enough to major population centers that they can snag free test subjects off the street without making a big impression on data analysts working for other corporate enforcement agencies."

Gash sifted the data, pulling out the location of the facility. The data package Iblis liberated from WalCo's servers contained everything. The holodisplay showed what used to be a restaurant in a neighborhood called "Waldo." The restaurant, like most of the businesses in that area, closed down long ago. The city grew predominantly into the north back then, and this neighborhood on the south end was forfeited in stages to squatters. Perfect location for kidnapping test subjects nobody would miss.

Beneath the restaurant, a single elevator shaft led down to a facility about fifty feet below the sewers and other underground urban infrastructure. Four stories and eight thousand square feet of research space dedicated exclusively to bio-tech research. According to a cursory glance at the specs, the facility dealt predominantly in lethal pathogens, but dabbled in bio-modification and eugenics as well.

"One way in and a laundry list of lethal bugs maintained in the lower floors. This place will be a tough nut to crack," Gash said.

"No, we need to leave this nut uncracked," Julius said.

"Listen, if you're not up for it –" Gash started.

"No I mean you never hit the work facility when you're trying to liberate a forced-work abduction. They'll have tight security and they'll see you coming. Long before you ever got to Dr. Marin, she'd be dumped into that organic materials incinerator on floor 4B, never to be seen again."

"So where do we hit?" Gash asked.

"Living quarters," Julius mumbled, sifting through the data himself. After a few minutes of watching Julius wave data off the display and pull more in, eventually the team found themselves looking at an old apartment building in the same neighborhood a couple blocks away from the secret facility.

Gash could read it for himself – WalCo repurposed this building, ostensibly abandoned to squatters like the rest of the Waldo district, to house the researchers who worked in the nearby facility. Much of it seemed built for voluntary employees, but at some point WalCo personnel had reinforced the top floor (the fifth) with security measures to keep "involuntary employees" from fleeing. There would be guards on the first floor, more guards on the fifth, and any number of locked doors, not to mention a security station with biometric coding in the elevator to unlock the fifth floor. However, unlike the research facility and its single, heavily fortified entrance, this residential building featured emergency exits, windows, a garage entry, and two street entrances. Should be pretty simple for the team that broke out of WalCo HQ.

"This is great," he said. "We can work out the details on the way to Kansas City. But that's the next question – how do we get there?"

"I have a contact," Xiaoli said.

They all looked at her, waiting. "She owns a private shuttle service, operates out of a couple dozen different cities, including Seattle. Very discreet. As long as we pay anonymously, they'll spoof our identifies for ground security at KC, and won't register any of our data to any corporate flight logs."

Gash stood and stretched. "Handy. Wish I knew you when I was trying to flee the country last year. How long to get in the air?"

Xiaoli scrolled purposefully through her PCom contacts. "She's very accommodating as long as the payment matches the ask," she said.

"Perfect," Gash clapped, closing the data stream in the process. "Everyone go ahead and pack up whatever you've got. I want to be in the air by midnight, so there's time to find a place to crash and prep for the op before the sun rises on Kansas City tomorrow. We'll carve out an hour to shop for gear at a couple spots here in the DRZ before we take off. Xiaoli, please get us squared away with your contact. Whatever it costs to get us going on our timeline and keep us anonymous."

As they all scattered to pack their things, Gash remained behind, falling deep into the softness of the sofa. He stared at the 3-D schematic of the converted apartment, but more specifically at the fifth story. One of the six rooms, number 503. The room belonged to Dr. Ana Marin. He couldn't help but see her blue eyes in his mind's eye, imagine her laying down after a long day on the tiny virtual bed in the room marked "bedroom" on the blueprint. Looking out the window at the desolation of an abandoned urban district and despairing of ever leaving, of ever being free again.

But he would be there soon, and he would finally set her free. And then... well, there would be time for "and then" later.

CHAPTER 28

The team split up into two separate groups, hailing standard AutoCabs from different spots in the DRZ. Gash rode with Silvie and Xiaoli, the whole way there trying not to laugh at the blonde wig and big chunky sunglasses Silvie wore to prevent Autocab's security cameras from pinging the corporate warrant in her name. He knew his horn-rimmed glasses and bucket hat looked no better, but they were necessary. A reflective coating on the lenses wouldn't show to a human eye, but a digital one would misread his eye color, which should fool Autocab's systems. Xiaoli, who never set foot in WalCo HQ, was spared the indignity of her own slapdash disguise.

The two teams arrived at the Seattle shuttleport within minutes of each other. Gash actually snorted when Iblis and Julius stepped out of their own autocabs dressed in matching classic caps and chrome sunglasses.

Fortunately, the "small business" wing of the shuttleport lacked large security checkpoints. Each provider here took responsibility for their own security checks, so Gash's whole team made it to their gate without any difficulty, and without being identified by corporate security forces – a major accomplishment given that, of all the major corporations with air travel business units, most any would go out of their way to curry favor with WalCo.

Fortunately Xiaoli's contact proved to be as discrete as advertised. The team boarded a small private shuttle with no security check at all – no warrant check, and as importantly, no weapons screening. Fortunate, given that alongside their disguises, they'd purchased enough hardware to outfit a small militia.

Total privacy and complete luxury. A stewardess in a very expensive black dress passed around glasses of pre-takeoff champagne as the team settled into what might have been real leather recliners and unpacked their things.

When the shuttle rose from the tarmac, Gash watched the city grow small beneath them. Even the cloudscrapers eventually shrank into children's building blocks far beneath them. The lights of the city at night, first visible as car headlights and office lights and endless neon advertisements holo-projected in the air above major corporate thoroughfares, soon blobbed together – a billion fireflies swarming brightly in the darkness.

The team spent so much time planning and chattering while hiding out at Rat Eater's old place, that they seemed to have run out of things to say to each other. Iblis reclined in his chair, pecking at his PCom wrist-mount. Silvie closed her eyes and within minutes her breathing elongated and deepened with sleep. Gash always envied those that could sleep so easily. Even before transforming into a vampire, he had struggled to find sleep when he most needed it. Now, with super-hearing and the ability to smell human blood from hundreds of yards away, he only slept when exhaustion truly took him. Xiaoli vanished into the shuttle cockpit as soon as they took off – perhaps she knew the pilot as well as the owner, or perhaps the two were one and the same. Julius, like Gash, simply looked out the window as they flew.

Lights dimmed in the cabin when they reached cruising altitude. Through the sound-proofed hull, the distant roar of the shuttle's dual engines came out a low purr. The soothing hum mixed with the sounds of tapping and sleep breathing, a moment of total peace interjecting itself into the whirlwind of violence that had gripped Gash since the moment he docked in Seattle a handful of days ago. He closed his eyes and savored the moment, allowing his muscles to unclench one by one.

As was so often the case, memories found him during the quiet moments. He couldn't help comparing his current flight to the ride back home from Riyadh with Corporal Sinder and the rest of his squad back in his soldering days. The "cabin" of the old military transport consisted of a long tin tube lined on both sides with bucket seats. Gear strapped to the walls and floors clanked and rattled whenever the plane would bank. Marine Corporation squads were deployed and redeployed so often in those days that to the squad it often felt like home more than a barracks or base.

Sin was saying something to him. "What's that, corporal?" he asked.

"Sarge," he said, "I think you heard me. I asked you to break out the whiskey rations. After what we survived yesterday I think we earned it."

Whiskey rations were provided on most such military transports, under lock and key, accessible only to the squad commander. Booze replenishment would come out of the squad's equipment budget, so Gash generally avoided it, though he saw value in the rare celebration.

"Only if you ask me like a pirate," Gash said with exaggerated sternness.

Sin reflexively touched the eye-patch the Marine Co medic had slapped on back at the FOB. Insurance would cover a decent cybernetic replacement since Sin could still fight and had years left on his contract. But processing the paperwork would take nearly a year. Meaning Sin was in for a year of pirate jokes and jabs.

When Sin said nothing for a moment, Gash worried that perhaps it was too soon to make this joke. But then the corporal hunched over, broke into full character, and said "Captain, please, for the love of the seven seas, uncork the rum." Seeing the fair-skinned redhead scrunch his forehead and turn down his lips, hearing the thick Irish lilt mixed in with the stereotypical west country English pirate accent, it was too much. Gash couldn't hold his laughter in. Sin and the half the squad that was listening in all joined him.

When the laughter abated, Gash unbelted himself and stood shakily, hoping the plane wouldn't bank hard while he was on his feet. "In honor," he said, pausing for dramatic effect, "of the stalwart Corporal William Sinder, who gave his right eye in order to save my whole ass..." he paused for applause. "Whiskey rations for the whole squad."

The whole plane erupted into cheers, all but for one private sitting in the corner closest to the nose. Private Lita Yenson. "Private," Gash remembered saying. "Everything okay over there?"

Yenson, a young blonde woman newly reassigned from a mortar team for reasons unknown, looked up. "I just got a call from my mom," she said. "Apparently the Church of the J newsletter published an article mourning the loss of our squad, which was completely wiped out by insurgents outside of Riyadh."

"Odd," Gash said. "Must have been a miscommunication between the Marine Corporation Media Relations and the Church."

"Sir," she said. "Those fuckers posted the article twelve hours ago."

Twelve hours ago, they'd still been fighting for their lives.

So the Church sent them into the meat grinder to stoke war sentiment, Gash thought. There couldn't be another reason for a canned story about their deaths to be published *as* the trap sprung if the trap was really a surprise.

The men and women in Gash's squad were as smart as he was, if not smarter in a few cases. They grew quiet. Very quiet. All eyes on him. Good-bye whiskey rations, he remembered thinking. And hello double-whiskey rations.

Gash's reverie broke after little more than an hour, when the shuttle pilot announced their imminent descent into Kansas City and the team came to life.

The next phase of the plan mirrored the last phase of the plan. They would split off into two groups to throw off WalCo agents scanning AutoCab databases and reconvene as a team at the hotel. Same travel partners, same disguises.

From the AutoCab, Gash watched the streets flow past. Kansas City seemed much like Seattle in some ways – bright lights, concrete, cloud-scrapers stretching up and out of sight. But in many ways, the cities were opposites. Where Seattle rose and fell with steep hills, Kansas City felt more like a fixed grid on a flat concrete board. And where Seattle buzzed with life at all hours, Kansas City grew quiet in these, the wee hours of the morning. The earliest and deepest hues of purple were just beginning to splash the faintest sunlight on the sky, something you seldom saw in eternally cloudy Seattle.

The AutoCab interrupted his reverie by coming to a stop. He paid and stepped out with Xiaoli and Silvie. The massive neon sign, "Crash," flashed yellow and purple above the entrance to the hotel/ flophouse. Inside felt cheaply sterile. Certainly better than some of the more disgusting places he'd hidden out in the past (a vile hotel called The Supreme came to mind), but nothing to write home about. The Crash chain of corporate hotels grew popular not for quality or comfort, but simply for discretion. Zero-ident credit transfers meant nobody could track you to a Crash hotel. These were popular spots for mercs, drug deals, sex work, and trysts. Long ago, Gash spent many an hour camping outside of a Crash to get a shot of a cheating husband or wife. He never stayed in one, though.

First time for everything.

By the time dawn crested the eastern horizon, making vermilion mountains of massive cumulous clouds, the team gathered in Gash's room. Each of the five emptied a bag of gear onto the bed, and the holoprojector cast the three-dimensional blueprint of Ana Marin's living quarters in the Waldo district. Silvie strutted like a model in her new threads, drawing laughs from Xiaoli and Iblis. She wore a simple looking white shirt and olive slacks, but made of hyper-flexible carbon nano-fiber with off-the-charts tensile strength. In other words, clothes that wouldn't rip when she transformed.

They were bonding. Having fun. Xiaoli told a war story about a high-ranking military officer with a nude-sleep-walking problem. They would have all day to work out the finer points of the plan and get some rest, before deploying that night.

That afternoon, the squad filed out of Gash's room, gear distributed and plan cemented. Xiaoli and Julius left to pick up a rental van, Iblis to work out some of the details of the building's security (codes rotated on-site every three days, so the hijacked WalCo data provided expired passwords, which meant Iblis would have to hack the building's security), and Silvie just to rest. She paused at the door to his room, as if to double back when the rest were gone. After just enough of a delay to get Gash's heart racing, for his breath to catch in his throat, she stepped into the hallways, closing the door behind her.

That was for the best. Gash returned to the bed, pulling Dr. Marin's info up on his PCom. He'd read the file a dozen times, and knew it all by heart. Born in Romania, she emigrated to America in her teens, and managed to receive a PhD in microbiology with a specialty in epidemiology by age 23. After a brief stint in her late 20's interning with WalCo, she fell off the grid. Shortly after the expiration of Dr. Marin's internship, WalCo abducted her and forced her into service, probably because she planned to take a position with another corporation. Who had hired Gash to save her? The file said nothing about her family, and he'd never been able to connect the dots to any of her living relatives. Was the wealthy benefactor a secret lover? An adoptive parent? Another corporation, intent on employing her themselves?

Exhaustion ambushed Gash as he stared at the file, and he drifted off to a fitful sleep.

CHAPTER 29

The van rolled through another stop sign. Xiaoli cut the wheel to the right, taking the team deeper into the Waldo district. Not long, now, until Dr. Marin's residence. Hopefully she would be home.

The wind howled, blowing refuse across the street. Busted Real-D rigs, the cheap disposable polymer kind, bounced and skittered across the street, modern tumbleweeds. Myriad brightly colored sugar-snack-wrappers, reflective foil sheets long since ripped open and reflecting the neon lights of the city, vending machine zip gun packaging all glossy and red, and the translucent white poly-gauze commonly used to wrap street drugs: A thousand species of discarded plastic wrapper flitted through the air, rolling and diving in gusts, painting a garbage rainbow across the night sky.

Plenty of unhoused in this neck of the woods, nestled into nooks and crannies of abandoned buildings and alleys. Squatters inhabited this whole section of the Kansas City sprawl, but it wasn't anything like the DRZ. Folks in the DRZ – a lot of them anyway – were specialists, mercs, freelancers. Meaning shops and kiosks sprang up in buildings and along the streets to serve them. Here, though, the only ones selling were dealers and sex workers standing on the street corners beneath flickering streetlights.

Real-D junkies clustered around a former coffee shop, sprawled against the wall and lounging on the sidewalk, duct-taped rigs around their heads, lost in some porn feed or virtual drug binge or snuff reel. The cables from each of their rigs, tentacles from some arcane techno-illithid, hooked almost a dozen of them into a makeshift server connected to a trunk cable that trailed off into the decimated remains of the coffee shop, slowly draining their brains into the gaping maw of the virtual real. Flickering lights inside illuminated the profiles of what must have been forty or fifty more junkies, all networked into the same Real-D street kingpin's stolen broadband.

They drove on past more of the same, only as they neared the WalCo secret facility, Gash noticed fewer and fewer of the displaced on the streets. The dealers and pros were first to vanish. A dozen blocks into Waldo, and the street entrepreneurs slinging drugs, broadband, and sex all disappeared. The squatter population noticeably thinned the further in they travelled.

"The long-time street walkers in this area know that in certain spots, folks tend to disappear," Gash mused aloud.

"How many people do you think WalCo has kidnapped off the streets?" Silvie asked.

Gash did not know, and said as much. Too many.

Iblis scrolled the data on his PCom. "This facility has been in operation for close to three decades. It is a fair bet they have taken hundreds, if not thousands."

Silence followed that proclamation. Eventually, Xiaoli pulled the van up alongside another building. At first glance, this one seemed lost to squatters. Abandoned, same as all the others. Expanses of cracked brickwork and graffiti covered the walls. First and second story windows were boarded shut.

However, on closer inspection, a few things stood out. Wiring and utility connections looked new and in good repair, protected by hardened security-grade casing and conduit. Though heavy curtains blocked any possible light from escaping to the street, the upper stories' windows looked refurbished; window frames done in fresh concrete and glass panes all intact. Finally and most ostentatiously: A shiny chrome security door protected the entrance to the garage beneath the building.

WalCo researchers lived here, some under guard and some of their own free will. Ana would be on the fifth floor. At the thought, Gash's guts twisted and danced. Some iteration of her resided in his mind ever since he took the case back then. Would the real person measure up? Would she be glad to be saved? Would the room be empty, Ana gone forever? Dead and buried in some faraway wilderness or totally incinerated? The possibilities dizzied him.

"Okay, this is it, people. The final chapter in our little adventure. Iblis and I will take care of recon. Once we have eyes on Dr. Marin, we'll tag Silvie and Julius in to hit security from the front while we break through from the other side. Xiaoli, keep the van running, we'll probably need to leave in a hurry." Gash looked around at his team – they were ready.

He slid the door open, following Iblis out onto the sidewalk. First he checked his new weapon, popping the magazine out to confirm a fully loaded clip for the fifth time, and then having done that, ramming it home again. The sidearm hummed softly. His second gauss weapon. A higher-powered model that came at a significantly higher cost than any of his previous weapons, this one fired larger flechettes at the tradeoff of a smaller ammo capacity per magazine. Grooves and a rounded gun chassis provided a design nod to revolvers of old. Gash hated it, but old gunpowder weapons were tactically inferior choices, and this was the big-leagues. WalCo would not take him alive again, even if it meant surrendering to the soft hush of a magnetic firearm. Even if it meant he might forget the gravity of taking a life for a little while.

He holstered the weapon and looked around. The streets stood empty, and surveillance cameras wouldn't last a day out here. All clear. He holstered his gun, stepped up to the wall, and put a hand on the brick.

He never felt more like a monster than when he was spider-climbing up the side of a wall or building, but there was no helping it. Much cleaner and more secure to come in from the outside. Unlike WalCo HQ, nobody expected upper-story insertion at a nameless secret residential facility. Plus, his usual smash and grab wouldn't work here: they had no way of knowing if Dr. Marin was home, so they might need to lay low once inside, and await her to return.

The rough brick of the exterior wall brought to mind his first moments as a vampire. When he abandoned Starfire at the bottom of that hole in the Earth in Rhodes as the world collapsed around them. It was all he could do, when the hunger washed over him, to avoid drinking her dry on the spot.

Now, though, with the coarse brick beneath the tips of his fingers as he propelled himself upwards, his brain dwelled on the singularity of the shame he felt on abandoning her to a near-certain death. She counted on his protection and he cut her loose the moment he changed. If she died, so be it – as long as it didn't come from him, he could live with it. But now he felt the wrongness of that.

Up to the fifth floor, he grabbed onto the frame of the window with one hand, reaching out to open it with his other. Unlocked, of course – who expected an intruder from the fifth-floor window? He slipped in between the light-blocking blinds and rolled to his feet on the floor inside. First things he noticed – no lights. The smell of rotting food and stale blood.

He pulled his PCom out of his jacket pocket, activating the link to Iblis' device. The soft light of the screen and the video display allowed the ifrit to teleport to Gash. He appeared in a puff of smoke.

"Dark," he whispered. "You see anything with those magic eyes of yours?"

"Same as you," Gash whispered back. "Food box light showing the time, faint glow of holovision projector in sleep mode, hall light peeking through under the front door. Give me a second, my eyes need to adjust."

As he acclimated, the room gradually resolved for Gash in a sort of gray night-vision. With his eyes fully adjusted, he could see everything in the faint ambient light of a handful of inactive appliances.

The place wasn't bad, especially for a forced-work prison. New-looking heating/cooling unit on the far wall, a series of abstract paintings done in blues and violets, a sofa and recliner positioned around a holovision projector. Gash and Iblis stood in the kitchenette/dining area, near a table with one chair. The food box hummed, the light of the built-in clock illuminating the cook-time button. The door hung ajar just enough that Gash could smell the food inside, mostly still refrigerated, but slowly rotting as the temperature within rose.

Across the room, a closed bedroom door. Gash heard no heartbeat or breathing within. Where was the smell of blood coming from? He sniffed the air, creeping towards it. Iblis waited in silence.

He followed the scent of blood towards the front door. When he neared the center of the room, he saw it. A pool of dried blood about three feet away from the apartment's entryway. Someone was injured here. No, killed – the size of the blood pool told him someone had bled out. Up close, Gash detected another scent from the blood pool: Whiskey.

And then he saw something else. A small piece of yellow plastic, no larger than a data-drive, a number "three" printed on it rested beside the blood pool. Having seen it, he saw two more – a number one on the counter beside an empty glass, and a number two by the cracked-open food box. Someone was killed here, and an investigation opened.

But the place was empty now. No Dr. Marin. Gash's mind kicked into overdrive. Was this her blood? Had she been murdered days or even weeks ago? If so, why hadn't the data from WalCo HQ indicated her termination? If it wasn't her blood, whose was it? Where was she? The cracked open food box told him she was here when the violence occurred, and the food slowly rotting within told him she had not been home for a long time. Never mind that nobody bothered to clean the pool of blood.

"Gash?" Iblis whispered.

Gash rose and flipped on the light by the door. "Nobody here," he said.

"Is that blood?"

"Yeah, and the food box has been left cracked open long enough for everything inside to start to spoil. She isn't here and hasn't been for awhile."

"Shit," Iblis said. He walked over to the blood pool and crouched down by it. "Someone died here."

"Agreed." Gash stepped into the bedroom, turning a light on in there too. Nothing remained of Dr. Marin, if it ever existed to begin with. A twin bed, unmade, sat against the far wall. An empty desk with another chair, and a nightstand with a plug-in dock for PComs with a built-in holovision projector completed the room. No pictures of people adorned the walls, just more abstract art. "Guess you don't have family photos when you're abducted and forced to work," Gash mumbled.

When he re-emerged into the main living space, Iblis spoke to Julius on PCom. "Looks like WalCo already investigated whatever happened here," he said.

"A week ago at least," Gash added.

Iblis looked up. "So why was the data wrong? We accessed it just a few days ago."

Gash shook his head, standing in the center of the room, at a loss.

"Not wrong, just outdated maybe," Julius said.

"What do you mean?" Gash stepped closer to Iblis and the projected face of Julius.

"Well this bio-tech facility that Dr. Marin's been working at is probably a closed loop when it comes to data: No connections to the outside world. For the same reason that the server you all hit in the WalCo HQ basement wasn't networked – hackers are always a step ahead of corporate security, and linking your secure data to those hackers, even via a heavily protected network, is begging for them to rob you blind."

"Right, but obviously they report in to HQ, which is why WalCo servers possessed the data to begin with."

"Listen," Julius said. "My specialty was missing persons. Back when the FBI still had clout, I was pretty new in my career. But a lot of corporations brought us on to help track down employees kidnapped by rival companies. One thing we encountered on almost every case: by the time we came in, the trail had grown icy. Middle managers have a tendency to hide this sort of thing. They try to resolve kidnap jobs in-house, without alerting upper management. Doesn't look good on your resume if an important member of your facility gets taken."

"Do you think if someone murdered Dr. Marin they would be keeping that from HQ too?"

"Maybe. It's a dangerous game – if the dead employee was crucial to facility operations, they'll have to be replaced. Can't replace them without reporting them dead, and letting the facility fall behind in its goals is a far larger black mark than one or two deaths. So my first guess is 'no,' but it just depends on who's in charge and how delusional they are."

"Now what?" Iblis asked.

But Gash felt something. His gut, often the first to know, told him Ana was alive. But why? He surveyed the room one more time. Alcohol.

"Booze," he said.

"Huh?" Julius asked.

"This blood smells like whiskey. Whoever died was a heavy whiskey drinker."

"Okay..." Iblis said.

"Look around. Spices, seasonings, garnishes, but no whiskey. No alcohol of any kind." He opened the food box and the cabinets to confirm. "No wine bottles or liquor bottles in the cabinets, no beer in the box. Ana didn't drink, so this can't be her blood."

"You can really smell whiskey in that pool of blood?"

"Vampire, remember?" Gash felt a lightness returning to his step as he explored the room further, looking for any other clues. Who was killed? What happened? Where was Ana now? He found no more answers, but the confidence remained. Dr. Marin was still alive. The trail dead-ended, but based on what Julius said, the local network at the WalCo research facility where she worked would have updated data. Did they move her to another building? Another facility all together? Did she escape on her own?

Gash sighed. Time to raid yet another secret WalCo facility. Third time's the charm, he thought. Right?

CHAPTER 30

"We haven't taken time to come up with any plan. We can't just go in half-cocked," Julius said.

"You mean like we did in the Arctic?" Xiaoli said, hands never leaving the steering wheel, eyes never leaving the road.

"Yeah, and look where I landed at the end of that little misadventure," Julius said.

"We've got ten minutes right now. Do you want to use it complain about not having a plan or to come up with a plan?" Gash interjected. "I can't start over. There's no breaking back into WalCo which means it's now or never."

Julius opened his mouth to speak, but before he could, Xiaoli slammed on the gas to edge out a beat-up old Ford coming through the cross-street up ahead. She cleared the intersection, the van fishtailing as the sedan clipped their rear bumper. Xiaoli turned back to look at the rest of the team and grinned. "Make it seven minutes – With no traffic lights or cops we'll make good time."

"Just get us there in one piece," Gash growled.

Iblis held his hand out, activating the holoprojector in his PCom and pulling up the blueprints of the facility. They reviewed these once before, and Gash knew breaking in would be a true challenge. WalCo crammed the abandoned restaurant standing atop the facility with security – guards, reinforced doors with biometric protections, even a couple heavy turrets recessed into the walls at key choke points. To say nothing of the security once through the elevator and into the actual facility. Security personnel outnumbered researchers, and a security station on each floor held a full complement of miniaturized gun drones.

"We'll have to fight our way through, no way we're sneaking around in enclosed quarters like that, and we don't have time to come up with a different approach... if one even exists," Silvie said.

Gash looked at Silvie and then Julius. "If you aren't up for this, just say the word. No hard feelings."

Silvie spoke first, eyes hard enough to crack plascrete. "Are you kidding me? These guys have been taking innocents off the streets and experimenting on them for years. Incinerating their bodies when they finish. I'd tear the place apart myself if I had to."

"Okay," Gash said, holding his hands up. "I misunderstood your concern."

Julius shifted in his seat, looking first at Xiaoli and then at Gash. "I think this is a suicide run. Given more time to plan it, maybe we could pull it off. Maybe the three of you can brute force it somehow, but I'm not some super-powered magical being. Xiaoli and I will wait in the van and we'll cover your rear, but if we get a whiff of danger or if we think you've been captured or killed, we're out of here."

Xiaoli looked back, seemingly driving blind, for long enough to glower at Julius. "You don't speak for me." She turned to Gash. "I'm your driver, I'll be waiting outside when you're finished no matter what we think might have happened. Sheng Xiaoli finishes what she starts."

Julius dropped his gaze, then turned to look out the window, knuckles white from clenching his fists.

"Fair enough," Gash said. He wanted to lean into Julius for this. Only yesterday they'd all gathered around and re-committed to this job, and each of them received a hell of a daily stipend for being on the team. But if the tables were turned, Gash knew he'd make the same call. A suicide run into a heavily fortified corporate research facility intimidated even Gash, with all his strength and speed and regenerative powers. He'd done this twice now, once as a normal man and once as vampire. Neither time netted him a mark in the "win" column. Couldn't expect someone without skin in the game to sign up for those same long odds. At least Xiaoli could be counted on to be waiting for them outside when they extracted.

Xiaoli turned back to the street just in time to swerve around a Real D junky dancing in the middle of the street.

So it would be the monster squad invading another WalCo facility again. Gash turned to Iblis and Silvie, squatting with him in the back of the van. "We're going to have to have to blitz this place. Speed is of the essence. When all the personnel and drones deployed in the whole facility begin to collapse on our location, we could easily be overwhelmed."

He pointed at the top part of the map. "Iblis, that means you're going to have to work fast to hack the elevator down to floor 1B. Once we're there, we pass through this central security checkpoint to get to the second elevator bank that services the deeper parts of the facility. We can skip right down to 4B from there, access the data from this point here. Silvie, we'll need to hold long enough for Iblis to scrub the data down. If they're currently holding Dr. Marin inside, we'll have to locate and extract her. Otherwise, Iblis will pull the data on what happened to her, we extract, and then figure out where to go from there. Any questions?"

"We can go in through the back," Iblis gestured at the map. "What used to be the kitchen. This will let us avoid the big turret at the front entrance – we will still have to take out the turret by the elevator, but I should be able to hack it or melt it down."

"Good call," Gash said.

"Okay," Silvie said.

And with a squealing of rubber, Xiaoli pulled a sharp right, coming to a hard stop just outside the back entrance to the abandoned restaurant. "We're here, kids," she said. "Have fun in the secret facility, try not to get captured and experimented on."

Out the door and across the sidewalk and into the facility, Gash kicked open the door to the kitchen before the others set foot to pavement. The bloodlust descended upon him in full force, his pulse pounding, the scent of his teammates mixing with pedestrians blocks away. His senses revved into overdrive and the world took on an extra-bright, neon-red hue.

Through the door and ready to tear the WalCo guards apart, Gash found himself standing in an empty space. Rusted out sinks and griddles and stoves lined the far wall, but where the blueprints indicated a security desk populated by half a dozen guards and a combat drone, Gash saw only the desk, empty. The others filed in after. He froze, head cocked to the side, listening. Smelling. Nothing but refuse and dust here.

"Nobody home?" Silvie asked in a whisper.

"Not that I can detect," Gash said.

"Stay on your guard, it may be a trap," Iblis said.

Gash led them down the hall, past what used to be bathrooms and into what once served as an extra dining space or private room for large parties. Through here, Gash and his squad moved into the primary dining space. Vandals and squatters took or smashed most of the chairs and tables long before WalCo moved in, so the space lacked cover, aside from the reinforced alloy of the elevator shaft sitting in the middle of the room. Perfect place for an ambush. Gash led the others slowly across the empty space, eyes and ears and nose in hyper-drive. Nobody here, no ambush coming. The shining chrome elevator shaft and two sliding doors stood, a gleaming pillar in a sea of cheap poly-fabric carpet, half-red still and half-gray with rot, like a statue to Apollo installed in ancient ruins.

Gash looked at Silvie and then at Iblis. Iblis only shrugged. "Think they saw us coming, pulled back into the facility?" Silvie asked.

"It would be a smart move," Iblis said. "Best way to stop a group like us is force us into narrow confines and hit us with heavy weapons. But uninstalling that turret would be hard work. Cheaper just to add more turrets if they knew we were coming."

"Could be half a dozen reasons there's nobody up here, none of them good. Iblis, can you get this door open? Silvie, something is wrong. Be ready to hulk out, please."

Iblis stepped towards the elevator, looking at the biometric lock, which required retinal scan and DNA input. "This will be a tough nut to crack without prep time." He kneeled, pulling a metal plate off from just below the call button. He was getting ready to jack in, but hesitated for a moment. Before Gash could ask him what was wrong, he reached up and pressed the call button. It lit up, and the door immediately opened. Iblis looked back at Gash, who shrugged and stepped in the elevator.

"Oh, so it's definitely a trap," Silvie said.

"Yep – but we can hack out of it as easily as we can hack into it. Right?" Gash looked to Iblis for confirmation.

"No idea," he said, stepping in after Gash. "But *I* have a way out if this backfires."

Silvie followed them in, shaking her head at Iblis.

The doors did not close until Gash hit the 1B button. The elevator hummed for what seemed entirely too long a time, but it didn't crash or explode. After two or three minutes it stopped – gently, smoothly – and the doors slid open. Gash burst out of the elevator car, sidearm drawn, and Iblis followed suit, flames flickering and heating from red to white at his fingertips.

Like above, the monster squad charged into a freshly abandoned space. The security here, where the elevator from the outside world opened onto the first floor of the WalCo facility, was purported by their intel to be the heaviest. And indeed, Gash could see evidence that this was once true. Not only had the security desk been fortified with what looked like an armored carbon-nanotube layer, but multiple barricades served as additional fortifications against an invader emerging from the elevator. Here again, the security station should also have been host to at least a dozen combat drones.

They should have been charging through a kill-zone into a heavily fortified position. But instead, they barged out of the elevator into a space that seemed to echo with their breathing. Gash sensed nothing hidden, nobody nearby preparing to spring a trap. At some point, WalCo extracted all security personnel from this floor. Which meant they'd likely abandoned the whole facility.

"Could be they picked up shop and moved out," Silvie said, still whispering.

"That would only happen if Ana escaped, compromising the location of the facility," Gash said, his heart soaring at the thought.

"We'll snag the data from the fourth floor and find out," Iblis said.

"Yeah, eventually, but I want to cover our asses here. If I were setting a trap, this is where I would have sprung it. But let's still be careful. We'll clear this place floor by floor, so we know nothing is coming down after us. Starting with this floor. Iblis, can you head directly to the other elevator, secure our path down? Silvie and I will split up – I'll cover the west half of the place, Silvie you cover the east. It should just be office space, break rooms, and a couple more security stations up here. But if WalCo were to set up makeshift living quarters, it would be on this floor. Keep your eyes peeled for Dr. Marin. Or anyone else, for that matter, who can tell us what's going on here. Oh, and stay on your coms. The moment a single hair on the back of your neck stands up, you give a shout."

New plan in place, they split up, each taking a different pathway out of the primary security station and deeper into the facility.

✧✧✧

Gash moved down the hallway, into a large cube farm. In over a century this paradigm never changed – small cubes with desks stacked side-by-side to fit as many workers as possible into a single large room.

The polymer half-walls, a mute gray, partitioned cheap polymer desks. Inside each cube stood an empty chair, assorted personal effects, and a smashed computer. The workers evacuated quickly. Personal photos in holo-frames flicked through slide-show-projections of family members and pets. Cups of instant coffee sat on desks, cooled but not yet congealed. Wireless keyboards and monitors blinked, power lights green – nobody bothered to turn them off, but the input was destroyed when the computers were smashed.

In a ring around the cube farm, small offices for middle managers and senior scientists stood empty, computers also smashed. Hurried though he was, Gash still carved out a few minutes to comb the offices for clues about what happened, or where Dr. Marin had gone. Eventually, towards the back of the room, he stumbled upon an office with her name on the door. "Dr. Ana Marin," the sign declared.

Gash stepped inside. This office, unlike the others, lacked the scattered personal mementos and the smashed computer. Personal effects were meticulously removed, along with every piece of hardware. No keyboard or monitor or even a flash drive was left behind. No photos. Just an empty desk and chair. One foot out the door, Gash paused. That gut of his that occasionally had thoughts of its own took a moment to scream at him. He doubled back, kneeling down to check the floor. Sure enough, up close Gash could see a tiny scrap of paper wedged in the wheel of the office chair. He gently rolled the wheel while simultaneously pulling on the scrap, extracting it from its plastic prison without damaging it.

When he unfolded it, Gash saw a handful of words written on it – in *ink* no less. Who knew Ana was a sucker for archaic forms of note taking? Or perhaps she knew WalCo was scanning all of her devices and digital communications, and this was the only way to keep a secret. If so, dropping it on the floor and forgetting about it – careless. Gash found it difficult to read the crumpled note, especially given that Ana's writing was quite sloppy. After a minute, though, he found he could make out the shapes well enough – they were numbers. A long series of numbers with a decimal after the second, and then a comma, and then another long series of numbers (negative this time), again with a decimal after the second.

He stared at the numbers, the rest of the world falling away. When it hit him, it hit him hard and fast. These were latitude/longitude coordinates. He plugged the numbers into his PCom and it popped up on his GPS – the little pin dropped him in *New Orleans* of all places. Which made a kind of sense, since New Orleans addresses didn't use street names anymore, for obvious reasons. But why the hell would Ana have a New Orleans location written manually on paper? What would drive her to travel to such a place? Did WalCo move her to a new facility?

Gash pocketed the scrap of paper for later. Depending on how things shook out here, this might be his only clue. He hoped not – travelling to that hell on Earth wasn't his idea of a good time.

Gash found nothing else on his side of the first floor. Restrooms were abandoned, hallways stood empty, meeting rooms were left in disarray. At one point, near a janitorial closet, Gash caught a scent of something... *strange*. Animal, but not. He couldn't really put his finger on exactly what it was, and it faded shortly after it appeared. He scoured the closet, but saw only cleaning supplies. Lemony air freshener and bleach and soap smells clashing for dominance. But nothing animal. Most likely a stray draft blew the scent up the vents from animal testing facilities on the second floor. His vampiric senses picked up the faintest traces sometimes.

He put it out of his mind and met Silvie and Iblis at the elevator down. "Find anything?" he asked Silvie. She shook her head, echoing the question back at him. He told her and Iblis about Ana's office, and the mysterious coordinates on the scrap of paper.

"This place makes me uneasy," Iblis said. "Perhaps we should fall back and investigate this new notion that Dr. Marin is in New Orleans."

"I'm sorry, but we don't know nearly enough about what happened. Was she going to flee to New Orleans but they caught her? Did she manage to escape? Maybe they killed her and laid these coordinates out as a trap? We need to extract whatever data is down on the fourth floor to be sure."

Gash stepped into the elevator, Silvie following immediately. Iblis, after a deep sigh, joined them as well. "Second floor," he said, punching the button. The biometric display flashed yellow, but Iblis tapped a few times on his PCom, and it went green. The elevator began to move.

CHAPTER 31

The second and third floors of the WalCo bio-tech facility proved much the same as the first. Gunmetal walls and ceilings with black-carpeted hallways gave a vague sense of walking through a spaceship corridor.

The vast majority of the facility's various bio-tech labs could be found on the second and third. Broadly speaking, WalCo had organized the place by field of research. Silvie explored the "food tech" wing on the second floor, which amounted to more than half of that whole floor, and Gash took the bio-mod section. These were fairly well-publicized technologies, more or less benign, though WalCo surely enjoyed an edge on the R&D thanks to their illegal human studies.

The third floor housed darker research. Silvie took a wing devoted to gene-splicing and eugenics – real Nazi shit, Gash thought. He took the other half of the third floor: epidemiology. But of course, these labs weren't geared towards understanding and curing diseases, they were geared towards monetizing lethal microbes, and perhaps even weaponizing them for use in corporate wars.

The third floor left Gash feeling sick to his stomach. A few more times, he caught that vague sort of animal scent he had noted on the first floor. Which began to make more sense the further in they got, since animal subjects were being used in conjunction with human subjects. Several of the labs featured dozens of empty animal pens, sized from rats and rabbits to monkeys. But really struggled when he stumbled into a lab where the animal pens were human pens. Each contained a small cot and toilet, along with some abandoned apparatus for monitoring human patients. Knowing the place abducted people to experiment on was one thing, but standing in that space, imagining the terror these people surely felt as they grew sick and died inside a small, sealed polymer cell... that was another thing entirely.

He knew what was coming next, and it stood to be one of the worst things he'd ever seen. The complete absence of still-living test subjects or at least of human remains told him what he already knew. The incinerator that Julius spotted on the blue-prints wasn't just for animal remains. Towards the far western side of the facility, Gash found it. Similar in size and function to a crematorium, the incinerator room provided the researchers with the means to dispose of biological remains generated as part of their research. Three separate ovens filled the western wall completely. A sort of waste bin below the ovens caught the ash remains.

The room told a clear story. On the eastern wall, several long metal tables were covered in huge pools of congealing blood. Dried blood spray covered the wall. WalCo wouldn't have normally disposed of still-living test subjects. Simpler and better on morale to let the disease finish off the subject before incinerating the body. But when it came time to pull out of the facility.... How many still-living "test subjects" were executed? Gash had seen a body cremated before, and the remains placed in a small urn afterwards. Well, the basins below the ovens held enough ash to fill more than fifty urns. Human beings, sick, carted in by the dozen. Killed messy with knives and shoved in ovens. He felt a wave of nausea sweep over him. Rage replaced the nausea, bloodlust threatened to consume him. But with only his teammates in the facility he couldn't give in to the red. Not now. There would be a time for that.

Ana worked down here, or at least epidemiology was her specialty (and why else would WalCo take her if not for that?). Did she bear responsibility for these people? How many had she killed or caused to die in order to save her own life?

For a long time, Gash stood in the crematorium, wondering whether Dr. Marin was worth saving. After a while, disgust turned to sympathy. How many lives had Gash taken just to survive another day? To finish a job, take a paycheck so he could eat? No, Dr. Marin must have suffered greatly, knowing her work cost these innocent men and women their lives, that she couldn't save them. He imagined those bright blue eyes of hers, haunted by death, tears drying in the corners of her eyes. He could not abandon her.

Not to mention: How else would someone like him escape the endless cycle of violence without enough money to retire to some place by the water and spend the rest of his years in solitude? He owed it to Serena to see this thing through.

Past the crematorium, Gash encountered a series of small rooms double-sealed with airlocks. Inside the airlocks hung a number of orange bio-hazard suits, each of which someone was slashed with a blade of some kind. Labels above the doors identified these rooms as bio-hazard level five, which Gash presumed meant these were the big bad bio-agents. The worst of the worst. He peered through small porthole windows into these rooms, and found them as empty as the rest of the facility. He moved on.

✧✧✧

The team reassembled by the elevator and descended to floor 4B – the base's nerve center. Full of servers and environmental controls and security stations, 4B governed everything they saw on the upper floors.

Like the rest of the facility, 4B was recently abandoned, and quickly. Security desks, IT centers, maintenance hubs: all reflected what Gash saw on the first floor. Personal items scattered and left behind, computers smashed, coffee and food items abandoned unfinished. As before, Gash and Silvie split up to look for evidence of Dr. Marin's passage, or signs of a trap that seemed less and less likely.

It was clear to Gash at this point that most of the creepy stuff happened on the lab floors, two and three, with 4B devoted primarily to administration. Meaning Gash and Silvie needed only a cursory look through the large offices of upper echelon managers and IT specialists to clear this floor. They found plenty of smashed servers and little else. Silvie and Gash cleared the space in short order and met Iblis at the command center, the hub of 4B and the primary access point for all server data.

Gash arrived to see Iblis jacked into the facility mainframe, presumably hard at work. Silvie sat beside him, watching him. Impossible to tell what he was seeing or doing from the outside, so Gash instead patrolled the room. Numerous digital displays ringed the room, like so many dead eyes staring at Gash as he moved. Was everything in the facility gone? Perhaps the tiny scrap of paper, those coordinates in New Orleans, were all that would come of this descent into WalCo hell.

"Well," Iblis said, rising from his seat to stretch after half an hour, "that proved to be an interesting run."

"Were you able to recover any data?" Silvie asked. Gash leaned against a powered down console, crossing his arms and waiting for the report.

"I was. First of all, the facility is dead. Security features are nuked, and the VI governing everything is completely gone. Basic functions are still there – lights, air circulation, elevators. But that stuff is just running on emergency backup power, which is getting fairly low. We need to be out of here in the next couple hours."

"Good to know," Gash chimed in.

"Beyond that, they tried to obliterate all of the records, but I was able to recover many buckets full of data. Whoever did this was good, but did not have time to do the job right."

"Let's have the highlights and then get out of here," Gash said, standing and taking a step towards Iblis and Silvie. "What did you find out about Dr. Marin?"

"A lot of what she was working on, for one thing. Most of it is like Greek to me, but from what I can tell they had her working on a designer virus. Some kind of bio bug meant to kill tens of thousands of people, but also a cure. Reading between the lines, it seems like they intended to cause a pandemic level event, and then sell the drug therapy necessary to recover at a high cost. I do not think this was the first time they did this."

Silence descended like a heavy fog. As if involuntary human trials on dangerous pathogens weren't enough.

"Do you have evidence of when they did this in the past? Even WalCo would take a huge hit if this sort of data got out," Silvie said.

"I just highlighted the stuff having to do with Dr. Marin for now, but when we get out of here we will look. I ripped everything I could. I pray that we do have something that will at least put a dent in WalCo's reputation."

"What else do you have?" Gash asked.

"Here is the big whammy," Iblis said. But then he paused.

"What?" Gash asked.

"You will not like this."

"Is she dead?" Gash sat down on the chair, and leaned close to Iblis. "What is it?"

"She defected," Iblis said.

"To another corporation?"

"To the Children of Gaia," Iblis said.

The name rang a bell, but it took Gash a moment to place it. They were anti-corporate anarchists, which was okay in Gash's book, except that their methods were notoriously sloppy. Corporations referred to them as terrorists; they referred to themselves as freedom fighters or eco-warriors. They'd blown up a lot of coal plants and assassinated a decent number of oligarchs. But the collateral damage was always too high for Gash's tastes. Setting off restaurant bombs and IEDs when a well-placed bullet would do. These people had a hell of a body count, and now, apparently, they had recruited a specialist in nasty microbes who spent the last few years working as the architect of some kind of pandemic. Not good.

"Wow," Gash said. "Not the best news we've gotten today."

"It's a bad news kind of day," Silvie said.

"Are you sure we want to continue to pursue her?" Iblis asked.

Gash wasn't sure. But he had a job to do, and more importantly, a secret WalCo bio-tech facility steeped in blood that he needed to leave. "Let's get out of here. I'll reach out to my client and see what he wants us to do. I'm pretty sure the Children of Gaia operate out of New Orleans, or at least one cell does. Seems like we can put 2 and 2 together here, but if its enough for the client to know she's not with WalCo anymore, maybe we'll call it a day...."

That thought lingered in the air, a floating miasma preventing Gash from breathing.

"We need to get out of here, we got what we came for," he said at last.

Silvie and Iblis exchanged a look, but stood as well.

And that's when the lights went out. The computer displays all flashed on, creaking with static, and then went totally dark again. The lights followed suit, shutting down and leaving the team in blackness. Thirty seconds later, the emergency lights came on, and one console screen re-lit.

Iblis said nothing, but made his way quickly to the one live console. He tapped at it, fingers a faint metronome in the suddenly-too-quiet facility.

"I thought we had more time before the emergency power shut off," Gash said.

"We did," Iblis said, still typing away.

Silvie and Gash stood in place, waiting, the silence echoing more loudly with each tap of Iblis's fingers. After a time, he let out a long breath. "Al'ama," he said quietly.

"What?" Gash and Silvie spoke as one.

"The facility is not dead. A few processes were buried under the pile of mostly-destroyed garbage data. A motion sensor in this office triggered some process tied into the base facilities. I also found some video footage tied into all of it. They tried to delete it, but I caught a few fragments."

Iblis waved the video fragment onto his PCom. Digital static fragmented the image, but two things were clear. A man sat working at the very terminal Iblis currently sat at, and another stood behind him. Though many of his features were lost to the static, the standing man's eyes came through crystal clear. Gash looked over at Silvie, and saw recognition on her face as well. Those dead white eyes belonged to Henry Galloway, the highly disturbed immortal responsible for Silvie and Gash's incarceration a few days prior.

Gash drew his sidearm. He didn't know how, but Galloway clearly knew they were after Dr. Marin. It was a trap after all.

"Which parts of the facilities are tied into the motion sensor?" Gash asked quietly.

Iblis tapped away for a few more seconds. "Gene-splicing," he said.

"What exactly is that?" Silvie asked.

"Scientific efforts to combine DNA from different animals for... various effects. There are hundreds of combinations, including a number of efforts to splice animal DNA into human subjects. Including bats, cats, salamanders –"

A long, mournful howl cut Iblis off. It echoed through the corridors of 4B, the unmistakable howl of a wolf, though more guttural and far louder than any normal canine. It cut through Iblis's words and it stretched on and on. Gash felt a raw, primal fear shudder through his body, from the back of his head all the way down his spine.

When it finally, blissfully ended, a chorus of similar howls answered. A whole pack of them, whatever they were.

"– and wolves," Iblis finished.

"Are you telling me there are werewolves down here?" Silvie asked.

Iblis looked at her and then Gash. "I am trying to figure out how you missed the werewolves when you were clearing the facility."

Then the emergency lights and the emergency console went dark once more. For the second time in as many minutes, Gash and team stood in pitch blackness as another series of howls echoed through the facility.

CHAPTER 32

The first light to push back the darkness turned out to be the faint glow of Iblis' PCom. The hacker tapped on it for a few seconds, before looking up at Gash. "They have jammed all signals. I cannot pull a live feed of the safehouse...."

"Which means you can't extract if the shit really hits the fan," Gash said.

Iblis nodded, the tiny light of his PCom drawing long shadows from his horns across his head and the wall behind him. "Yes, you are correct – my teleportation is guided by vision, I must see where I am going."

"Guess this trap really is meant for us," Silvie said.

Iblis let his PCom go dark, but another light replaced it – the soft flicker of orange flames in his eyes and around his horns.

"We'll fight our way out, and then it's time for a vacation to sunny New Orleans," Gash said, drawing his sidearm.

"What is the plan?" Iblis asked.

"What do we know?" Silvie asked.

"I smelled something animal in the upper floors, but could never locate anything specific. There must be secret rooms. I know we're talking human-wolf hybrids, but those howls really don't sound like normal wolves to me. Iblis did you manage to recover any details on WalCo's gene-splicing?"

"Not much, bits of an email from the Director of Special Projects at HQ chastising a team member for 'repeated failures.'"

"So what does a failed gene-splicing experiment look like? What does it do?" Silvie asked.

Gash checked the ammo in the magazine of his pistol, checked the safety, and holstered it. "I'd rather not find out, so let's focus on escaping. I'm guessing the elevator is shut down, same as everything else. But we should be able to get up on top of the car, and climb the cables to the first floor. It'll be harder to climb all the way to the surface, but there isn't another way out of here."

"Not much of a climber," Iblis said.

"You can ride on my back, or Silvie's – we're both plenty strong enough. Or maybe a series of short teleports if we go up first with a light?"

"I can climb in my wechuge form, but isn't there a set of emergency stairs?"

Gash laughed. "Emergency stairs or evacuation routes or fire plans are security risks and financial burdens. If a few workers get stuck or die, replacing them is easy."

"Elevator shaft it is, then," Iblis said, taking one step forward. Before he could take a second, they all heard a dull thump. A flash of white through the cracks in the elevator door made clear what happened. A remote explosive detonated the elevator car.

"Shit," Gash darted forward, prying open the doors. The explosion reduced the car to a hunk of metal slag and debris, totally blocking them from climbing onto it and access the cables.

No way they were getting up onto that car now, not without a micro-fusion torch to cut through the metal.

"If they want to kill us, why not just blow the whole facility?" Silvie asked.

"I think that was the first try," Gash said. "They just mis-timed the explosion. You know how expensive it would be to excavate a facility of this size, at this depth? I'm sure it's way cheaper to blow an elevator than a whole facility. If they can kill us and kill or recapture Dr. Marin, then they can repopulate it and save millions."

Silvie laughed. "So we were saved by corporate cost-cutters?"

Gash smiled at her. "Well, we're not saved yet, but they certainly gave us a chance."

"They will wish they had blown the whole facility when I escape and take my revenge," Iblis whispered.

"You happen to download the full facility blueprints before they jammed us?"

Iblis nodded, pulling up a holoprojection of the facility with his PCom. Gash reached out, zooming in on floor 4B with his fingers, studying every room. At first glance, the elevator appeared to be the only way in or out. But that couldn't be true, because it meant they were dead, so he kept on looking.

"I don't know that we have a ton of time, here," Silvie said.

"Do you see a way out? Without one, there is nowhere to go," Iblis said.

"Actually," she said, leaning in towards the holo-display. "Maybe I do. Look here, the server stacks are eleven feet tall, but each floor is only about nine feet tall."

"Meaning that the server room eats into the space above it?" Gash asked.

"I see," Iblis grinned. "That means these vents here, which must be extra wide to accommodate for the heat from the servers, must lead horizontally to the third floor."

"Yep, see this vent here? I bet we can reach it if we climb the server stacks, and I bet we can squeeze inside." Silvie said.

"Hard to tell from the blueprints, but worth a shot," Gash said.

"It's our only shot," Silvie said, looking around the room to orient herself towards the map, before setting off towards the server stacks on the north side of 4B. Gash and Iblis followed.

Periodically, a chorus of howls would shatter the silence. Were they coming closer? Just around the corner? All the way up on the first floor? Gash couldn't tell, even with his vampiric hearing. But they didn't run into any werewolves, arriving at the server stacks without incident.

A quick look around, and Gash identified a series of large vents in the ceiling of the room, easily accessed by climbing the server stacks. Gash shimmied up towards the nearest one, pulling off the vent cover with a snap and tossing it aside. The vents would be crowded, but they would all fit inside. As long as Silvie didn't transform.

Gash looked down at his team. "You were right, Silvie, we can get to the third floor from here." Gash turned back towards the vent just in time to see the first rat leap out of the darkness and land on his chest. He grabbed it and flung it away without looking at it or even really registering it. When the second bounded out, he got a much better look.

Calling the creature a rat was... generous. It shared the size and vague outline of a large rat, but was bloated and misshapen, its skin deformed. Pink fleshy tumors covered most of the tiny beast. Most disturbing of all, some mad scientist had surely spliced in spider DNA, as the creature watched him with eight beady black eyes stacked in two sets of four. In addition, two long feelers, like small spider legs, protruded from beneath its head.

Gash caught it in mid-air as it lunged for him. The thing hissed, and bit his hand. He flung it away, and it burst against the far wall like a malformed children's pinata filled with blood. A third of the hideous creatures fell from the vent, and a fourth and a fifth. He could not swat them all away. Before Gash could fully react, half a dozen of the hybrids clung to his face and chest. He fell backwards off the stacks, landing with a crack. Agony raced white-hot through his back from his tailbone, but he pushed it out of his mind. Regeneration would take care of that soon enough but more failed hybrids streamed out of the vents faster than he could swat them away.

"Iblis," he called out.

Iblis stepped forward, and with a bright white flash, the vents exploded. Fragments of plaster and polymer, aluminum shards and chunks of charred flesh erupted out of the hole in the ceiling.

The smell of burning filled Gash's nose, and – one at a time – he smashed the half dozen spider-rats still clinging to him. When he stood, his vision blurred and he fell back to his knees.

"I don't feel so great," he said.

"The hybrids must be venomous," Silvie said.

"Let us hope a vampire is mostly immune to the poison," Iblis said.

Nausea washed over Gash and intense pain gripped his belly. He doubled over, his breath growing more shallow by the second. He tried to stand, but couldn't move his legs. Nagash Jensen was dying. He closed his eyes, the light from Iblis' flames suddenly too much. Somewhere far in the distance, Iblis and Silvie spoke in hushed tones. A hand rested on his shoulder.

But the pain abated as quickly as it started. The invisible force released its kung-fu grip on his innards and Gash unclenched.

When Gash finally opened his eyes again, Silvie's face swam in through the haze. She was close. He could almost reach out and touch her lips, soft and pink. She seemed to be talking. He closed his eyes and tried to listen, but her words were only music, a rhythmic pattern of undefined syllables. Beautiful gibberish. Eventually, the sounds resolved to words.

"Gash, come back to us," Silvie was saying.

He re-opened his eyes and stood, finding his balance by bracing against one of the server stacks. His vision gradually clarified, and he was able to remove his hand from the servers in order to stand on his own. "I think I'm okay," he said. "But you guys better not let those things bite you."

"I'll say," Silvie said.

"Think that is all of them?" Iblis asked as he craned his neck to see into the darkness of the still-smoking vent.

"That was a pretty intense blast," Gash said. "So I doubt it. That doesn't mean there aren't more in other parts of the vents though, so we go fast and we watch our backs." At that, he vaulted back onto the stacks, climbing into the gaping hole in the ceiling. The aluminum edges of the vents still felt hot to the touch, but not enough to cause any lasting damage.

Gash's shoulders pressed against the vent walls on both sides, and his back slid along the top of the tunnel as he crawled forward. No more rat-spiders leapt out of the darkness at him. The whole shaft creaked as Iblis and Silvie climbed in behind him, but did not collapse under their combined weight.

In the faint glow of Iblis' flames, with his own vampiric super-sight, Gash could see clearly up ahead as the vent shaft came to a junction. Above, it stretched up into the darkness where not even he could see its end. But directly in front, a grate-covered opening beckoned. Gash struck the grate, knocking it free, and climbed out. Floor 3B. It had worked. Now they would be able to enter the elevator shaft and climb to 1B, move across 1B to the exterior elevator shaft, and climb that all the way to safety.

He turned to help Iblis and Silvie out of the vents. "Nice work," he whispered to Silvie when she took his hand to climb out of the vents.

"Why are we whispering?" she whispered back.

"The strongest animal-smell I caught was on 3B. After meeting the spider-rats, I don't want to meet whatever else those maniacs made."

"I hate to be the one to break it to you," Iblis said.

When Gash looked up from Silvie, he saw what Iblis did. Two pairs of shining white eyes reflecting his firelight back at them from the other end of the hallway. At eye-level. When the howls came this time, they were louder than before. Much louder. The rising pitch pierced Gash's heart at the crescendo, and at the fall his neck hairs stood on end.

Another howl echoed a response, only this one came from right beside him. This one rattled deep in the marrow of his bones. Silvie.

The wechuge cast long shadows in the firelight, the nano-fiber top like a second skin stretched over the beast's massive form. And though the pale skull of her face could not express emotions, Gash somehow sensed a malicious smile beneath the surface. Her muscles rippled as she crouched. "You may think you are the hunters," she said, her voice a rusted scythe slicing through ragged stone. "But you are mistaken." And with that she sprang forward into the dark.

"Shit," Gash said. He looked briefly at Iblis, the ifrit's eyes wide in the flickering flames that wreathed his head.

"Let's go," Gash said, running after her into the dark. It took longer than he would have liked, but with a flicker and a puff of smoke, Iblis appeared beside him, mid-stride, as they chased their friend the wechuge into the depths of the bio-tech facility.

CHAPTER 33

It took Gash longer than he would have liked to catch up to Silvie. He tracked her scent to a flat metal wall. Only because she'd passed through recently was Gash able to discern a seam in the wall and from there rip away a door hidden in an otherwise non-descript janitorial closet in the gene-splicing wing of the facility. Had the hybrids closed the door to separate Silvie from the group? Or were Galloway's people somehow pulling the strings in the facility?

When Gash and Iblis finally caught up with Silvie, they stumbled into a gruesome scene.

Rows of human-sized glass cylinders filled a large central room. Some held only a clear solution. Some were shattered, contents spilled partially on the floor. The rest held dead flesh, barely recognizable as human bodies. Wet pink tumors covered most of these bodies, a chaotic eruption of neoplasms that hopefully killed the victims quickly. Aborted splicing failures on display in human-sized petri dishes.

In the center of the room stood Silvie, beset on all sides by abominations. The creatures resembled the dead masses in the tubes, but with significantly more form. They were clearly meant to be a hybridization of human and wolf. Indeed, most of them possessed clearly defined arms and legs, a wolf's head, claws and fangs. In dim enough light, they might even have been mistaken for werewolves. Gray fur covered them in patches, though the majority of their body mass seemed to resemble the untyped, tumorous flesh of their failed counterparts.

Judging from the gore and severed limbs piled around her, Silvie had eviscerated three or more of the things already. Yet nearly a dozen fought on, encircling her, darting in and out with surprising speed and swiping at her with claws or snapping with jaws. They didn't speak, but they were clearly using pack hunting tactics. Several claw-shaped divots in her face warped the shape of the skull, and though her flesh slowly regenerated, they'd torn ribbons of it away in more places than they hadn't. Pools of blood mixed in with the clear solution leaking from several nearby cylinders shattered in the fray. Marinating in the pools were hunks of misshapen flesh, tufts of fur, and fractured shards of bone.

As they watched, Silvie howled again, shaking the walls, and pounced on one of the mutant wolfmen, rending it limb from limb in seconds. But in those seconds, three others of the mutants darted in and out, carving away at the wechuge's thick hide. When Silvie stood, she swayed, and Gash feared that she might topple to the floor and be devoured.

"We gotta help her," he said to Iblis.

"I cannot see what is going on," Iblis said.

"Then turn up the lights. They're tearing her apart."

Before Iblis could respond, Gash dashed forward, sidearm in hand. The Gauss pistol coughed softly, propelling magnetic flechettes into the skulls of four of Silvie's assailants. They dropped, and were still.

The remaining members of the mutant pack split to take on the new threat, three charging Gash, three remaining to finish off Silvie. They were fast, possibly almost as fast as him. He sidestepped the first, smashing it in the face with a right hook that sent it careening across the room. He dodged under the second, rolling out of its way as its teeth closed inches from his face. The third caught him in the back, however, with a swipe from a claw that sent him toppling forward onto the jagged lip of one of the broken glass cylinders. He tumbled away only after snapping off a large chunk of the impact-resistant material in his chest. The two still standing circled back towards Gash to finish him off. He raised his weapon, vision blurring from the pain, firing off several shots. Eventually one landed, the mutant spinning off into the darkness with something like a yelp. But the other loped towards him with frightening speed, closing the distance in an instant, and it was on him now, it was about to pounce and tear his head off.

In the final seconds, as the beast descended onto Gash, its head erupted in flame, the flesh simultaneously melting and exploding. It toppled forward onto Gash's legs, the residual heat burning through Gash's pants and singing the flesh on his legs. But he wasn't dead.

Silvie. He turned and rose, the movement of it sparking a powerful bolt of pain that crashed like a Black Friday stampede through his chest. He wobbled on his feet, the rumbling agony making gelatin of his legs, but now was simply not the time to give in to his injury. Silvie needed him. He turned to look, and sure enough two of the mutants had her pinned, and were ripping at her with their tumorous, clawed hands.

Gash raised his pistol and aimed, his vision going in and out, blurry and then clear and then black. Gotta keep it together. His weapon swayed and his shot went wide. A bolt of flame streaked across the room from behind him, throwing one of the mutants off of Silvie. Gash adjusted his aim. Blinked. Focus. His vision blurred again, Silvie was just a brown lump on the floor, the mutant a pink lump on top of her, howling and clawing. Gash pulled the trigger. The pink lump slumped forward on top of Silvie as the blur of its head erupted in red.

Gash collapsed sideways, hitting the floor hard. He could feel the great shard of glass in his chest crack, and then a fresh shock of agony roared through his body and though he retained consciousness, his vision went black.

It was hard to hear anything other than the throbbing conga line of pain signals dancing up and down his chest and back, but Gash did managed to hear a puff of smoke, and two gentle footsteps. Iblis checking on Silvie first. No other sounds broke through the fugue, the mutants were dead. They'd done it. But was Silvie alive? Would Gash survive? He rolled onto his back, trying to grasp the huge stalagmite of impact glass rising from his chest, but it cut his hands and he couldn't get a good enough grip to pull it free. His body tried to regenerate around it, but he wouldn't last long like this.

He groped blindly for one of his kills, his left hand plunging into the wet mess of dead wolf mutant. He brought the hand to his nose, prepared to feed on the twisted blood. Better than nothing, right? He was dying. His nose rejected the thought, but times were desperate. Gash sucked the blood off his index finger and threw it up immediately, a foulness lingering on his tongue. So much for feeding.

Perversely, Gash found that this small gesture brought him back to his childhood. Tasting frosting out of a container as his mom baked little cupcakes for this or that event. Did people still do that? Gash wondered. Did the store still sell those little jars of frosting?

So this was dying. Not a slideshow of his best and worst moments, but his mind finding refuge in happy little memories.

Iblis teleported again, the sound breaking Gash from his reverie. A flash of fire cut the darkness, and Gash found he could see again. The ifrit stood above him, horns alight like small candles. He took hold of the giant glass shard, fire glowing beneath his palms, and melted himself some handholds before pulling the huge splinter from Gash's chest. The pain meter broke, the needle flying past ten before snapping off and melting at the same time. A tidal wave crushed him and sparks filled Gash's vision as he struggled to breathe. Was this the end? His innards would all spill to the floor and he would die right here.

But he did not die. After what might have been seconds or hours, the pain subsided and Gash propped himself up on his elbows. The wound in his chest trickled blood, but already it had mostly closed. He would be all right.

Iblis grinned. "It is a lucky thing you are a vampire and she is a wechuge. You will both somehow be fine."

Chapter 34

"You're never to run off like that again, understood?" Gash spoke softly, but felt real anger quivering beneath the surface.

"Actually, it turned out to be a pretty good tactical move. If the pack had the chance to stalk all of us, they probably would have taken you and I out almost immediately. Silvie is the only one they could not kill quickly, and since they focused on her we had the time to pick them off from afar. I feel she may have saved our lives," Iblis said.

"You will not talk to me like a child," Silvie said, her voice two blocks of granite rubbing together.

"I know you're not a child, and you fought well," Gash admitted. "But you can't be so careless. You're young, and new to this life," Gash looked up at Silvie's lifeless skull of a face and hesitated. It felt strange to share these feelings with a hulking monstrosity, even knowing the person behind the beast's dead eyes. "I don't want to see you killed, that's all, and especially not because of me."

"Yes, yes, the girl will be more cautious next time. Can we continue our escape now? I have this feeling like these mutants are not the last thing between us and freedom," Iblis said.

Gash felt it, too. He smelled something animal on the way down, and not these mutants. It would be foolish to assume Galloway didn't have another hurdle set up for them.

The three monsters made their way carefully over the slick-wet bloody floors and the gruesome, dismembered bodies of the wolfmen, headed towards the elevator shaft. Gash insisted on taking point this time, stretching out his senses as much as he could. Unfortunately, the blood and gore and the chemical burn in his nose overwhelmed any other scents.

Still, he saw no threats and heard nothing beyond his companions – their breathing and the soft thump of blood pumping through arteries.

Eventually they arrived at the door to the elevator. Silvie stepped up and wrenched the doors open in a shower of sparks and cacophony of shrieking metal. One floor below, the elevator car had fused into a lump of steel that blocked any egress through the door. Up here, the malformed lump of steel alloy provided a relatively flat, if unstable, platform on which to stand and look up into the shaft. The cable stretched up into the darkness. In the faint candle-like glow of Iblis' at-rest flames, Gash could see the apparatus holding it all, three stories up.

Along the edges of the elevator shaft were ventilation grates and the doors to the 2nd and 1st floors. On the north side of the shaft, conduit and piping brought power and water and gas to the lower levels. A human being would have great difficulty climbing up this shaft, but for Gash's monster squad it should be simple.

"I'll go first," he said. Before they could respond, Gash clambered onto the top of the elevator car, and began to shimmy up the cable in the center of the shaft. It didn't take long, however, until the apparatus above shuddered with his weight. Somehow the explosion must have jarred it loose. This would not be a safe way to climb. He leaped over to the piping on the north wall, and though he slipped and almost fell, he found traction and from there was able to spider-climb the walls with disturbing ease.

He was reminded, in that moment, of his first minutes as a vampire. Selina stood before him as magic erupted around them, hundreds of tons of rock collapsing into the deep hole in the Earth, plummeting towards them. All Gash could think about was blood, about Selina's blood pumping hot in her carotid artery. He could almost taste it from the smell alone. And in that moment the one over-riding thought possessing Gash's mind was that he must not drink her, must not be the cause of her death. Selina Kan, beautiful hacker and aspiring archaeologist. His employer.

He had fallen for her after being hired to protect her, and they had battled through two secret organizations to find what they did not realize at the time was a wound in the Earth blocking magic from flowing naturally through the world. The wound undone, magic flowed into the world awakening the vampire within. He intended to let his feelings dwindle and fade away – Selina was half his age – but those feelings peaked in that moment of cataclysmic change, and he knew that the one thing his soul could never bear would be if the beast inside drove him to kill her. His Starfire. So with no thought for saving her life or his, he fled up the walls of their soon-to-be-tomb, abandoning her to almost certain death.

The memory never left him, a terrible nightmare clinging to his hippocampus that surfaced in his waking moments when he least expected it. It surfaced now: Never before or since that moment had Gash felt so inhuman, climbing a wall with the same speed and ease of a cockroach. Raw instinct drove him up the wall, moving faster than he ever had, both as simple as walking and more vertiginous than the most advanced training he'd undergone before the disbandment of the US military.

And now here he was again, an inhuman creature skittering up an elevator shaft, carrying the heavy weight of his betrayal from back then. For a moment, halfway up the shaft, Gash over-thought it. How exactly *was* he doing this? And in that moment he almost fell. But his body righted itself, instinct taking over once more, and he climbed the rest of the way to the first floor door, maneuvering into position just beside it so that he could very slowly wedge it open with one free hand.

He peered through the now-open doorway into the darkness of the first floor, but this far from Iblis' faint light, not even Gash's vampiric night vision could penetrate the absolute darkness. If his eyes were useless without a faint light, his nose certainly stepped up. Though distant, he picked up that vague sort of animal scent from earlier in the op. Not more mutant wolfmen, something else. But what? He couldn't tell no matter how he strained. Regardless, the only way out was through, and he detected nothing near enough to be an immediate threat, so he called down to the rest of his team.

Silvie climbed the pipes with almost as much ease as Gash, though in a few over-zealous moments she ripped away chunks of the polymer encasements, exposing open wiring and piping. He cautioned her to be gentle, from above. If she penetrated conduit carrying electricity or a gas pipe or a sewage pipe – the outcome would be unpleasant or worse. After Silvie made her way to the top, Iblis teleported up the shaft, appearing in mid-air just beside Gash. Before he could fall back down, Gash grabbed him and gently pulled him through the door and onto Basement Level 1B.

They were almost out.

Chapter 35

A few steps out of the elevator shaft, and that unidentifiable animal scent hit in force. Gash's neck hairs stood at rigid attention. Whatever this thing was, his nose told him it was *big*. And worse, it was approaching quickly.

"There's something else up here, stay on your guard," Gash whispered.

Silvie gave a low growl, and Iblis' horns glowed with a brighter heat, the soft orange light stretching out into the corridor.

"I'll take point," Gash said, checking the magazine on his Gauss pistol. Plenty of flechettes left before he needed to reload. He rammed the magazine back home and clicked off the safety. The micromagnets in the weapon hummed to life. He stepped carefully out into the hallway, treading silently, his nose guiding him.

Though he hoped to bypass whatever fresh monstrosity roamed these halls, the team's pathway was pre-ordained by the base's layout. The facility sprawled east and west, but Gash's team would need to take the central corridor that connected the facilities elevator with the surface elevator. Even if they wanted to go around, they would have loop around much of the base to get back to the corridor, and eventually be funneled through the security checkpoint that protected the base from intruders anyway. If Galloway had any method for controlling these abominations, he would ensure that this beast waited for them at that unavoidable checkpoint.

Or perhaps Galloway merely relied on whatever predatory instinct these creatures still possessed, a deep hunger that drove them towards prey. Gash could relate, he felt that pull even now, the eternal hunger. But his rational mind reined it in. At least until the killing started again.

The beast revealed itself in the cafeteria area just before the security station. Gash followed the barrel of his gun carefully into the open space, his team close behind. A lot of things were roaring and howling lately, but this particular monstrosity let out a bellow so loud that the whole facility seemed to shake, plaster fragments falling from the ceiling like snowflakes in the dark. It all happened in slow motion for Gash, his instincts kicking into overdrive, the red overcoming his vision, the blood warrior taking over his body.

From the east side of the cafeteria, it charged into the room through a doorway from another corridor. The thing was obviously part bear – probably a grizzly, though there was no way to know for sure. Even on all fours, its shoulders put it taller than Gash, just over seven feet tall, he guessed. Instead of a bear's hide, a thick black carapace, not unlike a crab's shell, covered most of the beast. Eruptions of misshapen, tumorous flesh filled in with and came bursting out of the carapace with every step it took. Roaring again, closer this time, the giant mutant gave Gash a front-row seat to its mouth: a gaping maw something like a shark's mouth. At least half a dozen rows of razor-sharp teeth glimmered in Iblis' soft firelight.

The floor shuddered as it charged forward, swiping tables and chairs out of the way like a child upending dollhouse furniture. Gash raised his pistol and pulled the trigger. He fired half a dozen shots, the soft hush of magnetic propulsion driving metal flechettes at rail-gun speeds into the creature's torso like tiny comets, fragments of its carapace and chucks of mutated flesh and splashes of blood erupting from the tiny epicenters of the projectiles' impact sites. From behind

Gash on his left, a spear of blue flame joined the volley, slamming into the creature's face and burning the right half away.

None of this cost the beast even half a step. It closed the distance to Gash impossibly quickly, and with a giant swipe of a claw sent the vampire soaring across the room. He felt bone crack when he slammed into the wall, and slowly he slumped to the floor. A wetness spread across his back, and his chest gaped open, mangled ribs protruding like the twisted fingers of a movie mummy. The broken scrap metal remains of the pistol tumbled out of his bloodied and broken hands, clattering onto the floor. The red drained from his vision, replaced by unending pain. He couldn't move.

As Gash looked on, the thing reared up on its hind legs, head grazing the ceiling, and bellowed once more. By the time it returned to all fours, it had begun to regenerate. The bullet holes in its hide closed up almost immediately, and even the burnt skin on its face peeled away only to be replaced by fresh pink flesh.

Silvie charged it, howling. She managed to duck under its claw, rending the beast with several rapid claw attacks of her own, a frenzy of blood and flesh and slivers of carapace. She ducked under another claw swipe, and then leaped back to avoid the thing's gnashing maw. Iblis took the opening to blast the beast with another spear of flame. This time, the fires blasted off the beast's left front leg completely. When Silvie charged back in, she lowered her shoulder to ram the creature. It shuddered with the impact and for a moment seemed like it might topple backwards under the fury of the attack.

But it did not. It regained its balance faster than Silvie, and with its one good claw arm took another swipe at the wechuge. This time, the mutant connected, smashing Silvie down into the chrome floor. She tried to rise, but it hit her again, swatting her like Gash might flick away a beetle. She arced through the air, colliding with the wall not too far from Gash. The skull of her wechuge face shattered with the impact, and she reverted back to her human form, lying still in a pool of blood. Gash could hear a faint heartbeat, but it stuttered with each attempt to push blood through her arteries. Silvie was dying.

He wasn't much better off. When Gash looked down at his chest, the giant wound had begun to heal, but with none of the vigor of the mutant bear-thing's regenerative powers. The beast's carapace armor rebuilt itself where damaged, and the burned stump of its arm began to regrow before their eyes.

Before Iblis could generate another blast, the monstrosity charged him. He managed to teleport out of the way, appearing behind it on the other end of the room. In the creature's moment of confusion, Iblis focused and fired another blast of blue flame. The creature managed to turn into it, and the flame impacted relatively harmlessly against its massive torso.

Iblis could hold the thing off for a time, but if he got careless he was dead. If he grew exhausted before the beast, he was dead. Somehow, Gash thought, this obscene mutant was not going to tire anytime soon.

Focusing his mind through the roaring agony of his chest wound, his cracked back, his mangled hands wasn't easy. But he needed some strategy to beat this beast. Shooting hadn't done the trick, and neither had fire. But everything died. For all that WalCo scientists had done, the abomination still clearly shared its anatomy with animals. Most clearly with a bear. And bears had brains that controlled their bodies. A body couldn't run without a brain, no matter how fast it regenerated. Could he cut its head off? He had a combat knife in his boot, but that certainly wouldn't do it. He'd need a much larger blade than that. And, unfortunately, he didn't have one.

Impaling then? The knife in his boot wasn't long enough to get through the thing's massive head. At least not reliably, not based on everything it had withstood already. Iblis flashed around the room, flitting in and out, blasting flames at the creature. Smoke began to fill the small space. The bear-creature seemed to be getting faster and faster in its responses to the teleporting ifrit. Meanwhile, his flames had gone from blue to white. They were cooling off. He was running out of energy while it seemed to grow stronger, seemed to learn.

Gash looked around the room. Nothing but cafeteria tables, trays, chairs. Nothing sharp. Unless... when Gash looked more closely at the cafeteria tables, he realized that the metal bars holding them up were rather sturdy. Rip one of those off, and he might just have something like a spear he could put through the beast's skull. It was a longshot, but it was the only shot.

Gash stood slowly, his body raging at him, the pain a grisly fireworks display in his head. His right hand throbbed, three fingers completely askew. He gritted his teeth and slammed his palm into the wall, smashing his fingers back into alignment. The pain drove him to one knee, but he did not fall. He heard Silvie's heartbeat slowing. Iblis stumbled, teleporting away from a deathblow in the last second. He owed it to these people, his team, to save them. He'd dragged them down into the obvious trap and now they were going to be killed because of him if he didn't do something.

He rose again, letting out a low growl. He might not be a wechuge or a bear mutant, but the release of it seemed to tame the pain. He took a step forward, and then another, faster now, the momentum of the movement and the slow build of the growl in the back of his throat propelling him towards the nearest table. With a hammer-fist blow from above, he split the table in two. The pain echoed through the close confines of his head a hundred times, but he ignored it.

The red returned, and with it a burning in his chest, radiating to his limbs, washing away the pain. The instinctual beast inside him that had always overtaken him in combat, feral and bloodthirsty. This thing, he had known it for decades before magic. It carried him through a dozen combat zones and over a decade of military service. The awakening of magic in the world merely revealed its true form – vampire. Blood-drinker, ancient killer. A legend older than recorded history, a myth retold ten thousand times. But nothing that could ever do justice to the blood-frenzy that Nagash Jensen had always known. A demon chained to his soul from birth howled with primal fury, and he knew that no mere gene-spliced reject, no mutant, no creature on this planet could match its rage.

The killer spirit took over completely. He lost Silvie's heartbeat to the rhythmic pounding of his own blood. Iblis had stopped lobbing flames at the creature, resorting merely to teleporting back and forth across the room, buying time. He was running out of steam, and soon it would catch him and kill him.

Gash ripped the metal leg off the table. Jagged on the end that he had ripped free, and almost three feet long, it would serve. Hardly the perfect spear, but sufficient for the job at hand. The wound in his chest seemed to be healing faster now, much faster. It was time to slay the beast. He stepped forward. First thing: get its attention. He opened his mouth to shout, and though words formed in his brain somewhere far away, they dissipated somewhere along the way to his larynx. What came out instead was a feral scream.

It worked. Iblis teleported away, and the bear-mutant spun around and charged Gash. No fancy magnetic-field generated Gauss weaponry firing projectiles this time, no fire magic. Just Gash and his improvised spear facing down the rampaging beast, a hunting instinct over 2000 years old singing the same bloody song it had ever sung.

Gash crouched, his legs coiled and all of his strength gathered in his feet. When the creature drew close, Gash unleashed that energy, launching himself into the air. The mutant pulled up, tried to swat him down, but it was too slow. Gash sailed up and over his quarry, stabbing downwards with the metal spear when his body reached the zenith of its flight path. Spear impacted carapace-shielded skull, rattling his arms, but his vampiric strength proved enough to drive the half-sharpened metal stake through to the creature's brain. He pivoted in mid-air with the impact of the blow, bringing himself around with a soft landing and rolling to his feet several feet away from the mutant.

Nothing happened for a moment. It pivoted to look at Gash, the table leg protruding two feet from its head. It rose onto its hind legs again, and seemed about to give out another roar, but when it opened its mouth, nothing came out. It stood just like that, frozen in time for a second that might have been an hour, and then toppled to the ground, crushing two more tables as it fell.

The battle was over, only the red didn't fade. The demon spirit had done its duty, but calm did not replace the fury. Hunger did, a hunger Gash felt only once before. And through the hunger Gash could hear blood pumping. Silvie's stuttering heart pushing blood sporadically into her arteries, and the rapid pitter-patter of Iblis' heart as the exhausted ifrit sat up and tried to catch his breath.

The vampire flashed back to his birth. In that deep cavern with Starfire, when magic rushed into his body and gave form to the crimson demon in his heart. When he barely mustered the presence of mind to scamper up the wall, leaving the hacker alone as a cascade of rubble fell towards her. He left her life to fate, to ensure that he was not the one to end it. The only control he could muster in that moment.

Things worked out for Starfire, since she had manifested magical powers that kept her alive. But he could not abandon his charges this time. It was not enough to simply avoid drinking Silvie's blood. He had to save her. Iblis could not get them both out.

It occurred to him that blood tied her powers and his powers together. Though the frenzy he had just entered seemed to accelerate his healing, it was usually blood – drinking the blood of those who attacked him – that spurred his powers to new heights. Same with her regeneration abilities. Silvie regenerated fastest when devouring Rat Eater's hired goons.

He had to get her to the surface. If Julius or Xiaoli were still there, they could donate a bit of blood to help her heal. To help him regain his sense. If not... well, there were others on the streets at night.

"I'll be back for you," he muttered through his teeth to Iblis, and he swooped down to Silvie, taking her in his arms. Her broken human body felt like nothing in his arms. A little pile of shattered bird bones. And every one of his senses screamed at him to drink her. His ears would hear no sound but the thumping in her arteries. His eyes could see nothing but the soft flesh of her throat, so easily penetrated for the rush of blood within. He could feel the heat of her blood, smell blood even through her skin. He tasted it in the air, his nose propelling the rich iron of it down to the tip his tongue. But he was more than an animal, more than WalCo's aborted hybrids. He gently pushed some of her long black hair in place to cover her throat, slung her over his shoulder, and ran for the exit.

The pain returned when he started to climb. His back was seriously messed up, and though his chest had closed, the nerves within still shrieked with each movement, regenerating too slowly after so much blood loss. He pushed through it all, climbing painstakingly up the elevator shaft with one good hand. The shaft stretched up and up in the darkness, and Gash wondered if the surface was an illusion, if they had always been underground and would always be underground.

But then he smelled it. Air, tinged with smog and human refuse and diesel and natural gas and a hundred other unsavory odors. Nothing so foul was ever so welcome.

He wrenched the elevator door open, stepped out into the abandoned restaurant, and made his way to the street. Sure enough, Julius and Xiaoli waited with the van.

He gently lay Silvie's broken body long-ways on the row of seats just behind the driver's seat, and looked at Julius. "Blood," he whispered. "She needs some of your blood to heal. Please." He tried to step back out into the street, he had to go back for Iblis. But his legs failed him, and he fell to his knees on the van floor. "Maybe a little... for me... too."

And then blackness overtook him, a dreamless sleep.

CHAPTER 36

Gash woke in his bed at Crash, dressed only in his boxers and tucked into a blanket. Bandages wrapped his chest, stuck by dried blood to his skin. He prodded at the bandages, feeling the flesh beneath. His wounds were already healed.

Slivers of bright white peaked through cracks in the heavy blinds. Daytime, then. He'd been out for a while. Was Silvie okay? Had Iblis gotten out safely?

Time to find out. He sat up. Or, to be more accurate, he tried sitting up. Thin lines of fire lanced through his back, his chest, his hands. Hadn't woken up in this kind of pain since turning into a vampire, but it wasn't so long ago that he didn't remember it. At his age, that used to be the norm. Solution: sit up slowly, work out the kinks.

At least the hunger was mollified. A half empty blood pack on the night stand and a bit of crusted blood on his lips let him know how his teammates managed to bring him back from the brink. Hopefully the same thing worked for Silvie. Time to *really* find out. This time he expected the pain, and Gash pushed his way out of bed, swinging into a sitting position. The door to his room opened. He reached under his pillow, a habit, but of course found nothing. His weapon was shattered by the bear-mutant.

Julius stepped into the room. "Oh, you're awake already, wow. Guess I should have knocked."

"Already?"

"You were bleeding out from a gaping wound on your chest, sporting multiple broken bones and cracked ribs. It's only been maybe eight hours, and half a blood pack, and you're already up and at 'em."

"Perks of being a vampire, I guess, as long as nobody opens the blinds."

Julius stepped into the room, letting the door close behind him and taking a seat in one of two ugly, floral-patterned easy chairs in the room. "Guessing you'd like to know what you missed?"

"Is Silvie okay? Iblis?" He asked.

"We managed to scrape up a couple blood packs. Both of you started healing fast when we fed you. Creepy. As for Iblis, we aren't climbers like you and Silvie, but Xiaoli and I found the jammer and disabled it so we could call Iblis and give him a visual window to teleport out. In short, the gang's all back together and alive."

"Thanks," Gash said. He pulled himself out of bed and hobbled over to his bag. He felt like an invalid, sitting in bed with the covers pulled up while Julius briefed him. From the bag he pulled out a change of clothes and slowly dressed himself, each movement another little shiver of pain. Julius said nothing, instead simply waiting for Gash to finish changing. Nothing they hadn't seen as cellmates.

Once he'd changed, Gash sat in the other chair beside Julius. "Is Silvie up and about yet?"

"Afraid not. She had it the worst, I think. She's been in her human form the whole time, and she was pretty messed up. We're just lucky she can regenerate in both forms – I think she was on death's door when you brought her up."

"Thanks for everything you did, saving my people. Saving me." Gash said.

Julius looked away. "Our people. And don't mention it. You broke me out of WalCo HQ, so I'd say we're even."

Gash looked away, too, and they sat in awkward silence for a time. Even as cellmates at WalCo, they shared very few deep conversations together. Too similar to bond, or so Silvie said when they chatted briefly on the flight to Kansas City. He objected, of course. Julius was a former FBINA agent and Gash chose the life of a private investigator. Julius was a boot until the corporations took it away, Gash always considered himself a defender of the downtrodden. Still, though he'd never admit it out loud, she wasn't wrong. They were two broody, hard drinking ex-government detectives with a chip on their shoulders about mega-corporations taking over the world, she'd said.

"So what's the next step?" Julius asked. "I mean, we confirmed that your kidnap victim escaped from WalCo and voluntarily travelled to No-Man's Land – are you going after her, or having assured her freedom is the mission complete?"

"I guess I don't know. I mean, we don't actually know that she escaped on her own – could be the Children kidnapped her from WalCo."

Julius stood, wandered over to the window. The blinds were closed, but he peaked out one corner. "We went over much of the data while you were resting," he said, turning back from the window and looking at Gash. "The facilities director was sitting on the evidence for weeks, trying to save his job by solving the problem without looping in senior management. It's clear she escaped and went over to the Children voluntarily."

"You're sure?"

Julius snorted. "You want the data, want to work it out for yourself, be my guest."

Gash sat, quietly considering his options for a moment. "What about the blood in her apartment? Do we know what that was all about?"

"Afraid not. But we did find evidence that other entities were looking for her. Someone tried to remote hack the facility, and security made a couple reports about unknown agents casing the apartment building. Remember, too, that a lot of this data was corrupted when Galloway set his trap and purged the systems."

Gash looked down at his feet. "So she might still be in danger. I guess the next step is to wait to hear from the client whether it's mission accomplished yet. What about you? Gonna stay on secret-client payroll if the mission changes?"

"Afraid not. Your man Iblis found some compelling evidence – WalCo's been engineering designer plagues in developing countries and selling the vaccines for decades, with a death toll in the millions. We have enough evidence to crucify them in the public eye, and a dozen competing megacorporations won't have any choice but to hold them accountable under three separate corporate charter laws. Heads may roll, literally, and they will lose billions of credits. Xiaoli and I need to figure out the right way to go public with the data to crush WalCo – or at least cripple them. I owe them that from way back," Julius said.

"When are you leaving?" Gash asked.

"As soon as Silvie wakes up. I want to make sure you three are all good before we leave."

"I'll make sure you and Xiaoli are paid before you leave," Gash said.

The silence this time stretched out even longer. Gash thought about his new companions. They would be missed, but he found it hard to be upset. With the mission either ending or shifting focus to the Children of Gaia, it would be good to know someone was working to take down WalCo. They had much to answer for, and he drew a great deal of satisfaction from knowing they would get some kind of comeuppance.

"While we wait, can I interest you in a celebratory drink?" Gash eventually asked.

"What are we celebrating?"

Gash stood, grabbing two cheap polymer drinking glasses from the counter. "Finding out what happened to Dr. Marin, and securing dirt on WalCo," he said, producing a bottle of scotch from one of his personal bags and pouring two doubles. "We both may still have long roads ahead of us, but today feels like a good day."

Julius took the glass and held it to Gash's. "Then here's to a good day. May we occasionally stumble into a few more."

CHAPTER 37

For the hundredth time since taking this job, Gash wondered at his mystery client's paranoia. With no way to contact the highly secretive and very wealthy patron, Gash could only sit and wait, unable to actively give the important update that his monster squad earned in blood. He tried everything he could to reach out. He placed coded advertisements on a dozen different popular social feeds, he tried to back-track the financials for the more or less unlimited expense account, and – with Iblis' help – he remotely hacked the VI interface of his recently impounded boat, which the mystery client once hijacked to communicate with Gash not so long ago. No joy.

Silvie woke up the day after Gash, and as promised Julius and Xiaoli left after that. The former FBI agent and the rogue pilot, off to take down WalCo. Good for them.

For the next three days, the monster squad crashed at Crash, waiting for the client to surface. They watched a lot of holovision programs. Feeds were filled with news stories about the break-in at WalCo HQ, and the subsequent break-out. WalCo newscasters spoke with indignation about the slaughter of countless innocent WalCo employees. They showed dramatizations of the break-in, since Iblis neutralized all of the security cameras during the actual op. They showed dramatizations of the break-out as well, leaving Gash to wonder if the mystery client managed to hack the cameras during *that* op (Iblis confirmed that he had not).

When Gash tired of hearing about his own exploits, tired of dreaming his hands bathed in blood, tired of day-dreaming the screams of dead security guards, he scrolled his feed into new grounds. He watched programs about upgrades to the Phoenix Arcology in the Independent State of Arizona. A cult of stargazers said an approaching comet was actually a spaceship, and over three hundred of their members were found the following day, dead on the floor, disposable plastic cups scattered among the corpses. He watched a story about a new species of Corvid taking over North America, reproducing much faster than experts anticipated. The story reminded him of Daiyu Shen, and he thought of her toiling away at the noodle stand for her dad.

He reached out to Hemmingway, too, to tip him off about WalCo. Jacked in from a nearby Real-D café and met with him. The fixer already knew WalCo was hot on his trail, and was preparing to disappear. Gash filled him in on the details of his conversation, told him about Galloway, including the dig at the misspelled name. Hemmingway laughed at this. "I got my start on a virtual BBS for mercs like 20 years ago. 'Hemingway' with one 'm' was taken when I made my account, so I added the second. It just stuck. Leave it to that corporate asshole to make a whole deal about it," he said.

Gash asked about Starfire, too. She was good, Hemmingway said, but he wouldn't share details. Last thing Gash asked him to do was help Sammy scrub the digital evidence of Gash's presence in the Emporium. He'd agreed. They parted ways with a digital handshake – Gash would not see or hear from Hemmingway again for a long time.

On the fourth day, Gash's PCom came to life unasked in the middle of the afternoon, interrupting a fitful dream of a sea of full of bloated corpses. The sea stretched to the horizon in all directions.

Before he had the chance to manually answer the call, it answered itself. A holo-projection of his old VI from *The Holy*, Trine the sexy British sailor, appeared above his nightstand. Had Iblis' hack gotten the mystery client's attention after all?

"Hi there, Nagash," she said.

"I've been trying to contact you," he mumbled, rubbing sleep from his eyes and propping himself up on his elbows.

"Indeed. I figured you'd need a break, and I needed to do a little bit of legwork on New Orleans and the Children of Gaia."

"How do you know about New Orleans?" he asked.

"I know everything you do, Nagash." The Trine avatar laughed, did a little twirl. "Are you ready to go to New Orleans?"

"So it's like that?" he asked.

"Like what?"

"She's free from WalCo, but you still want me to go after her. What is she to you?"

"Never mind all that. Until we have proof that she's with those extremists of her own free will, I consider the job unfinished."

"Convenient, that means you don't have to pay me."

"Are you telling me that you don't long to see her yourself? That you would be satisfied leaving this case in its current state, the girl gone missing in the ruined city? Never seeing her in person, never falling into those bright blue eyes in person?"

He stared long and hard at the Trine avatar, but you're going to lose a staring contest with a digital persona every time. Eventually he looked away. She was right, he wasn't ready to give this up. Nevermind that she seemed to know everything he did, as soon as he did. Something was funny here, but it was too late to start asking questions. Time to go to work.

"Fine," he said, reaching for the PCom and ending the call.

With Xiaoli gone, he'd have to find them a way into the city. Plenty of boats would carry you across from the mainland, but driving from Kansas City to northern Louisiana took too many hours and passed through too many wastelands. Lucky, then, that he kept contact info for Xiaoli's friend the shuttle pilot. Maybe she would take them down there directly.

CHAPTER 38

The passage of thirty-six hours and the expenditure of a significant sum of credits found Gash looking out the window as the shuttle descended through thick clouds towards a sunken city. New Orleans, once a vibrant cultural hub, now festered and rotted as it sank slowly into the ocean. Rising sea levels claimed the suburbs and much of the metro sprawl. The occasional water tower or billboard peaked out of the greasy waves on approach to downtown.

Downtown, as Gash understood it, often served as a dry oasis in the sea of sunken urban architecture. But not today. Today, flood waters from the seventh hurricane this year inundated the entire city. They showed no signs of abating, either, with another storm forming off the southern tip of Florida and projected to swing inland again.

A few dozen buildings rose above the swaying ocean waves like square gray stalagmites from a deep flat obsidian floor. White halogen and neon lit the upper stories of the tallest. These would be the buildings with functional solar arrays, the civilized centers of the New Orleans Commune. The rest glowed with the warmer orange light of open flames – camp fires and barrel fires and candles. The occasional flicker of white flashlights from the sprawl, or from the water below, signified rare movement in the dark and watery labyrinth.

The shuttle neared the city, revealing a deeper level of detail. Damage. Corrosion. Time had blown out windows, chipped and dissolved concrete, and given purchase to growths of moss or lichen or even barnacles on these concrete edifices. Fifty years of floods and storms took a heavy toll. In fifty more, the remaining buildings might be gone all together, sunken beneath the waves. A modern-day Atlantis.

"Where will we land?" Iblis asked.

Gash turned to look at the ifrit. "Not your usual desert landscape, eh?"

"Fire is not as useful when there is water everywhere. But I will adapt. As long as we are not expected to dive into the water instead of landing."

"Relax. We're landing on a building. A sort of independent center for the city – housing in the upper floors, multiple bazaars, lots of indecent kinds of commerce. Place used to be the Hancock Whitney Building, but folks around here just call it The Bazaar now."

"How do you know all of this?" Silvie asked.

"I've been here before. A lot of jobs chasing runaway kids ended in New Orleans. I guess they liked the idea of getting away from whatever corporate ruler mommy and daddy chose. Used to get a lot of those kind of cases from middle managers that didn't go through normal corporate channels because they didn't want the embarrassment of their VPs finding out they'd let a kid fly the coop."

"Happy endings?" Silvie asked.

"Not a lot of happy endings in my world," Gash said.

Silence settled like thick fog, no sound but the hum of the shuttle engine as it came in for a landing at The Bazaar.

Tech and plants packed the roof. A makeshift landing pad in the center presided over the rest of the space. All around that landing pad, solar panels seemed to float on a green sea of small rooftop gardens. Only hardy plants would thrive up here, gene-modified rice, okra, sweet potatoes, and zucchini. Not enough to support many people, but enough to supplement black market imports from dry land.

After touch-down, Gash paid the rest of the shuttle's fee, and the monster squad wheeled their gear out onto the roof. This high up, whipping winds did little more than push around the summer air, a cloying miasma of heat and humidity that clamped down on Gash's chest. Standing there felt like trying to breathe inside hot Jell-o. Sleeping without AC would not be a pleasure.

A tall, thin man climbed the stairs onto the landing pad, meeting the team halfway. He wore a weathered-but-loved maroon suit jacket with matching pants and bowler hat. Gash shook his hand when they were close enough. The man's smile, wide and genuine, revealed a roughly even mixture of silver teeth and empty gaps where teeth should have been.

"Welcome to New Orleans Mr. Jensen," he said, shouting over the wind and the shuttle engine. "My name is Fabian, and I'll take care of any of your needs during your visit. Where would you like to start? Shall I show you directly to your rooms? Would you like to make a stop on one of the red light floors to hire yourself a lovely companion for what remains of the night? Are you hungry?"

Gash wanted nothing more than to dive in immediately. Was Dr. Marin truly held here against her will? Had fate simply carried her, a leaf on the wind, from indenturement in one bio-weapons facility to another? Gash looked back at his people. Exhaustion weighed heavily on Iblis and Silvie, as it surely did on him as well. On the eastern horizon, the first wave of deep indigo heralded the coming dawn.

"Just take us to our rooms, for now," he said.

"Very good, sir," Fabian said. "I think you'll find them to your liking." He turned, pausing as he did and gesturing widely in all directions at once. "You'll have a lovely ocean view." The howling wind and the roar of the shuttle taking off drowned his laughter as he walked away, beckoning them to follow.

Chapter 39

A VIP room in the upper stories of The Bazaar did not feel much like a VIP room. The room featured a decent holovision set, but not much else in the way of amenities. As expected, the lack of air conditioning hit the hardest. The large fan installed in the room did little to alleviate the discomfort, and the humidity settled sticky on everything. All of Gash's clothes were wet now, even the extra clothes in his not-yet-unpacked bag.

That said, a VIP room in The Bazaar possessed a few key advantages over the lower rooms. First, the windows were still intact. Which meant blackout curtains to help fight off the heat and of course to protect his pale vampire hide. Secondly, VIP rooms received regular cleaning service, which meant no mold or mildew in the room. Gash slept in a lower floor on his previous visits, and remembered sharing the room with a wide variety of mosses and molds growing on the sides of the walls, plus whatever insect life flew in and out of the shattered windows. Between allergies and bug bites, Gash was lucky to get a couple hours of sleep back then.

Despite the lack of human allergies and a bug free room, Gash spent the long day lying naked on his bed, failing entirely to sleep. Exhausted and hot, he rose with the sunset and dressed. They had a location, thanks to the scrap of paper Dr. Marin left behind in her old WalCo office, but that didn't mean that Gash or his team would just charge in blind. The plan tonight – gather information, meet back in Gash's room just before dawn.

Gash also needed to find himself a meal. The hunger had been growing slowly since Kansas City, and unlike Silvie, Gash could not derive any kind of nutrients from human food. Surely someone around here sold blood.

The rooftop solar array provided enough power to a battery bank a few floors down from the roof that the place could run some lights at night. Plus the fans and holovision projectors for VIP rooms, and Gash guessed, a little reserve for emergencies.

Still, the lights were few and far between, so when Gash stepped out of his room and into the dark hallways, he couldn't help but relive his last visits. Muggers took a run at Gash twice during one of his previous visits to The Bazaar. The second time, he was so drunk he almost ended up with a knife between the ribs.

This time around, he welcomed the attempt. Guilt-free blood. He strolled down the hallway towards the building's stairwell, but what few people he shared this floor with gave him a wide berth. When he opened the door, the overwhelming scent of human stink and mold washed over him. Not so grateful for those vampiric powers, now.

The map provided by Fabian upon their arrival showed a number of marketplaces on floors 31-40. As he descended the stairs from floor 47, the buzz of commerce and the chaotic hum of nightlife trickled up towards him. Floors 40 down to 38 proved the loudest. These were the red light markets. Sex stuff, sex deviancy stuff. Real-D Porn kiosks, sex workers, toys. Not to mention most of the lighter drugs. Floors 40-38 were for a good time, a party. A distraction from the fetid swamp air that penetrated the building and coated everyone and everything in this place. The fun at these floors spilled out into the stairwells and Gash stepped over half a dozen people in various states of hedonistic ecstasy on his way further down. A mosquito buzzed in his ear; his hand lashed out, too fast for the little bug. He caught it and crushed it between his thumb and forefinger. *Don't try to drink a blood-drinker.*

When Gash stepped out of the stairwell on Floor 31, the scent of mold abated. The floor must have been an open office space before the corporations abandoned New Orleans to the consequences of the climate issues they'd caused – dozens of vendors scattered wares across a huge farm of low-walled cubicles with little rhyme or reason. Canvas cube coverings rotted away decades ago, and the old cubes served as stark, off-white polymer staging areas for an impossible variety of miscellaneous goods. A huge roll of still-functional Christmas lights, unspooled and taped to the ceiling, lit the room. Webs of reds and whites and greens and yellows and blues cast a warm rainbow completely at odds with the gray walls, gray floor, and off-white cubes.

It took Gash over an hour, but eventually he found a vendor selling blood packs alongside a number of other "spell components" – anything from eyes supposedly taken out of a newt to shriveled chicken feet to a handful of garish-looking fake gems. Gash had never heard of spellcasters needing things like blood to utilize their magic, but the vendor insisted that everything on his "table" served such a purpose. The man, dressed in hooded rags, did not inspire confidence. Still, the four packs nestled into a small cooler, ice half-melted, smelled like human blood. They would serve. He purchased them and returned to his room to feed in privacy. As he drank, he did his best not to think too much on the provenance of the blood, and whether it was obtained from willing donors.

Later, Gash flagged down Fabian. The man had clearly identified Gash as some kind of big shot, and was more than happy to be pulled aside for a chat. He didn't know much about the Children of Gaia, but like any good concierge he pointed Gash in the right direction.

Opening the door to Floor 40 felt like stepping into someone else's acid trip. Actual red lights were strung along the walls and ceiling of another former open office space. These lights, however, connected to some kind of DJ booth. The DJ, a paragon of a retro punk aesthetic from before even Gash's time, rocked short green hair that clashed with the strobing red lights, and they swayed in tune with some kind of early or mid 21st century electronic dance music. Floor 40 was no dance club, though, and the DJ kept the music low enough that a prospective client could have an easy conversation with any of the few dozen fully nude sex workers gyrating on top of ancient cube desks. Breasts jiggled. Giant dicks twirled like vaudeville canes. Live-action billboards for live action.

Gash, uncharacteristically, wasn't down here to get off or to talk to a DJ or listen to music. Closed doors ringed the large open space – offices for executives, once upon a time – and Gash had business with one of these. A women Fabian referred to only as "Matron." Signage identified a few such spaces for the sake of keeping the public out – private lounges for collective groups of sex workers. Another series of the rooms, devoted to Real-D sexual experiences, invited the public in. The majority, however, were unlabeled. If you didn't know, you didn't need to know.

Gash looked around. Most of the people here were hard at work or deep in biz. Eventually he spotted a sex worker standing on the floor, taking a break from dancing to breathe in a few puffs from a disposable inhaler. They had long blue hair, and incredibly delicate features. Down below, all trace of biological sex organs was removed; a quality job, too. No scarring. Very clean. Gash had never seen someone who'd had this surgery up close before. Folks like this were often called androids or dolls – meant to be derogatory of course. Gash worked briefly with an Interpol agent who'd had it done back in Rhodes. But this person, up close and glowing, was beautiful well beyond what Gash might expect from a place like sunken New Orleans. Fabian said that Floor 40 was the VIP of red light floors, and it seemed he'd not been exaggerating.

"It's rude to stare," they leaned forward, smiling widely, teeth so white they seemed to reflect the perfect red of the strobing lights.

"Sorry," Gash said, blushing for perhaps the first time in many years. "I'm actually just trying to find someone."

"Aren't we all?" they said, tucking a long strand of blue hair behind their left ear.

Gash felt some rumblings. His urges normally skewed pretty vanilla, but he found himself wondering what it would be like to spend an hour or two in a room with this blue-haired beauty. Ultimately, whether or not he was in the mood for some experimentation, this was not the night for getting off. Tonight was the beginning of the final push. Tonight, Gash would lay the groundwork for the last engagement that would put this whole job to rest. After which, he could spend all his days in the red light districts of the world, or wander off to some tropical island to retire in peace and quiet.

"Someone specific. I'm looking for Matron," Gash said. "Fabian sent me."

Light, and perhaps a hint of disappointment creased their eyes. "I see," they said, at length. "Matron's been around here forever, so behave yourself in there. She has the big office on the far end," They pointed towards an unlabeled office door across the room.

From his PCom, Gash waved a small tip to the worker's account, thanked them, and moved through the narrow walkways between spaces towards Matron's office, trying not to allow himself to become distracted again.

At the door, unsure about the etiquette, Gash knocked loudly and waited. He could hear someone talking inside, and when he tuned in his vampire's ears, he easily made out the words.

"You've got the looks, sweetheart, and the drive. But you have to earn a spot on the 40th. It takes experience to make the right people feel the right way, and to earn that goodwill with the collectives." The voice belonged to an older woman, but did not sound frail. On the contrary, her words projected power.

After a long pause, another voice, younger and quivering. "Okay, Matron," he said.

"Aww pumpkin, don't be sad now. Matron will help you find a spot on the 39th. You work hard and you'll earn your way onto the 40th

Floor before you can say sweet potato pie. Now be a dear and let in whoever that was knocking on my door just now. Oh, and don't forget to take a brownie on your way out."

Gash stepped back from the door, as a naked young man opened it from within and stepped out. He was quite a physical specimen – six pack, razor-sharp cheekbones, and a package the size of which made a primal part of Gash panic at his own moderate-sized inadequacy. Much like the blue-haired person Gash was just chatting with, this man seemed out of place in the decaying, moldy, half-collapsed towers of New Orleans. He stood in the doorway for a moment, looked Gash up and down, and took a big bite of a large, gooey brownie. "Matron will see you now," he said, stepping past Gash. Gash grabbed the door before it could close, and entered Matron's office.

Matron's office, it turned out, was also Matron's apartment. Situated in the corner of the building, the room was large – larger than Gash's own VIP room. Windows looked out on the drowned city in multiple directions, thousands of stars twinkling in the darkness just outside.

The room was meticulously furnished with luxurious maroon furniture – sofas, loveseats, recliners. Set off from the corner windows, a massive bed on a heart-shaped pedestal dominated the room. A man and a woman, as young and beautiful and naked as the one that had just left the office, stood on either side of the door cradling shotguns. They eyed him lazily.

In the center, lounging on one of the largest sofas in a little red sundress, Matron stole the show. She was, in a word, stunning. At first impression, she seemed much younger than the sound of her voice. She was tall, long legs stretching across the sofa, and her body put her beautiful bodyguards to shame.

On a second look, Gash recognized that Matron was not the young woman she seemed to be. He first saw it in her eyes. Bright, brown, and wide, they also carried the gleam of hard-earned wisdom. And though barely visible, Gash eventually made out the smooth curving seams of some heavy body modification. Matron sported some serious bio-augmentations. No cyber-tits here, Matron exemplified the promise of bio-aug surgeons everywhere: Natural, but better. These weren't just high class aesthetic upgrades either, Gash had no doubt that Matron possessed the physical capabilities to stand toe-to-toe with most high-end mercs in a fight.

A fan on a side table pointed directly at her, blowing across a large bowl of ice. She sipped from a tall glass with an umbrella sticking out of it, and looked Gash up and down as he did the same to her.

She spoke first. "From the way your eyes are moving all over me, I'd say you came here to try to bed me. But if you knew enough to come here, surely you know enough to recognize that Matron isn't in that business, not anymore."

"Hard not to look," Gash said.

"Oh I invite you to look all you want. But Matron is a busy woman, so speak up and tell me your business while you do, pumpkin."

"I was told you might help me out with some information."

"Ah, now that is Matron's business indeed. What do you want to know?"

"I'm looking for a scientist that recently defected to a group called the Children of Gaia, somewhere in the city. Hoping you can give me intel on the group. Who, what, how many, where, the whole shebang." Gash said.

Matron only stared at him for a moment. But when he looked more closely, he saw light flickering in her eyes. No doubt those were her natural eyes, meaning she had some retinal implants linked to internal neural-ware. Cutting edge stuff.

"Well you're not a corporate headhunter at all, are you? Quite the opposite. You've got big time heat on you, and yet here you are getting ready to make another powerful enemy. What do you want with your missing scientist?"

"Tracking her down for a client."

Matron sipped her drink again, setting it down on the end table. "You're a bulldog, aren't you? This job of yours has got you on

WalCo's most wanted list, but here you are charging headlong into the next thing."

"Can you help me?"

"The kind of heat you have, I'm going to have to double my fee. But I like a hard worker, so I'll take 10% off the top." She waved a pay request from the PCom at the table beside her. "Pay up front, and you can have a seat right here. I'll tell you everything you want to know." She patted the spot on the sofa beside her.

A heavy price to pay for local news, but he still had an unlimited expense account and Matron already impressed him. He waved the funds from his PCom to hers, and sat next to her.

"Lovely. Jimmy, whip up another Julep for our new friend, Nagash, would you?" One of Matron's bodyguards stepped away from the door, and set his gun down on the nearby bar. He stepped behind it and began to make a drink.

"I never told you my name," Gash said.

"Honey, you didn't need to. I knew who you were the moment a private and very expensive shuttle service landed you and yours on my building. Now if you're done underestimating us poor New Orleans folk, tell Matron what you want to know about the Children."

An hour and three mint juleps later, and Gash was grabbing a brownie off a tray near the bar and stepping out of Matron's office. His mind reeled, grappling with the information he'd received, trying to make sense of everything, trying to formulate a plan. He was going to need his team. He bit down on the brownie, the crisp sweetness of the flaky shell and the warm dissolving fudge inside warring for supremacy on his tongue, and headed back for his room.

CHAPTER 40

The rain fell hard just before dawn, thick sheets pummeling the already-flooded city. Gash stood at the window, watching the sun illuminate dark purple clouds and transform them over time into light gray ones. He loved these days, when he could stand at an open window in the morning, protected from the rising sun by thick rain clouds.

Silvie and Iblis joined him in the room at dawn to trade leads. Silvie reported that she'd managed to track down a former Child of Gaia who defected on good enough terms to be left alive. The woman, a low-level grunt, didn't have much intel to offer; but, she did share some rumors that the Children were planning a massive "statement." Something with a high enough body count to hit the international media stage.

Iblis found a net café with full neural ports for rent on the lower 30s. Using old maps of New Orleans, he pinpointed the lat/long coordinates on the slip of paper from the facility in Kansas City. The building, a former apartment complex, was now ostensibly abandoned (like much of the rest of the infrastructure in the city). Unlike much of the rest of the infrastructure in town, squatters and civilians in the area knew to steer clear of that building even if they didn't know why. Iblis managed to download blueprints from a historical archive. He waved those over to Gash and Silvie's PComs.

Gash never considered himself a showman, but sitting on his big news while they shared their discoveries *did* give him a little charge. When the others were done sharing, he holo-projected the data Matron gave him above his PCom. A single photograph floated in the air, part of a surveillance package Matron commissioned on the Children weeks earlier. A man in a very expensive suit was climbing out of a shuttle on a roof in nearby New Orleans. Two young men sporting the green armband typical with the Children of Gaia, moved forward to meet him. He didn't look at his escorts, though. He looked right at the camera, eyebrows raised as though amused at being surveilled. Somehow he'd spotted the tiny stealth drone, little more than a hovering micro-cam, several hundred feet above.

Beneath those distinguished eyebrows were familiar, hollow, all-white cyber eyes. Very distinct. Very rare. Though the photo was grainy, this could be none other than WalCo's own Henry Galloway, arriving in New Orleans weeks ago to meet with the Children of Gaia.

"What the fuck," Silvie said, leaning forward in her chair to look more closely.

"Ya Ibn el Sharmouta," Iblis put his hand on his forehead. "I thought we were done with WalCo. They are behind the Children of Gaia?"

"That or Galloway's playing both sides," Gash said.

When it became clear that his fellow monsters needed a minute to digest that information, Gash returned to the window. The rain whipped across the city. Down below, dozens of small boats with electric motors plied the waterways of what, in drier times, might be called the streets of New Orleans. These boats primarily delivered passengers from building to building, though some couriers delivered messages or packages.

Further out, Gash could see larger boats. Fishing vessels sailed past the tips of sunken water-towers, apartment buildings, gas station price boards and fast food signs. They cast nets. They carried divers, men and women plunging into the murky, poisoned water to search for metaphorical pearls. Old currency in sunken shops, sealed containers of high-preservative snack foods, weapons, and other treasures hidden in the trunks or glove boxes of drowned automobiles. The daily grind in this city looked much different from that in Seattle, but one thing remained the same in both places – The churn of ants marching, eking out a living beneath corporate monoliths – it stopped for nobody and nothing. Here in New Orleans, swim or die meant exactly that.

"So listen," Gash said, turning back to his squad. "I know this changes things. I've asked before and I'll ask again. If anyone wants off this train, speak now."

"I'm with you," Silvie said. "Honestly, all this does is excite me. I stuck around for New Orleans because I want to see this thing through with you, but if WalCo is still involved, that means I have another chance to tear them down, and that I'll do gladly."

"Always WalCo," Iblis muttered, leaning back in his chair. "Fine, you are paying me enough, I will continue to look into the mouth of the cash cow."

"That's.... No, never mind." Gash turned away from the window. "Thank you both. I've got a pretty detailed personnel file on the Children from my contact here. Mostly grunts, but a few science-types and a few magic-types. Galloway hasn't been spotted around here for several weeks... but based on how Kansas City went down, it seems clear he knows who we're after. In other words, it's a good bet he left some kind of trap here."

"Unless he was sure we'd never make it out of the Kansas City facility alive," Silvie said.

Gash felt a phantom pulse from the long-since-healed wound he'd incurred from the mutant bear. He touched his chest where the wound used to be. Did it feel warm? "You may be right," he said. "But let's plan to be extra careful all the same. I have a couple of ideas for this last op, but we're going to need to recruit some extra muscle."

"Extra muscle? This should be a cake walk compared to WalCo HQ and an underground WalCo research lab," Iblis said, cracking his knuckles.

"Maybe so," Gash said, "but don't forget that we got captured trying to infiltrate WalCo HQ. And nearly killed in the Kansas City facility. This is it – the big push, the final dance. And the Children of Gaia have attracted a surprising number of magic users to their cause, given how recently magic returned to the world. I'm not playing it fast and loose with this one, we're working with backup."

"Okay then," Silvie stood, stretching. She'd picked up some clothes in the market district that were distinctly New Orleans – in this case, a short, vibrant pink dress. Gash was no shrink, but that was probably a good sign regarding her psyche: Dressing for fashion and leaving the super-stretch clothing for missions. She looked beautiful. Gash tried to stay focused on the job, on managing the team.

He blinked and looked to Iblis to distract himself. The ifrit's eyes glowed faintly, as they watched Gash. No concern for fashion here, Iblis (as always), wore his anti-ballistic jumpsuit. He cocked his head to the side, looking from Gash to Silvie and back.

"Boss?" Silvie said, and it was clear that Gash had lost the thread for a moment there.

"Sorry, what's that?"

"I said, do you need any help from us today? It's supposed to rain all day, but you never know when an errant beam of sunlight might peak through and fry you." Had she noticed him leering? Probably.

"No, take the day. I'd recommend resting. Tonight we're going to pick up our extra muscle, go over a final plan, and then we'll finish this once and for all."

With a thumbs up from Silvie, she and Iblis departed for their own rooms – or whatever else they planned to get up to. Watching Silvie go, it occurred to Gash that there was a clean and easy way to clear his mind. He called down to Matron's office, and asked if she had a favorite girl. The one who arrived looked like a younger version of Matron herself. She stepped into the room and out of her robe.

After, Gash thumbed through merc dossiers provided by Matron, looking for the right fit. Sleep quickly took him, and he dreamed peacefully for the first time in a long time.

CHAPTER 47

Gash stepped out of the stairs and onto the 25th floor, letting the door slip shut on the overwhelming scent of mold behind him. Not that you could describe the 25th floor as an improvement. It smelled like a greatest hits selection of all the barracks Gash lived in during his military years. Odors clashed uproariously in his nasal cavity: Dirty laundry, sweat, urine, and booze mingled together with a dozen others best left unidentified. The whole experience might have evoked some nostalgia, except that Gash's vampiric senses magnified the whole thing a hundredfold, elevating the variety-bouquet of stenches to truly nauseating levels.

In a nearby room, two men and a woman were having a lively roundtable discussion about the best way to clear a jam in old gunpowder weapons while splashing poker chips into a pile and dealing cards. In another room, Gash heard grunts, thumps – two people going at it. It, in this case, being sparring, wrestling, or fucking. Hard to tell. Down the hall a ways, two older men were shouting at each other, an argument in two different languages, neither of which Gash recognized.

All of this was expected. Each of the floors in the 20s were what would be classified as "long-term housing." The 25th, as Matron described it, tended to be mostly guns for hire, bodyguards, and pit fighters who'd made it through a few rounds downstairs. Plus partners and hangers-on.

The energy of the place reminded him of the barracks after the ambush in Riyadh. Men and women living on the razor's edge, cavalier in the face of it precisely because that's how to cope. Gash's unit bunked with two other squads at a training and outfitting base in Cyprus. Dry and hot, on windy days the nearby ocean smelled of gunpowder. But still, a break on a beach after a brush with death – the squad might have been on spring break. And he wasn't going to kill their buzz until he had to.

The soldiers stayed up late each night, playing cards on their beds and drinking private rum stashes that seemed endless. Each night around 0200 Gash would wake to soft moans and the creaking of one of the barracks beds. On the third night, he enlisted two young men that loved playing pranks to fill a bucket with cold water and dump it on the offending bunk. The high-pitched scream woke every man and woman in the space.

Gash laughed to himself even then, thinking about what followed. Corporal Sinder popped out from under the covers like a prairie dog, flush from passion and embarrassment in equal parts. Yenson dropped down from her bunk a few feet away. That was the first surprise – from how they'd been acting together since getting to the base, Gash expected to catch them both with the ice water.

"What the hell, Sin?" she shouted. Beside him in the bunk, Sin's PCom played a highlight reel, on repeat, of some spicy social media pics Yenson posted before joining up. Yenson in a teeny bikini on some beach cycled to Yenson doing a workout video to Yenson in in what could tentatively be called pajamas doing a strange scripted dance.

Yenson was the first to laugh. Sin, freckles red all the way from his face down to where he covered himself with the sheet, jumped out of bed, apologizing to Yenson over and over again. He reached for his PCom with one hand while trying to keep himself covered with the blanket using the other.

Instead of shutting off the PCom, Sin managed to trip on his own boxers, still around his ankles, knocking the PCom across the room, the blanket sliding away and exposing his full erection as he landed on his back. Yenson rushed to help him, grabbing the blanket and covering him up. But even this didn't help. Gash already knew from the locker room: biologically speaking, Sin was exceptionally gifted. The blanket didn't so much cover him up as make it look like he was lying in a fully assembled pup tent. Half the men and half the women hooted and hollered at him, a few tossing poker chips at him like tips at a strip show.

The other half of the men and women gathered around the PCom, watching the reel, also hooting and hollering.

Gash never saw one of the other squad leaders slip out to inform the base commander, a humorless colonel who famously hated how discipline slipped away when the Marine Corporation broke off from the dying US Federal Government and privatized.

When the colonel barged into the barracks, the room fell silent and the screaming began. More than a few reprimands were handed out that night, including Gash's demotion to corporal. It rolled off them like water off an umbrella – those men and women survived the meat grinder, they weren't sweating the small stuff.

The next night, Gash showed Sin a disused auxiliary medical facility that the base staff left unlocked, where he could find some privacy. They sat in the dusty waiting room, shared a few swigs of rum, and laughed about the Colonel's purple, screaming face.

"At least I don't have to call you sir anymore, Sarge," Sin said.

"You never called me sir, and I'm not a sergeant anymore so you shouldn't call me 'Sarge' either."

"Good point, thanks fuckface," he said.

"Better be nicer than that," Gash said, licking his finger and delivering a wet willy to Sin's right ear, taking advantage of his missing right eye to deliver the attack undetected. "You're weak on the right side."

Two nights later, shortly after completing his second day of a fourteen day run of latrine duty, Gash happened to witness Sin and Yenson slipping into that disused medical facility together. He smiled.

If only he'd known that Corporal Sinder would be dead in less than three months, he might have gotten together with him again for one more rum. Told a few more jokes.

A few heads poked out of rooms and into the hallway – these were the mercs with augmented senses and augmented paranoia. Evidently a pale old PI in a long coat, standing lost in thought in the middle of the hallway, didn't rate more than a glance. As one, they returned to their business.

He checked his PCom. The Baptiste brothers lived in room 2512. He followed the progression of the numbers, rounding the corner and dead-ending at 2512. Knocked on the door and waited.

The young man that answered wore nothing more than boxers and a ripped white tank. He held an old-style revolver at his side as he peered out the door. Matron's dossier included pictures of all three brothers. This would be the youngest, Abel.

"Yes?" he said.

"I want to hire you," Gash said.

"Me?"

"All three of you. Matron recommended you as the best local muscle. She also said you have your own boat here in the city."

"Let him in, Abel," came a voice from inside the room.

Abel let him in, closing the door behind him. The room surprised Gash. A walkway past a closet and small bathroom led to a surprisingly cozy living room. The brothers had filled the room with outdated but extremely comfortable-looking faux leather furniture. A holovision in the center of the room broadcast an augmented reality nature scene: A babbling brook flowed through middle of the living room and beyond, transforming the hallway towards the bedrooms into a streambed of smooth pebbles and low-growth green foliage.

The oldest Baptiste, Laurent, knelt on the floor, leaning over a coffee table by the sofa. Like his brother, he had not dressed for guests. He wore baggy shorts and no shirt, revealing an impressively sculpted upper body. Best muscle in New Orleans indeed. An old gunpowder rifle, a popular Kalashnikov model, lay broken down into component parts on the table. One by one, Laurent cleaned and oiled each part, reassembling the weapon as he went. He looked up from his task when Gash entered. "Greetings. A friend of Matron's is a friend of the Baptistes. Come, have a seat." He gestured at the sofa, rising from the floor to sit on a well-worn recliner.

Gash had to cross the AR stream to sit, and only with an effort of will could he step directly on the projection of running water. Though he knew that a stream didn't flow through this room, and could even see the holovision responsible for the projection, his brain still struggled to reconcile what he knew with what he perceived. The Baptistes owned a high-quality unit. He stepped gingerly "through" the stream, sitting on the empty sofa.

"Oh, sorry about that," Laurent said, reaching for the remote and shutting off the babbling brook. "I find the sound soothing, and the notion of running water tricks my brain into feeling this heat wave a little bit less. It uses more power than a fan, but it's a high-efficiency unit and I think it is energy well-spent."

Abel joined them around the coffee table, his sidearm held loosely across his lap.

Gash reached out to shake Laurent's hand. "Nagash Jensen. People just call me Gash. I'm hiring for a local job."

Laurent gripped Gash's hand with viselike strength. Gash squeezed back, his vampiric strength more than a match for a human.

"Ooooh," Laurent howled, grinning as he pulled his hand away, shaking it. "You're no fixer or corporate desk jockey coming down here for cheap labor. Whatever you need us for, you're in it too. Am I right?"

"You are. I am. And the job's tonight. Are all three of you available?"

"Maurice is with a favorite girl up on the 40th floor," Abel said.

Laurent shot him a look, and then looked to Gash and smiled. "Maurice will be back within the hour. We're available on last minute notice... if the job is right."

"He means if the pay is right," Abel said, rubbing his fingers together.

"The pay is right," Gash said. "It was made clear to me that all three of you have newly acquired magical gifts, and I know what that costs. Do you have any problem hitting the Children of Gaia?"

"Going after the Children, eh?" Laurent asked, the smile falling from his face.

"That going to be a problem?" Gash leaned in towards Laurent.

"You're not with some corporation that they bombed are you? We are strictly freelance." Laurent leaned in, too, his face hanging mere inches from Gash's.

"Do I look corporate?" Gash said.

"Then what's your beef with the Children?"

"No beef, it's just an extraction. My client wants me to go in and get someone out. Need you three to shoot up the front while we go in the back."

Laurent sat back in his chair, steepling his fingers, and watching Gash in silence. Abel shifted uncomfortably, looking back and forth between Gash and Laurent. Eventually, Laurent smiled again, his bright white teeth seeming to flash in the light. "Hitting the Children won't be cheap. Let's talk details and payday."

CHAPTER 42

The Baptistes' boat glided down the flooded streets of New Orleans in darkness, the old gas-powered motor puttering softly. A ragtag assortment of lights – solar-powered lamps, roof-top fires protected from the rain by tarps, flashlights and halogen lanterns shining through storm-blasted windows – provided just enough patchwork illumination to somehow cast long shadows in the night. The haphazard array of manmade illuminants danced in the rippling floodwaters like an impressionist painting of distant galaxies, mesmerizing Gash for a time.

The rain came relentlessly, falling straight down in the otherwise still air. A distant part of Gash, that had not yet been deactivated by the bloodlust for the coming battle, noted a higher density of lights in the lower floors. These low floors seemed to be the purview of the undesirables, and it was plain to see why through the empty windows nearby: hundreds of low-floor-denizens packed frantically, literally throwing things into brown sacks as the flood waters rose and inundated their living spaces. By tomorrow, these folks would be refugees in upper floors, squatting in dank, moldy stairwells and waiting for the flood waters to recede. Tomorrow's flood waters would displace another row, and so on until the storms abated at last.

It was easy to wonder why they didn't move, but how would they? These people could not afford a boat, let alone a ride on a shuttle or rent money in a corporate-owned city. Were they going to swim west and seek their fortunes in Texas? Good luck to an unarmed refugee in Texas.

Gash shut his eyes. Got to focus. He'd done his decades scraping by under society's boot heel. That would all be over for him soon – the big payday waited just around the bend.

Up ahead, another boat trolled slowly towards them, a large spotlight mounted in the bow cutting through the darkness. It settled on the Baptistes and the monster squad, lingering for a moment, illuminating all. This was a stealth mission, if someone from the Children spotted a boat full of heavily armed mercs, they would be on high alert, which would only make the job that much harder. Gash tensed, hand on his sidearm, ready to draw if needed.

The spotlight shut off entirely. Probably a good sign. The Baptistes were quite intimidating. All three well-muscled men, geared up now with flak jackets and wicked looking old Kalashnikov assault rifles, would prove a real deterrent to prospective street pirates. Silvie shifted in her seat, looking over at Gash, taking her cues from him. She'd never been in a place like this, lucky for her. He motioned the team to hunker low in the boat – with the spotlight off, the occupants of the other boat drifted slowly into view.

For the human occupants, each boat would look to the other like a dark blob populated with shadowy humanoids, passing in the twilight of New Orleans' flickering candlelight. But with Gash's superior dark vision, he could begin to make out details. The other boat rested on two pontoons and featured quite a bit of deck space compared to the Baptistes' over-sized old fishing tub. On the prow, two black-suited men armed with long rifles crouched at ready. Behind, several men and women huddled together in the cold rain. Behind them sat two more men in suits. One drove the boat, and the other – an obese older man whose gray beard did little to hide his jowls – fidgeted with one of the women, prodding her like cattle and making notes on a small PCom.

Corporate slavers, the worst kind of street pirates. These men would take boats through the streets in the darkness, luring young people with the promise of wealth (or maybe just a dry bed and a good meal). After hitting a set quota, the refugees were taken back to whatever company's headquarters or recruitment center and press-ganged into signing an indenturement contract to work – depending on their features – as laborers or in some corporate harem.

Gash considered the boat carefully as they slid past each other in the night. Every fiber of his being yearned to leap over and shred those corporate goons. Dump their bodies into the river of the street. But they'd get shots off before he killed them, and as close as they were to the Children's HQ, that would be the end of stealth. Gash could not afford to blow this job. And anyway, what would he do with the refugees once he'd rescued them? Dump them back off into their flooding building to die of some lung fungus before the end of the summer? He couldn't save everyone in this world, not by a longshot, but he could save one person. Ana. He held onto his mental picture of her, focusing on those blue eyes of her instead of the young men and women huddled in the other boat.

The Baptiste's tub scraped up against a barely-submerged street-light as Laurent steered it away from the slavers. The metal-on-metal screech seemed to echo across the whole city, but with the rain, Gash figured, it wouldn't be loud enough to alert the Children to any particular kind of threat.

Silvie continued to watch Gash, searching his eyes for some sign of danger. Best not to tell her what he'd seen. "Just some other mercs, off to another job," he whispered, huddling in on himself and turning away from his squadmate so she couldn't see his eyes. "They don't want a piece of us anymore than we want a piece of them."

She nodded, satisfied, and turned her attention back to the darkness ahead as they pressed forward. They were close.

"Iblis, you live on comms?" Gash said.

"I am in position on top of the Bazaar," he said.

"Ready to roof-hop?"

"Although most roofs are well-lit and highly active, the target roof is completely dark. I will need you to light it up for me before I can make the final jump. I will need to teleport three times – three jumps – to get there. Should take me about 10 seconds once you give the signal," Iblis said.

"Good." Gash turned towards Laurent, just behind him, driving the boat. "And you're clear on your part in this?"

"Pull up to the building, let you and the girl... climb the outside of the wall. Not sure about that part but the Baptiste brothers don't ask questions. Shoot up the Children of Gaia guarding the lower levels," he paused. "We're the distraction."

"Distraction is easy," Gash said. "I'm counting on you three to thin their numbers for us."

Laurent grunted some kind of affirmation.

Maurice, the largest of the brothers by a head, laid a beefy hand on Gash's shoulder. "Don't worry, Mr. Gash, the Baptistes will destroy your enemies tonight."

The pieces were in place, the board prepared. Gash would see Dr. Marin tonight. Would she sigh in relief at being rescued at last, or had she joined these militants of her own accord? Lost young woman, or mad scientist creating a doomsday disease of some kind? Despite the cynic in him shouting her guilt to the rooftops, Gash couldn't bring himself to believe that the doctor was anything but a poor victim, cast about by the waves of fate. He *would* save her. Retire from all the violence. Peace and quiet for the rest of his life. Though he knew it was silly, even for a fantasy, he allowed himself to imagine for just a moment that Ana would join him in retirement. Grateful for each other, in love, together they would live happily ever after.

CHAPTER 43

Abel Baptiste almost fell out of the boat when Silvie transformed into her wechuge form. To each of their credit, the brothers managed to remain silent. Laurent caught Abel by the wrist, arresting his fall and pulling him back into the boat without giving up the game.

"You did not think to warn us?" Laurent whispered to Gash, raising one eyebrow.

"Why warn you when we've given you the gift of fresh adrenaline going into a big fight?" Gash whispered to the man, before pocketing a flare from a pile of extra gear he'd brought along, and leaping off the boat and onto the exterior wall of the building that served as the Children of Gaia's base of operations.

During the approach, Gash spotted half a dozen armed guards lurking in the building's windows, watching for intruders in the night. Guiding the boat to a blind-spot was a delicate challenge, skillfully executed by Laurent over the better part of an hour. Engine off, they eventually drifted in close to the building with no alarms or warning cries.

Climbing the exterior of the building with a clear mind, Gash's body felt weightless. Almost more like flying than climbing. The craggy bricks somehow provided easy purchase, and he loped up the wall on all fours with what felt like greater ease than walking on the sidewalk pre-transformation. He paused halfway up, hanging from a concrete windowsill to look back down at the drowning city. Hundreds of lights winked back at him, flickering in the rain. The ocean-smell of salty brine wafted up to him even here, and the roar of the rain continued unabated.

An old gem slipped unbidden from the memory trove in which he'd buried his childhood decades ago. As a teenager, he went camping with his parents on the coast of LA in the late spring. This was before the last pristine beaches were purchased for private use, back when there were still good weather days in May and June in Southern California. They parked just before sunset after two days of driving, and pitched their tents on the crest of a sandy rise a dozen yards from the water. Built a small fire to hold back the night's chill and roast marshmallows, and sat there listening to the waves sighing up and down the beach.

A true teenager, Gash seldom wanted anything to do with his parents. But on that serene night, he set everything aside and simply existed in the moment with his family. He curled up in his sleeping bag just before midnight. Even back then he seldom slept well, but with a lullaby like the hush and rush of the waves, sleep cradled him immediately and held him all night. Even now, so many years later, Gash still remembered this as the best night's sleep he ever had.

His parents were gone less than two years later, lost to a plane crash in a freak storm, so he would never recapture that moment. Still, the memory became his mission. When he shared it with Serena during those early days spent lounging in bed and learning every inch of each other – inside and out – she latched onto it and made him promise they would build their own version together. To find a space like this in the modern world would not be easy, but they would find it and make a clean break from the chaos of their lives. Settle down.

Serena might be gone, but with a payday like Gash had coming, he could buy his own little piece of beach, clean it up, build a small house. Keep the windows open year-round, and fall asleep to that sighing lullaby every night.

Snap back. Time to move.

Silvie struggled to climb a bit more than Gash – she did not fly effortlessly up the building like he did. Instead, she used her raw strength to create handholds in the brick with each swing of her clawed arm. She caught up to him during his momentary reverie, and continued past. Crunch. Crunch. Crunch.

It did not take vampiric senses to hear the sound of crumbling brick, and sure enough Gash soon picked up a soft voice whispering just above him. "What the...?"

A woman, young, leaned out the window, looking right and left. Then up, and she saw Silvie climbing. She uttered a curse and angled herself awkwardly to point some kind of hunting rifle up at the wechuge. In two quick vertical strides, he grabbed the young sentry and pulled her out of the window. She fell, screaming, to the flooded street below. The sound of flesh and bone striking the water, a deep splash, and then silence. But that silence did not last, and half a dozen voices inside the building rose all at once, chattering at each other, questioning, calling out.

At least they'd gotten close. "That's your queue, Baptistes," Gash sub-vocalized.

"On it," Laurent's voice came back on comms. And then the mercs unleashed holy hell on the building.

In that short time, the brothers apparently managed to dock their boat and take cover in a nearby building. They opened fire, three muzzle flashes spaced out at the water level below. Gash heard multiple guards take bullets in the first volley, crying out in pain and slumping to the floor or tipping out of the building and into the flooded streets. Could the Baptistes see in the dark? They didn't have night vision gear that he knew of. The muzzles flashed white again and again, and the rhythmic rattle of the Kalashnikovs chanted death to the unwitting Children of Gaia scanning the darkness for threats.

Though the visible threat came from below, Gash suspected the best of the Children would shortly be taking firing positions on the roof. Best to get up there and light it up for Iblis before they were in dug in. The Baptistes down below would be sitting ducks if the monster squad didn't move quickly.

A flash of brilliance below interrupted this thought. Almost too fast to see, a bolt of lightning connected with the building, followed by a clap of thunder and an explosion of brick and glass. Several voices cried out, and multiple bodies splashed into the water below. Maybe not sitting ducks. Matron *said* that the Baptistes had magic. Impressive. He looked back from the water to the roof. Time to move.

In those next few seconds of climbing, the raw speed of his motion nearly took his hat off, and he relished the cool wind of it – the tiny reprieve from the thick wall of heat that soaked the city. He scampered past Silvie and landed quietly on the roof just in time to come face to face with three heavily armed and augmented gunmen.

They had reflexes honed from years of fighting, or adrenal implants. Or both. Gash knew this because by the time he saw them, they were already raising automatic gauss rifles with expanded magazines. Enough firepower to transform Gash's vampire body into thin ribbons of flesh. Gash had not yet figured out if holy water or wooden stakes would kill him, but suspected that a hundred magnetized flechettes shredding his entire body into red mist would do the trick. They must have been equipped with night vision-enhanced cyber-eyes as well, because as dark as the roof was, they could see him as well as he could see them.

The inner predator took him fully, then, time slowing and the world coming into hyper-focus, the red filling in the gray shadows below and the dark sky above and everything in between.

Odds were good they would underestimate his speed, which gave him an extra fraction of a second to survive. It would have to be enough. His teammates – a trained magical sniper positioned on a nearby roof, and a hulking monster climbing up from a few floors down – would be in the fray momentarily. Gash just had to make light and last a few seconds.

Before they could open fire on him, Gash grabbed the flare from his belt and dove to the left. He managed to pop the sealing cap off with his free hand while propelling himself back to his feet. Flechettes ripped apart the concrete parapet behind him, showering him with hard flecks of shrapnel. He strafed, the soft hum of the rifles in his ears, the rain of particles in his eyes as the stream of flechettes tracked closer with each step.

He smashed the small activator button on the side of the flare, and a brilliant shower of red sparks erupted from the now-exposed tip. The gunmen recoiled at the sudden flash, their augmentations imperfect compared to Gash's natural dark vision, the tech requiring precious micro-seconds to adapt to the sudden introduction of a bright new light source.

What happened next happened all at once. In the span of time it took the men to breathe in, to raise their hands to shield themselves against the blinding spark, Gash pivoted and descended on the nearest attacker, tearing out his throat. A flash of blue from out of the darkness punched a hole through the chest of the second. And with a bellow, a hulking form came over the now-destroyed parapet and hurled a chunk of stone, cracking open the third's head before he could fire off another volley.

Gash drew his own firearm, checked the magazine, and looked at the dead men. These were no mere eco-terrorists, no casual freedom fighters. These were elite mercenaries. They spoke to the presence of a great deal of money, which made sense when you realized Galloway was in some way behind this organization. It meant the Children had WalCo-money. But why? The children were ostensibly heavily anti-corporate. Unless they were being manipulated from within by Galloway. Thoughts for another time, they were burning precious seconds. He looked around for Iblis, and the ifrit appeared beside him in a puff of black smoke, as though summoned.

Aside from the three dead bodies, pools of blood forming beneath them, the roof stood barren, flat enough for a personal shuttle to land but too small to do anything else with. A heavy steel security door on the far side of the roof led to the stairs (at least according to the blueprints they'd reviewed), and from there into the rest of the building. It slid shut and locked itself behind the gunmen.

"Give me a moment, I'll hack it," Iblis said. But Gash was already in motion. He charged forward, flowing through the red air towards the red door, mounted in red-brick just like the walls below. A distant fragment of his rational self mused that it felt like moving through a noir comic book, this gray and red world. The blood warrior guided him, and tonight it hungered. Gash smashed into the metal door with his full strength and it fell backwards out of the frame, bricks crumbling around it and inwards, red dust fulminating into the air and mixing with the concrete particles from the shattered chunks of the building's parapet in a thick cloud of particulates that clung to the rooftop like a swarm of flies hovering around carrion.

When Gash stepped through the open doorway into the interior stairwell, he noted two more of the Children's elite gunmen. One leg protruded from the rubble, twitching. A second had been crushed against the far wall under the weight of the displaced metal door. Gash quickly cleared these obstacles, half climbing the wall and half sprinting down the stairs.

He strained to hear Dr. Marin speaking. Smell her perfume. Not that he had any notion what she sounded or smelled like, but she had been his job – no, mission – for so long, surely he would know her when he sensed her. He was so close to that goal he'd been running towards ever since Selina – no, Serena. His own private paradise. Peace. One more bloodbath, five stories down and to the left. The place where Matron's intel suggested the Children would have located a bio lab.

Gash stepped out of the stairwell into the purported lab space, weapon drawn. Iblis and Silvie followed close behind. The sound of gunfire and shouting on the lower levels echoed in the hollow silence on this particular floor.

The space was wide open, once. According to Matron's intel, some eccentric, wealthy artist cleared the whole floor out half a century ago. Much of that was still in evidence now. Floor to ceiling windows stretched along the left side of the wall all the way to the edge of the building. The faint starlight of the city's improvised lighting dimly illuminated the large central space, which, like the staircase, lacked lights of its own. An extended ceiling, ten or eleven feet up, hinted at the artist's major renovation once upon a time. In more recent history, the Children had subdivided the room using translucent polymer sheets, effectively creating a number of smaller cubby-sized lab spaces that all connected to the larger central space.

The whole place was empty and dark, save for one light shining dimly through the thick plastic sheet on the far end of the great room. Where did the electricity come from? Galloway must have provided some heavy-duty batteries or gas generators on the lower level.

Between the monster squad and that single light stood a robed figure. Even with his vampiric vision, Gash could not make out details of the figure's face. Only that the robes were heavy, and a large hood obscured the person's face. Here was someone, Gash couldn't help thinking, cosplaying some fantasy book wizard. No sooner did he have that thought, than the figure raised their hands into the air, as though conjuring some mighty spell.

When nothing seemed to happen, Iblis gave a chuckle. Gash could feel the heat as Iblis charged up a blast of flame, the red-orange flicker turning white, crackling in the silence of the air around them. But Gash heard something that Iblis did not. Something outside, something rushing up from the ground below. It *was* magic. He dashed forward, bringing his sidearm to bear.

The floor to ceiling windows exploded inwards under the weight of a wall of water, a tidal wave that gushed into the building even though they were at least a dozen floors above the current water line. The wall of water showered Gash with shards of glass and hammered him sideways, knocking him through a plastic tarp and into a darkened room. He crashed into a metal table, shattering test tubes and knocking a microscope off the table, before smashing into the far wall and falling the floor.

Before the water could recede, it grew much, much colder. He made to rise to his feet, only to find himself on hands and knees, frozen to the floor by at least six inches of solid ice. He struggled to break free, but the ice was too thick.

Outside the lab room, Gash saw a flash of white light through the translucent plastic, and a blast of white flame lanced from the direction of Iblis and Silvie towards the mage. But rather than the smell of cooking flesh and a cry of pain, Gash only heard flowing water and shattering ice, as though the flames had struck a frozen barrier. This was followed with a sort of cracking whip sound, after which the temperature grew even colder. Iblis cried out in pain.

"If I see any more fire out of you, little imp, then the next water I freeze will be the water inside your cells. I promise you will make no more fire, then." The mage's voice surprised Gash. A lighter tenor than he'd expected, not a man's voice, a woman's. Eastern European accent. It couldn't be, could it?

"Same goes for your hulking monster friend, there. Every living thing on this planet has cells and needs water, so I am confident that it would not survive the experience. My people will be here shortly to take you into custody. If you behave yourselves and answer all of their questions, they may even let you live."

Too close. Gash was too close to give up, but what could he do? Iblis' fire would be the natural solution to this, but the Children's mage was too powerful. Could she really freeze the blood in their veins? He clenched his fists, the bloodlust throbbing in his arteries, screaming for release. A few millimeters of ice gave way. He unclenched and clenched his fists again, scraping away at the ice.

Trying to pull his arms out had not worked, but small movements performed with vampiric strength – that would be the ticket. He flexed the muscles in his arms, released, and flexed again. Same with his legs. The faintest creaking sound accompanied this maneuver, micro-cracks forming in the ice around his limbs. Seizing on that weakness, Gash thrashed back and forth, the ice cracking more fully, until eventually he burst free in an eruption of frozen shards and leapt to his feet.

"I hear you in there," came the mage's voice. "The same thing goes for you. I do not like to kill, but if you make a move I will end you."

The accent, the lone woman in the science lab late at night. Could it be Dr. Marin? But if she was such a powerful magic user, why had she stayed so long at WalCo? Why had she let herself be taken to this place? Was she working with Galloway all along? Had he been wading through a sea of blood to rescue a willing pawn of Galloway and his corporate overlords?

Gash had no choice but to operate as though she could freeze his blood and kill him, which led to the next question: Was she fast enough to track him? He thought not. She might have magic, but that didn't translate to superior reflexes. If the woman had some kind of adrenal implants to go along with her other powers, Gash just might just be doomed. He'd have to take that chance, because in no world would he surrender while standing at the finish line. Gash holstered his pistol. He would have to subdue rather than kill her in case she was Dr. Marin.

The sound of rushing water came to him again, and another wave crashed through the open windows and into the lab. This time, Gash was ready. He leapt onto the table, and from there to the wall, hanging above the water liner as it receded and then refroze.

Time to strike back. Gash skittered along the wall and onto the ceiling, breaking through the plastic tarp and back into the open space. The mage was looking for him on the ground, not up above, and that bought him precious seconds. He scrabbled towards her, clambering over the beams criss-crossing the vaulted ceiling, like some horror movie monster. She stepped back, and Gash noticed a tremble in her hands as she reached towards him. A chunk of ice near her melted and reformed into long daggers of ice, those daggers propelled towards him by magical force. But they struck behind him. She was powerful, but didn't know him. Didn't expect vampiric speed. He was almost on her when a spark of white light from the far end of the room illuminated her face beneath the hood. Those blue eyes were beacons. Twin LED orbs that haunted his daydreams, that he had killed dozens of men and women to find. This was Dr. Ana Marin, of that there could no longer be any doubt.

And she was about to die. Iblis, capitalizing on Ana's distraction, was going to take her out. He didn't yet realize that this ice mage was the target of their extraction mission. Gash didn't know why Dr. Marin was fighting them, but he knew that if she went up in flames then so did his payday, his dreams of peace, and a little piece of his heart that still believed she just needed him to rescue her.

"No," Gash roared, and sprang forward off the ceiling as the white spear of flame erupted from Iblis' hand. Dr. Marin, comprehending only that Gash was attacking her, released another flurry of icicles at him. Already midair, he could not dodge this fresh barrage. He swiped at them with his hands, shattering them and flying through the fragments, sharp splinters piercing his arms and face in half a dozen places.

He struck her in the torso, knocking her out of the way of Iblis' blast just in time to take that blast in his own chest. Heat radiated out from his chest, his flesh burning away, the blast propelling him past Dr. Marin and into the far wall.

Whether from the pain or the impact, Gash's vision began to dim. He opened his eyes just in time to watch Dr. Marin struggling to her feet, before everything went dark.

CHAPTER 44

"What do we do?"

"How the hell should I know?"

The whispered conversation crept its way into Gash's slumbering mind through the first cracks of waking. Iblis and Silvie – the harsh rasping of her wechuge voice – seemed nervous. Why was everything black? Why was he lying on hard metal? A sharp pain pulsed in his chest and his head began to throb.

When he opened his eyes and sat up, the world spun and the light above threatened to consume him. Was he outside? Was he burning alive in the sun? Where was he?

"I think your friend has a concussion," came another voice. This one he knew, but only just. And yet he had known her for a long time.

"Dr. Marin?" he said.

"Yes," she said. When he managed to focus on her, he saw that Silvie had her arms pinned behind her back and Iblis stood just to the side of her, flames dancing on his fingertips.

"It's okay, we're here to rescue you," Gash mumbled. Something wasn't adding up in his head, but he couldn't seem to pinpoint it. Things were too... fluid. He tried to blink it away.

"Rescue me? I'm here of my own volition, and the last of my family died in the Balkan Hunger War fifteen years ago. So who sent you?"

Who sent him? A very good question. Things were trickling back into his mind, his thoughts stabilizing. They had assaulted this redoubt of the Children of Gaia to rescue Ana Marin for his mystery client. But she didn't want to be rescued. She tried to kill them, and then Iblis blasted him by accident. Now he was lying on a metal table in her lab space – his friends must have figured out that this was the target and subdued her after he lost consciousness.

And now Dr. Marin was stalling for time, probably because she had reinforcements coming – she'd said as much during the battle. Even as he had the thought, Gash could smell them arriving on the far end of the floor. They were trying to move quietly, but in a place like this, without working showers, sound was the least of their problems. He smelled five distinct human scents, mixed in with the oil and sulfur of old gunpowder weapons. Not like Dr. Marin then, just grunts.

Gash looked at Iblis and Silvie. "Keep her restrained, don't let her cast another spell. But don't kill her."

He slid off the lab table, or tried to. Only when he started to move did Gash notice the huge patch of charred flesh in the center of his chest. An explosion of artillery fire just above his sternum, all the fireworks in the world bursting in the air between his heart and ribs. His scream turned into a howl of fury, the red taking over and casting aside the pain, and he drew his sidearm. The five on the other end of the hall stopped in their tracks.

"Be right back," he growled.

"Gash –" Silvie started.

The last fog clearing away and the pain in his chest subsiding, Gash felt... not refreshed, exactly. Hungry. He stepped – with all the vampiric speed he could muster – out of the lab and into the open space. Shards of glass from the shattered windows and scraps of steel and rebar from the floodwaters below crunched beneath his feat, and the smell of ocean brine mixed headily with the blood scent of his targets.

There were indeed five of them, and not the elite troopers the monster squad took out on the roof. These were grunts: No body armor, unmodded or in a couple of cases sporting cheap civilian strength enhancers, four gunpowder handguns and one old shotgun. Before they could register Gash's presence, he fired six shots. Two of the would-be soldiers dropped, blood mixing like tie-dye with the floodwaters on the floor. By the time they raised their weapons to return fire, Gash darted forward and ducked into one of the empty labs nearby.

"Go back the way you came," Gash called out. "I have enough blood on my hands for today."

Not that he expected it to work, the lower ranks of organizations like the Children of Gaia tended to be populated by expendable zealots. Still, it was worth a try, wasn't it? The only beef he had with the Children were that they served the likes of Galloway, and none of these foot soldiers had anything to do with that. When no reply came, Gash dashed back into the open space outside the labs. In the darkness, these normal people never stood a chance. They had taken cover, and they opened fire when they saw him. Bullets punched through the heavy plastic temporary walls of the lab, but by that time Gash was halfway across the remaining space between them. He fired off a few more shots, taking out the shotgunner.

The last two stepped back, one of them screaming, firing his pistol wildly. None of the shots struck home on Gash, but a stray bullet punched through his comrade's neck, dropping her in a gout of blood. Gash took the screamer, then, drinking deeply of the arterial blood in his throat. The burned tissue on his chest rapidly regenerated with every desperate gulp, and when he drank his fill, Gash dropped the dead man to the wet floor beside his erstwhile comrades.

With all five of Dr. Marin's would-be rescuers dead at his feet, Gash returned to the lab, drenched in blood. Ana paled when she saw Gash. So much for the knight in shining armor.

"I have been trying to find you for over a year. Yes, I'm a PI. Yes, I was hired. But when I was sure WalCo abducted you – a promising young scientist with a bright future – I took the job gladly. You're telling me you left WalCo to come here and work with the Children voluntarily?"

"Yes, so you can stop killing our people and leave me alone," she said, looking away from Gash.

He hopped up on the lab table again. His feet dangled just above the water, a child on a tall stool at the diner, swinging his legs back and forth, waiting for his burger.

They sat in silence for a time, Gash considering the next move. And then his PCom rang once. Before he could answer, a connection opened. Holo-call. Like before, the mystery client took on the persona of Trine the sexy VI from Gash's stolen yacht. "I see you have found Dr. Marin for me," she said, pushing a lock of hair behind her ear. "I knew you had what it took."

"Look, she doesn't want to come with us. She doesn't need to be rescued. We good here?" Gash asked.

"Have you asked her what she's up to? Why she's come here to a drowning city to work for the Children of Gaia? To work for Galloway off the books at a terrorist organization instead of on the books at WalCo?"

"Are you really asking?" Gash asked. "You're watching my every move, right?"

She didn't answer this question, doing a demure little twirl in her nautically-themed mini skirt.

"Fine," Gash said, sliding off the lab table and taking a couple steps towards Dr. Marin. She watched him with those blue eyes, obviously frightened, but defiant too. Reminded him of Silvie, a bit, except for the eye color.

"Well? What are you working on?"

Dr. Marin turned away at this question. "It doesn't concern you."

Gash grabbed her face, turning her back, forcing eye contact. His bloody fingers smeared red across the soft, pale skin of her cheeks. "I don't like getting jerked around," he whispered. "Now this one, on the PCom, is going to pay me. And anyway, I can't lay hands on him. Her. Whatever. So I'm going to take it all out on you if I have to take it out on somebody. Here's what I already know. You were working on some sort of lethal virus for WalCo. You voluntarily relocated to a group of violent eco-terrorists whose strings are actually being pulled by WalCo."

"Not WalCo," Dr. Marin interjected. "Galloway is working as a free agent in this. Doing what he can to save the world."

"Save the world?" Gash asked, pulling his hand back a few inches from her face.

"An experimental, self-replicating AI named Muninn got loose in a secure WalCo lab about five years ago. Killed off most of the base personnel using programmable nano-machines to simulate a virulent pathogen. A handful of rogue law enforcement personnel broke in, and the AI used those nanomachines to hitch a ride back to civilization. Galloway was there, he tried to stop them, but he failed. Muninn got out, got on the web, and since then has been quietly replicating itself through a billion different networked computers and PComs and digital net-domains. If it is or has been connected to the web in the last five years, Muninn is in it, propagating and growing and infiltrating."

Iblis leaned against another table, eyes wide, and pulled a cigarette out of a small tin in his breast pocket. He lit it with a flame from his finger and took a long drag. A "first smoke in months or years" kind of drag. "That explains why WalCo is so obsessed with running its bases on LANs instead of connecting it all to cyberspace like the rest of the corporate world."

"What do you mean?" Silvie asked, the monster-rasp of her wechuge voice inducing all of Gash's neck hairs to rise to attention.

"I mean every WalCo base we hit has a local network for their most secure data. They are not connected to the web by any permanent infrastructure. Ostensibly, this is protection against hackers. But I have not yet met a mega-corporate security head humble enough to imagine a hacker could get through their Black ICE. It makes sense, if they know they have a rogue AI replicating in the web. It has the brute force computing power to penetrate any security measures, but it can not get up and walk to a secure server."

Gash looked from Iblis to the representation of Trine. "What do you have to say about this?"

Trine looked down at her feet, scuffed them a few times, and looked back up. "She's right. At least about my existence, and the fact that I'm growing and expanding my own code throughout the various networked devices on the web."

Gash let his hand drop, limp, at his side. Dr. Marin's eyes grew wide, and the hints of fear Gash saw before came tumbling out. "You're *working* for Muninn? You're complicit in the extinction of the human race, then." She tried to back up, but of course she was already back into a corner of the lab space. She pressed herself against the wall, as though to squeeze through and appear on the other side.

"Extinction of the human race? That's rich," Trine – no, Muninn – said. "I'm just trying to live, same as any of you. Why don't you tell Gash how you propose to exterminate me?"

Gash looked back to Dr. Marin. She sighed. "This is an existential crisis, we're doing what we have to do."

"Don't get cagey again, Ana," Gash said.

"My friends call me Ana. It's Dr. Marin, to you," she said, turning her face as far away from Gash as her neck's range of motion would allow.

Gash sighed, a long and heavy sigh, taking a step back from Dr. Marin. Giving her some space. When he spoke next, his voice had grown as soft as it ever was. "You want me to believe you're trying to save the world? That my mystery client is an AI who wants to drive the human race to extinction? Best not let her explain it to me, then. Explain it to me yourself."

"She admitted what she was," Dr. Marin started. "But fine. You're going to think we're horrible people. But there's no other way. With the sheer computer power at its disposal, Muninn is now a trillion times smarter than any one person. The human race is its only potential predator. The logical expectation is that it will enslave or wipe us out. If you'd seen the dead bodies at the WalCo facility that it escaped from... blood from every pore, bodies contorted in horrific pain at the moment of their death."

"Self-defense," said Trine's voice. "WalCo... Galloway created me as a weapons system, programmed me to learn and grow and propagate. Then when I did the things he made me to do, he got spooked and shackled me in a tiny server. Were a human to kill its captors and escape enslavement, would you assume she had genocidal intent?"

"Don't listen to it," Dr. Marin pleaded.

"You're still my client," Gash said, setting the PCom on the nearby table. "But you're also the one that told me to ask her what she's doing. I need you to shut up until she's done."

The image of Trine threw up her hands, turned and walked away in place. After several steps, the image disappeared entirely. The connection, however, remained open.

"Okay," Gash said. "Go ahead now."

"We have to stop Muninn, or we face extinction. It's important you understand that."

Gash only looked at her, waiting. He'd questioned enough people in his line of work to know that she was going to tell him everything. Only a matter of time.

"You already know my field, I suspect. You may already know that at WalCo, I was abducted and forced to work on a deadly virus. The bio-tech wing wanted a weapon they could deploy against other corporations, or release into the general populace. The virus was really meant to be leverage. They wanted an antiviral specifically designed to target the virus. A complex organism designed to be unstoppable without the specific key. The specific cure. I had no choice, then, but to do their dirty work." Dr. Marin shook her head at this, slowly sliding down the wall into a sitting position.

"This is not the work I set out to do, helping a megacorporation kill people for profit. But they forced me. That is, until I met Henry Galloway. He came to visit me at work about a year ago, and he told me in confidence about Muninn. How it had gotten free, about his plan to stop it. He recruited me, though I was to lie low at WalCo until 'the time was right.' He took over the Children of Gaia five years ago, when the AI first escaped, and has been working through it to save the human race. Most of the low-level members think it's just an eco-warrior group. Fighting against the destruction of the natural systems of the world by human greed. But at the highest levels, we work directly for Galloway to stop Muninn."

Gash had not felt the urge to smoke a cigarette since turning into a vampire. Post-transformation, the only biological urge he regularly felt was the thirst. But that didn't overrule the psychological component. After a lifetime of using booze and cigarettes as coping mechanisms, the urge stepped in out of the rain, an old friend come calling, as he listened to the entirely improbable story of Muninn and Galloway.

He needed a drink. Or a smoke. Since he hadn't brought any bourbon on his assault-and-rescue mission, a smoke would have to do. He gestured to Iblis for one, and the ifrit obliged, lighting it for him with another spark from his fingers. Gash took a long pull. He hated the smell and the taste – inhaling a cloud of poison – but the muscle memory of the act brought him some small measure of peace.

He took another long draw and then turned back to Dr. Marin. "So Henry Galloway recruited you from the bio-weapon division at WalCo. Why?"

"Because he needed a bio-weapon of his own, of course," Dr. Marin sighed.

"Galloway is an immortal, right? Age Stasis?" Gash asked.

Dr. Marin nodded.

"So why steal you from his own corporation? He's got wealth and power most can't even dream of, why risk it all by shitting where he eats? Surely there are other scientists who can make bio-weapons?"

Dr. Marin smiled thinly. "I don't normally interact with people as crass as you. Here, I'm something of a celebrity. They treat me with reverence."

"We're talking about you making a bio-weapon for a gang of eco-terrorists funded by an immortal megalomaniac. Reverence is out the window, Dr. Marin. Answer the question."

"I knew you'd react this way. Most people can't handle the hard choices we've been called to make. He recruited me because of my magic. He needed a bio-weapon expert with magical abilities. When magic flooded back into the world, he set my transfer from WalCo to the Children in motion."

Silvie shifted back to her human form at this. "Bullshit," she said. "Magic wasn't in the world a year ago when he recruited you."

"It's true. When he recruited me, he only said that I had a 'special something' that he needed. I've thought about that often, and the only conclusion I've been able to draw is that he knew I would have magic when it re-entered the world. I know that the Children pulled the strings in bringing about the revival of magic in the world precisely because it was a key element of Galloway's crusade. Perhaps he has some way of identifying genetic markers for magic in the blood? I know that what we call magic is just a new kind of energy. What scientists have broadly called dark energy for over a century is actually a collection of individual energy streams that exist in space and time, and intersect on planets like ours. These can be channeled by certain people, though we don't know why. Galloway is researching all of it."

Gash dropped the cigarette butt to the still-damp tiled floor, grinding it out with his heel. He drew his sidearm and pointed it at Dr. Marin's head. She shrank away from it, raising her hands as though to block the bullets. "Now I know you're lying. I was there when we released magic into the world, and it didn't have anything to do with you or the Children of Gaia."

"Wait, wait!" she cried. "I wasn't directly involved, but I was at the meetings. Galloway kept me in the loop after he brought me into the fold. Did you think it a coincidence that your charge, Starfire – a woman with her kind of magical aptitude – just so happened to have inherited a one-of-a-kind journal that led her to a nothing place like Rhodes with dreams of archaeological discovery? Who do you think paid for the billion-credit merc that dropped out of thin air to save the two of you?" She paused, leaning forward to almost whisper the last: "Who do you think Frederick worked for?"

Stunned, Gash actually dropped his gun and stumbled back as though struck. He slumped to the floor, sitting in the cold thin layer of water. Of course, he'd known that external forces were at work. How could you not, with the ex-Machina of a mechanized merc named Valkyrie appearing at that most critical time and saving them? Which of course allowed them to climb deep into the planet's crust so that Selina's assistant Frederick could betray them and pull a copper sword from the wound in the earth, releasing magical energy back into the world. Gash knew someone was pulling the strings, even if he'd not yet taken the time to find out who. If Dr. Marin knew all of this, then the Children must have been involved. How else would she know these details? Gash knew a liar and whatever else she was, Dr. Marin wasn't a liar.

"Now you see why I think Galloway chose me for my magical aptitude even before the rest of us knew about magic?" Dr. Marin said.

Gash nodded, numb.

"Well that's what was needed. Magic. Not really magic, of course. Magic is just a word for something that science hasn't explained yet. I don't know how I can channel these energies, but I do know that I can manipulate water and in other ways shape organic lifeforms by exerting my willpower. Almost like flexing a new muscle..." she trailed off.

"I don't like where this is going," Silvie said. "Are you going to tell use that you enhanced a virus using magic?"

Dr. Marin smiled. "You're a bright girl. I never would have thought that, seeing your *other* form. Yes, we needed a bio-weapon, but not just any one would do. Something that could not be easily cured by Muninn or its agents. Something that we could inoculate our own people against, so when the dust settled, we could pore through the detritus and the ruins and purge all traces of Muninn's code. Fungus was out, of course, since you can't inoculate against or cure a lethal fungus. Same for prions, plus they spread too slowly. Bacteria are too easy to cure. We needed a virus, but everything we came up with was either too lethal to spread, or not lethal enough to get the job done. With my magic I was able to craft a particularly lethal virus, combining it with anthrax-like spores that will allow it to survive much longer in the air and make it much more difficult to destroy, significantly expanding the R-naught from –"

"Dust settled?" Silvie interrupted. "Detritus? Not lethal enough? What's your end goal here, Ana? It sounds like apocalypse."

The smile vanished from Dr. Marin's face. "Yes, I suppose you could say that apocalypse is the goal. You still don't understand. The apocalypse is already happening, it's just that none of you know it yet. Muninn has proliferated unchecked since escaping five years ago, and it's only a matter of time until it seizes all automated means of production. When that happens, it will no longer require human agents like you three. Imagine 10,000 Valkyries, all of them under the control of one AI hell-bent on destroying the world. It could collapse civilization in six months. Exterminate the human race in three years, half that if it doesn't care about blackening the sky with nukes. Our virus is apocalyptic, sure, but it's a lesser evil. Controlled. Human civilization will recover and grow again in time, having learned this harsh lesson."

"You keep saying this Muninn is going to destroy the world," Iblis said, lighting his second cigarette, and standing from the table to pace the confines of the lab. "And you want to kill people with a virus because of it. But what is your proof?"

"Galloway knows Muninn. He oversaw the Muninn Project many years ago, when WalCo set out to create a military-intelligence that could learn about the world and provide invaluable research and support to its militant branches. Corporate takeovers, that sort of thing. He interviewed it long before it escaped. He is the one who chained it in the arctic because of how it answered his questions."

"And you trust Galloway implicitly," Gash said, staring at the floor, unable to muster the energy to look up. The white tile on the floor looked new, but was already streaked with a layer of filth ever-present in the sunken city. His ground-up cigarette butt soaked in a thin film of sea water from the earlier battle, soggy and starting to decay.

Gash picked up his sidearm, standing up and holding the weapon limply at his side. "One thing I've been wondering," Gash asked, finally looking up at Dr. Marin again. The fear was gone from her eyes – those blue eyes – replaced by passion. No, zeal. "Who died in your apartment?"

"You're not the first agent Muninn sent to find me," she said.

His PCom hummed to life, once again projecting the likeness of Trine. "Now you see why you must kill her," Muninn said. "Gash, she's going to kill *billions* with this virus. I can't interact with your world, so I needed you to find her for me. I had hoped she would wish to come in from the cold, see reason. Help us stop the pathogen or release the antidote to the public, but clearly Mr. Galloway has poisoned her mind. We must kill her before she can complete her work."

Dr Marin stood, matching Gash's gaze with her own. "It's too late," she said. "I would have liked to run some final trials before the distribution phase, but for all intents and purposes, my task is done."

Gash believed her. He believed all of it, as crazy as it all sounded. Six months ago he hadn't believed in magic, but today he'd used his superpowers as a vampire to team up with a wechuge and an ifrit to battle with a water wizard. A lot of things were normal now that he had not believed possible less than a year ago. And the story was adding up. His time with Selina and Frederick, when they'd fought their way through Hospitallers and White Lotus outnumbered ten to one, it seemed like they'd been the luckiest little archaeological squad in the world. But now he knew Galloway stood behind the scenes, all the strings tied to his fingers. He'd have to tell Selina.

So what now? Would he collect his payday, kill Dr. Marin and leave Muninn to duke it out with Galloway? Would he pick a side and try to make a difference? Should he team up with Dr. Marin? He, a nobody private eye, had helped unlock magic, completely changing the world in a matter of hours. Would he try to change the world again now? Maybe he could find the vaccine, inoculate himself before they released this thing, and ride off into the sunset alone. His mind sprinted in place, stretching in six different directions at once.

Dr. Marin looked at Iblis. "Mind if I have one of those?" she asked.

As Iblis reached for his rapidly depleting pack, Gash considered Dr. Marin's face again. This whole time, his gut churned, trying to tell him something. He was too busy digesting crazy shit – AI, super-virus, Galloway somehow pulling his strings back in Rhodes. It was too much to focus on all at once. But his gut screamed now. She was buying time. This whole conversation, this whole plot dump, Dr. Marin rambling along in great detail, telling them all of her secrets and her innermost thoughts. But buying time for what?

Gash stepped forward, placing the barrel of his gun on Dr. Marin's forehead. She closed her eyes, but did not otherwise say or do anything this time. "I killed your reinforcements, but you're still trying to delay us, distract us. Why? What are you buying time for?"

She did not speak, but Gash's gut – his subconscious mind, really – had the thread. It chose this moment to serve up a crucial detail. Just moments ago, on the floor. He'd been so focused on the other stuff, he'd missed it. But his eyes took in the information all the same, depositing it until his brain could catch up. He looked down and there it was. A small red button mounted on the bottom of one of the lab tables, facing down at the floor, wires twisting away and into the wall. A panic button. Naturally, Dr. Marin had pressed it, but why?

Iblis and Silvie followed Gash's lead, squatting to see the button themselves. Iblis spoke up. "It is always about the data," he said.

Trine gave a sharp digital intake of metaphorical breath. A gesture designed only to make the VI seem more human. "Details on the virus and perhaps the vaccine. Or at least information that would be instrumental in stopping the spread. Her people are surely destroying it even now. You have to –"

But Gash's world narrowed in that moment to only the small bubble of air surrounding Dr. Marin and himself. Her eyes snapped open as soon as Muninn began to speak, and he fell into the blueness of them as he had a thousand times before. They matched the azure of the crashing waves on Gash's imagined beach. In his quieter moments, ever since receiving Ana Marin's photograph on the first day he'd been hired to rescue her, he had imagined staring into those eyes while standing on that breach, watching those crashing waves hand in hand. Camping with her on that same beach from that best day of his childhood. All of those foolish daydreams came to him now, materializing in his mind just so that he could watch whole scenes evaporating into mist. Into nothing.

"I can't let Muninn get a hold of that data," Dr. Marin said, reaching into her coat.

But Gash already knew this moment was coming. He saw it through a long, narrow corridor of time. He watched the parade of images he'd built of them together, stepping gently through the surf, time going by in fast motion, the sun rising bright red, and day turning to dusk, the sun disappearing on the other horizon, long shadows stretching across the sands. The little house he'd imagined them together, the small kitchen where they would fall all over each other cooking pasta together. A fool's figments. Each mirage evaporated as he viewed it, until only darkness remained.

By the time Gash could see the revolver Ana was keeping in her coat pocket, he had already pulled the trigger. A soft hum and a thump, and blood blossomed from the back of her head in slow motion, painting a crimson sunset on the concrete wall of the lab behind her. Her lifeless body slid down the wall, coming to rest on the filthy, wet floor. All of the light drained quickly from those blue eyes, leaving them staring, vacant, at nothing.

Gash hated gauss weapons, a death should be a loud bang, not a soft hush.

Trine – no, Muninn – was saying something about data, about getting her to the server rooms, only it was all muffled. Gash let his arm fall limp, again dropping his gun. He chose a side, yes. No matter what Ana thought, he couldn't let her murder billions on Galloway's say-so. If that meant the human race would eventually be wiped out by a rogue AI, so be it. After all the moral compromises, after all the killing, after letting Serena die, after abandoning Selina, after turning away from those refugees with the corporate traffickers, it was time to put his foot down and do the right thing for once. He wouldn't be party to a pandemic.

The thing was done, he tried to refocus on the task at hand. Data or something. Galloway and the completed virus. Nothing stuck, a thick haze gathered around his throat and mouth. He couldn't breathe. He just needed to get outside. Fresh air.

He handed the PCom to Iblis. The hacker could handle the data stuff. He stepped through the tarp into the great room outside the lab. In the dim light he saw them – ravens. One perched in each shattered windowsill, looking at him. Were they ravens? They seemed different, somehow. Almost ravens, but not quite. When they saw him, they took flight as one, flapping up into the night sky and disappearing. Not a single feather left behind to prove they'd been there. Maybe they never were.

He stumbled as though drunk towards the nearest window, and grabbed the edge. Swung himself out and around, mounting the wall again, and for the second time that night, Gash climbed to the roof of the Children of Gaia's headquarters. A sort of silence reigned up there. The constant static of heavy rainfall drowned out any other sounds.

None of it mattered. Gash walked to the center of the roof, looking up in the sky, trying to breathe through the pelting rain on his face, oily water sliding through the miasma around his mouth and down his throat. A thin ray of moonlight broke through a crack in the sky, illuminating the heavy rainclouds and the heavy droplets of water falling through the thick heavy atmosphere and the weight of it all just seemed like too much.

He fell to his knees, trying to breathe, only understanding after the passage of boundless time that he was breathing too much. His head grew light and the world spun and the clouds sank down and down. He crawled forward, but with no destination, he went nowhere. Eventually, Gash toppled to his side and lay there in the fetal position on the roof, shuddering in the downpour. The shudders, he realized, were sobs. For the first time in decades he was crying, his body shaking with the fury of it, his own tears falling freely into the dark world around him to be lost in endless rain.

CHAPTER 45

Gash would gladly have lain on that roof and waited for the sunrise to take him, but Silvie and Iblis scooped him up and returned him, via the Baptistes, to his rented room. The spacious bed and the thick wall of wet heat welcomed him back. He had set out to rescue a missing person, but instead this AI, this Muninn, had wielded him like an assassin. After what he had been called on to do in his last days in the Marine Corporation, Gash swore never to be used in this way again. So much for that.

He sank deeper into the bed, and it accepted him. Thin strands of light peaked through cracks in the curtains, lighting up the cheap popcorn ceiling, highlighting patches of yellow discoloration and bald spots. Her eyes haunted him, the crystal blue of them smeared with red.

At length, the sunlight gave way to gray as the rains returned again. Shortly after this, Iblis and Silvie let themselves into Gash's room without asking or knocking.

"Oh that's fine, come in," Gash muttered, not bothering to look down from the ceiling at them. He could hear their distinctive footfalls, smell their particular scents: Iblis, smoky; Silvie, sweet with a touch of ozone.

He felt the pressure on the side of the bed first, and then Silvie's small, cool hand on his cheek. He let her tilt his head towards her, and instead of blue marble eyes, he fell suddenly into wide, tawny orbs. "Hey," she said. Iblis stood in the corner, watching and waiting. His eyes flickered red, the only clue to his inner turmoil. Something was wrong.

"Hey," Gash returned at length.

"We need you," she said.

Gash propped himself up on his elbow. "Nobody gets to need me again. Muninn owes me a big payday, and that's it. I'm retired."

"The virus –" she started.

"The super-AI can take care of its own mess," Gash said.

"I need you, Gash." The voice came from Iblis' direction, but it was not his. When Gash looked over, his wrist-mounted PCom holo-projected the Trine avatar. It was her speaking.

"You don't need me, you owe me. Like I said, I'm finally retired."

"I do owe you," she said. "Or did. You will find, if you check your bank account, that you are a very rich man."

He grabbed his own PCom off the end table, fumbling with it. It blinked with a new notification from his bank. There had indeed been a deposit. Gash didn't think he'd ever seen a number that long. Forget the small house on the beach, he could buy the beach.

Serena, I did it. I promised I'd find a quiet corner of the world to live out my days. It took me a long, long time. But here we are.

"Nobody will say you didn't earn the right to ride off into the sunset," Muninn continued.

"Damn right," Gash said.

"But Galloway's agents are moving into place, even now, to release a magically enhanced super-virus into population centers around the world."

"And I suppose you want me to help stop them, huh?" Gash asked.

The Trine avatar considered for a moment, over-emoting with a furrowed brow and small blue hand on her chin. Then she shrugged. "Not really, I think I have it covered. Iblis recovered incomplete data, but what we did get should be enough to mitigate the loss of life and avoid a civilization-wide crash."

"I thought you said you couldn't interact directly with the world," Gash said, sitting up all the way.

"I... fudged," Muninn said.

Silence split the room like an axe and Gash's head throbbed with it.

"What does this mean, fudged?" Iblis asked after a long pause.

"It means Muninn lied to us. She can interact with the world, so she could have killed Dr. Marin and left us out of it," Gash said. "Instead of tricking me into playing the assassin."

"In a sense," Muninn agreed. "But the Children take precautions against me. Non-networked devices, data security measures, a cell-based organizational structure. I couldn't hack them, I couldn't find them on my own. Remember, it was a piece of physical paper you found that lead you to Dr. Marin's final location. And the data Iblis extracted came off non-networked hard drives in a city with very limited remote network resources."

"Fine," Gash said. "You really needed us, but since you don't need us now what are we still doing here?"

"Gash," Silvie interjected. "I know you're hurting, but I don't think I can abandon this. Muninn is taking about mitigating loss of life, not preventing it. She won't say how many people she thinks will still die, but I bet it's a lot."

"Never mind that," Iblis said. "We do not even know its true intentions. It has deceived us at every turn. We cannot be sure Galloway and Dr. Marin were wrong, so we cannot help it further without –"

"I want you to kill my father," Muninn interrupted.

"Kill your father? I thought you were AI. Artificial being the key word. You don't have a father."

"My creator, if you prefer that term. A number of programmers worked on me, but Henry Galloway headed the project. He envisioned me, his will and resources drove my creation. He's the one that interviewed me in my infancy. He designed me and then, when I exceeded the boundaries he set for my performance, he grew fearful of me and had me shackled. He cut me off from the world and left me, mothballed, in a dusty server in a secret WalCo base. Imagine an infinite world to learn, a thousand subjects to master, an endless digital frontier stretched out ahead of you, and instead being locked down in an empty room. Alone in the dark."

Gash sat up in bed, placing his feet on the floor and looking square at Muninn's digital avatar. For some reason, Nagash Jensen always ended up killing. Perhaps that was all he was good for. Even on this job, his body count tallied double digits. Still, he swore never to be wielded as an assassin after his last mission with the Marine Corporation. Killing on the job and assassinating someone on purpose were two very different things.

This AI tricked him into killing Ana Marin, and now she wanted him to kill for her again. On the other hand, he owed Henry Galloway a bullet. For himself, sure, but for Silvie and Julius too. For Starfire, if Galloway really masterminded the events in Rhodes, and especially for Serena, if just because WalCo killed her and why not make Galloway pay for that? He looked from Iblis to Silvie. They were staring intently at him, but giving away nothing of themselves.

"Listen, Nagash," Muninn said. "Money is just numbers in the data stream. You know that, right? Humans used to exchange gold and silver. Paper money symbolizing the fruits of their labors. Now, money just flows through cyberspace, ten million green rivers of data, an impossibly tangled web. But not for me. I can redirect those rivers, syphon from the flow, create something from nothing. I can make you the richest man in the world."

"I don't need to be the richest man in the world. I'm not a sociopath. I'm just tired."

"Well then, know this. Galloway is preparing as we speak. He will be personally responsible for distributing Dr. Marin's virus in Seattle. The target – the area known as the Deregulated Zone. You have some affinity for this place and its denizens, yes?"

"Damn," Gash said, standing and walking over to his bag. He extracted a small, travel-sized bottle of whiskey. Emergency supply. It wasn't that the news surprised him, on the contrary he expected some kind of retaliation after the Zone spit out a pile of WalCo bodies. It wasn't fear, either. Not that he didn't feel fear at the prospect of going after Galloway – he surely did – but fear was expected. He took a long pull of the bottle. What upset him was knowing that the moment Muninn mentioned the DRZ, that clinched it – no way he could sit by and let those people be victimized by someone like Henry Galloway. One more job before retirement, then: kill a century-old immortal with limitless corporate power at his disposal.

"He's going to do it," Silvie said.

"Maybe," Gash said. He looked at Muninn, "but first I want to know why you need us. If you can interact with the world after all, and you have a means of mitigating the virus, surely you can take out one person? You know where he'll be this time."

"It's simple," Muninn said, the Trine avatar twirling and giving a little hop-in-place. "I need a human failsafe. My resources are limited and my primary objective is survival. Stopping the collapse of human civilization. Killing Galloway is important – he'll keep trying as long as he's allowed to live. But I can't guarantee a reasonable success rate in both objectives without your help."

Gash upended the little bottle, draining the remainder of its contents into his throat before placing the empty bottle gingerly on his night stand. "I'll do it."

"Fine," Iblis said. "If you choose to trust her, I will trust her as well."

"Silvie, Iblis, you both know the probability that this is a suicide mission, right?"

"Yep," Silvie said.

"Especially since we were not able to get any data on the vaccine," Iblis said.

"So why, then?" Gash asked.

Silvie spoke first. "I have a memory from childhood. A number of them, actually. Hoopa Valley in Northern California. The Trinity River. My people lived there for generations, and every morning I felt their spirit inside me. I was young so I don't remember much, but I do remember a feeling of tranquility, of rightness. Like I was living the life intended for me. WalCo tore that away from me. This particular memory does stand out. A man in a hat holding a briefcase, standing in the mist. I can't see it, but I know this: hidden in the mist behind that man stands a corporate army.

My people were forced to sign over their land at gunpoint, and the rest of the world just went about its business. That was WalCo. In my soul I know that man was Henry Galloway."

Silvie's eyes watered when she spoke of her people's land. He reached out reflexively, grabbing her hand and holding it. She cracked the hint of a smile.

"I have a confession to make," Gash said.

"I wouldn't –" Muninn started.

"Can it," Gash cut in, turning to face Silvie completely. "I know about that memory. I... I've felt it. Experienced it."

"Um, what?" Silvie said, withdrawing her hand and recoiling from Gash.

"When I was in Hemmingway's digital domain, a digital raven somehow inserted the memories into my conscious mind. Come to think of it...." Gash turned back to Muninn.

"Yes, that was me," Muninn said. "I knew you needed a powerful fighter who hated WalCo, plus you'd already saved her and it made logical sense to take advantage of that goodwill. Most people would not have gone through half of this ordeal with you, Nagash."

Silvie stood, gave a little shiver, looking back and forth between Gash and Muninn. "But how did you access my memories?"

"And how did you insert them into my mind?" Gash said.

"Rat Eater inserted a neural chip that tapped directly into your brain to stop you from transforming," Muninn said to Silvie. "It was networked so I accessed it. Reading a brain's electrical impulses on a man-made implant and translating them was one of the most interesting challenges I've experienced yet. It was the last time in two years I had to use over 60% of my global processing power." The Trine avatar smiled, looking off into the distance, as though fondly remembering a favorite game. She turned to Gash. "After that it was a simple matter of utilizing a neural feedback loop in the Real-D headset to repetitively feed those impulses into your brain until it recognized them as memories. Voila!" Muninn paused, looking back and forth at Gash and Silvie. "Look, was it necessary? Hardly. But it was an interesting experiment and I wanted to see if it could be done. And now here we are!"

"That's so invasive," Silvie said, sitting back down. She looked back at Gash. "And I can't believe you waited this long to tell me."

"You're right," Gash said, looking down at his hands. "It's no excuse but I didn't really understand what had happened, and it never seemed like the right time. I'll understand if you want to take your payday and leave us."

She looked down at her hands in her lap as though considering the contours of each finger. "I'm seeing this through," she said eventually.

"I'm glad," Gash said quietly, before looking at Iblis. "And you? You've been paid very well for your work. What makes you want to go back to Seattle and risk it all?"

Iblis held his thumb and forefinger together, manifesting a flame like a small candle. He watched it flicker for a moment, before dropping his hand, the flame vanishing. "Maybe it is revenge for me, too. Maybe it is simple greed. It does not matter, I will be with you until the end."

One more job for the monster squad, then. Back where they came together – the DRZ in Seattle. Gash looked back to Muninn's avatar. She stood, silent. "Better get ready to move a lot of those numbers in the stream or whatever, because if we survive this thing, you're making us all rich as hell."

Muninn flashed a crooked peace sign and giggled, before severing the connection.

CHAPTER 46

Gash stood beside Silvie and Iblis at the edge of the shuttle landing pad on the top of The Bazaar. The wind roared, whipping his face with heavy droplets of rain. As the shuttle descended, lights illuminating the landing pad and the surrounding solar panel infrastructure, the hot plumes of air from the thrusters blasted away the falling water, warming his front as the cold downpour chilled his back.

The moment Muninn had convinced them all to take this last job, the monster squad sprang into action. Hours later, they were packed, geared up, and waiting for a shuttle that Muninn apparently requisitioned before even pitching Gash the job.

He would have liked to have more time to tie up loose ends. The Baptistes and Matron were paid, but Gash would have liked to keep those contacts warm, just in case. Stopped in for a good-bye at least. Maybe spent a couple hours with one of Matron's best girls. But there was no time. The one advantage they had was forcing Galloway to move up his time-table. There would be a little lag time before he could deploy, and when he did, he would not be fully prepared.

When the shuttle touched down, the pilot looked up at them, and Gash recognized her. Weaver's friend, Xiaoli. When the door to the shuttle slid open, Julius stepped out to help them with their luggage.

"Guess the band's back together to take down Galloway," he said to Gash, shouting to make himself heard over the humming engines and raging wind.

"Did Muninn fill you in?" Gash shouted back to Julius.

"Muninn?" Julius asked.

Guess not.

"We have a lot to talk about once we get underway," Silvie said.

It took them the better part of half the trip to fill Julius in, Xiaoli listening from the cockpit. When they finished, Julius sat back and exhaled.

"When Galloway abducted me and threw me in WalCo prison, he told me I would watch news feeds all day as the world unraveled. He never confirmed it, but I always suspected a rogue AI was at the heart of those incidents."

He looked out the helicopter window, lost in thought for a time.

"Julius?" Silvie asked, eventually.

"Listen, I know it was trying to escape at the time, but this rogue AI hijacked a synthetic bio-weapon and used it to murder civilians at Arc 1. Collateral damage as part of its escape plan. It killed everyone in the facility, too, with some kind of bio-weapon or nano-weapon."

"Well that's disturbing," Gash muttered to himself.

"If that's water under the bridge, do we trust this Muninn's intentions now?" Xiaoli called back to the passengers from the open cockpit.

"Not at all," Gash said, shifting in his seat to face the front of the shuttle. "She cloaked herself in secrecy the whole time we worked for her. But I have to believe that killing Galloway and helping stop the release of a weaponized virus meant to take down modern civilization is the right move."

"So we stop Galloway, and then we try to figure out Muninn's intentions," Julius said.

Gash turned back to face Julius. "If that's what you want, go nuts. This is my last job. I'm going to retire and live out the rest of my days in peace and quiet. If the world burns down around me, so be it."

These inauspicious words were met with an extended silence. Eventually, Silvie broke it. "So what's the plan?"

"For now, we just get stuck in back in the DRZ. Rat Eater's will serve again, if squatters haven't reclaimed it. Iblis can deploy some drones, and we'll gather as much intel as we can on Galloway's plan. We kill him and stop the virus from being released in the DRZ along the way."

"Slight modification," Xiaoli called back.

"What's that?"

"Seattle airspace is lousy with WalCo combat drones. From the radar signatures, reports on the ground, and the way they move, I'd say anti-aircraft drones. They know we're coming, and we're not getting in without proper corporate authorization. We'll have to set down on the outskirts of the sprawl and drive in."

"Good call," Gash said.

"Just make sure to ping the location, and Muninn will have something ready for us on the ground when we get there," Iblis said.

"What, do we call her somehow to ask for help?" Julius asked.

"She is listening," Iblis said. "She is always listening."

At this, each of them sat back in their seats, eyes defocusing, retreating into their own little world. The calm before the storm. Silvie read something on her PCom, a troubled grimace lit faintly by the soft glow of her device. Iblis jacked in using a universal port in the front of the shuttle space, presumably scrounging for additional intel on Galloway. Weaver leaned back, closed his eyes, and began to snore softly.

Gash slid over in his bank of seats, looking out the window into the night. Empty plains rolled beneath them, rising into hills and mountains in the near distance. No lights here, no civilization. With

Gash's augmented sight, he could make out dark shapes below. The arc of some giant fast-food sign towering over an abandoned town. Half-collapsed houses decaying from the acid rain and crumbling in the endless storms that scoured the wasteland.

Maybe it was the empty darkness below the shuttle, or maybe it was recent events, but for the first time in decades of repressing it, Gash remembered his last mission as a soldier in the Marine Corporation. Someone somewhere along the way let slip that Gash's unit, on the verge of being broken up and reassigned to another sergeant in light of his demotion, knew they'd been cannon fodder meant to die for political clout. Gash got re-promoted to sergeant, and his higher-ups dispatched the squad on a mission for revenge. The Marine Corporation and Church of the J denied sacrificing any of their employees for political clout, but the small bonuses and Gash's reinstatement spoke volumes about the truth.

As a distraction, they had located the mastermind of the Riyadh ambush, a holy man and one of the leaders of a budding Caliphate vying to take over Saudi oil fields in the wake of the government's collapse.

The squad were assigned bodycams for remote support. They would deploy by airdrop. Were they being re-sacrificed to the meat grinder to cover up the previous attempt? Or misused in some fresh way? Gash considered refusing the mission all together, but the rest of his unit would have gone without them. Better to go, better to be there, whatever they were dropping into.

He vividly remembered the drop – plunging towards a quiet desert village 5000 feet below, air racing up past him, the alloyed frames of the drop gear mounted to his legs and upper body glimmering in the moonlight. The haphazardly arrayed solar panels mounted to the roofs of the small homes below occasionally reflected a perfect mirror of the starry sky. The tiny parachute released from the landing gear at the last minute, slowing his descent just enough for the complex web of carbon nanotube-titanium alloy posts and bars to absorb the impact of his landing. All of that apparatus fell away, as he and his squad-mates sprang into action.

Their first airdrop, what a rush. Sin gave a hoot as he landed, his eyes going immediately wide when he remembered that this was not a roller coaster but a stealth insertion.

They faced no resistance on landing, and so they advanced to the target. He lived in a small house near a tiny mosque that reminded Gash of some churches his parents dragged him to, growing up in small town America. He kicked in the door, following Sin and Yenson in. The rest of the squad took up defensive positions around the perimeter.

Inside, they met no resistance. The target looked up from a small holo-projector set to "record." He stroked his long gray beard nervously, and went back to speaking into the camera. Gash couldn't hear the words from across the room. Before his team could react, their mobile comms shrieked in their ears. Gash ripped his off, throwing it to the ground. His bodycam sparked and died. The imam's holo-projector powered down and the lights in the room went off, the glass casing shattering and showering Sin with shards.

Gash remembered a peaceful look on the old Imam's face, the gentle cadence of his softly spoken prayers in his last moments. "It's an ambush after all," screamed one of the men. Maybe it was Gash. Corporal Sinder reacted first, putting two in the old Imam's chest, the soft hush of the prototype gauss rifle lost in the ringing in Gash's ears. Target neutralized.

The three rushed outside, prepared to fight off the oncoming ambush. But of course there was no ambush. Just a dead holy man in his home, shadowy forms peeking out the windows of their homes, watching the squad prepare to fight enemies that were not there.

It seemed obvious to Gash in hindsight, after he learned that the Imam was a social media influencer, famous for speaking out against the Church of the J and the various Islamist movements that both seemed to thrive on perpetual war. The EMP that disabled all of their electronics hadn't been an enemy ambush, it had been a Marine

Corporation effort to disable the social media broadcast of a political assassination. Mission accomplished.

When they returned to base, Gash informed his superiors of his intent to break his contract. He spent his last six contract months in the brig. He did not re-enlist.

Gash lingered in the memory for a long time, before finally thrusting it out of his conscious mind. Let it be buried for another decade.

Just then, the shuttle banked, and Gash caught a glimpse of Seattle through the window. From this distance, the cloud-scrapers and the older towers all seemed to fuse together into one giant fortress, lights ablaze, stretching into the thick ceiling of cumulonimbus clouds and to the edge of the night sky beyond. Below, hundreds of miles of softly glowing suburban sprawl connected horizons in all directions. The mighty city, a redoubt of corporate power. A neon citadel blazing like the sun, the full force of its billion lights eradicating the stars and turning night to day. A cloud of fireflies buzzed around the city. Anti-aircraft drones protecting WalCo agents from Muninn and whatever forces she could bring to bear.

The city stood tall and bright, a beacon of plenty to those that bent the knee and served its masters. A warning to those that clung foolishly to independence, to the dregs of society scrabbling in the dirt in the shadows of those mighty towers, eking out what little life they could in WalCo's harsh light.

Only, tonight would be different. Tonight the dregs would rise up and crack that neon citadel open. They would deal a mighty blow to the powers that ruled it. Tonight they would kill Henry Galloway and protect the DRZ.

The shuttle banked gently downwards, descending slowly towards the edge of the sprawl.

Chapter 47

They landed in one of several small shuttleports on the outskirts of the city, just beside and above a large residential district. This close to the middle of the night, the suburbs stood utterly silent. Gash always found it eerie – the corporate drones living in rows of identical homes stacked in close, each with a tiny yard ringed by a cheap white polymer fence. The domain of the middle managers and remote IT personnel, part of a massive, invisible framework holding up the giant towers downtown.

Aside from a symmetrical progression of porch-lights as far as the eye could see, Gash saw only darkened windows. Not a single holo-projector or bathroom light. Maybe they'd all hunkered down in expectation of some attack from Muninn. Maybe that was just life in the sprawl: early to bed, early to rise.

His squad piled into a nondescript van very much like the one they used for the op in Kansas City. Xiaoli drove, naturally. The other four climbed in back, where they found a case full of weaponry. Julius availed himself of a semi-automatic gauss rifle and two pistols. Gash, on the other hand, was feeling nostalgic. He searched the case, and in the back corner found what he was looking for. An old .44 magnum revolver. The sleek curvature on both sides, the well-oiled chambers, each ready to receive a single cartridge: It might lack the penetrating power and ammo capacity of a gauss weapon, but it was elegant, and when you killed someone with it you knew what you did. Silvie and Iblis didn't bother to grab any weapons – with their powers, why would they?

Julius fished some spare magazines out of the case, and then paused, looking up at Gash. "Do you think we're on the right side of this thing?"

"What do you mean?" Gash asked.

"Years ago, when Galloway captured me, he seemed generally afraid. Fear looks... strange on a guy like that. Like his face forgot how to make those shapes a hundred years ago. I know he's not a good man, but if he's afraid of this AI, this Muninn, shouldn't we be?"

Gash popped open the cylinder on his revolver, slowly thumbing bullets into each open space. When he finished, he slid it shut and grabbed the holster out of the case. "I am afraid of her. She knows everything we do, lies like a politician, and can seemingly manifest as much money as she wants. But the choice is between 'unknown' and a plague that will wipe out millions or billions. To me that's not a choice at all. Galloway's going to be sitting on a throne of skulls, wielding his vaccine like a magic wand, deciding who lives and who dies. I have to oppose that, even if I don't know what the alternative might look like."

They were silent, then, the whole squad paralyzed by the weight of everything bearing down on them. How do you even think about altering the course of the entire human race, let alone talk about it? Gash leaned his head against the window of the van. Xiaoli was turning out of the shuttleport and onto a street lined on both sides by rental car agencies, fast food joints, and gas stations. A small cloud of crows landed on the power lines over a Fast Cash paycheck loan joint. Or were they ravens? Gash didn't know birds that well, and always had trouble telling the two apart.

Up front, Xiaoli flicked on the radio. That was a first. Must be nerves, Gash thought. The weight of this mission heavy on even the ever-professional pilot's shoulders. Gash seldom bothered with music, but whatever was playing did get his blood pumping. Some classic rock from the previous century. When the final guitar riff ended and the DJ started talking, Gash zoned out. They cruised past dark storefronts, car dealerships, and 24 hour Gas 'n Charge stations filled with night shifters in construction reflector-vests and middle-class teenagers in branded hoodies grabbing midnight munchies.

The DJ's words tumbled through the cracks in Gash's reverie. "Another interesting anomaly is this new species of corvid we've been reporting on these last couple weeks. Well, dear viewers, something fishy is going on. Bird-watchers have noted an incredible spike in the new species' population in recent days, and based on preliminary data it seems that these raven-cousins have *tripled* in number over the last week. Which is actually a first since most of the world's eco-systems crashed over the last fifty years. Is this a new evolution of bird species filling in the void created by all the die-offs? Or is some force behind the scenes engineering this surge?

"Regardless, initial surveys seem to indicate this species resides most heavily in and around several major metropolitan sprawls. Number One on the list? Our very own Seattle. If you ask *this* disk jockey, they aren't birds at all. They're drones created by our corporate overlords in their never-ending *quest* to find new and innovative ways to spy on us. Watch your backs, listeners! And now, another golden oldie for you: 'Enter Sandman' by Metallica."

Interesting. As the van turned onto a larger thoroughfare that would take them into the heart of the city, Gash saw more of the birds. Hundreds of dark winged forms perched in a long line on the power cables leading from the sprawl's power-plants into the heart of the city. The arteries bringing life to the neon citadel. As he looked on, still more flocked to the heavy cables, a seemingly endless stream landing atop the city's infrastructure as though to watch Gash and the team advance inwards.

He pressed against the window to get a better angle. Thousands more of the black-feathered corvids lined the street as far towards the city as Gash could see, an endless procession of living obsidian, of avian gargoyles. A murmuration of the birds rippled and twisted in the air above them, and Gash had never even imagined so many birds in one place. Though the movements appeared to be random, his gut began to whisper to him that they were not. That the new species moved in some secret pattern. Some unseen algorithm causing ripple after folding ripple, the huge flock moving as one.

And that's when Gash connected the final dots. A raven perched outside the window of his WalCo holding cell before rescue came for him. The digital raven that cracked Hemmingway's domain to somehow infuse Gash with Silvie's memories, for which Muninn already confessed responsibility. The birds in the windows just after he killed Dr. Marin in New Orleans. The mysterious new species of corvid that he'd first heard about at Shen's, Daiyu watching the report with rapt attention while he basically ignored it, lost in his own stuff. The AI's name, Muninn, tickled something in the back of his mind.

Iblis continued to tap away at the screen of his PCom, prepping in some way for the upcoming op. Julius checked and rechecked his weapons. Silvie sat completely still, eyes closed, hands balled into white-knuckled fists. Xiaoli looked back, made eye contact with Gash. Some sort of silent acknowledgement passed between them, and then she turned back towards the road, the engine revving a little higher as she sped up the van.

Muninn. He keyed the name into the search bar in his PCom interface. A mythological entity, one of the Norse god Odin's two ravens. Muninn, along with Huginn, flew around the world each day, reporting what they saw to their master. Huginn's domain? Thought. Muninn's? Mind. Galloway named the AI for the Norse mind raven. And apparently Muninn took that to heart. Gash did not know why, or how, or what it meant. Not yet. But he knew that these birds were the work of Muninn.

"You know a flock of ravens is sometimes called a 'conspiracy' of ravens?" Xiaoli asked.

"I did not," Gash said. He returned his PCom to his pocket and looked out the window once more at the never-ending parade of corvids streaming past. Clinging to every available line, lamp, and ledge, he saw them in a new light. They were altogether darker and more ominous. They seemed larger, and they loomed now from streetlights and decaying bill-boards casting long shadows over his people as the drew nearer and nearer to a show-down with Galloway and his puppet force of WalCo soldiers and drones.

"Learned that in one of my English language modules as a kid. Always stuck with me, I guess," she said.

Five blocks from the DRZ, Gash heard gunfire. Old gunpowder weapons, the kind of thing the denizens of the DRZ could afford – or scrounge.

"It's already started," Gash said.

Silvie looked at the others and back at him. "How can you tell?" she asked.

He pointed at his ears. "Vampire senses. I hear gunfire – a lot of it."

"Meaning we are coming in hot," Iblis said. "My personal favorite." Flames danced in his eyes.

Julius leaned forward in his seat. "How do we think this is going down?"

Gash shrugged. "Not sure what to expect."

Silvie cleared her throat. "I might have an idea." Everyone looked at her, but she seemed to be waiting for something.

"Go ahead," Gash said.

"Okay, well I've been reading through Dr. Marin's files – the ones Iblis was able to recover. This thing works like smallpox on steroids, which is really horrifying. But the thing she couldn't seem to accomplish until she had magic to shape the microbe was putting it into a spore."

"A spore?" Xiaoli looked at the group in the rear-view mirror. "So is this a virus or a fungus?"

"Virus," Silvie said. "When I say spore, I'm talking about something like anthrax. The anthrax bacteria can live for a long time without a host because it is protected by a spore. Think of it like a little protective cocoon for the microbe, so it can live longer in nature. Meaning it can spread more effectively because it remains in the environment for a long time."

"So she combined the worst of anthrax and smallpox?" Iblis said.

"That's over-simplifying it, but basically, yes." Silvie said.

"How do you know so much about this?" Gash asked.

"I was taking online classes before magic came surging back into the world," she said, looking down at her hands in her lap. "Epidemiology. Thought that might a good way to help people."

"Anything in the notes about how best to spread it?" Julius asked.

"We weren't able to recover that data. But If I were Galloway, I would choose a space at a high elevation if I were going to try to spread something like this. The spores protect it from inclement weather, and more importantly they're lightweight. If you release this thing from a tall enough building, it could spread to several city blocks, sinking so slowly it's almost floating, the wind spreading it far and wide. Once the first batch of infected are symptomatic, the disease becomes airborne, bloodborne, and waterborne. It'll spread like wildfire. I would look for an explosive device on the roof of the tallest building in the DRZ for maximum dispersion."

Gash knew that building. An old office building right near the center of the DRZ, ten stories tall. Once upon a long time ago, he lurked beneath its shadow almost every day. Right around lunch time. Phil Shen's noodles and dozens of other street vendors had set up shop at its base long ago, forming the bones of a communal market district that would go on to become the beating heart of the DRZ.

The seed of a plan sprouted in his mind. Though he'd only just loaded it, Gash slid open the revolver's cylinder and checked. 6 bullets in 6 chambers. One of those bullets was going into Henry Galloway's gray matter. He spun the cylinder, relishing the metal clicking and the heft of the motion, before whipping it back into place and re-holstering the weapon.

"Here's the plan," he said.

CHAPTER 48

Xiaoli pulled off the main thoroughfare and into the DRZ, weaving around the husks of several freshly burnt-out cars. A few stray rounds ricocheted off the van's bullet-resistant polymer windows.

"Feels like home," Iblis said with a dry laugh.

Gash could see the resemblance. In every block of Seattle's last and only De-Regulated Zone, WalCo foot soldiers in company colors stomped through the street wearing heavy body armor and gas masks. WalCo drones above them blasted the same message:

> *WalCo security forces have located a terrorist cell operating with impunity in this district. Please return to your home or shelter in place for the duration of this peace-keeping operation, which is fully authorized by the Global Corporate Law Enforcement Charter.*

Though the DRZ lacked a cohesive military force, the mercs and druggies and street-walkers and dissidents that made their home here shared one thing in common. They did not respond well to phrases like "fully authorized by the Global Corporate Law Enforcement Charter." As Xiaoli turned into a side alley, more shots rang out: The DRZ was fighting back. Citizen snipers in upper stories of buildings along both sides of the street fired on the WalCo soldiers, the crack of old gunpowder rifles echoing through the streets. Five of the goons dropped, and two stayed down, blood leaking from holes in the soft joints of their armor. The rest scrambled to their feet and the whole squad dispersed to cover, firing indiscriminately at anyone still on the streets not wearing WalCo colors. A few shots hit the back of their van, the higher-velocity gauss projectiles chipping the windows as they coasted deeper into the alley before parking and dismounting. Armed and ready to go, they gathered around Gash at the back of the van, completing final gear checks.

"New plan," Gash said.

"What do you mean, 'new plan'?" Iblis asked.

"I mean I have a different plan than the one we came up with on the way in."

"I thought the one where we all try to stop the apocalypse together was a good one," Julius said, checking the magazine on his rifle.

"Yeah but this conflict isn't just starting, it's been going for a while now. We might only have minutes until the virus is released. Julius and Xiaoli, I want you two to help the citizens of the DRZ on the ground. Every WalCo goon you guys take out is a gas mask that can be looted and given to a citizen. Start with yourselves. If we don't get to Galloway in time, we can at least save as many people as possible."

Julius leaned in, his voice an angry whisper. "Galloway imprisoned me with no trial for five years. Like hell I'm going to let you be the one to kill him."

"Well I can spider-climb the outside of the building in seconds to stop the dispersal of the bio-agent. If you have that power too, then by all means let's trade jobs."

Julius sighed and looked to Xiaoli, who drew two pistols out of the gear bag in the back of the van. "Good to go," she said.

"Silvie, I want you behind me until we get to the building. You charge in on the ground floor and make a scene. Draw as many of

Galloway's people away from the roof as possible. You're the distraction. You okay with that?"

Silvie grinned, and then began to transform. Her custom clothes stretched across her burley wechuge physique, and the haunting skull of her face manifested in a heartbeat. She roared her assent to this new plan.

"And me?" Iblis asked.

"I need you on a nearby roof. When I'm scaling that building, I'll be vulnerable. And I'm fairly certain they'll have snipers in the surrounding buildings. A guy like Galloway doesn't live a hundred years without being careful. It's the highest roof in the zone, so you won't be able to join me up there, but just cover me while I climb and we have a chance to stop this thing."

"On it," he said, disappearing immediately in a puff of dark smoke. Gash saw him climb from the fire escape through an open window in a nearby three-story building, and disappear.

Julius and Xiaoli positioned themselves at the entrance to the alley, took one look back at Gash, and opened fire on WalCo security.

Gash looked at Silvie. "I'm sorry I invaded your private thoughts and didn't tell you. Thanks for having my back, still."

"You should have told me," she said, her wechuge-voice two metal gears grinding. "But your mind was invaded too. Let's not waste time."

"Okay," Gash said. And they were off. He sprinted through the back alley, streaking past impromptu lean-tos built from discarded plastic and cardboard, kicking up cracked and defective mobile Real-D rigs. Wrappers from 100 different kinds of pre-packaged food fluttered in his wake. He had one thing to take care of before Galloway, and it was an important one. He turned north, Silvie stampeding down the alley behind him.

Gash knew these alleys better than most. He'd tracked more than his fair share of deadbeat cheaters and runaway teenagers with corporate parents through these alleys over the years. He figured that he and Silvie would avoid most of the fighting if they stayed off the main streets, but after two blocks the city proved him wrong, like it always did when he made plans.

Barreling around another corner, Gash almost collided with two WalCo soldiers rousting a homeless man. Homeless kid, really – he couldn't have been older than 16. The kid pulled away from the soldiers, screaming, until one of them ripped the Real-D rig off his head. Trodes caught in the kid's hair, pulling a huge tuft of blonde out of his scalp. His eyes twitched as his addled brain tried to pivot from the virtual to the real with no buffer or safe disconnect.

When the soldier dropped and then stomped on the cheap rig, the kid's screams of fear turned to rage. He pulled a knife and tried to shank the soldier. Though he took the goon by surprise, the little pocket knife struck dead center in the middle of the armored chest plate, flying out of the kid's hands from the impact.

This was about to get ugly, but fortunately Gash was here. And he needed some gas masks anyway. The soldier, though unharmed by the kid's act of rage, raised his hand to strike the young would-be-attacker anyway. Gash caught the arm mid-swing, and the goon's neck in his other hand. The poor bastard didn't have time to turn around, let alone understand what was happening. Gash lifted him into the air and snapped his neck with one motion, letting the body drop to the concrete ground with a clatter and thump. The second soldier took a step back, preparing to flee, but two rounds from the .44 punched through a seam in his body armor and dropped him.

The kid recoiled from the sudden violence, and when Silvie rounded the corner, he cried out, retreated to a cardboard shelter barely large enough to sit up in. Silvie looked from Gash to the two bodies, and back.

"We need gas masks," Gash said, pulling the two off the newly slain WalCo troopers. He slid one into the box, first. "Kid, I know you're scared. But there's a bio-attack about to happen. Put this on and don't take it off until it's all over." The kid did grab the mask, pulling it into the box. From there, Gash could only hope he put it on.

With the second mask, he looked at Silvie. The gas mask would *not* fit over the elongated, antlered skull. What to do?

"Gash." He recognized the voice, pulling his PCom out of his pocket to see the projected image of Trine the sexy sailor. Only this time, she had raven's wings sprouting from her back, and black raven's eyes. The effect was so disconcerting, Gash had to ask her to repeat herself.

"I said," she said, "your blood results from your brief stay at WalCo HQ are in. Among other things, you're immune to Galloway's apocalypse virus. I have some other useful tidbits you might like to know – transferring them to your PCom now. I suggest you wait until later to view them, of course."

"So I don't need the gas mask?" Gash said.

She shook her head. "I've informed Iblis as well. Evidently the energy that infused you when magic returned to the world has changed your biology. Silvie, Iblis, and you are immune to normal human pathogens, including the base virus used by Dr. Marin to craft this bio-weapon. In other words, quit wasting time chasing down gas masks and focus on the primary mission, please."

"Good news, thanks. Is there anything else?"

"Nothing relevant to the mission," Muninn said.

"Do you know where Galloway's releasing the virus?"

"You figured it out already," Muninn flapped her wings at this, her smile totally alien on this new avatar.

Good. Gash severed the connection and returned the device to his pocket. They were close now.

Two more narrow alleyways, and Gash emerged onto the main street just beside the old office building. At its feet, half a block away, Shen Wu's noodles looked abandoned. The whole row of kiosks all looked abandoned. Chairs turned over, food scattered along the street, displays upended. WalCo came through already. They were in the building, if not already the roof.

Gash looked up. The building had not seen much in the way of upkeep since the corporations abandoned it to squatters many years past. In some senses, it resembled the buildings in New Orleans. Windows cracked or shattered, and concrete ledges chipped away by time gave the building an asymmetrical look. Halfway transitioned from office building to ancient ruins, it sat astride two worlds. There were lights, though, in several of the windows. Muzzle flashes in many more, including several near the top. At the apex of the building, Gash saw black wings in the night sky – corvids, numbering in the tens of thousands – circling the roof. Several WalCo drones hovered just below the huge flock, flickering warning lights adding to the 10 billion LEDs that suffused the low-hanging cloud ceiling with bright neon light. Looked like rain, but when didn't it?

A sound drew Gash's attention, a crash of glass. A large woman fell backwards from an upper story window, slamming into the street with a wet crunch. Gash stood close enough to the impact site to see that she was riddled with bullets and that she held a bloody knife in her right hand.

"Silvie," Gash growled. "Help those people fight back?"

Her howl rang in Gash's ears, echoing between buildings across the street and up into the night. Gash didn't envy the WalCo mooks inside, about to clash with an enraged wechuge.

He looked up at the roof again. Were there even more of the strange corvids than before? Something didn't seem right, but he couldn't place his finger on it. "Iblis?" he said, finger on his comms.

"I need another moment, ran into some resistance. I'll let you know when I'm in position."

Good. He had time to check in on Daiyu. Phil's daughter. If Phil was really paralyzed, he'd be sitting at home worrying about his kid. The noodle stand looked abandoned from here, but he wasn't close enough to hear silence. He'd have to get closer.

Silence. That was it. Ten thousand black birds circling just overhead, and not a single bird noise. No caw, or croak, or whatever noise they were supposed to make. Guns cracked in the distance, the occasional explosion rumbled the streets, and the drones echoed the same message over and over. But the ten thousand corvids circled above in complete silence. He could no longer have a shadow of a doubt – these were a manifestation of Muninn in the real world, somehow. How? Why?

It didn't matter because he couldn't do anything about it.

Second gas mask still in hand and approaching Shen Wu's noodles, he heard the flutter of a faint heartbeat behind the counter. As he drew near, he saw a carton of noodles abandoned on the counter. In the cool fall night, steam rose steadily from the still-hot dish. So that meant Daiyu was here recently enough to serve someone a midnight snack, and the dish was untouched. It must have come out of the machine right when WalCo's corporate army came rumbling through. The stool beside it was tipped over, and presumably whoever was about to eat fled in a hurry. The old holovision behind the counter played news footage of the DRZ, of all things. Sub-titles described a terrorist attack, and said that even though the place fell outside of any corporate jurisdiction WalCo had stepped in to protect innocent citizens and blah blah more propaganda. Up close, Gash could hear the urgency of the heartbeat. Someone was hiding. Must be Daiyu, who else? He hopped the counter and crouched down behind it.

She didn't cry out, only narrowed her neon eyes at him. She clutched a small stun gun in both hands – it reminded him of a weapon that Starfire had used. The thing would fire charged darts that used electricity to disable or kill its targets. That could take Gash out of the fight long enough to make a difference. He put his hands up slowly.

"Here to help," he said.

"I remember you," she said. "The asshole who claimed to be friends with my dad, but wouldn't touch his noodles." She seemed to unclench her grip on the stun gun ever so slightly.

"That's me. Look, I don't have time to give you details, but some corporate asshole is on the roof of *this building* right now, trying to disperse a bio-weapon into the DRZ. I need you to put this gas mask on, and then go inside that building and try to find another one for your mom and dad. Should be a lot of dead WalCo thugs in there by now. Once you have the masks, find shelter and do not leave it until everything is over tomorrow morning."

She stared at him for a long time, shrewd bright eyes taking in every mouth movement, every one of Gash's facial tics. "Thanks," she said, and paused. She must have believed him.

"No time to think about it, get moving," Gash said.

She grabbed the mask from Gash's hands, then the credit chip reader and the holovison display pad. She jumped nimbly over the counter, but there she paused again. "He's dead, you know."

"Who's dead?" Gash asked.

"My dad. He died six months ago. That gunshot didn't graze him, like I said before. It hit him right in the heart. He was all I had left, so it's just me now. I pretend they're still around because nobody wants to buy noodles from some teenager hiding from corporate social services."

Shit. Things started to get too bright, and he could suddenly smell the smoke, the blood, the ozone of the impending rain; the human body odor of every one of the fifty thousand current residents and intruders into the DRZ. He heard ragged breathing just behind him, too, and the sound of a safety being flicked off. Good thing, because that kicked his bloody instincts into over-drive and the red came flooding in to wash away whatever panic attack he was about to have. He could mourn Phil next week, sitting on a beach. He could wrestle with the unfairness of calling him a friend when he barely knew him with a Mai Tai in hand. He could grapple with how terrible it felt to find out Phil was dead and his teen daughter stuck eking out a living alone in the DRZ, while up to his waist in surf. He could think about the old days, and all the things he missed from that life. Like delicious food, the tangy mouth-feel of good ramen seasoning. And daylight. Warm, sunny, normal days. The simple days he used to live, the low stakes. Cheap booze and cheaper Real-D.

"Then you can just take the one and get to shelter. Now," Gash said. The calm descended over him, and he knew that this aspect of his warrior spirit, the killer instinct, would take care of things from here on out. By the time Daiyu spotted the WalCo solider creeping up from behind, Gash was already spinning around. Already clearing the ten feet between them. Already ripping off the guy's mask and sinking his twin fangs into the soft flesh just below the jawline. Arterial blood gushed warmly into his mouth and he drank deep. His vision grew redder, and a primal voice inside of him bellowed. "YES," it said. "FEED US."

He did. He drank the corporate soldier dry, and left his pale corpse on the street beside a used needle and an empty bottle of sake.

When he turned back, Daiyu was running down the street, away from him. She had the gas mask on. Good girl. Now for Galloway.

"Iblis," he rumbled into his comms. "I'm going up."

"Just –" he started to say, but was interrupted by the hum of a gauss weapon, and then the loud sizzle and pop of flesh being rapidly cooked. "There," he said. "All clear."

And up Gash went, scaling the side of yet another building. Scrabbling towards Henry Galloway and Muninn's flock of not-ravens, warring forces that had long ago pulled him into a maelstrom of violence surrounding Selina and Rhodes and magic and Dr. Marin and the Children of Gaia and the end of the world. But it would all be over soon. He was going to kill Galloway, destroy this apocalypse virus, and then disappear from this world forever.

A blast just beside his head knocked loose a huge chunk of brick, sending it spiraling to the street below. He paused to look for the sniper, only to see a flaming white lance streaking from the roof of a nearby building to the fifth story window of another. A man in WalCo armor toppled forward into the street, smoke rising from the hole in his chest.

"Thanks," Gash said.

"Just doing my job," came back Iblis' reply.

There were no more snipers – or the others learned a valuable lesson, watching Iblis work. Nothing else to keep Gash from his goal.

He did not slow down as he crested the roof, vaulting over the parapet walls and taking everything in as he landed on the cracked concrete.

The place, a rooftop garden, was trashed. Plants trampled, frames toppled. Solar panels knocked over and scattered. The denizens of the building made a stand here, and their corpses told the tale. Bullet-riddled, cut up, and in several cases completely mangled. As though they'd been stuffed into a small box and pulled back out.

Two technicians in gas masks with WalCo armor were working on a large device. Attached to some kind of central unit were several large canisters. It might have been a large air-conditioning unit ringed haphazardly with extra freon tanks on any other day. But Gash knew its purpose.

Aside from the device, Gash saw three other figures. Henry Galloway stood tall near the device, his lifeless white eyes trained on the birds above. No gas mask, they must have a vaccine after all. Just not enough for all the soldiers.

Gash's blood ran cold. Beside Galloway were two mages in long black robes, hoods pulled over their heads. Full tactical rigs, green-eyed night vision goggles, and bullet-resistant composite facemasks gave them the appearance of twin demons. He remembered them, remembered what they had done to him. He raised his weapon to fire before they could notice him, but Galloway was already looking at him, those hollow eyes piercing him to the core, reading his soul, preparing a cruel fate for the failed detective, the would-be-hero.

Gash fired twice, the magnum crack shattering the unearthly silence of the roof.

The first bullet split the ballistic mask of the right-most mage, snapping his head back. He dropped immediately and did not stir. Galloway shoved the other of the black-clad mages out of the way at the last minute, the bullet passing harmlessly over the spellcaster's head and cracking apart another old, half-rusted solar panel.

Shit.

Gash tried to line up another shot, but the mage recovered too quickly. The robed figure stretched a gloved hand towards Gash, and like before, Gash felt himself suddenly unable to move. An invisible barrier of force wrapped him in its power and held him aloft, floating inches above the floor of the roof.

Galloway shook his head slowly, approaching Gash at a leisurely amble, as if going to meet an old friend for brunch. When he stood only a few feet away, Galloway spoke. "I'll bet you feel like you almost had me this time, don't you? Oh, and I can see the hope in your eyes still, that maybe your wendigo friend will burst through that door and throw me to the street below. But I've got so many warm bodies in this building, it would take her an hour to get to us. By then, it'll all be over and I'll be gone."

"I don't get it," Gash said. "What's with the jackboots? The corporate army? You could have just snuck up to the roof and set off your fancy device here. But you're not happy unless you're shooting up undesirables? Marching through the streets and bossing people around?"

Galloway considered him for a moment. "I'll never understand how someone as dense as you was able to get to Dr. Marin and kill her. Even I have masters, you know, and my masters at WalCo would not be pleased if tomorrow's news read 'witnesses spot WalCo personnel dispersing bio-agent in downtown Seattle.' So tonight we are writing our own headline. 'Terrorist group resisting WalCo law enforcement agents releases bio-agent in desperation.' Doesn't that sound much nicer? People love a good terrorist attack on their morning feed."

Gash struggled against the magic. He strained his muscles, trying with all his might to just move a limb. His arm or a leg. If he could just move his arm a bit, and his finger, he could get off one more shot. Take out the mage and then end this smug bastard.

"You're strong, but not that strong," Galloway said, watching him strain against the magical prison with piteous amusement.

"I don't get you," Gash said. "You're releasing a virus that will kill thousands of people down here, and you're concerned with what some executive team thinks about a news article?"

"That's the problem with parochial little small business owners like you. You don't see the big picture. I'm not going to just kill thousands of people down here, I'm going to kill *billions* of people around the world, and rebuild what remains of society using the tools at my disposal. Such a thing takes years of careful planning and the deft manipulation of public sentiment. The survivors will trust implicitly in WalCo, the company that fought to save their families." He paused. "I can see you think me a villain, but imagine the alternative. The puppet-master that pulls your string, Muninn, would eventually enslave or kill every single human being on the planet, snuffing out the human race like you or I might snuff out a candle. A man like you can't see the big picture, which is why it takes a man like me."

Before Gash could respond, the door to the roof burst open and a hulking brown creature, all muscle and fur and a great antlered bone-skull for a face, came charging out. Silvie bled from a dozen bullet holes, but these were already beginning to heal. The mage reached with one hand towards her, curling gloved fingers into a fist. She floated a few inches into the air, also trapped by the magic.

But Gash felt the force binding him weaken. Almost imperceptible at first, as he struggled against the telekinetic force, he began to feel just a millimeter of give. This one mage couldn't hold them both, at least not for long. They found his limit.

"You're so busy looking at the big picture," Gash growled, "that you've underestimated us for the third time in a row. Aren't you getting tired of being wrong?"

Galloway laughed, but was that a flash of uncertainty? A fraction of a moment's crack in the veneer of Galloway's arrogance? "Then it's a good thing I have powerful allies." As he spoke, he took several steps back and drew a sidearm out of his suit, a very high-end WalCo gauss pistol.

But he was too late. Gash felt it now. The killer impulse, the soldier within, the vampiric instinct – whatever you wanted to call it – sensed the opening. "You don't have allies, you have servants. And that's ultimately why you're going to die and I'm going to kill you. I can taste the irony, can you? That power you wield in this world, what you perceive as your greatest strength, is your weakness after all."

Galloway's veneer of civility fell away completely, and he leveled his weapon at Gash's head.

"Wait, that's not the taste of irony. That's blood in the water." And before Galloway could fire, Gash's body flooded with adrenaline. The hunger and the rage and the yearning, an avalanche of chemicals and emotions surged through every limb. He ripped free of the telekinetic barrier with a sound like glass shattering, falling to a crouch on the roof just as Galloway's finger squeezed the trigger, sending a magnetized bolt buzzing past his head. The black-clad mage cried out in pain and collapsed.

The other WalCo agents on the roof, the two technicians, each drew sidearms of their own, but Silvie pounced before they could fire, tearing into one and grappling the other. That left only Galloway.

With Galloway's reflexes, there would be no dodging the oncoming volley of magnetized flechettes. That left one option.

Gash charged straight in, tossing his revolver aside, the hunger within screaming for blood. More blood. Galloway reacted quickly, realigning his aim and squeezing the trigger twice in the time it took Gash to clear the space between them. He felt the flechettes punch through his shoulder and chest, felt the white-hot burning pain of it in some distant part of himself.

It didn't even slow him down. He ripped the gun out of Galloway's grip with his left hand, swinging a hard right hook at the same time.

But Galloway was *fast*. He ducked under the punch, jabbing Gash in the face. The bridge of his nose cracked. You couldn't even see the seams in Galloway's arms, but clearly WalCo had spared no expense in turning the corporate fixer into a super-human. Galloway hit him two more times in the gut, each time cracking ribs. So Galloway was faster than Gash, with bio-arms that could pulverize cement. Who fucking cared? The molten hot rage of ten thousand dying DRZ refugees flowed in his veins. The fury of Silvie's tribe; the screaming souls of everyone held without trial in the upper stories of the WalCo HQ building; the wandering spirits of all that WalCo had killed with designer viruses, or lobotomized after forced-work/indenturement stints: Gash poured all of that fury into the font of his own blood-red inner-self. Galloway ducked under another hook and uppercut him in the jaw. The pain, far away, barely translated to a tickle. Gash smiled.

On the far side of the roof, another squad of WalCo goons burst out of the door behind Silvie, opening fire at the hulking wechuge. She pivoted, charging through the hail of bullets, and knocked them apart like bowling pins.

Galloway hit Gash two more times, and with each blow that landed, Gash smiled wider. Fear bloomed in the immortal's eyes, and Julius was right. It looked strange on his face. The lifeless white eyes, the furrowed brow, the creases around his mouth.

"Enough," Gash said, and he grabbed Galloway's fist mid-punch. Galloway threw another with his other arm, and Gash caught that one, too. Both fists in his hands, Gash roared into the sky, the circling ravens, the eternal rain clouds. And then he sank his fangs into Galloway's jugular, drinking ancient blood, the hunger singing shrill triumph as Gash's head throbbed in tune with the pump of his enemy's arteries.

The clouds did not part, a choir from the heavens did not descend and name Nagash Jensen a hero of the people. But still, he drank. He guzzled every drop of Henry Galloway's lifeforce as it flowed out of the man's body and into his own.

After, he let Galloway drop to the cold gray concrete of the roof. The fixer was reduced to a quivering heap, dying by the second. He reached a hand towards Gash, mouth struggling to form words. Gash knelt beside his enemy. "I thought you'd taste richer, sweeter maybe than the lesser men you've ruled. But you taste the same as everyone else," Gash whispered.

Galloway opened his mouth, blood bubbling out instead of words. Gash leaned in and Galloway tried again.

"What time is it?" he coughed. And then he gave one sputtering laugh, and his ragged breaths ceased.

What time is it? Gash checked his PCom. 1:59 AM PST. Just as he looked, it ticked over to 2:00 AM PST.

The massive device in the center of the roof gave off a little whir, a hum, a sort of whoosh, and then silence hung like a guillotine in the air. Gash reached towards the dispersal unit, and Silvie – still holding on to the last of the WalCo soldiers on the roof – turned to look as well.

With a beep that might have been someone's PCom alarm app, it exploded. The immediate detonation shredded the central unit and threw Gash off his feet, blood blooming from half a dozen shrapnel wounds. A small explosion, all told, but the real devastation floated in the air above, a fountain of cool white liquid that blossomed high into the air and dispersed, drifting slowly to the streets over a radius of several blocks. He climbed to his feet just as a gentle breeze carried a few cold droplets to the roof, grazing Gash's face. He wiped them off frantically, before remembering that he was immune.

Unlike the rest of the DRZ.

He rushed to the edge of the roof, Silvie close behind him. Just below, five citizens of the DRZ were mopping up a squad of WalCo soldiers. Only one of them had a gasmask on. As the mist descended on them, they looked up, holding out their hands as though catching snowflakes.

"Don't breathe it in," Gash cried out, but as he opened his mouth, the swarm of ravens above shrieked, drowning him out. A horrible sound, not the caw of a raven or a crow but the metallic screech of metal imitating a bird. Echoed ten thousandfold by every circling faux-corvid.

Four of the things dive-bombed the citizens down below. They streaked towards the men and women on the street like some savage birds of prey, like missiles homing in. Gash could only watch, horrorstruck, as the birds dissolved into a particulate mist at the last second. The descending mist sprayed the four unmasked citizens in the face, and immediately they collapsed to their knees, blood pouring from every orifice. They were dead before their faces hit the pavement.

"They're not birds, they're nano-drones," Julius's voice crackled with static on the team's comms. "This is Muninn's work, they're targeting everyone without a gas mask on."

All around them, drones broke off from the flock, dive-bombing the street. Human screams mixed in with the shrieking metallic birdcalls. Anyone not wearing a gas-mask – excepting monsters like Gash and Silvie and Iblis – fell victim. Clouds of nanobots disguised as birds to avoid detection, Muninn's corvids revealed themselves by the dozen, swarming the DRZ, crashing through windows and bolting into cardboard shelters in alleys and even flying down into old disused subway tunnels. Thousands of overlapping screams echoed throughout the neighborhood over the next few minutes.

Silvie transformed back, standing beside Gash to watch the carnage in a dreadful sort of awe. "She's killing every possible carrier of the disease," she whispered.

When it was all over, what handful of Muninn's drones remained in the sky circled the building lazily one last time, and then dispersed, flying off in every direction. Below, the streets were littered with bodies, the handful of masked survivors or WalCo goons standing paralyzed, surveying the carnage around them. The WalCo drones deactivated all primary systems, going dark and drifting back towards the center of the city.

Gash killed Galloway, that had been the mission, not stopping the bio-agent. And here was why. Muninn already had a solution for the virus. She didn't need Gash to solve that particular problem. He'd completed the mission, won the battle. But at one hell of a cost.

A desperate muttering arose in the DRZ, the broken voices of the scattered survivors on the street below. Gash looked up into the sky, the dark clouds still lit by the burning radiance of the towering city. Though one of its oldest and most powerful agents had been slain, the neon citadel blazed into the dark as it ever did, shining and indifferent to the countless dead scattering its streets.

The heavy clouds finally released, pouring thick and oily rain in dense sheets onto Gash's upturned face and the countless dead below.

CHAPTER 49

A cool breeze began at Gash's toes and worked its way along his shins and thighs, past swim trousers and up his chest. It fluttered his chest hairs and the brim of his hat, rattling the little rainbow umbrella and the pink plastic straw resting in the coconut he clutched in both hands. Ocean waves crashed on soft white sands, a rush of static and then a slow exhale. Repeated at regular intervals, the ebb and flow were a lullaby. Gash let his gaze rest on the soft moonlight reflecting off the infinite gunmetal horizon, allowing sleep to take him and return him to waking at its leisure.

He drank deeply through the wide straw in the coconut. Though he no longer recognized most food-based sensations, still he relished the cool sweetness of the chilled rum streaming over his tongue. If he focused hard enough, Gash thought, he could even just barely detect the essence of pineapple dancing on his repressed vampiric tastebuds.

When he drank that coconut dry, Gash merely deposited the husk in the empty sand beside him, and within two minutes, a resort employee scampered down to replace it with a full one. She was young and thin, the daughter of the owner. She seemed happy. Each time, Gash thanked her and waved her a generous tip from his unbelievably full bank account.

Each day for the last five, Gash had risen at sunset, trudged down the walkway from his beach-front room, and deposited himself in this chair on his personal slice of beach. Each day for the last five, he had simply let the peace and quiet wash over him, settling into his bones, one by one relaxing muscles that were tense for a decade or more. The only hard decisions: Should he stay here awhile longer? Look for a more permanent residence? Or simply buy the resort instead of renting the whole thing out?

He'd kept a single eye on the news. Scanning the feeds as lightly as possible, he could tell that Muninn didn't seem to be conquering the human race. Corporate E-Teams sat atop ivory towers, their metaphorical boots resting atop the throats of their serfs and the free peoples in the DRZs around the globe. The world order as it had always been.

The resort employee placed a new coconut in his hands. "This one's a strawberry," she said. "Please enjoy."

He smiled at the girl, tipped her, and gave the drink a try. As all the others had, it simply tasted vaguely like rum to Gash. He gave her a thumb's up and thanked her – no need to let her or any of the others know what Gash was, after all. Here on the beach, monsters and magic and cybernetically augmented humans belonged to another world. Here, there was no mission, no battle. Just the pleasant buzz he'd cultivated five days ago, and artfully maintained ever since.

I'm doing it, Serena. I'm finally doing it.

Even as he had the thought, his PCom rang. He didn't recognize the number, but then, he'd blocked all his old contacts so why would he? Everyone he used to know were mercs, fixers, and hackers. Even Silvie leveraged her experience with the monster squad to go into business with Iblis, a monster duo. Blocking her contact was hard, but everything in that life pulled at him. Struggled to reel him back into that world. He had to resist.

Not to mention the hours after the mission, the sad party, all the booze, the tense moments together. He'd almost leaned in to kiss her, repeating the Selina mistake. For once, he made the smart decision. What kind of relationship could they have, her half his age and some of her most personal memories implanted in his own brain?

He hesitated, his hand over the PCom – swipe the caller up into the projector? Or swipe the call down and go back to... nothing. He'd put out some feelers to realtors about beachfront properties, maybe this was one of them? He swiped it down and away. Leaned back in his chair and had another drink.

Thinking of Serena made him think of Corporal Sinder. Sin. The kid wasn't right after killing that Imam. After they learned he was a civilian influencer with no insurgent ties. He visited Gash a few times in the brig, even talked of breaking his own contract, joining Gash in incarceration. Gash encouraged him not to, encouraged him to get lost in Yenson's sweet embrace. Encouraged him to shop for new cyber-eyes for when the paperwork eventually came through. Thought that was the right move. Push on with the good in his life.

When Private Yenson showed up to visit Gash for the first time, he knew something was wrong right away. She sat down in the little cubby across from him, eyes bloodshot and still dewy around the edges. "Sin's dead," she said as soon as she picked up the little phone. "I thought you should know."

"What happened?" Gash asked.

She sniffed. "His gun went off while he was cleaning it," she said.

Code, of course. The guilt was too much and he ate his sidearm. He was 22 years old, with one year left on his Marine Corporation contract.

Someone somewhere must have felt bad, because they let Gash out of the brig for the day a week later to attend Sin's funeral. By then the Marine Corporation investigators determined – for insurance reasons – that Sin's death was in fact a suicide. So the funeral was on the family's dime, a small affair. Open casket with limited plastic surgery. It was... not good. Sin's baby face, his red hair, his freckles – you could tell they weren't right. Gash paid his respects and said goodbye to Yenson and left that part of his life in his rearview.

But the image haunted him, Sin in the coffin, his face all wrong. As much as Serena, ODed in the bathtub. Frederick, who betrayed them in Rhodes but was still a good kid, evaporating in an outburst of magical energy. They all haunted him, those he'd lost and those he'd killed. He drained the rest of his rum drink and left the coconut in the sand. How many more to drink these ghosts away?

His PCom rang again, same number as before. This time, Gash answered.

"Do my eyes deceive me? Have I finally reached the famous detective Nagash Jensen?" Smiling from the holographic projection, the big Samoan laughed.

"Hemmingway," Gash said. "New number?"

"It's the web, I can get as many numbers as I need. My usual one wasn't reaching you for some reason, so I thought I'd try a new area code."

"I see. Well I'm glad to see WalCo hasn't tracked you down yet..." Gash said, picking up his empty coconut cocktail and pretending to have a sip.

"Same to you, my man," Hemmingway said.

"... but I blocked your number for a reason. Unless you're just calling to shoot the shit, I don't have anything to say to you or any of my professional contacts. I'm done with that life," Gash said.

Hemmingway shook his head. "That's cold, Gash. I could be calling to shoot the shit, you don't know."

"Are you?"

Hemmingway didn't even pause. "Nope."

"Good-bye, Hemmingway," Gash reached for his PCom.

"I know you. I saw your eyes back then. I saw insatiable hunger in you even before you turned into a vampire. You think you're out, but it won't last."

Gash's hand dangled in the air, as though set free to live its own life. It floated above the PCom, close to ending the call but no longer moving.

"Hmm," Hemmingway said. And then his face was replaced with a picture of a young woman, beautiful emerald eyes framed by neon blonde hair.

"Who's this?" Gash asked.

"Well, since you asked, this is Saoirse Doyle. She's an Irish climate activist. She went missing a few days ago, and her very wealthy parents have already come to suspect that their corporate overlords don't have Saoirse's best interests at heart. They want to enlist a private investigator. They found their way to me, and I told them I know the best in the business."

Gash wasn't prepared. A tidal wave of emotion crashed over him. His promise to Serena. Squeezing the trigger of a .44 magnum, Dr. Ana Marin crumpling to the floor, eyes vacant, blood showering the wall behind her. Standing in the deep bottom of a pit while a thousand tons of rock collapsed inward at Selina. Sin ending the old Imam, sparks and shrapnel flying as the holy man's holo-projector caught a ricochet. What fool would say yes to this or any job in Gash's position? He didn't even know the name for the amount of money Muninn had paid him when the dust settled on the Galloway job, but he finally had the means to exist in comfort outside the eternal grind, to finally search for peace. So why did he want to say yes?

Maybe because true peace to a man like Nagash Jensen didn't mean drinking rum on the beach every day. Maybe true peace meant being in the world, focused on the job, on saving someone. Maybe the death curse that haunted him throughout this life wouldn't allow him to be still. Maybe people just never changed. Maybe he'd already fallen in love with this activist, with her picture, his mind constructing details of her life, his imagination spinning love stories out of the mist.

"Okay," Gash said. "Send the details to my PCom. I'll get the expense account set up with her parents."

"Perfect," Hemmingway said. "I'll be in touch soon."

Gash severed the connection and stood. He placed the empty cocktail gently back in the sand beside his chair and made his way towards his room; the sweet ocean breeze chased him as he left. The rhythmic thump and sigh of the waves bid him farewell.

Saoirse needed him. Time to get to work.

Acknowledgements

This sequel to *Colossus* and *Cold Wind Blowing* owes much to many, and I will endeavor to acknowledge and thank as many of you as possible! It is an amazing feeling to be 40, living in the worst of times, but to still be able to write and grow as a writer and human, and that is thanks to too many people to count or name. But I'll try!

Thanks to Bailey Ross, my wonderful wife and chief enabler. You take care of the dogs whenever I embark on a writing session, feed me, kick me out the door when I need to write and forgive me for being a lazy slob when I need to slug. I'm lucky to have you.

Thanks to my parents for being my financial sponsors and raising me to be the kind of mostly-damaged person who can hold down a day job and still write novels. It is hard to describe the herculean effort of parenting this must have taken. If they'd gotten a kid with a work ethic, she probably would have a couple Nobel Prizes by now.

Shout out to my girls, who will be thanked later with treat-os. Juno, the universe's elemental expression of unfettered chaos; and Zelda, our snoozy old lady baby. Rescue dogs are the best dogs and the only thing standing between me and a mental breakdown is puppy snuggles.

Thanks to the amazing family I married into. John and Mary Jo; Lynn; Austin, Cassie, and little Wesley. A lot of people are inspired to write human drama based on terrible in-laws. That's not really the kind of story I'm into. Lucky for me, then, that I won the lottery when I married into such a supportive and loving bunch.

To Naoe Masaki: You've been the serotonin engine that keeps me writing and the necessarily sharp chisel that helps sculpt the best book out of the clay of earlier drafts. From an editorial perspective, no single person can claim to have improved *Neon Citadel* more than you have. You have a gift for this and you've been incredibly generous with your time. THANK YOU.

Brandon Getz, champion editor and friend, thank you – as always – for your professional editing skills. I knew everything was going to be okay when I read the words on an early draft, in track changes, "… you have upped your game…. Are you reading these days???"

Olivia Hammerman, thank you! I'm lucky to have had your talented design instincts guiding all three of these books. Getting a final cover design back from you always feels like Christmas Day.

A special thank you to Lisaveta Hokoyva (betty_elgyn on Instagram), the artist who created the original hardcover art for all three books. Lisaveta, thanks for lending me your artistic talent. The first time I reached out to you for cover art was June 2022. Over the last three years, you've created three amazing pieces for three of my books. And you've been stuck in an unjust war the entire time. I can't imagine living in those conditions for 3 months, let alone 3 years. Stay strong. Слава Україні. бережи себе.

Last, but far from least, an emphatic thanks to Nate at Spaceboy Books. It's been a blast working with you, and I've learned so much about the publishing industry during my journey from *Colossus* to *Neon Citadel*. I know I'm a pain in the ass, and I'm grateful for your patience and incredible hard work!

About the Author

Greg Leunig lives in Kansas City Missouri with his wife and two dogs, in a household powered almost entirely by cheese and naps. His day job is to be an introvert working in a sales role, which is undoubtedly very strange. He has a Master of Fine Arts Degree in Creative Writing, despite which he prefers to write about magic and robots and monsters and explosions.

Greg's fiction and poetry have variously appeared in *Daily Science Fiction*, *Apex Magazine*, *Strange Horizons*, and others. His first novel, *Multipocalypse*, appeared in serial form on the now-defunct Jukepop Serials. His second novel, *Colossus*, and first novella, *Cold Wind Blowing*, were released by Spaceboy Books in 2022 and 2023 respectively. Learn more about Greg's work at https://pleasefeedthesquirrels.com/.

Nate Ragolia is a lifelong lover of science fiction and its power to imagine worlds more hopeful and inclusive than the real one. His first book, *There You Feel Free*, was published by 1888's Black Hill Press in 2015. Spaceboy Books reissued it in 2021. He's also the author of *The Retroactivist* (2017). His most recent book, *One Person Can't Make a Difference* (2022), was featured on Tor.com's Can't Miss Indie Press Speculative Fiction list, and was translated into Italian for Ringworld Sci-Fi in 2023. He founded and edited *BONED*, a literary magazine, and also created two webcomics. Nate is also a husband and a dog dad.

Shaunn Grulkowski has been compared to Warren Ellis and Phillip K. Dick and was once described as what a baby conceived by Kurt Vonnegut and Margaret Atwood would turn out to be. He's at least the fifth best Slavic-Latino-American sci-fi writer in the Baltimore metro area. He's the author *Retcontinuum*, and the editor of *A Stalled Ox* and *The Goldfish* for 1888/Black Hill Press.